MW01228607

PRAISE FOR THOMAS M. WING

"Building on the tradition of long-established writers of nautical thrillers such as P.T. Deutermann and David Poyer, Tom Wing has crafted a naval thriller that grips the reader and never lets go. As only an insider can, he has painted an authentic picture of modern surface warfare that the men and women aboard U.S. Navy ships will likely face in an era of peer competition. While some thriller writers craft stories that border on science fiction, *Against All Enemies* paints a scenario that is not only possible but probable, making this novel eerily prescient. Not confined to the world's oceans, this book delves into the political intrigue spawned by war and takes the reader to political machinations in Washington, Beijing, and Moscow. *Against All Enemies* is a tour de force that will not only entertain but inform."

—GEORGE GALDORISI, AWARD-WINNING
AUTHOR AND RETIRED NAVAL AVIATOR

"Authentic. Intense. And sobering. Kudos to Commander Thomas M. Wing, USN (Ret.) for his masterful presentation of what is wrought when the world's power brokers push us beyond the brink of disaster and hurl us directly into the arms of global chaos and nuclear destruction. Intelligently crafted from start to finish, this novel entertains and informs the reader. It also reminds us of the need to safeguard our national sovereignty while also employing a moral compass when dealing with both allies and adversaries on the world stage. Five stars!"

—LAURA TAYLOR, SIX-TIME ROMANTIC
TIMES AWARD WINNER

"Dig into this techno-thriller and prepare to stay up late. Tom Wing has constructed a compelling tale of modern nautical warfare in the vein of Tom Clancy. Wing draws on his extensive Navy background and today's headlines to create an all-too-realistic story of a world led to the brink of nuclear disaster by a calculating Chinese premiere, an egomaniacal U.S. president, and a Russian leader determined to reconstruct the Soviet Union. You don't want to miss this skillfully executed novel."

—MIKE MURPHEY, AUTHOR OF THE
AWARD-WINNING *PHYSICS, LUST AND
GREED* SCI-FI SERIES

"*Against All Enemies* explodes with intensity out of the opening pages and doesn't let up until the finish line. It's a gripping story that perfectly captures the isolation of a ship alone at sea and a crew up against the world. An authentic, overwhelming, and harrowing experience awaits you!"

—BENJAMIN SPADA, AUTHOR OF *FNG* AND *THE WARMAKER*

AGAINST ALL ENEMIES

THOMAS M. WING

FROM THE TINY ACORN...
GROWS THE MIGHTY OAK

Printed in the United States of America. For information, address
Acorn Publishing, LLC, 3943 Irvine Blvd. Ste. 218, Irvine, CA 92602

www.acornpublishingllc.com

Interior designed by Kat Ross
Cover design by Damonza

ISBN-13: 979-8-88528-054-9 (hardcover)
ISBN-13: 979-8-88528-053-2 (paperback)
Library of Congress Control Number: 2023903879

To my wife, Elisa, and my daughter, Emily, for their love and support; to my late parents, Bill and Donna, who told me I could be anything I wanted to be; and to all Tin Can Sailors, past, present, and future.

PROLOGUE

2300 Zulu (Greenwich Mean Time), 26 Oct
1500 Pacific Time
Naval Information Warfare Center Pacific, San Diego

A familiar yet out-of-place sound intruded. John Wilkins looked up from his Mongolian barbecue.

He and Russ met for lunch twice a week. The cafeteria on the fourth floor of the main building at the lab atop Point Loma provided a commanding view of the San Diego harbor below the hill and the city skyline beyond.

It was one of those beautiful fall days, the kind most San Diegans took for granted, just a hint of cool in the air. A slight haze obscured the distant mountains, the sky above crystalline blue. He'd been appreciating the one hundred and eighty-degree view from Old Town to Tijuana and the Coronado Islands of Mexico. The blue awning stretched over the veranda ruffled slightly in the breeze.

The low-pitched buzzing rapidly increased in volume and pitch, then dropped as a low-flying object shot past overhead.

A cruise missile? His unbelieving brain rejected the idea. He blinked several times as he looked over at Russ. "What the hell was that?"

Russ shook his head. "Somebody really messed up big time. Looked like a Tomahawk."

Both were former naval officers, surface warfare qualified in destroyers. John's brother, still active duty, commanded a destroyer deployed to the Western Pacific.

"Man, I'd hate to be the CO of a ship that accidentally flew a T-bird over the city," John said.

They stood to look down the hill to where the missile had disappeared. More noise sources cropped up. Trails barely visible, dozens of small dots stormed in from the sea across the harbor channel that separated Point Loma from North Island.

Half a mile away on the other side of the channel, explosions rippled across North Island Naval Air Station. The day turned dark and ugly. Pillars of black smoke climbed across the panorama.

John's heart raced.

As waves of missiles swept in, they blasted hangars, squadron buildings, the Fleet Air Control Facility, then the aircraft themselves. His stomach heaved as a taxiing helicopter vanished. Its rotor emerged from the flames, shedding pieces as it spun madly across the runway.

John's hands curled into fists and his jaw locked. An enormous ball of angry dark orange flame and black smoke rose just a hundred yards in front of him, blocking his sight. The thunderous boom that accompanied it dwarfed every other sound. His skin prickled from the heat. The acrid smell of burning marine fuel assaulted his nostrils. He gagged.

The fuel farm.

The ammunition pier took a hit, followed by an even larger cloud infused with black and shedding white sparks that erupted from the air station. One of the ammunition bunkers had been breached, the ammunition stored within exploding. The building shuddered as the massive shockwave pummeled it.

A cascade of shattered glass filtered through his battered eardrums as the windows on the floors below blew inward. Hurled back, he fought to grasp the unfolding events. He picked himself up and brushed absently at his clothes. Nearby, Russ disentangled himself from a chair. A mighty thunderclap pounded his already battered hearing.

In the distant harbor, thin columns of white smoke jetted upward, propelled by hard points of brilliant light. But those interceptor missiles, fired from Navy ships that had somehow gotten enough warning time to activate their combat systems, were far too few to make a difference.

His mouth hung open as the clear noontime sky blackened with smoke from burning buildings, planes, helicopters, fuel, ammunition, and bodies.

Around him people shouted, cried, and screamed, in rage or fear.

"Someone's pissed," Russ shouted, though they stood only a couple of feet apart.

John snorted and his senses returned. Russ could always be counted on to remain calm.

"We may wanna get folks out of here." John gestured toward the growing crowd. Turning, he shouted, "Get inside, now. Head down to the parking lot. We need everyone off base, fast."

Russ ran to the other end of the veranda to do the same. John followed the last person inside.

As he did, the building leaped into the air and shook itself. Six distinct, powerful shocks knocked nearly everyone off their feet. The floor to ceiling windows that separated the veranda from the cafeteria proper had been protected from earlier blasts. Now they too shattered, slicing arms and faces. The lights flickered and went out. Only the pale brown, smoke-tinged light streaming in from the abandoned veranda remained. Ice stabbed his heart as intensely hot breath exploded from the stairwell. Those nearest the door toppled like bowling pins.

John's effort took on new urgency. The building was solid

concrete, but those were massive warheads. If it collapsed with people still inside, the toll would be horrific. "Get moving. Down the stairs now. Move!" He wiped at the sweat coating his brow.

Those in front needed no urging. But a few held back, fearing the heat that boiled up. A cacophony rose with it: breaking concrete, falling walls and ceilings, and the crackle of flames. The emergency alarm's mechanical voice, nearly indistinguishable amidst the avalanche of other sounds, directed everyone to leave via the nearest exit.

A man's forward fall triggered a domino effect. Behind him, others tried but couldn't hold back the flood. The stairs became a twisted mass of people. At the top, linked arms with hands locked to the rails gave the disorder time and space to untangle.

Three more explosions shook the dying building. Flames reflected on the walls. The smoke in the stairwell became a choking cloud.

The crowd flow reversed.

John glanced over his shoulder. Russ joined him. He'd also failed to stop the chaos.

Then the back wall, from the drink cases to the grill, the grill itself, and the serving line, all disappeared. As it fell, a maw of flames erupted. Brilliant orange light combated the darkness.

Those who could pushed back outside, onto the veranda.

Across the bay, huge pillars of smoke scarred the blue sky. Incredibly, the bridge that linked Coronado and North Island to the mainland was missing at least two segments. The broken ends stood starkly above the bay.

As he turned toward his long-time friend the floor under him groaned and twisted. *This is how it ends.* Calm settled in his mind as weightlessness overtook him.

The faces of his wife and daughters, and brother, swam before him.

Then the waiting flames swallowed him.

CHAPTER
ONE

2240 Zulu, 26 Oct
0540 Local Time, 27 Oct
USS *Nicholas*, South China Sea

Bill Wilkins hefted himself up into the captain's chair on the bridge of USS *Nicholas* (DDG-189). Today, the ship steered a southerly course toward Fiery Cross Reef in the Spratly Island group. She cruised smoothly at fifteen knots through a gentle sea, rolling easily with winds off her starboard beam. A pre-dawn blaze of golden glory stood above the eastern horizon, framed by scattered clouds, deep gray by contrast. On the forecastle, the men and women of First Division prepared to chip and paint metal fittings in their never-ending war on rust.

One of the newest *Arleigh Burke* class guided missile destroyers, *Nicholas* was two months out of her homeport of San Diego on her maiden deployment.

She was also Bill's first command.

He shifted, trying to get comfortable. Missed workouts the past three weeks showed in the tightness of his trouser waist. The breeze coming in through the starboard bridge wing door ruffled his thinning hair. Later, the doors and windows would close in favor of air conditioning. For now, the fresh moist air cooled the bridge. The hum of electronics succumbed to the soft tones of the breeze entering through partially open windows.

He held a mug of his preferred beverage in his right hand — orange pekoe tea with milk and sugar — and in his left an e-book displaying a novel about Revolutionary War privateers. He luxuriated as he surveyed his domain, enjoying his seat at the pinnacle of a surface warfare officer's career.

"Sir, you wanted to know when we were an hour out from the twelve-mile arc around the reef," said Lieutenant Michelle Barrister, the ship's navigator.

"Very well, Nav," Bill responded.

She hesitated before continuing. "With your permission, sir, I'd like to conduct a loss of GPS exercise over the next few days. My quartermasters are getting pretty good at celestial navigation. Turning off the satellites'll boost their confidence."

A gangly six-foot brunette, Barrister's eyes weren't far below Bill's as he sat in his elevated chair.

"You sure they're up to it?" he asked.

"Yes, sir. I've had them shooting stars and sun lines twice a day and making local apparent noon observations. They shot moon lines and latitude by Polaris 'til the new moon made it too dark to see the horizon. They're ready, sir."

Bill smiled and nodded.

Quite junior, Barrister had only worn lieutenant's bars for a few months before reporting aboard. But she'd jumped into her new job with a vengeance.

"Okay, Nav. But let's get this FONOP done first. Start your exercise right after supper. Since it's a simulated system casualty, coordinate with the CSO and the Combat Systems Maintenance Center. They can use it for training, too."

The Freedom of Navigation Operation required they pass within twelve nautical miles of the reef to demonstrate the US did not recognize the People's Republic of China's territorial water claim. The Chinese had used fill to create a man-made island in contravention of international law. Bill had participated in FONOPs many times in many locales over his eighteen-year career. Normally, they were fairly routine.

Barrister smiled. "Aye aye, sir." She returned to the chart table at the back of the bridge.

Bill then addressed the officer of the deck. The OOD, the officer in charge of "driving" the ship for his or her four-hour watch, ensured continuity of the ship's routine and responded to emergencies.

"Kris, ask the XO to come to the bridge, please."

"Aye aye, sir."

Lieutenant Killingsworth reached for the ship's interior communications telephone and punched the code for the executive officer's stateroom.

"Yes, ma'am, this is the OOD. The captain requests you come to the bridge." A pause, then, "Aye, ma'am."

"Sir, XO's on her way."

"Thanks." Bill leaned back in his chair. "That Chinese frigate still on station?"

Killingsworth smiled. "Yes, sir, she's there. She couldn't keep better station if we'd ordered her to."

Two days ago, a *Jianghu*-class frigate of the People's Liberation Army Navy had plopped herself exactly three thousand yards on their port quarter and had remained relentlessly and silently with them since.

During the transit the XO would remain on the bridge while Bill went below to the Combat Information Center or CIC. He didn't expect any trouble, but he wanted the XO's greater ship-handling experience on the bridge in case the frigate tried to get in the way, something that had happened more frequently of late.

The tension was higher for this FONOP. In office for only nineteen months, the new president had been verbally hammering the Chinese government over dozens of issues, from disputed island claims to Taiwan and trade. He'd really heated things up when he'd ended the One-China Policy that for decades had governed US relationships with both the People's Republic of China (the PRC) and Taiwan. He'd then doubled down, formally recognizing the Taiwanese government as the Republic of China.

In retaliation, the PRC had withdrawn its ambassador to the US and reduced diplomatic contact to a bare minimum. As the war of words escalated, tensions ramped up on the Korean peninsula, and the president's verbal sniping with the North Korean dictator also exacerbated that situation.

When the XO arrived, Bill climbed down and headed below.

After a brief stop in the wardroom for a fresh cup of tea, Bill walked into the dim, blue-lit Combat Information Center and took his seat.

The brown padded leather chair, like the one on the bridge, sat mounted on a cylindrical steel pedestal right next to the Tactical Action Officer's station. As the only person aboard with the authority to fire weapons in the absence of the captain, the TAO was responsible for defending the ship.

The amber glow of electronic displays showed the status of sensors and weapon systems, radio circuits being listened to, callsigns of other ships in the strike group, and a plethora of other information of use to those who stood watch there day and night. The men and women at various computer consoles monitored radars and other sensors to track nearly every man-made object that floated or flew around the ship. Their headsets kept them in constant quiet communication. The low hum of cooling fan motors hovered just below the threshold of hearing, and the smell of warm electronics competed with the scents from a dozen or so cups of coffee set in cup holders throughout the space. The CIC Watch Officer — the CICWO, or "sick-wo" as the sailors pronounced it — supervised it all and ensured the TAO and CO had the information they needed.

In front of Bill, three Large Screen Displays showed what the ship's own radars saw, augmented with surface and air contacts that came in via computer data links. The latter currently included tracks from the MQ-4C Triton Unmanned Aerial Vehicle in an orbit over the central South China Sea. The Triton could remain on station for up to thirty hours, its radar and other sensors identifying, tracking, and reporting surface vessels over nearly the entire South China Sea. Augmenting the Triton's data was an intelligence broadcast that showed all the information that national intelligence assets had on the various colored air and surface tracks.

Nicholas's own sensors were limited by the fact they were only a few dozen feet above the sea surface and exclusively detected things in their line of sight and a little beyond. For floating objects, that meant perhaps twenty-five miles. But the Triton orbited above forty thousand feet, giving it a detection range far beyond *Nicholas's* relatively short radar horizon.

On the counter at which Bill and the TAO sat were two sets of three computer monitors, fed by both the ship's combat system and the desktop computers mounted on the deck at their feet. Bill had Third and Seventh Fleet, and the Carrier Strike Group command chat windows open, as well as his Navy e-mail and message traffic.

As he sat down, the TAO on watch, Lieutenant Commander Andy Pettibone, looked up. "Morning, Captain."

Pettibone was the ship's combat systems officer and he took his job very seriously. Though not a "screamer," in the eleven months he'd been aboard he'd displayed little sense of humor on duty or off. Today his face carried an even more serious mien, eyes roaming rhythmically from his computer to the systems' status displays above his head, then to the large screen displays.

"Anything change, Andy?"

Pettibone leaned back and stretched, arms behind his head.

"Not really, sir. Got yesterday's daily activity summary from PACFLT. Last night's surveillance flight along the north China coast got escorted a bit too closely. They narrowly avoided a mid-air collision. Looks like it got pretty hairy for a couple of minutes. Someone in Beijing must've thought better of it, 'cause the Chinese fighters suddenly pulled back a few hundred yards, like normal. But no change to the Rules of Engagement."

Bill grimaced as he donned his headphones. "One of these days, somebody's going to make a mistake and someone else will take a missile in the face." He sat back, took a deep breath, and faked a yawn. "But it didn't happen, so let's get on with our job. No ROE change is good. What's the count to liberty call in Singapore?"

Pettibone gave him a rare smile. "Nine days, sir. Ops keeps trying to tell me I've got duty the first two days, and I keep telling him what he can do with his duty." Pettibone's wife would meet the ship in Singapore, so he planned to take leave.

Bill grinned and sipped his tea. Idly, he rubbed the tip of his nose.

Yes, life is good.

"Vampire! Vampire! Bearing one two six. I say again, vampire bearing one two six."

The call across their headsets shattered the calm with silently urgent activity.

Bill stood and quickly looked left to where the electronic warfare supervisor sat near the port bulkhead of CIC. Despite his headphones, the SLQ-32's buzz was unmistakable. The radar-warning receiver instantly alerted if it detected an electronic emission that it decided constituted a threat.

Pressing the microphone key, he began, "Wha—"

Pettibone beat him to it. "Missile type? And are you sure?"

Pettibone's eyes were wide with alarm but his voice remained steady.

Bill imagined his own eyes were just as wide. His heart raced. He took a deep breath and deliberately calmed himself. He sensed furtive glances coming his way, his people checking his reaction.

Awaiting the EW Supe's response, he assured himself it had to be a false report.

"Yes, sir, SLQ's sure. Appears to be a YJ-62. We're picking up three separate seekers," responded the EW Supe. He sounded like he couldn't believe it either.

So much for a bad indication. One false report was very possible; three were highly unlikely. Bill's mouth went dry.

"Aye. ADC, TAO. See anything?" asked Pettibone.

The air defense coordinator, tasked with defending the ship against air and missile attack, had a combined radar and data link display at her console. She leaned forward, face barely a foot from her screen, staring intently.

"Nothing, si — no, wait, I have a tentative track at twelve nautical miles. Firming up . . ."

A pause, then, "Solid track, eleven nautical miles, bearing one two five, inbound at Mach point seven five. Composition three."

"Very well."

Bill and Pettibone both zoomed in and searched their displays.

Pettibone saw it first. "Got it, track three four eight six. Confirm ID?"

The ADC breathed heavily into her mike as she answered, "Based on EW, I make 'em hostile cruise missiles, sir."

"Very well. Take track three four eight six with birds."

Pettibone glanced quickly at Bill as he said it. Seeing Bill give a slight nod, Pettibone finished, "Batteries released."

"ADC, aye, taking track three four eight six with birds."

Bill looked over his shoulder as she punched commands into her keyboard. A sense of unreality kept his head swirling.

Pettibone touched his sleeve lightly. "GQ, sir?" he asked.

Bill didn't hesitate. "No, let's fight like we trained. Condition three. I don't want everyone running around in case we take a hit."

Pettibone went back to fighting the ship.

From the bridge, the boatswain's mate of the watch's (BMOW) voice came over the 1MC, the ship's announcing system. "All hands take cover within the skin of the ship. The ship is under attack. That is, all hands take cover within the skin of the ship. This is NOT a drill."

Someone had gotten word to the bridge, Bill noted with satisfaction.

As the announcement finished, six loud *whooshes* shook the ship one after another as the first interceptors slammed out of their vertical launcher cells forward and aft, leaping into the sky to deal destruction on the inbound missiles. Bill wiped his palms on his trousers.

"Vampire, vampire. Multiple vampires, bearing one two six. At least six more inbound."

Bill's head snapped left.

That made for nine. Definitely way up in the Not Good category.

"Combat, Bridge. The Chinese frigate just turned one eighty and kicked it in the ass. He's hauling butt the other way."

The words exploded out of the intercom, the "bitch box". The PLAN frigate didn't want to be in the target area.

She probably gave the reef the targeting data, Bill thought.

"TAO, handle the inbounds first, but as soon as you do, I want that frigate dead, understand? Don't let him live long enough to get outside his minimum missile range."

Pettibone glanced over at him then back to his console. His hands flew as they sent electronic orders to his team. Included were directions to the gun system to be ready to engage any missiles that survived the outbound interceptors, and to put the Close In Weapons System — CIWS — in Automatic mode. It would engage any "leakers" that got past the guns and missiles.

"Aye, sir. Kill the frigate before he can hit us," Pettibone responded. "Harpoon, TAO. Get a solution on that frigate."

"Harpoon, aye. Sir, it's inside min—"

Pettibone snapped, "I know. As soon as he's *not*, kill him."

The CIC crew worked like clockwork, as if it were a drill. Knowing if they missed one of those red icons on their screens, they wouldn't just get a bad mark on an exercise grade sheet, they all continued to do their jobs. The small vocal quavers and shrill tones had faded. The shock wouldn't hit until later.

"EW, TAO. Chaff and jam and drop decoys. Batteries released on all EW countermeasures," Pettibone said into his mike.

"Aye, sir. I been jammin' already," came the response.

Bill noted it for his after-action discussion with the team. While the EW operator's initiative was laudable, he should tell the TAO what he was doing.

His stomach lurched — there might not be a next time.

It suddenly became real for Bill. He shrugged off the chill that seized him. There wasn't time.

"Combat, Bridge. The frigate's training its gun at us," shouted the intercom.

Before Bill could say anything, Pettibone called, "ADC, TAO, take track three one two two with gun, whatever you got loaded. Bridge, TAO, come left hard to zero five zero."

Even as Pettibone finished speaking, the ship increased speed and heeled into the turn, the gas turbine engines winding up. He silently thanked God the XO was on the bridge. She'd aimed *Nicholas* right at the frigate, reducing the area it could aim for.

Within seconds the salvo warning bell shrilled from the gun mount topside. The five-inch rounds ripped out one after another, the ship jarring with each as the gun fired again and again, as if in an earthquake.

Another louder thud came from the portside. The ship shuddered out of rhythm with the gun. In eighteen years of naval service, he'd never heard nor felt something like it. As he reached for the intercom, it barked at him.

"Combat, Bridge. I'm taking evasive action. The frigate just missed us, port side."

So that was the sound and feel of a near miss, the 100-

millimeter round exploding in the water nearby. Bill pressed his lips together and held tight to the arms of his chair.

How dare they shoot at my ship?

Somehow, inbound missiles were less personal than four-inch gun shells.

The ship, already heeled over to starboard, abruptly careened back to port as the rudder shifted back and forth in a series of zig-zag turns. A steady course made them an easier target.

"Bridge, TAO. Don't turn so far the gun doesn't bear," called Pettibone.

"Aye, sir," came the response. "OOD has the conn."

Bill reached out and hit another button on the intercom, then pushed the switch to talk.

"Damage Control Central, this is the captain. Damage report from near miss, port side amidships," he said. Turning to Pettibone, he asked, "What's the range to that frigate?"

More vampire calls came from the EW Supe. A total of twelve missiles screamed toward them in three groups.

Moving his cursor over the track that represented the frigate and selecting it, Pettibone read off the range, "Five thousand and opening, sir."

Still inside their minimum range for launching missiles.

It would take a few more minutes for them to get far enough away. Topside, the gun continued spitting out rounds.

They had to have known about the planned attack, but they'd stayed on station until it was well underway to avoid giving away the surprise. He closed his eyes. The frigate captain had courage. *It may cost him his chance to get away and his crew their lives.*

"Combat, Bridge. We're hitting them, sir. At least five times."

"Give me a damage report on the enemy ship as soon as you can."

Funny, he mused. He'd just called it the enemy ship. How quickly he'd adapted to a new reality.

Just moments later, as still more missiles left their vertical launcher cells, the OOD called again.

"Combat, enemy ship's on fire aft and slowing. Her superstructure's a wreck. She's not firing anymore."

Bill heaved a sigh. They'd survived a surface gun duel with not a single hit. That was nothing short of miraculous.

"ADC, TAO. Break engage with gun. Standby for air action if we need it." Pettibone paused, then said, "Bridge, TAO. Come right to one two five."

With the frigate no longer a significant threat, Pettibone would use the gun against any surviving inbounds. Bill wasn't so sure. He opened his mouth to say something when the ADC called out.

"We've got leakers. Engaging with gun."

Bill sighed.

The concept for defending a ship in a modern sea battle depends on training the TAO to exercise good judgment quickly and decentralizing decision-making. Bill's only role was to step in if the watch team was going to make a bad decision. Thus far, they'd been like a well-oiled machine and there'd been nothing he would have done differently. Indeed, intervening might slow their response, add confusion, and increase the probability of taking a hit.

The concept had just been proved again. But it left him feeling useless.

After a short pause while the gun trained around to face the new threat, it began barking out more five-inch rounds. Two inbounds hadn't been killed by outbound missile fire or seduced away by jamming, decoys, or chaff. Around him, calm orders were given or acknowledged:

"Shift engage to track three six nine two."

"Splash one, continuing."

"CIWS confirmed in auto."

"Take track three one three two."

"Take track three one three two, aye."

"Splash track three one three two. One leaker."

"CIWS tracking."

Then came the tearing *brrrrrrp* of the CIWS engaging an inbound missile.

He closed his eyes and braced himself.

In the cacophony of battle came a distant explosion. Seconds later, rattles sounded on the main deck portside above his head.

"Combat, Bridge. CIWS got it. It exploded about a hundred yards out. Some pieces hit us, but it doesn't look like there's any damage."

"DC Central, captain. Call the Bridge and find out where the shrapnel hit us, then get some more investigators out. Report damage. But nobody goes topside."

"Aye, sir. I was about to call you. Minor damage from the near miss. Mostly things knocked off bulkheads. No hull buckling that we can see. We're pulling down some bulkhead insulation to make sure." A pause. "No casualties."

"Sir, want me to finish off the frigate?" asked Pettibone.

Bill sat back in his chair. With the frigate burning and unable to shoot back, technically he shouldn't take it under fire again. But part of him, the angry part, desperately wanted to punish its crew for the sneak attack.

His professional side won. He shook his head and reached for the intercom.

"Bridge, captain. Call the frigate on bridge-to-bridge channel sixteen. Order them to surrender."

What a strange word. Surrender harkens back to the age of sail. Do I have to think about a prize crew? No. We'll take the survivors off and sink the hulk. He continued, "Then close them to take on prisoners. Pass the word to muster the security force and station the boat handling—"

The frigate made a different decision.

"Sir, the frigate just fired something."

At nearly the same instant Sonar called, "TAO, hydrophone effects, bearing zero three five. Torpedo in the water."

"Bridge, Sonar, recommend emergency turn alpha."

"Bridge aye. Executing."

Pettibone also reacted, ordering an anti-air missile launched in an anti-surface mode.

Nicholas began an evasive turn designed to avoid the torpedo. As she heeled sharply to one side then the other, the CIC watch standers clung to their chairs, though they'd all buckled their seat belts as soon as the shooting started.

The torpedo ran up their wake. Unable to gain sonar contact on *Nicholas*, it kept going and disappeared. Meanwhile, an SM-2 missile screamed over the short expanse of water to rip into the enemy. Next, as the frigate came back into the firing arc for *Nicholas's* five-inch gun, twenty-one more high explosive rounds also slammed into the now savagely burning hulk.

Hoping the action was finally over, Bill unbuckled himself and rose. Despite the cool air in CIC, he wiped sweat from his brow.

Turning to Pettibone, he said, "I want to see Ops and his draft OPREP THREE ASAP. We need to get the report out most skosh."

As he headed out the watertight door, he paused and called back, "Just in case, let's get our Nixie torpedo decoy in the water at short stream. And get the tail out. I don't want to be surprised by a submarine."

CHAPTER
TWO

2325 Zulu, 26 Oct
0625 Local Time, 27 Oct
USS *Nicholas*, South China Sea

The white faces and anxious eyes of his sailors said he needed to address the crew.

"Captain's on the Bridge."

Crossing to the port side bridge wing, Bill stared over the gentle swells at the wreck. He noted with satisfaction *Nicholas's* gun mount remained trained on what was left of their enemy. Its barrel moved lazily up and down as *Nicholas* rolled, the gyro stabilizer maintaining a perfect aim point.

Watching the flaming ruins of the corvette, his knees began to shake. Men still hastened along its deck while others already swam in the water alongside. As he watched, more emerged from inside the skin of the ship, often dragging shipmates. They threw them over the side before jumping themselves into the expanding oil slick. Fortunately, it wasn't burning. *Yet.*

From the fires onboard the derelict a huge pillar of black and gray smoke climbed diagonally into the now piercing blue sky. The pall of smoke contrasted sharply with the peaceful seascape.

As *Nicholas* slowly approached the blazing hulk, the bow of the frigate disappeared in a large flash. An enormous ball of flame and black smoke erupted. Bill caught a glimpse as the gun mount climbed dozens of feet into the air before plunging into the water ahead of the vanished bow. Seconds later, the shock wave arrived and shook *Nicholas*, momentarily deafening everyone topside. Chunks of metal and other debris splashed down between the two ships.

Bill rose from behind the splinter shield where he'd instinctively ducked.

As the smoke rose clear, the frigate's stern rose quickly into the air, then slid down to a watery grave.

He stared, mouth open and unheeded, eyes wide, as the enemy ship passed from the light into the dark. He closed his eyes and paused for a moment, his anger vanishing. Opening them again, he looked out over the sea. Fewer men floated there than before.

He walked back inside and called out, "OOD, move in and take the survivors aboard. Rig fire hoses to keep the oil away from the side."

As he stepped to the 1MC microphone, he nodded to the BMOW and said, "All hands, Boats."

The man already had his pipe in hand. Raising it to his lips, he blew the piercing call that directed all hands to listen up. Archaic, nevertheless the call was traditional and most ships still required the use of the bosun's pipe to signal the various announcements made daily both underway and in port.

A bit of normalcy will help.

Bill raised the mike.

"This is the captain speaking. As I'm sure all hands are aware, *Nicholas* has just beaten off an unprovoked attack by the Chinese. The reef ahead of us must have coordinated with the frigate that's been shadowing us, and launched on us. Because you are *Nicholas* sailors, we lived to fight another day. The Chinese frigate was sunk."

He paused. Dead silence reigned on the bridge save for the hum of ventilation and equipment. He began again.

"I have no idea why they would do such a thing. There's no more tension today than yesterday or the day before. However, we will remain on alert. It's pretty unlikely this is an isolated incident. Attacks of this size usually aren't. We'll maintain Condition III watches, but we're going to stream Nixie and the tail to make sure we don't get surprised again.

"We have a proud tradition to uphold, a tradition built by previous ships named *Nicholas*, from the World War II destroyer that fought with distinction in the Solomons and throughout the Pacific war, to the frigate that served through the Cold War, Desert Storm, and Operation Iraqi Freedom. Samuel Nicholas himself, the first commandant of the Marine Corps, would be proud of you today, and I know you'll continue to do yourselves proud.

"As I learn more from the higher ups in the chain of command, I'll pass what I can on to you. That is all."

Bill handed the mike back and headed for his chair. The XO, Commander Joanna Irving, climbed down from her chair and followed. As they arrived, the bitch box squawked.

"Bridge, Ops here. Sir, we've been trying to reach Third Fleet on SATCOM. But I can't raise them, or anyone else, for that matter. Radio's checking the circuit, but they think the satellites are off the air. Given what's happened, they may be gone. But we'll keep trying. The hard copy's coming up to the bridge for your release." Frustration punctuated Lieutenant Commander Jason Campbell's voice.

Any ship attacked anywhere in the world had five minutes in which to report the attack to the Navy chain of command, the Chairman of the Joint Chiefs, and to the National Command Authority in the persons of the secretary of defense and the president. That report process started with a voice report to Third Fleet, *Nicholas's* operational commander. A hard copy heavily formatted message that also had to go out within five minutes followed.

The OOD looked over at Bill, saw him nod, and flipped the switch.

"Bridge, aye. Captain acknowledges."

Keeping her voice low, the XO asked, "Sir, what the hell's going on?"

Irving had fifteen years of service in cruisers and destroyers. A medium height, medium build woman, she could blend into a crowd and nearly disappear. She'd never distinguished herself but had no blemishes on her record, either. He'd found her a solid, all-around good officer. More importantly, in fifteen months, she would relieve him as *Nicholas's* commanding officer. His job was to prepare her.

He shook his head. "I don't know, XO. Intel's got nothing, unless they're hiding something. Third Fleet must be as surprised as us. But that doesn't mean someone up the chain in the Pentagon or White House didn't know something."

In the past there'd been occasions when folks at the pointy end of the spear had been left hanging by things the loony bin swirling inside the Beltway had known about but hadn't deigned to tell the operational forces. That had improved in the decade since the wars in Iraq and Afghanistan, but lately the pendulum had swung back. Secrets were being kept again in Washington.

"Meantime, can you go down and supervise the rescue?"

"Aye, sir. I've already mustered the Security Force to draw small arms, and the chief master at arms and his folks will supervise. The doc and his two corpsmen will be down there, too." She grimaced and stood silent.

"What's on your mind, XO?"

She closed her eyes and shook her head. "I can't believe I'm about to say this, but *should* we rescue them, sir?"

Bill rubbed his cheek. "I know how you feel. I came up here from Combat mad as hell."

He looked off at the horizon. To the west clear sky dominated, nothing to indicate the destruction and death that reigned to the east. "Part of me doesn't want to. But you know the ancient law of the sea. Not to mention the more recent codified laws. We're obligated to pick them up. Besides, we can't take what their government did out on them. Though it's awful tempting."

"But isn't that risky, sir? What if there's a sub around?" She took her ball cap off and ran her hand through her sandy hair.

Bill nodded. "I get it, XO. But if it was us in the water?"

She shook her head and was silent for a moment. Then she sighed. "Okay, sir, I give. We'll get them aboard and secure them below. For now, we'll use the starboard hangar to assess injuries, that sort of thing. With your concurrence, we'll move the helo out onto the flight deck. It might be good to have it in Ready Fifteen, anyway. They'll need dry clothes. I'll dig into the slop chest and augment from the laundry as needed."

"We'll end up owing reimbursement," Bill said.

The XO nodded and continued. "I'll have Suppo get the CSs to heat up some soup, too." The ship's Culinary Specialists worked for the supply officer and were responsible for feeding the crew.

"Good thought. Let me know how it goes." Bill grunted. "I'm not sure I want to feed them, but it's probably the right thing to do."

The XO shrugged. "Yes, sir. Good thing we had no casualties or I'd be worried about a few of our more, uh, boisterous folks. Anything else, sir?"

When he shook his head, she turned and walked toward the watertight door.

Bill rubbed his eyes. Just as she lifted the handle, he called out, "And tell Radio, do whatever it takes to get that report out. When I was an ensign, we didn't have all these high falutin' satellites. Let's think a bit outside the box."

Bill sat back to think. The XO was right. It would be good to have a helicopter ready to launch on fifteen minutes notice in case they detected a submarine or another enemy surface ship. He or the TAO should have thought of it.

Stress, he decided. *I'll have to watch for that. It won't do to miss something.*

He needed to make sure his leadership team was thinking through other potential problems. He counted on them to ensure nothing got missed. In fact . . .

Leaning forward, he pushed down on the lever of the intercom.

"TAO, captain. Go passive in the link with the drone and shut down SPY. I don't want the enemy tracking us with our own radar emissions. Set EMCON One Alpha."

"TAO, aye. Maybe they'll think the frigate got us, sir," came the response.

Setting Emission Control One Alpha required the mighty SPY-6 Aegis phased array radar be turned off. But it allowed them to still listen in on what the drone saw.

Nicholas settled into a complete radio and radar silent mode of operations.

It would be intensely uncomfortable for warriors used to knowing everything that went on around them.

The smell of marine fuel oil and burning debris fouled the air. The sea itself lay mute and flat, as if the floating detritus of death offended it. Surrounding *Nicholas* were the remains of what had been a ship and its human crew.

Nicholas pulled only thirty-nine survivors out of the water, of a crew that normally numbered over one hundred seventy. They also brought nine bodies aboard. A Chinese lieutenant and one of his senior enlisted men identified them. Then the dead were bagged and stowed in one of the meat freezers for later burial.

As the last of the living was hauled aboard, Barrister, who

now had the watch as OOD, approached Bill as he watched from the starboard bridge wing.

"Sir, TAO reports the Triton's circling about ninety nautical miles west. The center of its orbit is drifting west at about fifteen knots, consistent with winds aloft. He said it's still up in the link, but something's not right."

"Did he say what?" Bill asked as he rubbed the tip of his nose.

"He said it looked like it's in some kind of default mode. He checked track history. About five minutes after the island shot at us, it stopped its figure eight and went into this circular orbit. That's when it started drifting, too." She shrugged. "That's all he had, sir."

"Alright, thanks, Nav. As soon as the last survivor's onboard, let's get out of here. Best speed directly away from the island."

"Aye aye, sir."

It was the XO's turn next. She'd arrived on the bridge while he and Barrister talked. She waited until Barrister had gone back inside, then closed the watertight door so they could speak privately.

"Sir, we probably should talk about our own casualties. Turns out we had a couple after all."

Bill looked quickly at her.

She shrugged and continued, "We had three folks who, uh, didn't react well. Ensign Sandstrom was on the port bridge wing when the frigate started shooting. He froze up. Killingsworth took the conn, got the ship turning, then handed it off to Barrister. Boats called the corpsman, and they got Sandstrom down to the wardroom." She consulted the notes in her wheel book. Every officer and chief carried the small, dark green notebooks.

"Petty Officer Brownsfield was running aft in the portside second deck passageway, headed for Repair 5. The near miss exploded outside the hull near him and he wigged out. And when first division ran to take cover inside the skin of the ship, Seaman Jastrow was the last man off the fo'c'sle. He was just at the watertight door when missiles left the forward launcher. He panicked and ran down and hid in his bunk. Master Chief had to go down there to coax him out. They're all in sickbay. Doc gave them valium."

Bill leaned back and looked up into the sky. Instead of seeing the puffy clouds overhead, he saw the three men's faces. He should have expected there'd be at least a few who found combat difficult. It was no surprise they were among those who *hadn't* been busy defending the ship.

"Well, I understand Brownsfield and Jastrow. Sandstrom . . ." Bill said.

The ship's electrical officer, Sandstrom was a nervous type who always looked like he didn't know why he'd joined the Navy. Fortunately, the division had a strong leader in the chief Electrician's Mate. Bill and the chief engineer had decided to let the chief pull the ensign along and help him gain confidence. But now there was this.

"Okay, have Doc talk to me tonight about all three. For now, keep it between Doc, the master chief, their department heads and division officers."

"Aye, sir." The XO lingered for a moment, then said, "Sir, you know how it is. The bridge watch saw what happened with Sandstrom. Half of Jastrow's division saw him skedaddle, and Brownsfield ran *through* Repair 5 when he lost it. The rumor mill's already going full blast."

Bill shrugged. "We can't pretend nothing happened. But we owe it to the three of them to handle it discreetly. I'll talk to the wardroom tonight."

The XO nodded and headed inside. Bill rose and followed her, headed for the radio room.

It was time to get personally involved in getting the OPREP THREE off the ship.

CHAPTER
THREE

After hearing about Radio's efforts to bring up alternate comm circuits, Bill headed aft to the next item on his mental list: the prisoners.

Arriving at the hangar, he nodded to the guard, who wore a holstered Beretta 9mm pistol on her hip, the cover unclipped for quicker draw. She spoke briefly into the throat mike of the radio headset she wore.

"Go ahead, sir. They know you're coming," she said as she lifted the handle on the watertight door and held it open.

The sorriest sight he'd ever seen greeted him.

Thirty-nine cots clustered close together on the non-skid covered deck in the center of the closed hangar. On most sat or lay a Chinese sailor. A few others stood silently alone or in a small group. They all shared the same blank, haunted look, holding blankets tightly around themselves despite the late morning tropical heat. Doc, his two mates, and two other *Nicholas* sailors, bent over cots on the far edge.

Seeing him approach, the third class Hospital Corpsman – HM3 – nudged HM1 Wells, *Nicholas's* independent duty corpsman, universally known as Doc. As Wells stood and turned around, Bill waved him back down to keep at what he'd been doing.

Bill looked down at the men being treated.

The HM3 injected morphine into a badly burned man. When Bill looked at the blanket, his stomach turned and he closed his eyes briefly. Where the legs should have been, the material lay flat against the cot.

Next to the HM3, the HM2 stitched up an ugly jagged wound in another man's abdomen. Despite being nearly closed, blood seeped around the sutures. Two sailors held the unconscious patient down. Bill began to sweat even more.

He turned back to Wells. "How's it going, Doc?"

Wells didn't answer for a moment, then sighed. He stood and covered the face of the man he'd been working on.

"This here's the second one we lost, sir. First one was probably dead when we hauled him aboard. His arm was hanging by the muscle and nobody saw him bleeding out. Not their fault. We're gonna lose the one with Liddel, too. That's why he got morphine. And we'll probably lose the one Small's sewing up."

Bill nodded toward the now shrouded man next to them.

Doc shrugged. "This one had a long sliver of metal in the back of his head. Pretty unresponsive when we got him in here, so I just made him comfortable while we treated those we thought we could save." He swept his arm around the hangar. "There's one or two more we might lose, depending on infection. Their wounds were filthy with oil and other crap from their ship. Most all have burns of varying severity. We just have to see."

Bill remembered photos of survivors from the cruiser *Helena*, taken when they were pulled from the water by the first destroyer *Nicholas* in 1943. They'd had the same haunted look, been nearly or entirely naked, and covered in oil. He'd read the war diary of a first class Watertender serving in *Nicholas* and the profound effect it had had on the writer.

Now he understood viscerally. He'd never seen war at sea up close and personal. Few on active duty had. Now he prayed his crew would never suffer a similar fate.

The man with no legs died while he and Doc talked.

As they finished, one of the prisoners moved toward him, quickly intercepted by two guards. The man stopped and bowed his head. Bill held up his hand to keep them from dragging him away.

"You want to talk to me?" he asked.

In clear English, the man said, "Are you captain? I am Lieutenant Shi. I am senior officer. I thank you for bringing us aboard." He bowed his head again.

Not knowing fully what to say, Bill simply said, "You are welcome."

His face working, Shi asked, "What is next?"

"I do not know, Lieutenant. We will keep you safe for now and treat your injured. You are our prisoners. I require you to cooperate with my crew, follow their orders. Do you understand?"

"Yes, sir. Understand. I will." He bowed one last time and walked back to the small group of his men.

On his way out, Bill visited with the guards briefly. Afterward, he skipped lunch and went to his at-sea cabin to lie down for a few minutes.

The phone by his bunk buzzed, interrupting his rest.

"Captain."

"Sir, this is the Navigator. My folks have been troubleshooting GPS for the past hour with the ETs. We're certain it's not our gear. Looks like GPS is off the air completely." The Electronics Technicians maintained most electronic gear aboard ship.

"Huh. Well, I guess you get your celestial nav exercise earlier than planned. Still sure your folks are up to it?"

Without hesitation, she answered, "Yes, sir."

"Good, but let me know if you have the slightest doubt. Remember, CIC's blind, too, no radar or GPS."

As day turned to night, the OPREP THREE still hadn't gone out. Radio had been rotating through all the primary, secondary, and tertiary communication frequencies all day with no joy. Just as he sat down for evening meal, his phone buzzed.

"Captain."

"Sir, Ops here. Ensign Randall just called me. NAVFOR-JAPAN is up on HF."

"Great. I'm on my way. Get that OPREP out—"

"Sir, wait. They're broadcasting in the blind on a clear circuit. They're telling anyone listening not to respond or transmit under any circumstances. Then it repeats."

Bill let the handset slide down onto his shoulder for a moment as he considered the news. "So they already know about the attack. This confirms it was big."

"Sir, it means it was pretty devastating, too. If not, they'd have us up in a link so we'd have shared battlespace awareness across the theater."

"I agree. Keep monitoring it. If they put out any orders, take action first, then call me. I'll be up when I finish supper. And Ops, see if we can find an HF data link someone somewhere is broadcasting. It'd help to at least be receive-only and get some kind of picture."

Every fiber in Bill's being wanted to rush out of the wardroom to listen to the voice broadcast. But as he looked around at his officers, he couldn't. Conversation had died and they looked at him.

"Ahem. Radio's copying a broadcast from Commander US Naval Forces Japan. They're telling everyone *not* to respond. So, it sounds like the attack was pretty big and pretty bad."

As his audience stirred, he hurried to add, "But the good

news is that the chain of command is functioning. And there are other forces out here, underway."

He looked at Lieutenant Junior Grade Hawke, the electronic warfare officer and collateral duty intelligence officer.

"Emily, what friendlies were underway when this happened?"

Hawke closed her eyes tightly for a moment, then said, "Sir, as I recall, the *Reagan* strike group was underway for an exercise. Might have been with the Japanese? And I think the command ship, *Blue Ridge*, too, either with the CSG or nearby. I don't remember if Seventh Fleet's embarked or not, but I'll find out." She set her napkin down and moved to stand.

Bill waved her to sit. "There's time to find out after supper. Sit and eat." He broadened his gaze to include all the young men and women at the table.

"I'll let all hands know what I hear. Everybody's probably worried about their loved ones back home. Don't. The only thing we can do to help them right now is to stand in the way of those who've tried to hurt us. Everyone understand?"

He waited until he'd gotten nods from all of them. Then he turned to the XO and engaged her in small talk. Slowly, the noise level returned to something closer to normal.

When he finished eating, he rose and moved out the door. Once it closed behind him, he rushed down to the Comm Center.

He put his hand under the cover of the crypto lock and punched in the combination. Hearing the click, he opened the door.

"Captain's in Radio."

"Alright, Commo, whatcha got?"

Ensign Randall took him to the watch supervisor's desk where Bill could hear the broadcast for himself.

"It's just repeating, sir. Nothing new. But Chief tried something else about five minutes ago. I was just about to call you."

Bill nodded and Randall led him back into the equipment racks. Near the back of the space, technically the starboard side of the ship, Chief Williamson held a set of headphones to his ear. When he saw Bill, he held them out.

"I thought we should try the BBC, their old World Service. It's still up. Here, take a listen."

Bill stayed for the next hour as they reported on the devastating attack on the United States.

They were at war. In the middle of it, *Nicholas* sailed alone and unafraid.

But unlike a majority of Americans and the US leadership, they at least knew who they were fighting.

CHAPTER
FOUR

0300 Zulu, 27 Oct
2000 Local Time
USS *Nicholas*, South China Sea

An announcement followed the bosun's pipe. "Now lay before the mast all eight o'clock reports. Eight o'clock reports will be taken in the wardroom by the executive officer."

Bill put the headphones down. Finding the chief, he said, "Pipe this into my cabin, but don't put it on ship's entertainment. Not yet."

"Aye, sir."

Minutes later he walked into the wardroom.

"Attention on deck," called the XO.

"Seats. I'm going to interrupt for just a few minutes." He took his seat at the head of the table. "I've been listening to the BBC. I'll tell the crew about it tonight before taps, but I wanted you all to hear the highlights."

He spent the next few minutes laying out what he'd heard. As he spoke, Pettibone's head sank into his hands, covering his face. When Bill was done, Pettibone raised his head, eyes red, and stared at the wardroom clock.

"Any questions?" Bill asked, rubbing the tip of his nose. He looked expectantly at Pettibone, then glanced at the XO. Catching her eye, he pushed his shoulder slightly toward the combat systems officer. She nodded.

"Alright then. Tomorrow, we see what's what. Maybe Seventh Fleet will have something for us. Meantime, watch your folks. They're going to be worried about the folks back home. We can't afford that. I'm worried about my family. I know you are, too. But we've still got a job to do out here, and it just got a lot tougher. If someone asks to see me or the XO, that's fine. But I don't want us to spend our time handing out comforting words. You can do that, too."

Turning to Irving, he asked her, "How're our three medical cases?"

She raised her eyebrows and said, "I told Doc to skip eight o'clocks and stay with them. He says Sandstrom is more embarrassed than anything else. He's got the rev. I told Doc to turn him loose in time for his watch if he thinks he can handle it. Jastrow's still sleeping. Brownsfield may be able to return to duty first thing in the morning."

Bill turned to Pettibone. "Andy, if Sandstrom can't take his watch, what's your plan?"

Rubbing his cheeks, he responded, "I'll put the quartermasters in port and starboard. Put their chief in the JOOD slot. That may mess with Barrister's ability to navigate, though."

Bill shook his head. "She says they're all trained up. If that's what you have to do, go ahead. Give her a head's up tonight. Tell her if she thinks it'll be an issue, come see me." He paused for a moment. "You okay, Andy?"

Pettibone looked sideways at him before answering. "Yes, sir. I'm fine." He quickly looked away.

Bill sat silently for a moment, then said, "Okay, XO, I'll leave you to it." He rose, grabbed a fresh cup of tea, and headed for his cabin.

The already jarring news worsened as more reports flooded in. He tried to review the daily Situation Report — SITREP. A summary of *Nicholas's* status, he'd ordered Ops to go ahead and assemble it though it wouldn't be sent off ship. But he struggled to focus. Visions of burning bases and buildings invaded his mind's eye.

Just before Taps at 2200, he went to the bridge.

"Boats, all hands, please." As the pipe echoed through the ship, Bill reviewed what he'd say. He jumped when the BMOW handed him the mike.

"Good evening, *Nicholas*. You all know we're at war. We've been able to dial up the British Broadcasting Corporation on shortwave. There don't seem to be many American news stations operating right now because power's down in large swaths of the country. I'm sure they're working to get it restored." He summarized what he'd heard.

Then he turned to what his crew really wanted to hear. "I know you're all worried about folks back home. Well, it looks as though the enemy deliberately avoided targeting civilians. I wish I had specific information about San Diego. I don't. But based on what I heard about other places, I'm sure our families are safe. It's a big city. Even if they were on base, I'm sure the Chinese weren't trying to take out the exchange, the commissary, or any of the office buildings. They targeted the ships. But remember, those ships have the same weapons we do. I'm sure some put up a fight. So stop worrying. The best thing we can do for the folks back home is keep up the fight out here. I'll keep you all informed as I hear anything new. I'm sure Third Fleet understands our need to know, but that has to take a back seat to their job of hitting back. That's all for now."

"Thanks, Boats," he said as he handed the mike back. Striding to his chair, he sat.

Lieutenant Dolan, the electronics maintenance officer, had the deck until midnight and sidled over to him. "Sir, Ops said we've heard nothing from Third Fleet. And Seventh Fleet's just telling us to keep quiet. Do you really think we'll get anything else?"

Bill shrugged. "Hell if I know, Bob. But until I know something else, I have to assume the chain of command's functioning."

The door opened and a shape moved through it. After a few moments while its eyes adjusted to the dark, it came to them and spoke. "Sir, request permission to do the evening prayer."

Dolan added, "With your permission, sir, I'll pass taps on time after."

"Permission granted," Bill answered.

After the Protestant lay leader finished the evening prayer, the BMOW piped, then passed the word. "Taps, taps, lights out. All hands turn into your bunks. Maintain quiet about the decks. The smoking lamp is out throughout the ship. Maintain darken ship. Now taps."

Bill retired to his cabin.

He'd just sat down when a knock interrupted him. "Enter," he called.

"Got a minute, Captain?" Irving asked.

"Sure, XO. Whatcha got?"

She followed his wave and sat on the sofa. The wardroom mess attendant hadn't yet come in and converted it to a bunk.

"I talked to Andy. He's worried about his wife. Her last email contained more than her flight info for Singapore. She was taking her class of ensigns to one of the destroyers at the naval station for gun fire support training, all week. He thinks she might have been onboard during the attack."

"Shit," was all Bill could muster. "Why didn't he come up here himself?"

She smiled briefly. "You know, SWO guilt. He doesn't want to look like a whiner. Figures he's got to keep things bottled up. It took a lot to get him to tell me that much."

Bill sighed and bit his lip. "What about the others? What about you? Your sister's in San Diego, right?"

She shook her head and said, "Yeah, but she works downtown. I'm sure she's okay. But Landy's another one I'm worried about. His wife works at the child development center on Miramar. He says he's not worried, but he wasn't his usual boisterous self at eight o'clocks."

"Dammit!" He threw his head back against the headrest of his chair. Eyes sweeping the cabin, he finally settled on the photo of HMS *Rose* he'd placed next to the porthole. Finding calm as she sailed toward the camera, he asked, "Remember 9/11?"

She shook her head. "I was a senior in high school. I didn't go to UW til the next fall."

Bill put his hands behind his head. "I was in fire control officer school, in Newport. Just a dumb ensign. We had the TV on in the classroom, at least until they told us to go home. Once they opened the base back up, Thursday I think it was, we were back in class. One of the instructors came in. I don't remember what he was teaching. Countermeasures or something like that. But he kept saying things wrong. We kind of made fun of him. Bunch of stupid shits we were." Bill shook his head and smiled sadly. "Turned out his sister was in one of the towers. He was waiting to hear from her. He never did." He leaned forward. "Our whole crew is like that lieutenant now. They're all waiting."

"Yes, sir. So we keep them busy. Keep their minds off it. It's like the first week of deployment, make sure they don't think of home."

Bill nodded. "That's it exactly. But we can't run drills this time. Got something in mind?"

She grinned. "I might. Something we ought to do, anyway. There's too much flammable material aboard. We'll strip ship, get rid of unnecessary crap. That should keep all hands busy for at least a couple of days."

"What are you going to do with it?"

"We'll stow the stuff no one wants to get rid of back aft, in one of the storerooms. The stuff we can get rid of, we'll either put through the trash compactor or burn in barrels on the flight deck."

"Sounds like a plan. Make it happen, XO."

Irving rose to leave, then stopped and looked at him. "Er, how're you holding up, sir?"

Bill snorted. "I'm fine. Don't worry about me. I'm livin' the dream."

She smiled wanly and left.

Like an alcoholic with a bottle, he kept listening to the radio. He finally decided to turn in at two o'clock. But as he reached for the switch his hand froze. The London newsroom had just gone to a reporter in San Diego.

Bill slumped in his chair as listened to the woman's report.

"I'm traveling to the Cabrillo Monument," she said. "From there, I should be able to look over all of San Diego: Even from the street, I see massive pillars of smoke. The sun itself, when I can see it, is deep crimson."

Bill's muscles tightened.

"I'm approaching a police barricade. There's a great deal of smoke along both sides of the road ahead. I'm told there are government facilities up here."

Identifying herself as a reporter, the police waved her through. She continued her report. "Ah, the sign on the left side of the road says Naval Information Warfare Center. Across the street . . . I can't quite read it yet. There. United States Third Fleet. So this is the headquarters. Or should I say, was. The buildings along the road, well, in fact, all the buildings I can see, are burning. They remind me of photos of London during the Blitz. Burning, the upper floors collapsed onto the lower. It's complete devastation here. I see a few smaller buildings undamaged, but anything of a size has been bombed."

She kept up the running tally but he couldn't listen any longer.

His brother was probably dead. The e-mail he'd received just before the attack would be the last he'd ever get.

Bill couldn't quite grasp it. Should he weep? A pang shrouded his heart, but not the crushing sorrow he'd felt when his parents had passed. It wasn't even as strong as when his wife had asked for a divorce. Instead, it hovered in the background. *It's just not real. Not with everything else.* But he looked around his cabin, everything shrouded in gray mist.

The weight of command had never lain so heavy on his shoulders. In the past he'd relished it, itched for more autonomy. Now he had nearly complete freedom and he hated it. The Biblical injunction to be careful what one wished for came to mind.

He finally succumbed to sleep around 0300 only to wake again at 0515. As usually happened, his sleeping mind had weighed the factors involved, so he'd awakened with at least one significant decision clear in his mind. At 0530, his phone buzzed.

"Captain."

"Good morning, sir, this is the TAO. It's zero five thirty. The ship is on course two seven zero, five knots. Winds are light out of the northwest. Sea state one. SPY is in standby. Sonar's passive. Nixie is streamed at short stay. Condition Three watch is set, all weapons systems ready. Chaff and decoys are armed. I hold the Harpoon keys. The CIWS keys are in the console, but CIWS is in manual."

"Thanks, Jason. Hey, I want you and CSO to work up a plan to hit Fiery Cross. I don't want to keep operating around here if they've got reloads for what they shot at us yesterday. See what you can come up with. We'll head that way as soon as you have something workable, hit them early. They may expect it but not this quickly. Hopefully, they think they hit us yesterday."

He hung up and headed for his shower.

CHAPTER
FIVE

1120 Zulu, 27 Oct
1920 Local Time
USS *Blue Ridge,* Western Pacific, 400 nautical miles south-
southeast of Honshu, Japan

Vice Admiral Heather Simpson sipped coffee from her large
metal covered cup and leaned back in her chair.

Tight bundles of cables and masses of pipes crisscrossed the
overhead of the briefing room aboard her flagship, USS *Blue
Ridge.* The large screen which displayed the intelligence brief
took up almost half of one bulkhead. The other three bulkheads
held smaller displays and various electronic equipment, nearly
hiding the sound-absorbent tile that kept noise from the rest of
the ship out. Here at least what the Navy called robin's egg blue
replaced the haze gray, stark white, and light green — puke
green, sailors called it — that pervaded elsewhere.

Tall and athletic, Simpson's still mostly blonde hair hung just
below her earlobes, framing an open face. Her most prominent
feature was an incongruously large nose set between deep blue
eyes. She leaned back in her padded faux leather chair in the

middle of the long table. Embedded in the table in front of her was a display that could either mirror what the bulkhead mounted displays showed or access one of her classified computers.

Her senior staff had just finished giving her the fourth intelligence update in the twelve hours since the Chinese attack. She normally received only one per day.

"That's about it, ma'am," said her staff intelligence officer, Captain Proudfoot.

"Very good, Pete, thanks." Swiveling left then right, she asked, "Any questions, people?"

Her deputy, Rear Admiral (Upper Half) Jack Percy, call sign Perk, asked, "Ma'am, I know the question of why isn't all that critical at this juncture, but do we have any ideas in that direction?"

"No, I don't think we do. And it *is* critical. It would tell us what their objectives are."

She turned to face the junior staff who didn't rate seats at the table. The hard metal chairs of earlier decades had been replaced by three rows of relatively comfortable theater seats.

She continued. "To beat the enemy requires we know what he wants. I know some of you get frustrated when I harp on understanding the enemy, being able to do a center of gravity analysis, and the whole pol-mil evaluation thing. But if ever there was a time when it was important to know what the enemy's objectives are, it's now."

She took another sip of her coffee. "I don't believe this was a bolt from the blue. If you look back over the past nineteen months, you can see the seeds of conflict being sown. The only thing that surprised me is their ability to prepare for and execute the attack without us recognizing it."

Turning back to Percy, she continued, "The Operational Planning Teams are doing tactical and operational level analyses. I'd like you to get a small team together and do a thorough strategic-level center of gravity analysis. Given what appears to have happened to our national civilian and military leadership, we'll get little help from them. So we have to operate at the strategic level, too."

Percy smiled. They'd scripted this before the brief.

The door opened and a chief petty officer entered. He handed a classified tablet to the operations officer, Captain Letisha Brickman.

Simpson stopped. "What is it, Letty?"

Brickman held up a finger for a few seconds, still scanning the screen. Then she raised her head. "We just got comms back with what's left in Hawaii. The INDOPACOM deputy commander is acting. He's designated us both Joint Task Force Commander and Joint Force Maritime Component Commander. That's in accordance with the latest approved version of the CONPLAN." She glanced down, then continued. "The combined staffs are working to get a couple of subs and surface ships underway. Once he finds out what's left on the West Coast, he'll piece together a couple of task groups and send them our way. *Nimitz* and *Stennis* are both underway, but only *Stennis* has an air wing. She's also got the rest of her strike group. *Nimitz* was independent steaming." She paused again and sucked in a breath. "He's giving us OPCON of *all* US forces in theater. That's *not* per the CONPLAN."

Then she looked up at Simpson. "There's not much in terms of guidance. A short paragraph in the Admin section says there's very little left in Pearl or Guam. They even sank *Missouri*. This HF circuit is all we're going to have with them. He says he'll give us whatever he can, it's up to us to use it."

The chief returned and tapped on the tablet again. Brickman quickly scanned it and added, "Third Fleet's back up, too. The N9 is acting. He shifted his flag to ex-*Iowa*, in Long Beach. They're assembling what ships they can, but they won't be able to do much in the way of command and control. There's no SATCOM left."

Simpson gave a low whistle. "So, it's confirmed. All the head-quarters were ravaged." Shaking her head, she said, "I don't envy the survivors."

Turning again to face the drawn, weary, and anxious faces that sat behind her, she said, "With the exceptions of Fifth and Sixth Fleets, which are way outside the theater and busy with their own problems, this means we're the most functional staff left in any of the services. Well, ourselves, and the US staffs on the Korean peninsula. But I'd venture a guess they're busy trying to deter the North Koreans." Her face darkened. "Japan got pretty badly schwacked, too. I have to admit, it was pretty gutsy of the Chinese to attack them. Maybe it'll cost them in the end. The Japanese are going to throw everything into this they can, and you know how highly I regard their military profes-sionalism."

She leaned forward and ran her eyes over her team. "So, people, INDOPACOM made us the quarterback. We don't have a full coaching staff to back us up. Worse, there are no scouts at the top of the stadium to watch, to assess the other team. The chain of command will help us if they can, but I'm skeptical about what they can do. I hope it's more than I expect, but for now we're going to call the plays and run them."

Looking around at the more senior men and women seated at the table, she finished. "To do that, we need to know what their goals are. Then we'll set about keeping them from achieving them." She smiled ever so slightly. "We know one of their objec-tives was to destroy our naval power. Well, they didn't quite succeed, and we're going to make them pay for that. So let's be about it."

After the brief, Simpson and her senior staff remained behind. As the door closed, she took off the face she'd shown her junior staff.

"Okay, now that it's just us chickens, let's be candid. I've kept my mouth shut about how fucked up I think the administration's policies toward China have been." She snorted. "Hell, they haven't *had* any coherent policy. They just said stupid shit in the media and did everything possible to piss off a nuclear-armed country with nearly four times the population of the US."

"Ma'am—" started Percy.

She raised her hand. "I'm not done, Perk. This isn't about politics. I know we have folks from both parties on this staff. What I'm saying is for this audience only." She took a big sip of coffee and grimaced. "I take pride in the fact that none of you know my politics. But dammit, I've got to call an idiot an idiot. And look where it got us."

Percy shook his head. "I won't disagree about a lack of policy. But what the hell got the Chinese to a place where they thought attacking us made sense?"

"Well, that's something your team can look at, after you do the Center of Gravity analysis. Me? I think the convergence of our threats to North Korea, recognition of Taiwan, and the economic war we declared got us here. I'm sure the weapons sales we announced a couple of months ago poured gas on the fire. Who thinks it was a good idea to announce we'd sell Taiwan ten Aegis DDGs, six LA class attack subs, and five squadrons of Joint Strike Fighters? Anyone?"

No one spoke. They just looked at her calmly. Brickman chewed a fingernail. Proudfoot's chin was up as he stared at his boss.

Finally, Percy said, "But the PRC are long-term thinkers, and they never make rash decisions. This seems the ultimate in rash."

Simpson shrugged. "We can't know everything they were thinking, Perk. Maybe they saw something happening in DC we don't know about. They've got that place saturated with intel assets. Who knows? What's important is they leaped, and we've got to push them back." She stood and stretched. "As usual, the shit show in DC handed us a plate of crap. Now we've got to deal with it."

She walked out.

CHAPTER
SIX

1140 Zulu, 27 Oct
0640 Eastern Time
Oval Office, The White House

"What the hell happened?"

Jack Hunter hated it when the president shouted at him. He didn't like dealing with petulant children. Especially when he hadn't even had his coffee yet.

The president of the United States had often been angry since inauguration. Hunter believed that sometime during the oath of office, Travis Donnelly realized what he'd signed up for. Accompanying that realization had been another one: he didn't want the job. Donnelly hadn't run to govern. Like everything else he did, he'd run for prestige and fame. And to increase his wealth.

But Donnelly had refused to take the easy way out. Instead, he simply ignored the job. On the rare occasion he inserted himself in events, he usually made things worse.

Hunter sighed for the umpteenth time today.

Jack Hunter was a political operative cum unwilling presidential advisor. No one had expected Donnelly to win. In the aftermath of the expected defeat, Hunter *had* planned to parlay his role in the campaign into a lucrative lobbying job for some foreign power.

But that hadn't worked out. To his dismay he'd found himself pampering a novice in the Oval Office, trying to control the man's temper tantrums, base impulses, bad humor, and frequent rages.

Hunter was small in both stature and outlook. He held a life-long determination to fix whatever he perceived was wrong with his country. That included avenging himself on everyone he felt had personally wronged him. Along the way, he intended to amass great wealth. Being fifty pounds overweight and mostly bald, save for a rim around the sides and back of his head, didn't help his attitude. What hair remained was prematurely white. His bent nose, the result of a bar fight in college, completed the look of a gnome.

"Mr. President, I told you last night, all we know is someone attacked us on a massive scale. Normal communications are out. We don't know what's actual infrastructure damage, and what's been shut down by the opposition party to make it look worse. Unfortunately, it seems most of it is real. The BBC reports—"

"The BBC is bullshit. Fake news. They're out to make me look bad. Have been for years. They wouldn't know the truth if it hit them in the head. They're just as bad as our own lying media. Pathetic. I won't listen to that crap." His head tilted. "What does Freedom News say?"

Donnelly's thick Boston accent grew more pronounced when angry, so Hunter had to strain to understand him. He tried again to explain.

"Sir, Freedom News and all the rest of the US networks are reporting the same. The British Ministry of Defense told us there are big debris clouds where our military and some of our commercial satellites used to be. That, coupled with the fact we can't seem to actually *use* them, tells me they're really gone."

"Or it could be that our *special* friends have gone over to the

Krauts. Now they're lying to us, too," said the president. The man actually pouted.

Hunter sighed again, quietly, but chose to ignore Donnelly's jibe. "The secretary of defense's body's been found, sir. The fires in the Pentagon are mostly out. The chairman of the Joint Chiefs is out of danger at Bethesda Naval Hospital, but he's still unconscious. The secretaries of the Air Force and Navy are in their alternate command posts. So's the assistant secretary of the Army. They haven't found Secretary Atkins, but we're pretty sure he's dead. Despite all the damage to the outer ring, the Pentagon seems sound. The cruise missiles—"

An explosion from his president and master interrupted. "Cruise missiles, hell! Those weren't cruise missiles. How could they be? No one saw them, did they? DID THEY?"

Hunter took a deep breath. "Yes, Mr. President, actually they *were* seen. Hundreds of people saw them fly in from the east. More saw them when they hit. Radar also tracked them."

"Bullshit. If they were tracked on radar, why didn't anyone shoot 'em down? Tell me that. They weren't shot down because they weren't real."

Hunter lost it. "Sir, no one shot them down because we don't have any damned anti-missile batteries around Washington."

He didn't mention that there actually *were* anti-aircraft batteries — but only to protect the White House. It also wouldn't help to tell him that the only reason he still lived was because *those* batteries had shot down nine missiles, all aimed at the very building in which they now stood.

"Mr. President, walk to the damned window and look outside. The only lights on in this fucking city are here at the White House, in hospitals, and those few government buildings someone thought important enough to have emergency generators. Now shut the hell up and listen, will you?"

Donnelly stared at him as if seeing him for the first time. His jaw worked silently, his face crimson.

Hunter closed his eyes and took a breath. He would pay for it later. But for now, the president wasn't shouting. Maybe he was listening.

"The power is out because traitors shut it down. To make me look bad," Donnelly calmly said, as if it were the most reasonable thing in the world that the people who fought large corporations and big business in general somehow also controlled them.

Hunter ignored him and started again. "I just got off the phone with the Pentagon—"

"How could you if the phones are out? Hmm?" Donnelly smiled brightly.

Hunter answered from between grinding teeth. "It's a secure point to point phone that doesn't go through normal lines." He waited. "May I continue?"

Taking silence as assent, he did. "From what the media says — don't roll your eyes, sir, these are legitimate reports from local news, with solid video feeds — it looks like the Navy was hit hard. There's video of ships and headquarters buildings on fire. We haven't heard anything from INDOPACOM - that's Indian Ocean Pacific Command, Admiral West, sir," he said. "Interestingly, European Command and Africa Command weren't touched. The State Department thinks that's because they're headquartered on foreign soil. Central Command in Tampa got blasted, but their headquarters in the Middle East wasn't. That's all I know right now." Pausing to think for a moment, he continued, "I'll get the surviving secretaries or their actings over here to give you a full report. Do you want to be in the Sit Room for that?"

"How do you get solid video feeds if the internet is down and the power is out?" asked the president. The lilt in his voice showed he thought he'd found another flaw in Hunter's tale.

"Sir, local news stations all have emergency generators, and they still broadcast over the air, including the network feeds. We've got antennas here as backup. The news from Hawaii came from old-style ham radio operators."

The president looked at him for a moment, then said, "Okay." He looked down and shuffled some papers on his desk.

Hunter knew he no longer had the president's attention. He waited.

Donnelly raised his face to stare at him. Finally, he asked, "Is that all? Are you through?"

"Yes, sir. No, sir. Did you want to be in on the Sit Room meeting?"

The president's tone was deceptively calm as he said, "No." Then he asked, "Just who is supposed to have caused this widespread destruction?"

Hunter clenched his fists by his side. He wished he could avoid the next explosion.

"Military leadership believes the Chinese attacked us. The intelligence community—"

The president leaned back in his chair and put his hands behind his head. "Losers. Every one of them. They couldn't find an enemy spy if he grabbed them by the balls. They've lied to me every day I've been in this office, the deep state bastards."

Hunter raised his voice and talked over him. "—The intelligence community also believes it was China. They said a pretty sophisticated and comprehensive cyberattack hit the same time as the cruise missiles did."

Finished, Hunter waited.

The president smiled. "So, you expect me to believe that the Chinese, who can't find their ass with both hands, attacked us? With cruise missiles? Launched from China?" He rose, then moved to stand by the window, but facing into the room. "For chrissakes, Jack, the Chinese stole every weapon they have. How the fuck could they have built something that could fly all the way from China? We can't even do that, because 'til I got here, nobody had the balls to try." He flexed his hands, shot his cuffs, and smoothed his tie and suit jacket. "So don't try to sell me such bullshit. Find out what really happened. When you do, I'll listen." He smiled. "Besides, President Liu and I have an understanding. I give him a hard time, and he pretends to be pissed off. He knows I can kick his ass if I need to."

He shuffled papers again. "Meantime, I want whatever surviving generals and admirals there are to give me a plan to blast Iran and North Korea into the Stone Age, along with whoever else even smiles at me wrong. You and I both know Iran and a few dozen suicide bombers really did this." Donnelly took a big breath, returned to the chair and sat. "I don't buy the attack was that big. It's those fucking resisters making it look bad. Now get the hell out of here or you're fired."

Hunter left the Oval Office shaking his head.

As he walked into the corridor his secretary hurried up and tried to speak. He swung to face her and put his face down into hers — he'd deliberately hired a secretary shorter than himself, even if it meant having a less attractive one.

Shouting, he said, "Shut the fuck up. Go call the senior surviving Joint Chiefs. Get whoever's acting for service secretaries. I want them all in the Sit Room in an hour. Tell them to bring their plans for dealing with this shitstorm. And get someone over from Homeland Security. They owe me an explanation for how the fuck someone could sucker punch us like this. Now move."

She backed up all the while Hunter shouted at her, finally backing into the wall. She continued to shrink, trying to get away from the mouth that spit and cursed at her.

As he finished, she meekly replied, "Yes, sir. Right away, sir," and moved off.

Watching her hustle back down the hallway, Hunter felt better.

The president wasn't kidding. Hunter's continued employment hinged on solving the "mystery" of the attack.

He didn't believe it was a mystery. While he believed the intelligence community would always lie to forward their agenda, in this case they had no reason to. They all knew the president already hated the Chinese, believed them less than human.

But he couldn't fathom why nor how. That second question might be the most difficult.

Ann Selstrom scurried away. She'd learned that, if she just got out of Hunter's sight, he'd stop yelling and her heart rate and blood pressure would return to near normal. Eventually.

She'd been excited when first offered the position as executive assistant to the national security advisor. Having spent five years in the White House secretarial pool, where she'd subbed for anyone out sick or on vacation, the offer of something more permanent had been too good to turn down. Now, she regretted answering the phone that morning. Hunter had screamed at her that first day and on nearly every one since. She wished she'd quit months ago.

She sighed with relief when she finally connected with the last of the invitees. As she hung up, she tapped her pencil on the desk and fantasized about revenge.

She rose to get more coffee.

CHAPTER
SEVEN

"Be seated," Hunter said as he strode into the large Sit Room conference space, though only a few present had actually stood.

Only the president himself warranted every person in the room standing when he arrived. But Hunter considered himself as powerful as the president: he had the president's ear, after all. So why shouldn't he receive the same honor? However, when others in the Cabinet objected, he'd taken a simpler path: he ordered everyone to be seated as if they'd stood. Eventually, some had taken to standing. He relished it.

"All right, tell me what happened, who did it, and how. Starting with Defense," he said.

"Do you want to know what we have left, too, sir? Or, I don't know, maybe what we ought to *do* about it?"

The question came from the Vice Chairman of the Joint Chiefs, General William Norton. A forty-one-year Marine, the man was as tough as a Ka-bar knife and held little regard for politicians. A brilliant strategist, operational commander, and tactician, Hunter hated him. Norton, always careful not to directly confront political leadership, instead used his cutting sarcasm to great effect.

"Yes, General, I want your assessment of what is left, and if you can, tell me how the fuck we can use it to hit back," he said, biting each word off as if it were a nail.

Norton snorted.

Deputy Secretary of Defense Wilson took a deep breath, and asked, "Will the president be joining us at all?"

Hunter glared at him. In a grating voice, he said, "No, Mr. *Deputy* Secretary, the president won't be joining us. He sent me to get your collective shit into a single sock, if that's possible, before he wastes his time listening to your pathetic excuses. Now, speak."

He spoke. "Everything we have says the Chinese did this. They did a very thorough job, too. There's not a lot left, short of nuclear forces, and no one wants to use them?"

When Hunter glared at him, he continued. "The *Theodore Roosevelt* Strike Group is in the Arabian Gulf, fully operational. She's under the operational control — the military calls it OPCON—"

"I know what OPCON means, you useless piece of shit."

The DepSecDef paled, but struggled on, "—of Fifth Fleet in Bahrain. We've established communications with them using old-style high frequency from our emergency communications center in Crystal City, though it was a bear getting them to come up on the same freq—"

Hunter leaned towards him, eyes blazing.

"I don't give a *damn* how you talk to them. If you keep wasting my time, you can get the fuck out and never come back."

Wilson shrank. When he continued, his voice was higher and quavered. Haltingly, he got through the damage assessment for the Army's mobility. He finished with, "So the Army here in the States isn't going anywhere. Nothing in Europe was hit, thank God, though moving them any place where they could threaten China will be a copper-plated bitch—"

"Stop, stop, stop." He slammed his hands on the table. "I don't give a shit what we *lost*, dammit. Just tell me what we have *left*." Hunter threw himself back in his chair and rested his cheek in his palm.

"We still have the strategic bombers, nuclear weapons, and enough fuel for one or two long-range missions. The Air Force has the one Air Operations Center where they control those missions. But we've got no fuel for fighter escorts." Wilson paused.

"Wait, you mean there's no CAP over Washington?" Hunter leaned forward, eyes wide.

Wilson shrank again, but said, "No, sir, I mean, yes, sir. There's Combat Air Patrol over Washington now."

Hunter relaxed. Then he cocked his head. "Why can we fly CAP but only one or two bomber missions, and no fighter escorts?"

Before Wilson could speak, Norton replied, "Because bombers need more fuel for a mission. Bombers are bigger, you know."

Hunter glared at him.

Norton just smiled.

Wilson continued. "We're conserving what fuel we have for CAP. We took serious aircraft losses, too, and those can't be replaced in less than years." He looked very unhappy.

"Why did they miss the bombers?" asked Hunter.

"We don't know if those attacks failed or what," replied Wilson.

Norton snorted loudly.

"Would you like to add something, anything, useful, General?" Hunter spat.

Norton leaned forward and looked at Hunter. His eyes gleamed, but his mouth was set in a hard line of compressed lips. "Why, yes, sir, I would. It was a message."

Hunter's eyes went wide and his head jerked. "What the hell are you talking about?"

"Just this, *sir*. They didn't strike our strategic bomber force. They took out the fuel reserves, knowing we could run one or two long-range strikes with what they left us. I told your acting SecDef this, but, well, he didn't want to risk pissing you off by telling you the truth. They also left the fuel farm at Andrews. Plenty for CAP and the president's aircraft, but nothing else."

The general put his hands on the table in front of him. "Look, Mr. Hunter, this is how military operations work these days. They're either fought hard to win, or they're fought just hard enough to achieve some objective short of complete victory. I don't like it. No one I know does. But it's a *fact*, and we deal with *facts*. The fact here is the Chinese showed us they're not an existential threat to the United States."

Hunter stared at him, fuming. "So, you're trying to convince me that first, you *know* the Chinese did this. No one else does, but you, the great General Norton, knows."

As Norton visibly spun up to respond, Hunter said, "Never mind. Second, you're telling me that they destroyed the majority of our military power, and that this is somehow supposed to mean they're *not* going to take us all the way down? Because it sure as hell looks to me like they already have."

Norton shook his head. "Sir, they took out about half of our force structure, the part we use to project power to their doorstep. They did *not* take out those forces we'd need to defend ourselves from anyone *else*. And they left our strategic nuclear deterrent intact, despite knowing we might use it against them. That's a clear signal they aren't looking to end us."

Hunter looked around at the rest of the men around the table. Most of them, at least the civilians, apparently found the hands clasped on the table in front of them fascinating, because they were staring hard at those self-same hands.

"Does anyone else at this table buy into this bullshit?"

The military men nodded.

The other uniformed person also nodded and looked directly at Hunter. *I'll take care of her later.* "Continue, Wilson."

"Moving to the Navy. The Navy got brutalized. All three carriers in Norfolk were hit, at least five missiles each."

"So they're sunk?" interrupted Hunter.

"No, none of them sank."

"Then why the hell aren't they out to sea?" demanded Hunter.

Wilson looked back at him silently.

Down the table, Vice Admiral Tom Gadsden, acting Chief of Naval Operations, spoke up. The CNO had also been on the Hill, testifying when twelve cruise missiles had brought down the Capitol building. "Because despite being afloat, they all suffered extensive damage. The number two reactor in *Truman* was destroyed, and the interior spaces around it can't be entered due to radioactivity. It'll be months to get *Eisenhower* and *Bush*—"

Hunter threw down his notepad. The VCNO started, then glared at him.

"I said tell me what we *have*. Was I not clear?"

The VCNO's mouth opened, then clamped shut. He turned his head straight ahead and stared at the clock on the wall.

Wilson turned to glare at the VCNO for a moment, then returned his attention to Hunter. "*Nimitz* is at sea off San Diego for training. *Stennis* is north of Hawaii. She's coming home from deployment, so she's fully operational with a full air wing and her escorts. *Ford* is off Cuba training for deployment. She's only got a single squadron of fighter bombers aboard." He paused to shuffle his papers.

"That brings us to naval air forces. There's almost nothing else left. Most of the remaining aircraft were destroyed on the ground. So were the hangars, runways, fuel tanks, fueling equipment. All gone. The planes on *Roosevelt*, *Stennis* and *Ford* are pretty much all we have left."

Hunter interrupted again. "Are you telling me that over seventy-five years after Pearl Harbor, we still park airplanes wing tip to wing tip. Is that how the Air Force was destroyed, too? Did you learn nothing from World War II?"

Wilson stared sullenly at Hunter, then continued. "No, sir, our planes were not parked wing tip to wing tip. But modern missiles dispense submunitions. A single missile can destroy several even widely separated planes. The submunitions tend to be armor-piercing so bunkers don't fully protect them. Since World War II, our forward presence kept an enemy away from our own soil. So pardon me if this came as a bit of a surprise." Breathing hard, he no longer looked nervous. "We got complacent, even arrogant, thinking no enemy could ever do, well, exactly what's been done. The last enemy who could reach American soil was the Soviets. With them, it wouldn't have been conventional." Visibly calming, he pushed on. "Yes, sir, we've been caught with our pants down. No amount of shouting will change that."

He hesitated, took a deep breath, and continued. "We'll reconstitute squadrons from surviving airframes and pilot pools. We'll salvage what fuel and maintenance capabilities we can. Ordinarily, the Air Force would use Davis-Montham Air Force Base in Tucson to put together parts from their boneyard and get it where it's needed. But the enemy knew that. They blew hell out of the graveyard. Worse, they trashed the salvage hangars where parts were kept."

"Then where the hell are you going to get parts?" demanded Hunter.

"Museums. Air National Guard bases. Every airfield that operates vintage aircraft. All the airlines and air packaging services. Except for specialized military maintenance gear, basic servicing systems have a lot of commonalities, so we'll leverage that." He paused, not wanting to address the next part.

"Munitions. We lost more than half the inventory of bombs, missiles, and gun ammunition for large caliber weapons. We're still trying to figure out what's left. The fires aren't out yet and it's hard to fight fires when explosions keep killing the crews. Worse, the munitions factories were also hit. All of them."

Hunter stared at him. "How the hell could they do that? How could they hit that many places?"

Wilson looked down at his nails, flexing his fingers as he did so. Then he looked back up.

"Ever since the Soviet Union fell, Congress's been swilling the *peace dividend*. Sure, they spent billions on weapons programs and high-tech platforms. But they deregulated the defense industry. They encouraged consolidation in the name of efficiency, especially in high-profile congressional districts. Powerful congressmen incentivized companies to consolidate distributed sites or manufacturing facilities into large concentrations."

He looked Hunter directly in the eye, daring him to argue or interrupt. "It increases the tax base. More importantly, it increases the donor base for the next election cycle."

Hunter still didn't say anything.

Wilson continued. "So instead of having dozens of companies and factories building our ammo and weapons, there's a handful. A handful our enemy easily located, probably using Wikipedia, and targeted using Google."

All around, even those in uniform, stared sullenly at the table. They'd all known what had been happening.

Hunter broke eye contact first. Looking at Admiral Threadman, commandant of the Coast Guard and acting Homeland Security director, he decided to move on.

"Alright, you're next. You better have a good explanation for how the homeland you're supposed to be securing got hit so bad."

"Well, sir, I can confirm it was the Chinese, and I know how they did it," she said.

Hunter's eyes flashed and he sat bolt upright. "How the fuck do you know that?"

Nearly every eye in the room had turned to Threadman.

She began. "Merchant ships, specifically, very large container ships. I haven't seen the video yet. But our Search and Rescue Centers recorded three radio calls yesterday evening DC time. All reported seeing container ships firing what they said were hundreds of missiles toward the US coast."

"How the hell is that even possible?" The question came from Wilson.

Threadman started to answer, but the VCNO beat her to it. "We've been worried about someone using container ships to launch cruise missiles for over a decade. We spent a great deal of effort finding ways to detect and track suspect containers, but it's not glamorous or high tech. Congress didn't like spending money on such esoteric work. So we've been caught with our dicks flapping in the wind. But, hey, Congress got to funnel money to their favorite contractors, as Mr. Wilson so correctly pointed out," he said, adding, "Sir," after a lengthy pause.

It was Gadsden's turn to receive Hunter's glare. "But that would take hundreds of ships. How could they get that many ships near our coast without being detected?"

Threadman snorted. "No, sir, it didn't take hundreds. We don't know how many ships were used, but we worked with the Navy on this," nodding at Gadsden. "We assessed a single container ship could launch between five hundred and a thousand missiles each, assuming four missiles per container. And the Chinese land attack cruise missiles are just the right size to fit four per container." She paused for effect, then added, "And one of the reports said the container ship flew the PRC flag, a big one." She sat back in her chair.

Silence reigned, broken only by the hum of ventilation.

Finally, Hunter spoke. "That still doesn't explain why we let so many Chinese ships get near our coasts."

Threadman laughed. "Sir, we don't have a merchant marine of our own anymore, not really. Almost all our own shipping is tourist-based, except for some oil carriers, and there aren't many of them anymore, either. The Chinese move a huge percentage of the containers that circle the globe. Any normal day, there's at least thirty Chinese container ships in our ports delivering imports or loading exports. There's another thirty to fifty transiting within a few hundred miles of our coasts. We track them along with the rest of the merchant shipping, but only for safety of navigation. We don't interfere. That would inhibit trade, raise the cost of goods for American consumers. Congress would hear about it."

Hunter refused to let go of this thread, however. "With all the bullshit the Chinese have been saying about us, the tariffs we've both enacted, them pulling their ambassador out, no one thought to stop their container ships from coming in? Why the hell not?" he spat.

Threadman chuckled again and shook her head. "Because, sir, there's no reason to stop them. Like I said, Congress would be pissed if Joe and Sally Consumer have to pay more for their t-shirts and pants. I don't want Congress crawling up my ass asking me why I stopped their constituents getting their Barbie dolls."

Threadman looked Hunter in the eye. "Besides, sir, no one from the National Security Council, the White House, or my secretary ordered us to interdict Chinese ships. If they had, we'd have done so. But I don't have the authority to stop trade with another nation on my own, nor should I."

Hunter stared once more at her, grinding his teeth. He opened his mouth once, then twice, but closed it again. He felt like his head would explode. Finally, he sat back, and waved his hand for Threadman to continue.

The rest of her report wasn't any better. Thirteen of the

nation's twenty largest cities had no power and it barely hung by a thread in the rest.

Much progress had been made during previous administrations protecting the nation's electrical grid from cyber-attack. But the current administration had redirected funds to quixotic projects that energized its base voters. While a few central nodes for power distribution had been well defended against malicious ones and zeros, almost no infrastructure had been defended against flying bombs.

The internet, long vaunted for its stability and survivability, was also down across thirty percent of the nation.

The rest of the meeting went no better.

Before they adjourned, Hunter looked at Wilson and Norton.

"In three hours, I want your plans for the destruction of the Chinese government. If they really did this, I want, er, the president wants, to hit back with everything we have. The president wants bombs falling on government buildings in Beijing tonight."

The president hadn't said that, but Hunter didn't care. He'd take the initiative as he always did. The president would take the credit, for now.

Norton grimaced. "Sir, they'll detect the bombers and knock them down if we haven't properly taken down their air defense systems. If we use ballistic missiles, they'll assume we're going nuclear. They'd retaliate with nukes."

"They won't dare. If they do, we'll turn their whole damned country into a parking lot."

The two men stared at Hunter. Wilson's face was white, eyes wide. Norton's were narrow and blazing as he shook his head and looked away.

Wilson finally answered, "Yes, sir. We'll try to do that."

"You'll do it, Mr. Acting Secretary. Or I'll charge you with treason and have you shot. The president declared martial law, remember. I can do it," Hunter hissed and stormed out.

He'd had the president sign that declaration shortly after the attack. Now it might prove useful.

By the time the meeting ended, more than two hours had elapsed. Dudgeon was high, and the participants were in two camps: those who were angry at all the others and wanted them gone, and those who wanted to be gone. Nothing had been decided. Blame had been apportioned, reapportioned, and then spread widely, mostly on non-participants.

Business as usual.

CHAPTER
EIGHT

2300 Zulu, 27 Oct
0600 Local Time, 28 Oct
USS *Nicholas*, South China Sea

The first dawn of the war found Bill seated again on the bridge. Another brilliant day dawned to the east. His hand shook as he sipped his tea. He'd showered and shaved, but his bleary eyes and saggy jowls told a story.

"Zero six hundred, sir. Request permission to pass reveille."

Bill returned to the present. Killingsworth stood next to him, hand raised in a salute.

Bill blinked and nodded. "Permission granted."

Killingsworth pointed to the BMOW, who stood poised, pipe to his lips. He began the lengthy ritual piping, then announced, "Reveille, reveille, reveille. All hands heave out and trice up. The smoking lamp is lighted on the main deck starboard side smoking area. Now reveille." He piped again, this time a warbling call. "Breakfast for the crew. Oncoming watch has head of the line privileges."

Bill stood, stretched, and moved to the BMOW's station.

"Boats, pass all hands, please."

The shrill cry of the bosun's pipe brought every man and woman aboard to a halt.

"Good morning, *Nicholas*," Bill started. "I've learned very little new since last night. I'll repeat one thing: everything I hear is that civilians were spared." He looked around the bridge. All eyes were on him, save Killingsworth's, whose binoculars were raised as he stared out the forward windows.

He keyed the mike again. "However, in the absence of guidance from above, *Nicholas* can do one of two things. We can sit and wait, try to reestablish comms with the chain of command, and see what their orders are. Or we can take the war to the enemy and do whatever damage we can on our own initiative."

He unkeyed the mike for a moment. Rekeying it, he said, "I intend to take the war to the enemy."

A stir arose around him. Murmuring broke out, quickly silenced by looks from the BMOW and OOD.

Bill continued. "The enemy that attacked us yesterday sits on a heavily armed reef about two hundred nautical miles southeast of here. In a few minutes, we'll begin a high-speed run toward the reef. We're going to put some warheads on foreheads. Then we'll turn north and see what other damage we can do."

Someone cheered out on the weather deck, and he paused for another moment. "We'll sound GQ in a couple of hours or so, so I want all hands to get some hot chow now. We'll forgo sweepers this morning."

He smiled as he heard muted cries of "yes!" from behind him.

"Get up, get dressed, eat, and get ready. That is all," he finished.

Quiet conversation immediately broke out all throughout the pilothouse until the OOD called out, "Silence on the bridge."

Bill nodded to him and headed back to his chair.

He'd wait for a few minutes before he went below himself to the wardroom to eat. There would be time to tell the crew about what had happened to San Diego later, after the coming fight. Right now, he needed them focused on the mission.

The excitement his announcement generated quickly faded. A pall settled over *Nicholas* and an eerie quiet pervaded. Watch-standing rules discouraged idle chit-chat, but even the low conversations that typically took place anyway were missing.

With the exception of those whose duties required them to focus inside the pilothouse, all hands stared out at the horizon. Bill wanted to believe they were keeping an excellent lookout, but their blank stares spoke of minds that were elsewhere.

"OOD, rotate the lookouts every fifteen minutes. I don't want anyone losing focus up here. We don't have a radar picture, and an enemy could heave into sight at any moment."

"Aye aye, sir." The vacant stares disappeared as the watch galvanized into motion.

Two decks below the bridge, the officers awaited him in the wardroom. Walking quickly to his seat at the head of the long table, Bill told them to take their seats. As custom dictated, they'd stood when he entered and remained standing until he'd seated himself. He quickly scribbled his breakfast desires on the small paper order form and handed it to the mess cook. Then he looked down the table at the drawn faces and bleary eyes turned toward him.

"Questions or comments, ladies and gentlemen?" he asked.

"Yes, sir." Ops spoke up immediately. "The targeting team's headed back up to Combat. We can use Harpoon in an ad hoc anti-land-target mode. I also told them to gin up plans for Tomahawk?" he asked. The bags under Campbell's eyes empha-sized his fatigue. His eyes blinked often and his head weaved slightly.

Bill shook his head. "No, we'll save the T-birds for bigger targets. I'm taking out the reef partly because I feel a need to strike back. I appreciate the initiative, but for now let's hold those arrows in our quiver. When's the brief?"

Campbell's mouth opened for a moment and his eyebrows rose. "Uh, I need to talk to the XO. Zero seven hundred, sir?"

Bill kept his smile to himself. "Sure, that's fine if the XO approves. Next?"

Lieutenant Junior Grade Hawke said, "Sir, the intel broadcast is still up. Do you want to go after their fleet or some other targets, maybe on the mainland?"

"No mainland targets. Deep strike has a strategic effect. It's escalatory. For now, focus on their fleet. It's likely flushed to sea, so we'll have plenty to do just to find and hit it. That broadcast is the one comm link that isn't down, at least not yet, so let's use it. Get with the cryptologic officer. See if we can find some of those needles in the haystack."

"Aye, sir. Request to be excused?"

He forced a laugh. "Sure, though I didn't mean right now. Have you eaten?"

She blushed. "Yes, sir. I told Lieutenant Mortenson I'd be up in Combat about now." Mortenson was the aforementioned cryptologic officer.

Bill smiled and nodded toward the door.

A few minutes later, Campbell excused himself as well.

The question and answer session continued for nearly ten minutes more while the officers breakfasted. Bill usually forbade work talk at the table but today made an exception. When someone left to attend to duties or take the watch, their place was quickly taken by someone coming off watch.

When conversations finally died out, Bill excused himself.

On his way out he nodded at Ensign Sandstrom, who quickly looked down at his plate. Bill nearly stopped to talk with him but decided it was too soon. Sometimes letting an incident slide unremarked solved the problem.

The other two casualties were taking longer. Bill could only give them twenty-four hours.

Unfortunately, US Navy ships operated in something euphemistically called "optimal manning." That meant there weren't enough crew onboard to allow for casualties. Every man and woman aboard became critical, even a junior seaman like Jastrow. Having two people in sickbay and twelve more in a twenty-four-hour rotation guarding prisoners made for huge gaps in the watchbill.

Following the attack brief, the officers and senior enlisted filed out of the wardroom. Lieutenant Commander Nelson Dix stayed behind, along with the XO. The helicopter detachment Officer in Charge, Dix led the helo crews and maintenance personnel. When the door closed behind the last person, he asked, "Got a minute, Skipper?"

"Sure, what's up?"

Dix straightened. "Sir, about the aircrew—"

"I thought we'd settled this," Bill said, wagging his head.

"I just wanted to reiterate, I've got the most flight hours, the most experience. I ought to fly this mission."

"Yes, you do. That's why I want you onboard. Anything goes wrong, you can advise me. Me and the TAO."

"Sir, that's not the point. I can advise you just as well from the cockpit. And from there, I can make sure nothing goes wrong."

Bill shook his head. "No. That's final. You have no control over what the enemy does if you're in the bird. But here, you can help *me* control the battle. And you'll have a better handle on the big picture."

"Sir, you're going to be in EMCON the whole time. My bird will have just as good a picture as the ship." He frowned and tilted his head down. "Your call, Skipper. I'll make sure they're ready." He left.

Irving shook her head. "He just wants to lead from the front."

"I know, XO, but you can't always do that. Sometimes you need to admit your place is back where you can see the whole battlefield."

Irving shrugged and moved to rise.

Bill said, "Ops was a bit surprised I wanted a brief."

The XO sat back down. "He didn't say that to me, sir. I admit, I wasn't sure if you wanted one, either."

Bill nodded but said, "We always brief. Especially now. It's routine. Routine helps folks stay settled. Plus, there's nothing worse than going into a dangerous evolution without a brief to make sure everyone's on the same page."

Irving took a deep breath. "Aye, sir. Well, I thought it went alright. I know it was a bit rough, and they hadn't thought through all the questions you asked."

Grimacing, Bill said, "No, they hadn't. And they should have. I didn't think it went well at all. They need to spend more time thinking about what *might* go wrong."

"They don't have your experience, yet. Frankly, sir, none of us have any real combat experience, except for yesterday." She rose and refilled her coffee cup. "I'll talk to Ops and CSO, help them think through the risk management piece."

"That'll help. It's not rocket science." Bill stood and moved to the door. Just before he left, he turned to her. "Make sure they know — everyone knows — that all that stuff we do in peacetime doesn't end in war."

CHAPTER NINE

2345 Zulu, 27 Oct
0645 Local Time, 28 Oct
USS *Nicholas***, South China Sea**

As *Nicholas* raced at thirty-one knots toward Fiery Cross Reef, the attack team determined optimum Harpoon missile seeker settings and approach paths.

The sea was mild with small one-foot wind waves and gentle three-foot swells, both from the northwest. The shallow corkscrewing motion would have been soothing were it not for the tension that ratcheted higher with every mile.

The Triton had drifted out of radar range of the reef, so they were completely blind. Bill kept the SPY radar in standby, ready to come up at a moment's notice but not yet giving them away. It was an enormous gamble going in with all his electronics silent, but he couldn't give the enemy time to develop their own targeting solution. He'd also swung *Nicholas* wide first to the south then east so they wouldn't come in from the same bearing where the enemy had last seen their radar.

He'd agonized over the decision to make the high-speed run.

Fuel was a major consideration. While they'd topped off only a few days ago in Pattaya, Thailand, he needed to find their next gas. *Nicholas* burned fuel at a prodigious rate at high speed. But he also had to consider risk.

With the prisoners housed in the hangar, one of his two SH-60R helicopters had sat on deck overnight. He'd reduced it to Alert Thirty status at midnight, allowing the pilots and flight deck crew to sleep but still keeping it ready to lift off quickly.

Now it flew at low altitude well north of *Nicholas* to mitigate his blindness. Also operating in radar silence, it extended his visual and passive sensor coverage. More importantly, using the very tight-beam directional Hawklink he could see its tactical picture. Two merchant ships lay ahead of *Nicholas*, steaming northward thirty miles west of the reef. He would pass between them, further shielding his approach.

The likely abundance of fishing boats and other small coastal shipping between *Nicholas* and the reef concerned him. Some of them might accidentally absorb one or more of his Harpoons. Such ships often traveled with radars in standby during the day, so the attack team wouldn't know they were there unless either the lookouts or the helo actually saw them. *Nicholas* had already passed nearly a dozen in the past two hours.

The other risk they presented was that the PRC often used nondescript vessels and merchants as part of their national intelligence gathering system. They could give early warning to the Chinese forces on the reef.

Nicholas threw white water to both sides as she overtook the seas in her sprint. Her bow parted the waves, cleaving them deeply with her passage, rising and falling rhythmically as she rolled gently side-to-side in the bright morning sunshine.

The ship might be joyously charging through the seas like the greyhound she was as her crew prepared to deal death.

"Sir, we're twenty minutes outside their missile range." Pettibone's voice broke into his thoughts.

"Very well. Set GQ."

Pettibone spoke into his mike. Soon the shrill twitter of the bosun's pipe sounded. "General Quarters, General Quarters. All hands man your battle stations. Up and forward to starboard, down and aft to port. Set material condition Zebra throughout the ship. Make manned and ready reports to the bridge. General Quarters." They no longer passed "this is not a drill." Nothing was or would be a drill for who knew how long.

As the *bong-bong-bong* of the GQ alarm thrilled throughout the ship, few of the crew moved. Most had long ago found their way to their battle stations to ensure they got a good turnover from the normal watch, or to check and recheck their gear, especially damage control equipment. The entire ship had heard and felt the slam of the near miss. This time they might not be so fortunate. They also ensured everything was secured in place. Loose items could become missile hazards, flying off shelves and bulkheads in the spaces nearest impacts, injuring anyone in their path.

"Sir, bridge reports all stations manned and ready," said Pettibone.

"Very well," responded Bill in time-worn tradition. Then he sat back.

Nicholas settled into routine.

Setting GQ early got the ship to its maximum state of readiness well before they were in range of the enemy. More importantly, it let his crew work out their nerves.

All too quickly the real world intruded.

"TAO, EW Supe. I'm picking up a Wall Eye air search radar bearing zero nine three, right where it ought to be. The helo should pick it up soon." The Wall Eye gave the reef warning of any aircraft flying within the radar's range. But like *Nicholas's* SPY radar, the farther out from the antenna, the higher above the sea's surface the bottom of the radar beam lay.

Bill leaned forward. "Andy, make sure the helo stays below the detection envelope," he ordered.

"Already done, sir."

They were still a hundred miles out with little risk of either ship or helo being detected, yet. But the enemy searched using all its sensors.

He would close to sixty nautical miles before launching the Harpoons. That allowed the use of way points, intermediate destinations not located directly between the ship and the target, so the missiles came in from different directions. The enemy would find it more difficult to defend against or get a bearing back to *Nicholas*.

He didn't know for sure what the Chinese had left in terms of weapons, but he didn't want to make anything easy for them.

Nicholas continued toward the point from which she would launch her counterattack.

"Sir, we're at sixty-two miles," called out Pettibone.

"Very well. Everything ready?" asked Bill.

"Yes, sir. I just had them run a final BIT. All four birds test sat," the TAO responded. The Built-In Test checked all the missile circuits to ensure they were fully functional before launch. Launch failures after a satisfactory BIT were rare.

"The helo just reported a medium-sized surface contact eighteen miles northwest of the reef. We've got a passive track on it now. The Harpoon operator is adjusting the waypoints to miss it," said Pettibone.

"Okay, TAO, here we go." Bill rubbed the tip of his nose, then the back of his neck. "Batteries release for Harpoon launch at the designated point. Make sure the helo knows when we shoot."

"Aye, sir." Pettibone began to pass the well-rehearsed sets of orders. CIC became a hive of activity. Butts in seats shifted and backs grew straighter as the combat team worked their systems. An already taut combat crew became even more attentive.

"Harpoon, TAO, batteries released as planned. I'll call sixty miles. Estimated time to launch, four minutes."

Activity now centered on the Harpoon console where the

operator punched "buttons" on the touch screen to enable the weapons.

"All four birds ready, sir," she reported.

"ATACO, TAO. Tell the helo we launch in four minutes. We'll give them birds away when we do. Make sure they wait for my order to go in and get BDA." The Air Tactical Control Officer was the petty officer talking to the helicopter by the Hawklink's radio channel.

If the radars on the reef shut down at the same moment the missiles were supposed to hit, the helo would be ordered in to take a look and perform Battle Damage Assessment. If they didn't, *Nicholas* would break off. Bill didn't have any more long-range weapons that he felt comfortable using against a low-value target like the reef. He would save the TLAM and his remaining Harpoons for higher value targets.

Pettibone reached for the intercom. "Bridge, TAO, three and a half minutes to weapons launch. The captain gave batteries release for Harpoon. As soon as all birds are clear, we'll start our turn away."

The flurry of order acknowledgements came. Bill relaxed a bit. There was little more for him to do unless he chose to step in. His crew was well trained. He trusted them.

The minutes ticked away. Then, "Harpoon, TAO. Launch Harpoons."

From amidships came a momentary roar as each of the boosters ignited. Four nearly one-ton missiles sprinted out of their canisters, leaping into the air at a forty-five-degree angle. At apogee, their rocket boosters burned out and dropped off. The jet engines ignited and each weapon quickly descended and accelerated to fly over the horizon just above the wave tops.

As the fourth missile thundered off, Pettibone called, "Bridge, TAO. Last bird's away, execute turn."

He was barely halfway through the order when *Nicholas* heeled sharply to starboard. Bill grabbed his mug as it slid across the desk. Pettibone's momentary smile held a hint of ferocity.

"ATACO, TAO. Does the helo know the birds are outbound?" Pettibone said into his boom mike.

"Yes, sir. They've gone into an orbit."

The waiting began.

The Harpoon missiles flew sub-Mach, a little above five hundred knots, so they'd cover the seventy nautical mile plus flight paths through their waypoints in a bit more than eight minutes. Their seeker heads would turn on about twenty seconds before impact, giving the enemy very little warning.

Right on time, the ATACO called out, "TAO, ATACO. Helo reports Type 730 CIWS emissions on a bearing to the reef. Looks like they see the missile seekers."

A moment later. "All emissions ceased, including Wall Eye and CLC-3 air defense radar. Time coincides with predicted impact."

The EW Supervisor confirmed the information with the ship's own SLQ-32.

A small cheer broke out in Combat.

"All stations, TAO, silence," barked Pettibone.

The noise subsided but there were grins all around. The slap of a high five exchange sounded behind them.

He hoped there was reason to be happy, but the enemy wasn't stupid. Turning off their radars after a successful defense in hope of luring *Nicholas* in and ambushing her fell within the realm of possibility. He nodded at Pettibone.

"ATACO, TAO. The helo is cleared to go in for BDA, low and slow."

Thirty minutes later the helicopter reported. Bill normally had his left side headphone tuned to the internal communications circuit with the TAO; Main Control, which managed the propulsion system; and Damage Control Central. The right side held an external radio communications circuit, usually the command frequency for whoever *Nicholas's* "boss" was at the time. But right now it was set to the air control circuit.

"This is Sea Hawk Six Zero Eight. Lots of smoke on the horizon. We got a piece of 'em."

Communications with helos were normally more informal for two reasons. First, senior petty officers usually served as the ATACO. Second, naval aviators were notoriously informal in every way. Neither expected the CO to listen in, and the aviators wouldn't have cared even if they'd known.

The helo continued to carefully close the reef.

"Looks like we got the command shed, ATACO. There's two other buildings burning, too, and one covered shed that — holy shit. The shed just exploded. *Big* secondary. Wait one—"

Silence, then, "We're getting the hell out of Dodge. We're taking ground fire."

Bill keyed his mike on the internal circuit. "Light off Aegis. Let's get some 'trons in the air. I want to know what's going on with the helo, and I want the bad guys to know we're close."

He reached out to the intercom. "Bridge, this is the captain. Reverse course. Close the reef. The helo's been shot at."

He didn't say he wanted to be able to rescue survivors if it went down. He hoped they didn't have anything with longer range than their version of CIWS.

The ship shuddered as she leaned into the turn. The sound of the gas turbines winding up overcame the hum of electronics and cooling fans.

"TAO, be ready to take the reef under fire with guns. I doubt they can launch missiles again. But I don't want to assume anything."

"Aye, sir." Pettibone keyed his own mike and issued the necessary orders.

Then from Bill's right earpiece came the news he'd hoped for.

"ATACO, Sea Hawk Six Zero Eight. We're out of range. We were pretty much there when they opened up, but we've got some holes in the fuselage. Nobody's hurt. We're RTB," meaning they were returning to base.

Bill rose and headed for the bridge.

Behind his back as he left, Pettibone called DC Central and got a route for Bill to go to the bridge from CIC.

In case the ship took damage, it was critical DC Central knew someone was moving around, momentarily breaking watertight integrity along their path by opening and then closing watertight doors and hatches.

CHAPTER
TEN

0132 Zulu, 28 Oct
0832 Local Time
USS *Nicholas*, South China Sea

As Bill moved quickly up the ladders to the bridge, the 1MC spoke. "Emergency flight quarters, emergency flight quarters, all hands man your flight quarters stations. Remove all ball caps and stow all loose gear topside. Throw nothing over the side. Sea Hawk Six Zero Eight inbound with battle damage. Now flight quarters."

"Captain's on the bridge."

"OOD, as soon as we have the helo visually, maneuver to get the winds right and get that bird on deck. Then I want to haul ass again. Head west. Got it?" Bill ordered.

"Aye, sir," Barrister responded.

The junior officer of the deck, Ensign Bonnet, grabbed the "wind wheel", a simple device used to figure out what the optimal course and speed would be for flight ops, and stepped aft to the chart table to read the current relative wind. The plastic wheel spun in her hand.

Bill walked to his chair. The XO joined him.

"Flight corpen is three two eight, ma'am, at thirteen knots," Bonnet said.

Barrister moved to the starboard bridge wing and raised her binoculars to look for the helo.

The tension on the bridge dripped from the overhead like condensate from an air conditioning cooling coil. No one onboard the helo had been hurt and that was good. But "holes in the fuselage" sounded ominous. Everyone could imagine a crash on deck and the resultant fire.

"Forward lookout reports helo inbound, three one zero relative, position angle one," called the bridge phone talker.

Even in modern ships, a sound-powered phone circuit connected the bridge with the lookouts and CIC. The phone talker, posted at the back of the bridge, maintained a status board that listed the surface contacts *Nicholas* held on radar. She also had a console that gave her access to the ship's radar and data link display.

Barrister gave the JOOD a nod of approval.

Bonnet called out, "Left standard rudder. Steady on course three two eight. Engines ahead standard, make turns for thirteen knots."

"Left standard rudder, aye, steady on course three two eight," replied the helmsman.

The lee helmsman responded next. "Make turns for thirteen knots, aye." Manned only during GQ, the lee helm controlled the engines.

"Ma'am, my rudder is left standard coming to course three two eight," said the helmsman.

In a moment, the lee helm informed her, "Making seven five turns for thirteen knots, ma'am."

"Very well."

Bill grabbed his binoculars from the case bolted to the side of his chair. Striding to the bridge wing, he looked back over the starboard quarter. He still couldn't see the helo, but the lookouts stationed a deck above the bridge could see further.

They also have younger eyes. Bill snorted. A moment later his gaze followed a now-visible smoke trail to the helicopter itself. He hated the aviator mentality that made light of everything.

Behind him, the helmsman called, "Steady on three two eight."

"OOD, ask the helo if they can land safely," he called. Before she could call CIC, the bitch box sounded.

"Bridge, TAO, helo reports they're still fighting a class Charlie fire in the ASW console and the port engine is running hot. They'll try to make it, but they may need to shut down and ditch."

The XO said, "I'm headed for the boat deck," and left the bridge.

He cursed the helo crew. They'd just confirmed that it *was* worse than first reported. He stuck his head back into the bridge. "Tell them to try to get within half a mile before they put it in the water. And call the boat deck. Tell the first lieutenant I want that RHIB in the water in record time if we tell them to launch. And I don't want anyone hurt." He moved back out and stared again through his binoculars.

"Sir, flight quarters set. Request green deck," Barrister called from the pilothouse.

"Green deck," he replied.

Bill took a deep breath as he watched the inbound helicopter, conscious of the eyes on him as he stood there. He tried to never forget that the CO set the tone for the entire ship. Now he had to remain calm even as his stomach churned in worry for the pilots and the aircrew — his pilots and aircrew.

He wanted to slap the back of his chair. *If the helo pilot had just reported honestly. Next time. . .* Then he prayed there wouldn't be a next time.

The helo continued inbound. The smoke faded, probably the result of effective application of the onboard fire extinguisher.

With the winds now on the port bow at thirty knots, the helicopter made a fast, low approach, slowing only as it neared the deck. Bill moved aft to where he could see at least a small portion of the flight deck. A flat panel TV on the bridge afforded him a complete view of it, but he liked to see things for himself. The beating of the rotors overwhelmed all other sounds as the wind ruffled his hair.

His binoculars brought into stark relief the starred holes in the aft upper corner of the Plexiglas window on the helo's starboard side. As the helo turned, the shredded tire became visible, as well as the badly bent wheel and strut.

Despite the damage, the helo landed without incident and shut down.

He stepped inside. "OOD, Red Deck. Secure from flight quarters and General Quarters. Set normal Condition Three watch." Condition Three wartime steaming watch routine kept the ship ready to defend itself at a moment's notice. The Navy had been steaming in Condition Three since 9/11.

"Put the ship about," he continued. "Pick a point a couple hundred miles out, then head for it."

Nicholas turned away from the reef and increased speed. The noise of the wind whipping replaced the helicopter engine noise. He added, "Ask the XO —" He stopped as the XO stepped onto the bridge.

"The helo's a bit more knocked about than they knew, sir. It's going to take about an hour to cool the engine and then drag her into the hangar. The starboard side aft strut collapsed on landing."

"Yeah, I saw the damage when they made their approach. I just secured from GQ."

"I'll get the prisoners moved out of the hangar in the meantime. Put 'em on the mess decks while the helos get moved around, then put 'em in the other hangar." She paused. "Sir, what are you planning for the reef?"

"Nothing. We'll let what's left live, break off and head west then north. They'd have shot at us by now if they had anything left. There're plenty of other targets around, fortunately or unfortunately. And I want to see Dix in my sea cabin ASAP. I want to be very clear that we're not playing games with damage reports."

"Aye, sir."

When she returned from the phone at the back of the bridge, the XO moved close and said in a low voice, "You still sure we should go on the offensive, sir?"

Seeing Bill's face, she hurriedly added, "I know we're in an all-out war, but we haven't got any idea what Third or Seventh Fleet are trying to do or where we fit. We might throw a wrench into whatever's been planned."

Bill didn't respond immediately but instead walked back to his chair. He took a sip of his tea and grimaced. *Cold.*

"You're right, of course. We don't know how the Plan is being executed."

He meant the Contingency Plan, CONPLAN, that covered nearly every level of conflict with China, from isolated major incidents to full-scale war. Every theater commander had CONPLANs for potential conflicts within their theater. Indo-Pacific Command, or INDOPACOM, was no exception. But such plans were highly classified. Individual ship CO's weren't normally briefed in on them. So even knowing they were in an all-out war didn't help him know what pre-planned operations might be ordered into execution.

Bill rubbed the tip of his nose. "But here's the thing, XO. Based on what we heard on the BBC, I'm not sure Third Fleet's operational. It isn't hard for the Chinese to figure out what building houses what. All they have to do is look at the Third Fleet home page on the internet."

"Yes, sir, but Seventh Fleet is up, or at least it appears they are. Shouldn't we report to them for duty? In theory, they should know we're here."

"They're the ones telling us not to transmit. They probably assume we were attacked. But they may not know we survived." He shook his head. "I hear you and you're right to play devil's advocate. But I'd rather get called on the carpet for being too aggressive than for sitting around and waiting for orders that may take days or even weeks to come, if they come at all. Nope, we're going to take on our enemy and see just what damage we can do."

"Aye aye, sir." She glanced around the bridge, then took her ball cap off and ran her fingers through her hair. "Ops is digging up everything he can find on what the plan might be. He told me he'd let you know what he finds by noon."

"That's great. Maybe by then we'll have something more concrete from Seventh Fleet."

She nodded and put her ball cap back on. "I'll head back and see if the air det has any idea how long to fix the helo, or if it can be fixed."

CHAPTER
ELEVEN

0135 Zulu, 28 Oct
0535 Local Time
USS *Theodore Roosevelt* (CVN-71), North Arabian Sea

Rear Admiral (Lower Half) Gupta rolled over in his bunk and picked up the phone. "Gupta," he said.

"Admiral, this is Ham. It's zero five thirty five. We're eight miles from the turn south to leave the North Arabian Sea and head for the south tip of India. We just got word the *Monterey* Surface Action Group hit mines in the Red Sea."

Gupta came bolt awake and swung his legs out of the bunk. "How the hell did mines get in the Red Sea?" He'd been counting on the missiles those ships carried, both to defend the carrier and strike at the enemy.

"We don't know yet, sir. Fifth Fleet said they'll keep us informed." Gupta heard Delawr take a deep breath. "There's more. *Monterey* herself is DIW. She's got an anchor down to keep from drifting over any more mines. *Ross* is in the same situation. *Porter* split in two and sank, sir. *Leroy Grumman* was last in the column and avoided the minefield. She's providing search and rescue. Bahrain's coordinating with

Egypt and Saudi to get minesweepers and tugs there quick as they can."

Gupta scratched his head. "Very well. I'll come over. Tell Fifth Fleet I want to know if they think anyone could have sown mines along *our* transit route." He leaned back. "I planned to address the ready rooms before we hit the Chinese counter-piracy group. Guess this'll be one more thing I tell 'em about."

He hung up the phone. Rubbing his eyes, he stood and headed for the shower.

At around the same time as *Monterey* hit the mine, the air wing aboard *Theodore Roosevelt* was readying two dozen aircraft to launch a War At Sea strike. An operation often exercised, no American carrier had conducted a real one since a small attack against two Iraqi patrol boats in 2003. The last large-scale WAS strike occurred during Operation PRAYING MANTIS in April, 1988. An Iranian frigate and some smaller vessels had been sunk.

The target for *TR*'s strike was the Chinese anti-piracy SAG, now out of the Gulf of Aden and moving toward India. Intel assessed they were trying to intercept the carrier.

Admiral Gupta had no intention of letting them do that. While he'd informed Fifth Fleet of his plans, he hadn't asked permission, and they hadn't given it.

The Navy had shifted to wartime decision-making.

"Attention on deck!"

"Seats," Gupta said as he walked through the door and headed for the podium.

Ready Room Eight was the home of VFA-84, the Jolly Rogers. He put his hands on the podium and looked across the assembled pilots, back seaters, and other squadron personnel as they settled back into their chairs. Young faces peered back at him, a mix of bravado and anxiety, but mostly confidence.

"You've got your mission brief, so I won't belabor those points. But I want to emphasize a couple of things. First, you're about to throw the first punch at the enemy. Make it count."

A rustle moved through the room and most sat up taller.

He continued. "They'll be ready. They started moving this way six hours before their government rained destruction down on our homeland. Make them pay for their perfidy." He scanned their faces again. "Second, stop worrying about what's going on at home. You know as much as we do, from BBC and other news. Our families are most likely safe. There's nothing we can do from here, except fight. Focus on that." He paused, his gaze sweeping the faces of those gathered. "Third, don't worry about yourselves. You'll do fine. Put your fear of fucking up aside."

A chuckle ran round the room. He frowned then continued. "Lastly, I just got word about that friendly SAG headed our way from Sixth Fleet. They hit mines in the Red Sea. One of the destroyers sank. The cruiser and the other destroyer were badly damaged and are out of action. They're fighting to save their ships. So, keep the crews in your thoughts. And keep that in mind as you attack. The enemy's dangerous, so don't do anything stupid. Once you've got a mission kill, bring home any unexpended ordnance. We're gonna need it. But make damned sure you got the mission kill before you come home. Any questions?"

There were none. Gupta liked the determined looks that had replaced the anxious ones as he strode from the room.

An angry group of men and women were flung off *TR's* deck in their jets.

Three hours later the two Chinese warships, and the oiler that had accompanied them, were burning, sinking hulks.

Three F/A-18 Hornets had also gone to populate the bottom of the Indian Ocean. Two of the planes took their pilots with them.

The third was rescued by a passing South Korean flagged merchant ship and treated for her fortunately minor burns. A week later she was put ashore in Patras, Greece.

From there, the embassy secured clothing and airline tickets to Singapore for her, where she hoped to rejoin her squadron.

The military attaché had tried to convince her to go home, or at least to the military hospital in Germany for observation. But she displayed what might diplomatically be called a stubborn streak. Others might have called it a temper tantrum. Either way, she got sent forward instead of back, to return to the fight.

A Panamanian grain carrier rescued fewer than fifty sailors from the Chinese ships. A little more than three dozen survived long enough to be taken off to a hospital in Mumbai.

CHAPTER
TWELVE

0310 Zulu, 28 October
1110 Local Time
The Great Hall, Beijing

President and General Secretary of the State Council Liu Ji sat at the enormous table in the Council meeting chamber. Gathered around him at the table were the members of the much smaller Standing Committee. Tempers simmered under carefully maintained facades.

On three sides of them rose the rows of seats that formed the auditorium where the larger State Council had just finished meeting for the first time in five months. Normally, the entire body wouldn't have met for another month. However, today was special.

Twenty-four hours had passed since the People's Republic had launched the punishing strike at the United States.

The ornate hall had rung with discord. More had attended this meeting than in recent memory. The deep red and bright gold color scheme, the fabric-covered walls, and the soft lighting were supposed to contribute to harmony and peaceful understanding. It hadn't worked.

He and the standing committee members drooped in their seats.

Liu and the Council had carefully choreographed the meeting. The foreign minister, Zhang Yongyi, had briefed first, describing the road to war from a diplomatic perspective. All hell had broken loose when he'd mentioned the intelligence sources inside the American administration. The minister had revealed the access they'd gained to the new president's personal phone and the fact that he connected it to the classified networks in the White House, allowing the People's Republic of China's intelligence apparatus unprecedented entry into previously denied realms. He also divulged learning that the administration intended to manufacture an incident with North Korea, which would allow America to destroy the Kim regime. That information had been restricted to a very few, and the larger State Council members wanted to know why.

Finally, the defense minister briefed the very successful attack. Huang had nearly pranced as he spoke, such was the pride he took in what he believed to be the greatest military victory in all human history.

Liu snorted as he remembered, then looked around the table. "That did not go well," he said as he swirled the brandy in his glass. The others had their preferred beverages in front of them.

Zhang shook his head. "We knew it would not. When we committed to war without informing the rest of the Council, we set ourselves on a path to dissension. But it will pass."

Huang spoke. "It does not matter what the council believes or is concerned about. As the Standing Committee, we are authorized to act. We have an understanding of the situation they cannot possibly equal. If they persist in questioning us, they will be replaced."

Liu closed his eyes and rolled his neck. "That worked for Mao, and for some of my predecessors. But it will not work today. Like it or not, we must be more tolerant of disagreement."

He looked around at each of them. "That does not, however, mean that we will tolerate disobedience or public discord."

"Was not what was displayed here public discord?" Huang asked.

Liu had very little use for Huang. The man had spent a lifetime in the bureaucracy of the Ministry without absorbing any understanding of either technical or military capabilities. However, as an expert at political infighting, he'd managed to learn many secrets hidden in the closets of other ministers and People's Deputies. This had ensured his eventual advancement to lead the ministry. Huang was wise enough to leave the military planning and execution to his underlings and even to ensure a modicum of competent ones to do the work.

He turned to Zhang. "Have our embassies delivered our messages to the European nations?"

Zhang sipped his wine. "Yes, both in person and through appropriate electronic channels. For certainty, copies were provided to all major Western media."

The commander in chief of the army added, "Our cyber forces report that nearly every head of government has already been briefed on its contents, as have most of the NATO council ambassadors." Cyberwarfare fell under the People's Liberation Army.

"But do we know how those governments will respond?" Liu asked.

General Jiang bowed his head. "No, we do not. Not yet."

"Then we know nothing." He swallowed a slug from his glass. The brandy burned, adding to the fire already in his stomach. "We will be patient. We have achieved some of our aims. The rest will come. Once the Americans are completely contained, that will include ending the Taiwan situation. They will accept their fate and reunify peacefully." Turning again to Zhang, he asked, "What of our *other* communique?"

Zhang shrugged. "The BBC and other outlets have begun to

disseminate it. It will be days before we can assess its impact on the intended audience."

Liu finished his drink. "The NATO decision is important. But more important is what the American public does. We will meet again this evening. I expect at least an initial assessment by then." He rose and walked to the door. Turning, he said, "And Huang, there is that little matter of what happened in the South China Sea, the American warship. I expect by tonight you will report that it lies on the ocean bottom." He walked out.

CHAPTER
THIRTEEN

0700 Zulu, 28 Oct
0800 Local Time
NATO Headquarters, Brussels

The chamber of NATO's North Atlantic Council hummed with low conversation as the secretary general walked in. The noise did not entirely subside until he took his seat. On the wall behind the round table hung a large NATO logo, flanked on each side by the flags of each of the member nations, continuing along two of the remaining walls. The fourth held several large displays for teleconferences.

Karl Doenitz, distant cousin of the World War II admiral, sighed and reached for the gavel.

A veteran of the German navy, he'd deployed to the war in Afghanistan with NATO forces. Upon retirement, he joined NATO's bureaucracy. As a former senior officer and brilliant political analyst, he'd risen quickly on the staff of the German permanent representative. When that worthy had retired, Doenitz had replaced her. Six months ago, he'd moved into the rotating secretary position.

The election of a populist president in the United States had made NATO wary. Candidate Donnelly's attacks on NATO had sounded warning bells across Europe. During his first Heads of State meeting, President Donnelly had pronounced the alliance a throwback to ancient history, irrelevant in what he'd termed "modern times." In fact, Donnelly had described it as a danger to some poorly elaborated "new world order" that appeared to be a bilateral construct headed by the United States, and of all nations, Russia. The American permanent representative still occasionally attended meetings, but no longer actively participated.

Frustration had aged Doenitz. His once not-quite-blond hair was streaked with gray, and his face, already lined by decades spent at sea, now sported an unhealthy pallor. Defying ancestry, he was short and stout. He walked with a limp, the result of an improvised explosive device in Afghanistan.

Striking the gavel, he said, "The North Atlantic Council is now in order."

Immediately, silence reigned and the members straightened in their seats.

"This ad hoc meeting has been requested by the representative of the United States. Mr. Ambassador, are you ready to proceed?" Doenitz asked.

"Yes, Mr. Secretary, I am."

A large, flaccid man, the US ambassador's expansive forehead was perpetually beaded with sweat, even during the cold Brussels winters. Motion seemed a chore; movement quickly left him out of breath. Despite being over six feet tall, his girth led observers to believe him shorter.

"Mr. Secretary, representatives of our allies," the American began. A small stir greeted his use of the term allies; they'd not heard it from him before. "A great disaster has befallen my nation, reminiscent of another dastardly sneak attack in 1941. In fact, it has come from the same quarter of the world."

He paused, grimacing slightly before he continued.

"Gentlemen," — the female ambassadors bristled — "the

People's Republic of China has attacked the United States of America, without cause or provocation, and without warning. They have violated the norms of international relations and the laws that govern the United Nations. And they have perpetrated a heinous act against a member of this alliance. By the terms of the North Atlantic Treaty, I invoke Article 5, mutual self-defense. The United States, a member of this alliance, has been attacked. Therefore, we require all member states to comply with their treaty obligations and declare here that they stand with the United States against the horrific act of aggression committed by the People's Republic of China."

For nearly two years the man had steadfastly told member nations that NATO's days were numbered, called it an anachronism, and labored for its demise. The man's hypocrisy fascinated Doenitz.

His audience wasn't terribly pleased by the reversal, either. Some members, down deep in places they didn't acknowledge, had almost hoped something would happen to wake American leadership. Donnelly had antagonized most of the rest of the world, eschewing the friends and allies that had traditionally stood by the United States.

"Very well, Mr. Ambassador. Do you have anything else to add?" Doenitz asked.

"No, Mr. Secretary, I do not. I should think what I just said would be sufficient."

The representative from France, Marc Lebeau, spoke. "Monsieur Ambassador, it is customary to provide substantiating documentary evidence. Your Adlai Stevenson did as much in the Security Council, I believe, in 1962? Perhaps you remember the history of the Cuban Missile Crisis?" Seeing Henry's look, he added, "Not proof of the attack. Corroboration that the Chinese government is intent on destroying your nation, that they are an existential threat. It is hard to conceive that they would desire such a drastic outcome, no matter how, ah, provocative your own government's attitude has been."

The American ambassador looked across at Lebeau, nostrils flaring as he listened to the translation. When it finished, he stared for a moment before speaking. "Mr. Ambassador, I resent your implication that the United States somehow brought it on ourselves. How dare you! The United States has dealt fairly and firmly with China in the face of incredible provocations by *their* government. For God's sake, they initiated a trade war."

He cast his eyes down and flexed his fists on the desk in front of him. When he raised his eyes back up, they were calm. "Forgive me. I, along with my countrymen, are shocked by the events of the night before last. I, that is, my government, asks that you declare war on China and stand with us."

He sipped his water. "I respectfully disagree that we have somehow provoked this evil act. We have only protected our nation's economic well-being, as any nation in this room would do when faced with unfair competitive practices." He turned to look directly at the British ambassador, then continued, "Indeed, some members of this body have also recently unilaterally acted to protect their economic health, and while others disagreed, no nation here threatened war, let alone conducted a surprise attack. Indeed, such a cowardly act cannot be justified."

He paused and scanned around the table, then added, "If you don't stand with us, you must be on their side."

As the Spanish representative began speaking, Doenitz hid a sad smile behind his hand. This clash had been pre-coordinated.

The Spaniard started. "Yet, despite the advocacy of the American government, my nation for one will not rush to judgment and compound error. A declaration of war is not to be taken lightly. Actual facts must be considered, something that your government has of late, shall we say, found it difficult to do. What *is* clear is that your government is in no way concerned about truth. However, the rest of us—" he looked meaningfully around the room "—must concern ourselves with facts, for we live in the world the way that it is."

The American ambassador sat breathing heavily, perspiring.

"Am I to understand that my country's strongest allies, the nations whom we bled to save during World War II, now abandon us? Leave my nation helpless, cast aside, in its darkest hour?"

On the phrase "darkest hour" the British ambassador's eyebrows rose but she said nothing. Doenitz sat back and waited.

Jan Długosz from Poland spoke next. "We do not cast aside an ally. Your president, however, is known to deal with the world as he *wants* it to be, not as it is. He has a history of making statements that later turn out to be, shall we put it delicately, not entirely accurate? NATO must not rush to war. Perhaps the conflict is already ended. There are indications that it may be." He paused to pour water into his glass from the tumbler in front of him.

"There is another fact yet to be discussed," Długosz continued. "It is that Russia has been and remains the greatest threat to Europe. Your president refuses to accept this, despite the many provocative moves made by President Gregorivich. President Donnelly's lifting of sanctions imposed following the invasions and annexation of the Crimea and the rest of Ukraine, for example. Your president refused to acknowledge the independence of Ukraine. He said, and I quote, 'Ukraine isn't even a real country'."

His eyes bored into the American. "That could have been said of your own country in 1812 when you fought a second war with the British. Nevertheless, you retained your independence. Does Ukraine not deserve the same opportunity? Unfortunately, without America, NATO could only stand by and do nothing except protest. Russia is emboldened even more now, the result of doing nothing. We are stronger now than we were. But only if we stand united against the threat Russia poses. And only if we are not *distracted* elsewhere."

Finished, he folded his hands and continued to lean forward.

Eleanor Climber, from the United Kingdom, spoke. "Mr.

Ambassador, we acknowledge, as always, the unique relationship our two nations enjoy. Nevertheless, your president abused that relationship badly whenever it suited his purposes and ignored it when it did not. I will speak plainly, as a friend should. Your president has made it very difficult for this body to act in concert with his administration."

She looked around the chamber, then returned her gaze to Henry. "This alliance supports the United States—" She paused for the merest fraction of a second as Henry began to speak, then spoke over him. "—but to protect ourselves, let your president reap what he has sown."

She leaned back, lips pressed together.

Doenitz raised his gavel and held it in the air. Looking around, he asked formally, needlessly, "Is there any other business before this body?"

Długosz spoke up again, saying, "Nothing that concerns the American ambassador."

Doenitz looked at the American expectantly, willing him to go quietly.

He would not. "Gentlemen," he nearly shouted.

The female ambassadors sat upright, visibly angry.

He continued, "I find it incredible that this body, this alliance, which would not exist without the United States, would turn on its benefactor."

Turning on the Polish ambassador, he said, "You. Your nation didn't exist until we forced its creation."

He turned to Doenitz. "And you were beaten, destroyed. We rebuilt your country. Now you're turning on us, you ungrateful whelp."

He verbally assaulted several more ambassadors, excoriating them for past actions, though not with historical accuracy.

Turning to the United Kingdom's representative, he said, "You're the worst. We saved your ass. You wouldn't have lasted another month when we declared war on Germany. You were on the ropes, and now you stab us in the back. Winston Churchill is rolling in his grave, lady."

He sat back, staring at the other representatives.

Silence reigned for long moments.

Długosz broke it. "Mr. Ambassador, setting aside your impressive ignorance of European history, I disagree. We are not abandoning your nation. We are making clear we do not trust your *president*. His ignorance — deliberate, willful ignorance — as well as his shoot from the hip reaction to everything, and his intensely self-centered focus, has created this situation. Yes, you've suffered greatly, but nothing that cannot be repaired. And we will help. Our governments are even now readying aid. You have also suffered significant military losses. But again, nothing that cannot be rebuilt, given the enormous resources of the United States."

He shook his head. "We hope also that your president has learned a lesson. The world is a place where words and facts matter. Where nations must deal with each other, each other's needs, desires, hopes. Most importantly, where all nations are intertwined in ways that are unprecedented. It is a place where ultra-nationalism has no place. Some of us around this table have flirted with ultra-nationalism in the recent past. But in the end, our citizens have rejected it as the useless, harmful, damaging belief that it is." He grimaced. "I'm sorry, Mr. Ambassador, I cannot vote to support a war that did not need to happen. I will be blunt. There are those in my government, and I suspect elsewhere, who may consider your *president* the enemy."

When it was done, Doenitz announced the vote. "It is unanimous. The Council turns down the United States's request to invoke Article 5." He brought the gavel down. Rising, he looked at the American ambassador. "Please convey to your president that we will share any intelligence indicating additional threats to your country. There is no one here who wishes, or wished, harm to our ally. But we cannot defend ourselves against a much closer and very real threat if we go blindly off to what nearly all of us believe is a war brought about by sheer incompetence."

He moved toward the door but paused. "There are certain parallels with World War II, you know. The United States, an ally of Britain and France, remained neutral despite France being overrun. Only when the United States was attacked by Japan did it join the war. Now, Europe faces an enemy whose intentions are unclear, though suspected. Therefore, we will remain out of your war, at least for now. I wish it were not so. But we are all in agreement. I personally wish your nation well."

He turned back long enough to say, "And I will recommend a good book on European history since the start of the twentieth century."

He left the US delegation alone.

CHAPTER
FOURTEEN

0720 Zulu, 28 Oct
0820 Local Time
NATO Headquarters, Brussels

The ambassador sat back in his plush chair, not believing what had just happened. Behind him, his staffers rose quietly and began to put blank notepads into their briefcases. Still, he didn't move. Looking at one another, they shrugged and headed toward the door opposite.

"Don't fucking move." He stood as the expletive exploded, surprising even himself.

He turned on them, voice deep, angry, volume rising continuously until he shouted, "I want us packed and ready to leave this Godforsaken piddly-assed country within the next six hours. I want every trace of the United States's mission here scrubbed. Do you hear me? I want every miserable scrap packed or destroyed, and I, by God, want the ashes spread so thinly no one will ever even know we were here. I want the military out of here, too. They've got eight hours to pack up and get their crap out of this shit hole." He stared at their open mouths. "Move. Now."

The UK and Polish ambassadors waited for Doenitz in the hallway. The three walked together toward the ˋOperations Center.

After a few yards, Doenitz spoke. "Well, lady and gentleman, that went just as poorly as expected."

Długosz replied, "How else could we respond? Reports from listening posts near Ukraine are most alarming. Worse are the reports from surveillance aircraft monitoring Russian movements. Now we've lost the photographic intelligence the Americans were periodically sharing with us."

The UK representative looked sharply at the Polish ambassador, who laughed shortly and said, "Yes, they shared it with us. I know, you thought you were the only country special enough to get their high-resolution imagery. What did you think we'd requested as a *quid pro quo* for letting them build their Aegis ballistic missile defense system in the heart of our country?"

The UK ambassador smiled. "We assumed you wanted Yank dollars and knew it would defend your cities as easily as the rest of Europe."

"Those were considerations. But they needed our land more than we needed their dollars. And we don't fear Iran as they do. So defense was only a tertiary consideration. If the system protected us from Russia? Well, that would have been an entirely different matter." His smile became a frown. "Now that we are without access to intelligence, there are gaps in our ability to know what Russian soldiers across the border are doing. I will, of course, make a formal request for aid from both your nations."

He looked pointedly at them as they approached the Ops Center door.

Climber said, "Well, I expect we will work something out. We have sources of our own, you know. The Americans pooh-pooh them, but they are more than adequate. We can share with our allies. Perhaps it's also time we shared more of what we glean from American systems than our agreements with them allow."

Długosz inclined his head to the others as they entered the watch floor.

Doenitz sighed. "We warned Donnelly that his actions, and more importantly, his words, would have consequences. But he scoffed at any suggestion that someone somewhere might take exception and act. He must reap what he has sown."

The watch officer, a Belgian air force colonel, approached them. "You are in time for our shift change briefing. Would you care to listen?" Seeing them nod, he turned and waved at another officer. She moved to stand below the fifteen-foot wall of high-resolution displays. As she did so, the first of a set of slides was displayed above her head. A map of Eastern Europe from the Baltic states to Moldova came up next to her.

"Good afternoon, ladies and gentlemen. While we have no photo reconnaissance imagery today, reports culled from media of Russian troop movements within Ukraine indicate there is still a generalized flow toward the border with Poland and the Baltic states. Electronic communications intercepts continue to increase—"

Following the brief, the trio moved back to the conference room.

It would not be the first Atlantic Council meeting not attended by the American ambassador himself; but it would be the first without any American representation, and the first where none was desired.

CHAPTER
FIFTEEN

1300 Zulu, 28 Oct
1700 Local Time
The Kremlin, Moscow

Russian President Yuri Gregorivich smiled. He waited for the flash and electronic click to signal he could return to work.

The young girl at his side giggled nervously, her arm around his waist. When the expected cues came and went, the president gave the girl a squeeze and regained his own arm. Then he turned and walked back to his desk, the girl already gone from his mind.

Gregorivich sat and leaned back in his luxurious chair.

Defense Minister Pavlov Remkin, who'd stood just inside the door throughout the photo opportunity, came bustling forward as the photographer and the beauty pageant winner tried to exit. Remkin's girth nearly made the photographer drop his camera. Too cowed to say anything, he simply grabbed the girl's arm, pulled her through, and closed the door.

"Good afternoon, Mr. President. I presume you wish to talk about Ukraine?" Remkin asked.

"Of course. Is there anything else of import at this moment?" The president scowled at him.

Remkin sighed. In response to Gregorivich's waved invitation, he sat.

"Well, there is Belarus, or the Baltics. What else? Oh, yes, there is the war between China and the United States. Perhaps one of these is of interest today?"

The president looked a warning at Remkin, then relaxed and chuckled.

"All right, Pavlov, yes, all are of great importance. But let us finish one discussion topic at a time. The others will wait, surprisingly enough."

He leaned back in his chair and put his hands behind his head. "So, let's be about it. What have you for me today?"

"Today, sir, I have the report on the North Atlantic Council meeting."

The president's body shot forward, and he nearly leapt out of his seat.

"We have it already?" he said, his eyes wide, hungry. "Well, don't keep it to yourself."

"It is not what we hoped for, sir," Remkin said, his tone again entirely serious. He moved his hands to grasp his own knees. "The council rejected the US request for mutual defense. Worse, Poland reminded the rest of the members that we are still here, we are strong, and that we are currently not occupied, now that our Ukrainian province is, er, pacified."

Gregorivich stood and paced, his body bent forward, his strides pounded out on the thick carpet.

"They are right to fear me." He closed his eyes and stopped. Opening them, he continued, "But they should have met their obligation under the treaty." He pinched the bridge of his nose. "A part of me wishes to believe this may be the death knell for that infernal alliance. But no. We have too often thought so and been proved wrong. Still, perhaps Donnelly has made more progress in killing it than we hoped."

"Perhaps, sir, but one other item in the report may be of interest and shed light on the subject. I'm told that the American ambassador left along with most of his staff. Those that remain are clearing out their workspaces. He also ordered the withdrawal of all American forces from Europe."

Gregorivich snorted and moved to stare out the window. The trees in Red Square were turning in the crisp fall air. Below them moved dozens of men and women. Most moved purposefully. Some sauntered, taking in the sight. In the distance, light puffy clouds heralded light overcast and a change in the weather for tomorrow.

"He actually believes he has the authority to do that?" He barked a short laugh. "The American commander in Europe — what is her name? She will laugh when she receives *that* order." His head tilted to the side. "Still . . ."

Remkin didn't reply. He knew better than to interrupt the president's thoughts.

Gregorivich continued to stare out the window. "You remember I've been there, in that very hall. I observed one of the presidential level meetings. I even spoke. So many speeches about the *historic opportunity for peace* that my attendance foretold. That competition amongst nations was going the way of the dodo in favor of cooperation and collaboration."

He turned to Remkin, fists clenched in front of him. "It was all rubbish. Competition among nations will be extinct when one nation finally wins. Everything I have done, every action since *I* re-established the supremacy of the Russian Federation, has been to return it to its glory. To make the *Rodina* the country that finally wins. As the Americans phrase it, takes all the marbles."

Remkin had heard it before: Mother Russia was *destined* for world domination. The others had all failed *because* they'd turned on Russia. The *Rodina* had been the downfall of every aspiring hegemon. Therefore, Russia must *be* the hegemon.

Remkin heaved a sigh as his attention wandered. Gregorivich turned back to the window. Silence reigned.

After a few moments, the president turned back, eyes alight. "Still, you said the ambassador ordered American forces to depart Europe? Then perhaps Donnelly will reinforce that order. Perhaps he will also tell them not to help NATO." He resumed pacing. "His nephew still works for us? Can we communicate with him?"

"Yes, sir. He lives only a few blocks from our embassy in Washington."

"Then direct him to goad his uncle into endorsing the ambassador's orders." Gregorivich pounded his fist into his palm. "The Americans are alone. This leaves the rest of NATO without the American capabilities that integrate their own. There will be gaps to exploit. We will use the cracks in the NATO structure to drive wedges between the allies. This is *good* news, Pavlov."

"But, sir, I thought we needed NATO to go to war with Ch—" He stopped.

The president no longer listened.

Remkin stiffened in his chair, his heart racing. *He's going to do it. This is no longer an academic exercise. It's going to happen.*

Despite everything the president had done over the past dozen years, Remkin had doubted the next step would ever come. It was one thing to carve off sections of former Soviet Republics.

The president stopped pacing. "Tomorrow, we announce that because of global instability and the war between America and China, we will reinforce our borders. Due to an increased threat from NATO, we will place our forces on the border with Poland, Finland, and the Baltic nations on high alert. They will be poised to protect Kaliningrad and all Russian people."

"We cannot fool their intelligence agencies, sir. Their military leadership, at least, will not be misled. Satellite imagery does not lie."

The president looked at Remkin, gave a short laugh, and shook his head.

"Pavlov, we *will* fool them. The Chinese have been good

enough to destroy sufficient American space assets that NATO has been blinded, or nearly so."

"But the Chinese only destroyed the American satellites in the Pacific and Indian Oceans. My space intelligence people tell me that the satellites over Europe are still fully operational."

The president smiled. "Yes, Pavlov, but where does that intelligence go? Does it not all get collected at a central location? Do your operatives tell you whether that location is fully operational? And would the Americans continue to share it with allies who have just rejected their cry for help?" The president smirked. "The Chinese have given us an opportunity, and it never behooves anyone to miss an opportunity." He turned to gaze out the window.

Remkin stood and joined him. Together they looked at the spires and skyscrapers of Moscow, but what Gregorivich saw was the new capital of a great and growing empire.

CHAPTER
SIXTEEN

1330 Zulu, 28 Oct
0830 Eastern Time
The Oval Office, White House

National Security Advisor Hunter hadn't gone straight back to the Oval Office from the Sit Room. Instead, he went to his office.

As always, bad news wouldn't get better with age. But when he'd called the president's secretary, he learned the president had gone to bed with an order that under no circumstances was he to be disturbed.

Hunter decided to obey, despite the probable consequences.

Come morning, he got the video from the Coast Guard, thinking it might save him. It didn't.

As he summarized the previous day's meeting, the president fumed.

"What the fuck is wrong with those people?" demanded Donnelly, spittle flying. "They believe that Coast Guard bitch?"

Again Hunter took a deep breath. "Sir, trustworthy people analyzed the video. It's real. The flag is real, the ship is real, the missiles are real. They even confirmed when it was recorded."

"I'm not buying it."

"Sir, at least watch the video—" Hunter began.

"No. This has deep state written all over it."

The door to the Oval Office opened. The deputy secretary of state stuck his head slowly through it.

The president turned and blasted him. "What the fuck do you think is going on here, Phillips, we're playing tiddlywinks? Get the hell out of here."

Accustomed to the president's outbursts, Phillips ignored the curses that flew like bullets. He moved into the office. "Mr. President, you need to see this."

Phillips carried a tablet computer. His urgency stopped the president's bombast.

"What is it?" he asked in an almost normal tone.

"It's a broadcast from the Chinese government. BBC, Canadian Broadcasting, Sky News, and several others are carrying it."

Ten minutes later, the president sat at the big desk with his head in his hands, massaging his temples.

Behind him the sun streaming through the windows was heavily tinged yellow and brown by the smoke that still rose from destroyed and damaged government buildings.

Hunter sat on the sofa next to Phillips. Neither wanted to break the silence. Both expected another temper tantrum.

The president had begun screaming seconds after the video started. But as it played, the explosion had petered out. He'd watched the remainder in silence.

Hunter hadn't expected the Chinese to admit their treachery or make further demands. Seething, he plotted what would happen when the Chinese leaders were defeated, captured, and brought to Washington for trial. In his fantasy, American soldiers marching into Beijing was a possibility.

He glanced over at Phillips, who looked like he wanted to escape. He was the messenger Donnelly would want to shoot.

Ordinarily, Hunter didn't worry about that being a literal thing. However, given events of the past thirty-six hours, who knew? Martial law gave the president wide discretion and interesting new powers.

Donnelly raised his head.

"Who do those bastards think they are?" he asked conversationally.

"Mr. President, the intended audience isn't the American people. It's the rest of the world. They want the Europeans to stay out of it. Which they've already decided to do."

"How, exactly, does calling for the overthrow of the government of the United States achieve that?" Phillips asked.

"They said they won't try to take any land. They just want us to leave them alone, let them act as they see fit globally, but especially in east Asia. The translation, of course, is they want hegemony inside a line that basically starts at Tokyo and runs south to the west end of New Guinea."

He paused, but Donnelly listened, at least for the moment. He continued. "We were really the only ones standing up to them. With us out of the way, they've got a free hand. The Europeans don't really care much about the South China Sea, so long as commerce flows."

Phillips shook his head. "That won't wash. The Europeans don't want us out of the picture. We've been the source of world stability since the '40s. They don't want a return to the days before the war. And the Brits and Aussies *do* care about the South China Sea."

"They do, but they don't want to antagonize China unless we're along for the ride. And you missed the point, Phillips. They didn't call for the overthrow of the *government*, just *us*," Hunter said. He considered the possibility that Chinese leadership might understand the American people better than anyone in the Administration gave them credit for.

Perhaps, he thought, though he would never admit this to anyone, *better than we understand them, too.*

Not yet convinced, Phillips asked, "What does Europe gain by an American civil war?"

Hunter sighed and ran his hand through his hair. "What do they get? They get more say in global politics outside of Asia. There's a lot of men in European capitals who long for the old days when Europe called the shots. They won't figure out how expensive that is for a few years, until they have to police the world on their own."

"I'll never allow that," the president blurted out.

Both men turned to him.

Hunter had almost forgotten him. Donnelly usually didn't have the requisite attention span for deep analysis of international relations.

"They'll never run the world. I'll never give them that much power. Hell, they can't even take care of Europe, and we've been trying to make them to do that for decades," Donnelly said.

"Who do you envision taking that role on, then, sir?" asked Phillips, eyes wide, head tilted to one side. His tone conferred deference mixed with confusion. Hunter wondered if Phillips realized that he'd just stepped into the president's mine field.

"What the hell makes you think *I'll* give up that role?" demanded the president.

His face was red and his eyes bulged. He stood from behind the great oaken desk and began to pace up and down behind it. It struck Hunter how he was bounded on each end of his path by an American flag, two of a dozen he'd had installed, filling every nook and cranny in the Oval Office.

"I'll never give it up. I am the greatest nation on this planet. Europeans run things? Never. Fuck 'em. When I finish with China, I'll dictate their surrender from the Great Wall. Then I'll go after the Europeans. They'll rue the day they didn't back us. They'll come begging me to forgive them, and I'll tell them to fuck off." He was just getting warmed up. "I was the most popular president since Lincoln before their sneak attack. Now, I'm *the* most popular."

Hunter wondered silently how he'd arrived at that conclusion but wisely didn't ask.

"The American people will never rise against me. I'm the one who's going to *avenge* them. I'll kill every little yellow Chinese motherfucker on this planet."

He turned suddenly and sat back down in his chair.

"Go down to the Sit Room and get the secretary of defense on the line. Tell him I want every nuke-ular missile and bomb we have sent to China. I want every city and village nuked, then I want the dust bombed."

They sat staring at him. An electric shock pulsed through Hunter's body.

"Sir, I can't do that," he mumbled. For the first time, his stomach churned in Donnelly's presence. Seeing the storm gathering in the president's face, he quickly continued, scrambling for words. "You're the only person who can give that order, sir, and it has to be given in person."

Hunter could imagine the reaction of the acting secretary — he didn't intend to remind the president that the actual secretary was dead — if he tried to pass such an order. The man would hem and haw because he was a coward. But would he pass it on? Should he? Should Hunter?

The president stared at him, then spoke in that deceptively reasonable tone he sometimes used. Or at least, he started that way. As he spoke, however, his voice rose until he was screaming. "Are you not my national security advisor? Do you not advise me on issues of, perhaps, national defense? Do you not take your orders from me? Does the secretary of defense not take *his* orders from me?" He blinked several times. "If I give you an order, I damn well expect everyone to obey it. If you won't relay it, I will damn sure find someone who will. And I'll have anyone who doesn't, shot." He stared at Hunter. "Including you."

Donnelly sat fuming for a moment before he finished. "Now get the fuck out of my office."

Both Hunter and Phillips sprang up from where they'd been sitting. Bustling against each other, they fought to get to the door.

Hunter was last through.

He turned and whispered, "Thank you, Mr. President."

In the hall outside, Phillips waited. "You aren't seriously going to try to pass that order on, are you?"

"Do *you* want to be replaced by some other toady? Do you?" He took a few steps then rounded on Phillips again.

"First of all, what I do or don't do is *my* business and *my* job, not yours. Second, you ought to be rounding up support among our *allies*, not worrying about what we're doing militarily." He put his finger in Phillips's chest. "Third, get the fuck out of my face."

With that, Hunter spun and stalked down the hallway toward his office.

CHAPTER
SEVENTEEN

1600 Zulu, 28 Oct
1100 Eastern Time
The Situation Room, The White House

Hunter walked alone into the Sit Room. His "be seated" ritual complete, he once again took the chair at the head of the table.

He'd kept the meeting to just the acting secretaries of Defense, Homeland Security, Treasury, and State. In particular, he had not invited the vice chairman, though under the rules for what he was about to do, he should have.

He justified it by telling himself the vice chairman was only acting, though the fact that the other attendees were also acting put a crimp in that storyline. Hunter had really done it because he assumed Norton would defy him publicly and he didn't want to risk that.

"Acting Secretary Wilson, I have a direct order from the president of the United States. An order which he expects you to carry out immediately."

He paused, looking Wilson directly in the eye. Wilson flushed and cast his eyes down, then shrugged and looked back at him.

Speaking slowly, Hunter continued, "You are ordered to

conduct nuclear strikes against the mainland of the People's Republic of China. Target all of their major military bases, especially any base capable of launching ballistic missiles and long-range bombers. And destroy Beijing. All of it."

Wilson's jaw dropped. An audible gasp arose from the rest of those in attendance.

Even as Hunter spoke, a sense of unreality overwhelmed him. But he knew with every fiber of his being that this was his path, his destiny.

Wilson stared at him. His mouth worked but he uttered no sound.

Hunter had spent much of the intervening hour looking at the problem from every angle before arriving at the conclusion that the best option was to do exactly what the president had directed. He knew the order to be both legal and crazy at the same time. But it might work.

He'd also order the State Department to pass a message to the Russians, informing them what was about to happen. The destruction of China would create opportunities for them, as well.

Crossing the nuclear threshold was a bold step. But this was the time. Ordering it would also be the catalyst for other opportunities he'd sought.

If the men and woman here balked, he'd break them and remake the Security Council and Cabinet with his own selections. Donnelly would go along with his choices, he was sure. If they carried it out, he'd have iron-clad control of the four most powerful cabinet departments.

It would deliver the president, and by extension, himself, a great victory. Public opinion would be cemented in their favor. The Europeans would see that America was stronger by itself and didn't need them. There would be no civil war in America. It would give America permanent, undisputed world leadership. And rid the world of the Chinese menace.

It would also allow the final cleansing of the opposition

party. Their namby-pamby hand wringing would fall flat with real Americans, who would take matters into their own hands and purge such traitors. Those who survived would fall in line.

His epiphany had come when he'd realized how successful the Chinese strategy had been. Sure, it looked like they'd done what they'd said, avoided civilian infrastructure and casualties. But the administration could overcome that with messaging of their own, issued from the White House and the cabinet departments. Things were chaotic enough that no one would be able to refute any story they told. An angry and hurting American public would buy it.

Hell, a lot of them already buy every bit of bullshit we put out.

The Reagan administration had toyed with limited nuclear war back in the day. They'd even had a civil defense book published about surviving it: "With Enough Shovels."

Admiral Threadman spoke first. "You can't do that, sir."

Threadman's eyes narrowed as he met them. Her lips were compressed into thin white lines. "That order has to come directly from the president."

He'd expected this. The time to crush her had come. Leaning forward, he spoke quietly but firmly. "The president of the United States has given an order, Admiral. Are you saying you won't carry it out? That you will disobey a direct order from the commander in chief?"

He paused to allow his words to sink in. "You have no role in this, anyway. This is a purely military order, and *you* are not military."

Threadman's face reddened as Hunter spoke. Perspiration rose on her forehead. She opened her mouth, but Hunter interrupted her. "You're fired. Get out now, or I'll have security escort you out."

Hunter continued to stare at her while her jaw worked silently.

Finally, the admiral stood and moved toward the door. More

than thirty years of following orders had kicked her body into autopilot, physically overcoming her rage. But as she left the room, she turned and said, "This is an illegal order unless delivered personally by the president himself. Any of you who follow it will be judged, at least by history, if not by a war crimes tribunal. Assuming you live through it."

"Get out."

She slammed the door on her way out.

Hunter continued, looking at each remaining man individually. "Is there anyone else in this room who wants to challenge the authority of the president?"

The three men looked anywhere but at him. No one spoke.

"Very well, then. Acting Secretary Wilson, I expect you to carry out your order. Are there any questions? No? Good. I expect a report within an hour, and damage reports on our targets as soon as they're available. Dismissed."

The men didn't move for a few moments. Eventually they stood and filed out the door. Wilson hadn't said a word. He was the last out.

At the door, he paused. "She's right, it should come from the president. I'll do it, but they may not take the order from me. Why didn't the president call Major Whitely in?"

The Air Force officer tasked with holding the "football," Major Whitely carried the briefcase with the nuclear codes and procedures to be followed.

Hunter didn't turn around. Making it up as he spoke, he said, "Because Major Whitely can't order missiles re-targeted the way the president desires. Her function lets the president respond to a nuclear attack, not order one. This order requires intelligent execution, not a rote recital of a rehearsed ballet. Are you suggesting you will not carry out this order?"

Wilson quickly responded, "No, sir, I'm not saying that. But someone in uniform will ask me the same question, and I need to be able to answer it." He turned and hurried through the door.

Hunter smiled.

So far, it was working.

He returned to his office. There, he called the Justice Department and ordered the acting attorney general to have the FBI arrest Admiral Threadman.

The bitch never did fit in. Leadership is a man's game.

CHAPTER
EIGHTEEN

1645 Zulu, 28 Oct
1145 Eastern Time
Washington, DC

Wilson rode through the silent streets toward the Pentagon.

The martial law declaration kept civilians in their homes except for emergencies. Police aggressively enforced the curfew, as did the National Guard unit assigned to the city. Traffic was nonexistent.

Wilson didn't notice as he ruminated on the order.

Smoke still issued from a few smoldering fires in the massive edifice that housed the Department of Defense. Overall, it remained sound. The area hit on September 11th had been hit again, debris spilling out into the memorial garden.

As soon as his chauffeur pulled up to the side entrance, Wilson climbed out and headed for the elevator to his office. As he passed through security, he ordered the guard to have the vice chairman call him.

When the phone rang, Wilson took two deep breaths, stood and answered it.

"Wilson speaking," he spluttered, trying and failing to sound confident and in charge.

"This is Norton. You asked me to call."

"Yes, General, thank you. I am relaying an order from the president of the United States, issued this afternoon at a principals meeting of the National Security Council."

He could hear the prevarication in his own voice, and he hoped Norton couldn't. He relayed Hunter's order in detail. Then, he waited.

The long pause on the phone had Wilson thinking perhaps the connection had been lost. "General?"

"Yes, sir. I heard you. A meeting of the principals, huh? That normally includes the Chairman of the Joint Chiefs, *or his acting*."

Wilson closed his eyes. Norton's voice dripped sarcasm.

Norton continued, "Never mind. Admiral Threadman contacted me after Hunter threw her out of the Sit Room." Norton's breathing sounded over the encrypted Voice Over Internet Protocol phone line. "You don't really expect me to obey that order, do you?" asked the general.

Wilson cringed. He sat down. "Yes, General, I do. Threadman had no business discussing it with you. This order is valid and is from the president."

"How do you or I know that? How do I know that you are who you say you are? What proof do you have?"

The general was toying with him.

Wilson slogged on, perspiring though cool fall air drifted in through a window that opened onto the central courtyard.

"I am talking to you on a secure line, General. No one else has access to this line, and you called me. Is that good enough for you? Is it your intention to disobey this order?"

He'd decided to take the same tack Hunter had, but when his voice broke slightly at the end, it destroyed the effect.

Norton grunted. "No, sir. I'm telling you there *is* no order."

Wilson put his head in his hand as Norton continued.

"Mr. Wilson, there's a protocol for issuing a nuclear weapons order, and this isn't even close. That protocol was put in place to prevent accidental or unauthorized release of nukes. Until I get proper authentication, no order exists. Am I clear?" He paused, then added, "Sir."

Sighing, Wilson asked the last question in the world he wanted to. "What is the proper protocol, General?"

A moment passed before Norton answered. "Well, sir, let me put it to you simply. Major Whitely's team carries the football and the procedures. If the president wants to use nuclear weapons, he has to order it himself. He uses the process Major Whitely has in her briefcase. When the president does that, I will receive a properly authenticated order. Then, and only then, will I carry it out." Norton paused. "But until then, sir, you have a good day."

"Wait."

"What?"

"That process is designed for a retaliatory strike, is it not?"

A sigh from the phone. "Yes, sir."

"It was *not* designed for a first strike, then. You're suggesting I ask the president to use the process to do something it wasn't designed for," Wilson said. His voice stopped trembling. He felt on firmer ground, now.

The general's voice grated back. "You've been listening to that jackass Hunter, haven't you? He doesn't understand the first thing about civilian control of the military. Or the processes that ensure proper, note I say *proper,* authority is exercised. Sir, were we not attacked?"

Norton waited. Wilson knew what he was supposed to say but fought it. He didn't want to be lectured. In the end, however, the uncomfortable pause became too much to bear. "Yes."

"Well then, sir, would this not constitute a retaliatory strike? Second, sir, the process does not differ for a first strike, a retaliatory second strike, or even a third strike." Norton's voice rose

122 THOMAS M. WING

slightly as the general's patience wore thin. "The only damned difference, *sir*, is that we expect our nation to be in its death throes, or headed there, before we launch *any* nuclear strike. We're not there yet, not by a long shot. So, if the president wants to order us to cross the nuclear threshold against the recommendation of his military advisors, then he damned well better follow nuclear command and control protocol. Good day, sir."

The phone clicked then hummed as the crypto reset.

Wilson hung up the phone and put his head in both hands. He'd even forgotten to talk about the targets.

General Norton slammed down the phone.

He'd inherited a mess the moment the chairman went missing.

The afternoon before the attack, Norton had given a speech at the Naval War College in Newport, Rhode Island. He usually drove himself, but that day he'd used a driver. Partly, he wanted to enjoy the fall colors along the freeway. Mostly, he wanted to catch up on reports and reviews of operational plans.

The attack had hit as they'd passed through Philadelphia. Blossoms of flame and thick black smoke had leapt up over the Naval Shipyard. He'd tried to raise the Pentagon via the car's installed secure phone, but comms were out.

Traffic crawled on I-95, so much so that the driver had departed the freeway and gotten off on smaller state highways. Hours later, smoke billowed over Washington as they approached.

On arrival at the Pentagon and learning the chairman was missing, he'd taken charge of the United States military.

Not being selected himself as chairman hadn't bothered him much. He hated politics, and the vice chairman's job was less political. Such a twilight tour would take him into retirement.

Besides, he'd relished the thought that he could influence the military for the next generation.

Now, as acting chairman in the middle of a major shooting war, he had to deal with the politicians.

Especially the weak-minded, chickenshit Acting SecDef.

He called for his car to take him to Bethesda.

He needed help on this one.

CHAPTER
NINETEEN

1057 Zulu, 30 Oct
1757 Local Time
USS *Nicholas*, South China Sea

Only the furrows cut by flying fish as they flapped perpendicularly away from *Nicholas's* bow marred the mirrored surface as she steamed along a patrol line northeast of Singapore. The brilliant yellows and oranges of sunset reflected off the backs of the waves while the fronts lay in shadow. Armed with his sextant and stopwatch, the quartermaster on the starboard bridge wing sought Venus to the west, the first star he'd shoot for a fix.

Seventh Fleet had ordered *Nicholas* to clear a path into the South China Sea for the *TR* strike group. To remain hidden, she still maintained strict radio silence.

More importantly, the Rules of Engagement had changed: it was all out war. Any aircraft, surface ship, or submarine identified as belonging to the People's Republic of China could be destroyed as hostile. Bill already had his TAOs operating that way. But it reassured him to have official cover.

Conducting an anti-submarine barrier operation, the water

depth and bottom contours made for a patrol line eighty miles east-northeast of the mouth of the Singapore Strait, running north-northwest and south-southeast. Along it lay a slight underwater shelf where the water was deep enough to tow the AN/SQR-19 passive towed array sonar and the sound generated by any submarines would funnel toward them.

Bill, seated on the port bridge wing, considered his fuel problem. The *TR* strike group and its oiler were still nearly a week away. Therefore, with *Nicholas* down to sixty-three percent, he needed to conserve. But to fight required the ability to use speed as needed. So until he needed to fight, he would conserve, using a maximally efficient engineering configuration.

He pondered if any of the normally friendly nations in the area would let him pull in for gas. The law of armed conflict said that if a belligerent warship entered a neutral port, the neutral nation must prevent its departure, interning the ship for the duration of hostilities. Otherwise, the nation lost its neutral status and would be considered a belligerent. That law had been the basis for German protests during both world wars when the US had allowed goods to be shipped to Britain on American vessels. The US had maintained that, since they were not permitting British warships or merchants to enter US ports, they were compliant with the law of armed conflict.

But the geopolitical situation in the South China Sea for the past decade or more, coupled with the fact local nations had to know how badly the US had been hurt, left little doubt the answer would be no.

"Bridge, TAO. Intel broadcast shows a possible Chinese merchant departing the Singapore Strait, headed our way. Captain up there?"

He nodded to the OOD, who responded, "TAO, Bridge. Captain's here and acknowledges."

Bill put his head back against the headrest and closed his eyes. He didn't know how it was possible that broadcast hadn't been taken down, but he was damned sure glad he still had it.

The Triton drone had dropped out of the link the night before last, shot down or out of gas.

What do I do about that merchant? he wondered.

Legally under the new ROE, he could sink it. But he knew "positive" meant visual identification or VID. *That* meant closing the vessel to see its home port or flag. And if it were an intelligence collector, it would report his presence.

Even if he used his one working helicopter, the Chinese would know he was within a couple of hundred miles. Additionally, some Chinese merchants carried shoulder fired surface-to-air missiles. He couldn't risk it.

"Bridge, TAO. Captain to Combat."

The urgency in Campbell's voice made him leap from his chair. As he hurried through the door, he called out to the OOD. "Call the XO. Ask her to come to the bridge."

He was gone before the OOD replied.

Down in the dim blue light of CIC, the increased tension and drawn faces revealed a tired crew under stress. Three days of constant vigilance, fear for their families, and concern an enemy lay just over the horizon wore on them.

How bad will they look when it's been a month?

"Captain's in Combat," called the CIC watch supervisor.

Bill took his seat in front of the large screen displays. The TAO had a contact "hooked" on the tactical plot on the starboard side display. Campbell had the range dialed down to show only the area out to ninety nautical miles around the ship. The operational screen to port still showed the entirety of the South China Sea.

The information monitor above showed the characteristics of the hooked track: an unknown assumed hostile subsurface contact, held by passive sonar at ninety-seven thousand yards, forty-eight and a half nautical miles away. Sonar had tentatively classified it as a *Han* class nuclear-powered attack submarine, possibly approaching them at six knots. If neither vessel changed course or speed, it would pass astern of them at seven thousand yards in six hours and fifty minutes.

"Any indication they know we're here?" Bill asked.

"Can't tell yet, sir. We've got our prairie and masker systems online, so we should sound like a rainstorm. But it's unlikely they can hear this far."

"What's Sonar's confidence in the course and speed?"

Campbell shook his head. "Higher than it ought to be. I don't trust TMA solutions, automatic processing or not. We don't hold it on the 53, yet, either. So they're guessing."

The AN/SQS-53 hull-mounted sonar had both passive and active capabilities, but primarily operated passively. Passive sonar only gave bearings to a target, not range. TMA, Target Motion Analysis, provided a means to turn multiple bearings into an estimated course and speed based on an assumed range. However, it was only as accurate as the assumed range, the number of bearings, and the geometry of the courses and speeds of target and hunter.

Campbell continued. "They *say* they're pretty sure of the range, within a few thousand yards. It's a second CZ contact."

Bill grunted and sat back. Convergence Zones were concentric circles around a noise source. Sound from the target bent first downward toward deeper, colder water, then the water density at depth would bend it back up to the surface, forming the CZ. The water temperature "profile" allowed *Nicholas* to estimate how far apart those concentric rings were, and thus, approximately how far away the possible submarine might be.

The presence of the subsurface contact changed the situation with the merchant, too. If he maneuvered, they'd lose track of the submarine until the towed array sonar stabilized on their new course. If he didn't, they risked being seen by the merchant.

"ASWO, TAO, the captain's going to need your recommendation to kill the hostile."

Unwilling to publicly scold Campbell, he leaned over and said, "Jason, we need to ID it first. Believe me, I'm pretty sure it's hostile, too. But we need to make certain."

Campbell's head sank just perceptibly.

Bill sighed inwardly. Mentoring junior officers was a never-ending task. Each needed their own special style. Some were self-confident and recovered quickly. Others took even the smallest correction personally, letting it damage their self-esteem. Campbell was one of the latter.

"ASWO, TAO. Belay my last. We need to positively ID the sub."

Bill leaned back. Every bone in his body ached to walk over to the ASW coordinator console and look over Ensign Bonnet's shoulder, to see firsthand what she knew or could reasonably surmise. He could even walk into Sonar and talk to the sonar techs directly and get a read on what they thought.

But doing so would further cut into Campbell's confidence. It could also damage both Campbell's and Bonnet's authority, showing he didn't trust his subordinates to do their jobs without close supervision.

"TAO, ASWO. Sir, we've got solid machinery noise from their main circ water pump. It's a nuke, and the freq looks right for a *Han*. But there's some other sound that doesn't gibe. We need more time to analyze it."

"TAO, aye."

Bill sat back and forced a grin. "Remember, Jason, ASW really stands for *Awfully Slow Warfare*."

Campbell smiled briefly and took a sip of coffee.

"TAO, ASWO. Contact should pass out of the CZ in twenty-five minutes. If we turn away, bottom topography doesn't help us maintain contact. We'll lose it when we cross the shelf. Best course of action is turn toward and sprint 'til it pops up again in the first CZ. But no matter what we do, we're gonna lose it for a bit."

Campbell closed his eyes and rolled his neck. "What's your recommendation, then?"

"Sir, recommend we put the helo up with two Mark 54 torpedoes, full sonobuoy load."

Campbell looked over at Bill, who sighed quietly and nodded. He'd prefer if the TAO took such actions on his own. But because of the earlier reproof, Campbell was taking no chances.

"Bridge, TAO. Set flight quarters. Pass the word for the aircrew to lay to combat for a brief."

Seconds later Lieutenant Commander Dix tapped Campbell on the shoulder. "We've been over with ASWO. We've got the bubble. Whatcha got for me?"

Campbell gave him the surface picture, what they had of it, and the rules of engagement. When he was done, Dix turned to Bill.

"Anything else, sir?"

Bill nodded. "Yeah, why are you flying this mission?"

Dix shrugged. "My turn in rotation. Plus, I'm the one with the most time in contact with a real sub. No one else is even close." He smiled.

Bill scowled. "Next time make sure I'm there when you get the ASWO's brief." He paused and stared until Dix nodded. Then he continued, "Weapons tight, so talk to me before you drop any. And don't take any unnecessary risks. You see anything threatening, you hightail it and bring it home. How soon can you launch?"

"Aye, sir. You got it. I'll be airborne as soon as I get a green deck." Dix and his crew left.

A helicopter is the most effective weapon a destroyer has against a submarine. The greater the distance at which it can be attacked and sunk, the safer for the warship. The days of actively pinging away, chasing down the submarine and dropping depth charges over the side are long distant, not even hazy, memories. No modern warship captain ever wants to get into hull-mounted sonar detection range, let alone fire the ship's own torpedoes or even Anti-Submarine Rockets (ASROC). Naval officers term such a battle a "knife fight in a telephone booth." Thus, *Nicholas* would depend on the helicopter to use its expendable sonobuoys to find and identify the submarine.

And kill it if it turns out to be hostile.

CHAPTER
TWENTY

"Green deck." The Landing Signals Officer used the flight deck announcing system since the restricted EMCON meant no radio communications. Hearing it, the Landing Signals Enlisted standing in front of the helicopter raised his wands over his head. The light mounted next to the LSO booth above the flight deck changed from red to green.

Dix sat in the right seat of the SH-60R. The Helicopter Aircraft Commander, he'd chosen to also handle tactics while Lieutenant Zeke Craft flew the aircraft. Dix gave a thumbs up. Craft pulled the collective gently up to lift off the deck, then moved the cyclic right and slightly back, in order to back away from the ship before pushing the nose forward into the relative wind for departure.

Dix established communications on the highly directional Hawklink encrypted voice circuit. "Sea Hawk Six Zero One, ops normal, state one plus five zero, three souls."

Nicholas's Anti-Submarine Tactical Air Controller (ASTAC)

repeated the call back, then said, "Datum bears zero one three, four zero point three nautical miles."

"Copy, zero one three, forty decimal three nautical," he responded.

Craft turned the aircraft northeast. Dix swept the controls to ensure they had no lights showing. "I'm headed oh six five for ten miles," Dix told the ASTAC. They'd get clear of *Nicholas* before going directly toward the possible submarine, just in case a Chinese warship or intelligence collector happened to be nearby. It wouldn't do to give away the position of his bunk and the flight deck under which it resided.

He savored their speed as they flew along only two hundred feet over the moonlit wave tops. Every so often they changed heading to avoid a surface contact that appeared on the horizon. Twice traffic density made them pass between two contacts only a few miles apart. All were small coastal freighters.

"Hey, Dave, make sure you pass all these contacts back to home plate," he said over ICS to the sensor operator in the back.

The Hawklink blared. "Six Zero One, ASTAC. TAO says you're far enough out. Head for datum, bearing three three niner, nineteen nautical. Estimate last course and speed one eight zero, six knots."

"Damned ship drivers. Always tellin' us where to go," said Craft.

Dix grunted. "Yeah, well they think they own us. If they're not worried, guess I won't be."

Craft turned gently around to the north.

Ten minutes later, Dix called back to the sensor operator, "Got a buoy pattern for me?"

"Yes, sir. First drop is on your zero two five at five miles. Then turn left, two six eight for three miles, drop the second. Number three's another three miles beyond that one. We keep dropping every three nautical until six is in the water."

Dix shook his head. "Give us steers and drop calls."

As they approached the first drop point, the sensor operator called, "Stand by buoy one. Dropping now . . . now . . . NOW."

Dix felt the slight shudder as the first sonobuoy dropped out of its canister.

"Turn left, two six niner."

"Copy," Dix replied.

Three minutes later, he heard, "Buoy one's up. Stand by number two. Dropping now . . . now . . . NOW. Maintain for three nautical to buoy three."

After dropping the third sonobuoy, the sensor operator called, "Turn right, head two seven five."

Coming around, Craft settled on the new heading.

"Six Zero One, ASTAC. Sub musta heard your buoy drops. Sonar says they got a course change. Working the solution now."

"Dave, anything on our buoys?" He couldn't resist asking.

"Nothin', sir. I got the processor filtering out the surface contacts around us now. Coming up on the spot for number four. Dropping now . . . now . . . NOW."

"Extend the barrier both ways by two buoys."

"Copy. Maintain this head for six miles. Then we'll go back and get the east side of the pattern."

The helo continued to sow buoys.

"Six Zero One, ASTAC. Sonar reports lost contact."

"Six Zero One copies."

The SENSO said, "If they went shallow, we might not pick 'em up. There's a layer at ninety feet."

Dix shook his head. "No, they won't come up. The Chinese always go deeper when they think someone's looking for 'em. Besides, if they were at ninety feet, we might see 'em from the air. If we don't pick 'em up soon, we'll put a few buoys in with shallow hydrophone settings. But I don't—"

The SENSO interrupted. "Contact! Buoy four has contact. Matches the freqs Sonar gave us for the main circ pump and auxiliaries. It's in and out."

Dix pumped his fist. They had him, now they just needed to keep him.

"Homeplate, Six Zero One. Passive contact with unknown submarine, buoys four and five. We hold it on our two o'clock, six thousand yards. She's making a high-speed run to the west."

A pause, then, "Turning now. She's slowing and diving."

With the helo in contact, Bill ordered *Nicholas* to reverse course. The change had the added benefit of moving away from the possible Chinese merchant to the southwest.

The towed array would take time to stabilize after the turn, but they'd already lost contact with the sub. By increasing the distance, they might regain contact, and if the sub was armed with anti-ship missiles, *Nicholas* would be safer.

The submarine continued to try to evade. Apparently alert, it had detected the splash of the sonobuoys. Now it changed depth, course, and speed to get away. But the helo stayed on it, dropping more buoys to maintain contact. The water conditions favored the hunter.

Twice in the next ninety minutes the helo lost contact, however, as the sub changed depth, seeking shelter under thermal layers, warm water over cold that kept the sound from reaching the relentless microphones of the sonobuoys. But each time, they were able to reestablish contact.

"Jason, how close is the helo to Vietnamese land?"

"Just under thirty-eight miles, sir. Seems like the contact's headed that way."

"Tell the helo to keep an eye on that. Have them remain clear of nearest island by at least twenty miles."

Campbell relayed the order to the ASTAC.

"Still the mother hen, huh?" Craft replied.

Dix looked sharply over. "Stow it. It's their job."

"ASTAC, Six Zero One. Contact's over the shelf. Water depth six hundred feet."

"Dave, put a no-go line in the system twenty miles off the nearest land. When we get close, let me and Zeke know."

"Copy."

The chase continued.

———

"TAO, Sonar. Acoustic signature from the helo confirms. It's a *Han.*" The helo had been passing its data to *Nicholas*. Two sets of eyes, or in this case, analysts, were better than one.

"TAO, aye. What took so long?"

"There's extra noise lines at ninety-two and one-fourteen Hertz. Every once in a while, there's a bang. We finally decided they've got a fishing net tangled somewhere. The bang's prob'ly a float hitting the hull. When we filter that out, it's a near perfect match for a *Han.*"

Campbell rolled his eyes.

With every maneuver, Bill became more and more convinced it was hostile. The certainty of nuclear propulsion meant it had to be Chinese. No one else except the US or the British operated nuclear submarines in this area, and Bill knew there were no friendlies around. Now it was certain, even to the class.

Despite his certainty, he ordered the helicopter to use an active sonobuoy to ping out the universal signal ordering the submarine to identify itself.

"Sir?" asked Campbell. "Why not just kill it?"

Bill shook his head. "As sure as I am, as the sonar techs are, we can't afford a mistake. Right now, we're in control of the tactical situation. They can't hurt us. We can take the time to be sure."

They got no response. Moments later the helicopter reported

losing contact in the vicinity of a large mass of metal. Bill leaned forward and hit the desk in frustration.

"ASWO, TAO, how's our tail?" Campbell asked, reacting to Bill's anger. *Nicholas* had turned toward the enemy to close the range, then turned to the northwest to put the contact on the port beam.

Bill took a deep breath. It wasn't helpful for his crew to react more to him than to the enemy.

"Tail's still in the turn. We don't have anything yet. It'll be — seven minutes before it steadies out. But that hunk of metal's from World War II, Aussie destroyer sunk in '42. If the helo didn't pick up the sub leaving the area, it's probably still there. Recommend the helo ping 'em again."

This time, Campbell didn't look to Bill for confirmation. "TAO, aye. Do it."

"Are they fucking kidding?" Craft asked. "We should have dropped on it when we had the chance."

Dix said, "Calm down. Skipper just wants to be sure it's not a friendly or a neutral before we kill somebody."

"And if we lose it? It'll be out there looking for us. And what about the carrier, when it gets here?"

"That's why the CO gets paid the big bucks."

Craft snorted but said nothing.

"Dave, ping him again."

Finally, after more minutes of trying and getting no response, they heard, "Six Zero One, this is Homeplate actual. How sure are you the sub hasn't gotten away from the wreck?"

Dix keyed his mike. "Hundred percent. We got buoys on five points around the wreck. She must have bottomed right near it. We heard her go active for a few pings right before we lost contact. Probably guiding herself in. If she shut down most of her pumps, we won't hear her. Plus, the flow noise around the wreck masks low frequency sound."

Silence reigned. Finally, "Six Zero One, Homeplate. Weapons free, take the sub."

Dix grinned at Craft, who snorted again and looked out to the quiescent surface beneath which the enemy sub lay hidden. "Hope he's still there. It'd be a shame to blow up a war grave."

"Dave, prep one mark fifty-four, depth setting shallow, active seeker mode. Set the search pattern so it won't detect the wreck. We'll use one to get him to move. Then set the second one up, depth medium, passive. When he runs, we'll drop it on him."

"Copy, sir." After repeating the settings, the SENSO leaned forward, intent on his screen. "Sub's on the move. He's trying to slink away at two knots. Solid contact, pinger nine." A moment passed. "Activating pinger buoy eleven."

He paused for a few moments. "He's headed north."

"You sure it's not a school of fish?" Dix asked.

"Solid echo, metal. Want me to lower the MAD?" The Magnetic Anomaly Detector allowed the helo to detect large masses of metal moving underwater.

"No. That'll slow us down. I want to get a weapon in the water."

"Copy that. Turn left, two niner eight."

Craft maneuvered and settled on the heading.

The SENSO went silent for a moment, then called, "Dropping now, now, NOW." The helo jumped a few feet as the weight of the torpedo dropped away. Dix ordered a turn away to set up for the second shot.

Eternity crept by. Then ahead of them a white geyser rose in the darkness, bioluminescence giving it an otherworldly appearance.

"Holy shit," Craft said.

"Six Zero One, this is Homeplate. Report."

Dix replied, "Homeplate, Six Zero One. The torp must've hit

him. He went to high speed as soon as the fish hit the water." He looked out the small window.

"Hit the spotlight," Dix ordered.

The three men watched as a submarine hull breached in the middle of the foam from the explosion. The bow rolled to port, then slid back down and sank.

"There's a helluva big oil slick coming up. There's other debris." He paused, then said, "We got bodies, Homeplate. I'd say we got a kill."

"Six Zero One, bring it home," came Campbell's voice.

Dix acknowledged, "Aye, we're RTB." He grinned. Returning to base, Dix looked forward to hitting his rack.

Bill leaned back in his chair and wiped sweat from his face.

This is only our second day on patrol. What else is waiting for us? he wondered as he climbed the ladder back to the bridge.

CHAPTER
TWENTY-ONE

1830 Zulu, 28 Oct
1330 Eastern Time
Bethesda Naval Hospital, Maryland

At the Intensive Care Unit, the nurse told him the chairman was alert. They'd had to sedate him in the early morning when he'd tried to get out of bed to go back to the Pentagon. But he'd come out of it now and was better.

Norton walked into the room. It stank of medicine and raw flesh. A monitor beeped above the bed.

General Al "Hopalong" Cassidy had had a long and distinguished career in the Air Force as a B-52 bomber pilot, then in operational and strategic level commands. The first non-fighter jock to be selected as chairman, he'd brought sanity and rationality to the job in the face of a neophyte administration.

He'd been in his office in the C-ring when the missiles hit. Part of a wall collapsed on him, leaving him with two broken legs, several broken ribs, and a punctured left lung. He'd been lucky, though; he'd survived.

He opened his eyes when Norton walked in and tried to sit up.

"Don't sit up, Hoppy. The nurses tell me they'll have to shoot you full of sleepy juice if you do." Norton smiled and sat down beside the bed so Cassidy could see him by turning his head.

"Mph. They did that this morning. I still feel it. Damned medicos. Never let a man work." Cassidy's voice sounded rough, his speech slightly slurred.

"Well, you took a bad hit. We need you to be a full up round when you get back, so do what you're told for now."

Cassidy looked at him. "How bad is it, Bill? These bastards won't tell me, other than to say the Chinese did it."

Norton sighed. "Well, they probably don't know much. Hell, sir, *we* don't know all that much. But it's bad. They caught us with our knickers in the mud, and we're struggling to hit back. The good news, such as it is, is that they look to be done, at least for now."

"How do you know that?" Cassidy's question nearly disappeared in a spasm of coughs. His face squeezed shut as his body convulsed.

When it subsided, Norton continued. "Looks like they're in an operational pause, though there's reports of fighting in the South China Sea. There's a destroyer there that's giving them trouble." He waited while Cassidy breathed heavily and groaned. "They put out a diplomatic demarche, too. Copied everyone in the world. It basically says they met their military objectives. If we leave them alone, they'll leave us alone."

Cassidy began to cough again as he tried to rise. Norton put his hand gently on his boss's shoulder, both to calm him and to keep him from sitting up. That led to more hacking, but Cassidy sank back. When it stopped, he breathed silently for a few moments, each breath obviously painful.

A nurse came in and glared at both men. Norton put his hand up and shook his head. The man left, a disapproving look on his face.

"Stay calm, boss. We need you back, but you gotta be well first, or at least, more well." Norton took a breath. "Here's why I really came, though. Hunter ordered that prick Wilson to direct nuclear strikes on China. Easy, sir."

Cassidy laid back again, breathing deeply. His eyes were fixed on the ceiling above his bed, blazing.

Norton spoke gently now. "I know, sir. I told him where he could shove it. Mostly, I explained the birds and bees of nuclear command and control processes. Suggested he scurry back to Hunter and tell him to use it correctly." He shook his head. "But you know they might just do that, if it really did come from the president. For now, that'll hold them. And I've told Steve Bing at STRATCOM what's going on. You know what he said. No way he's accepting a nuclear launch order that doesn't follow procedure. So we're safe for the moment. But I need to know what you think, boss. I'm seriously considering disobeying a direct order from the president." He finished and sat back in the hard plastic chair.

Cassidy closed his eyes. Norton feared he'd fallen asleep or passed out. But then he opened them and turned his head again to face him.

Cassidy said, "You know I've been worried about these knuckleheads since they came into office. In forty years, I've never been more nervous about a president and the people who surround him. Oh, presidents and administrations made mistakes before, some of 'em horrendous. But they always wanted the best for America. They were always willing to listen to logic, to people who know what they're talking about. But these guys are deliberately stupid. Worse, they want to stay that way."

Cassidy exhaled harshly. "Okay, here's the skinny. And this'll get us both in a lot of trouble if it ever gets out. A lot of trouble." His eyes pierced Norton to the bone.

Norton nodded. Cassidy's face relaxed. Then they both looked at the door. Norton rose, opened it a crack, looked out for a moment, then closed and locked it. Sitting back down, he nodded.

Cassidy spoke quietly. "I made an agreement with SecDef Shackleton and SecState Kingston. If any of us got any off-kilter orders, we consult each other and make the decision as a group whether to obey it or not."

Norton's eyes widened. He sucked in a deep breath. This was an agreement between the secretaries of Defense and State, as well as the chairman of the Joint Chiefs of Staff, to mutiny against the president if they disagreed with him.

Cassidy wasn't done. "We agreed the most likely scenario was a nuclear launch. It's come now, and you must talk to them. Let them know I brought you into our little club."

Norton shook his head. "Shackleton's dead. He was on the Hill when the Capitol got hit. We don't know where Kingston is. Last we knew, he was hunting in Alaska. No one's heard from him."

Cassidy reached over and grasped his forearm.

"Then you're it, Bill. It's your call. But here's my advice. If we're not beat conventionally, it's not time to go nuclear. It's the old *existential threat* problem. And this is coming from the guy who grew up planning for a one-way trip into the Soviet Union with four one-megaton bombs in the belly of his plane."

Cassidy was wracked again. This time a red-tinged sputum formed on his lips.

Time to go. Norton had what he'd come for. He said a short goodbye and a short prayer for Cassidy's recovery and turned to leave.

"Keep the faith, Marine," came the strained order from the bed.

Norton turned back and smiled, then stepped out into the corridor.

Back in his office, he called Admiral Bing again. Norton filled him in and ordered him to ignore any nuclear strike order unless it was confirmed by himself via secure line.

Bing agreed readily, drawling, "Ah feel a sudden need to supersede the codes that Whitely's carrying in the football. I feel bad for the kid, of course, but that's life. She'll survive."

As he hung up, Norton reflected on what would surely be the end of his career.

Nearly forty years ago, he'd taken a sacred oath to the Constitution and to the nation whose course it directed. He'd sworn to protect that nation against all enemies, foreign and domestic.

But in all the times he'd renewed his own oath or administered it to others, he'd rarely considered what form a "domestic enemy" might take. When he had, it had always looked like an extremist, someone like the Oklahoma City bomber.

He prayed he hadn't made a grave error. Even more, he prayed he was indeed saving his nation.

The Four-Star Revolt was underway, and he hoped history would be kind.

CHAPTER
TWENTY-TWO

1830 Zulu, 28 Oct
1330 Eastern Time
Oval Office, The White House

Major Whitely's hand shook as she held the briefcase. The Secret Service agent standing by the door whispered into his wrist, then opened the door to the Oval Office. Captain Adams followed her through the door. Nuclear security required two persons to execute every step of the weapons release authorization process.

She'd been here a dozen times for exercises and system test events in the two years since she'd become the primary carrier of the nation's nuclear codes.

This would be the first time for real.

She'd been chosen for her mental stability and determination to follow orders. Nothing would change that. Nevertheless, what she was about to do would alter world history, not to mention result in the deaths of millions of people. People who were currently going about their everyday lives, oblivious to Death's approach.

It was sobering. Any sane person would be nervous.

The president stood behind his desk, framed by the window

with its golden curtains and view of the White House lawn. Beyond, tendrils of smoke still climbed into the sky. Hunter sat on one of the sofas.

Whitely had expected the chairman to be present. The acting chairman, she reminded herself. The chairman remained in Bethesda.

Oh, well, the most important person is here.

The two men both wore red faces and breathed heavily, as if they'd been running a race.

Whitely chalked it up to the same nervousness she felt.

"Get in here, Major," Donnelly said.

He ignored Adams completely. His voice sounded harsh and gravelly.

She'd not been impressed by this president. Despite public rhetoric about loving the military, in private he was dismissive, preferring the counsel of his closest friends and family, though none of them had ever served, over senior military leadership.

Well, it doesn't matter. He's the president.

"You know why you're here?"

"I suspect I do, sir."

"Then let's be about it. I want the Pentagon to conduct nuclear strikes on the enemy."

Whitely was confused. She froze for a split second. Then her training took over.

"Sir, I understand what you want. But we need to follow the procedures. First, I need you to look at my and Captain Adams's identification. Then I need to see your and Mr. Hunter's identification."

"Identification? What the fuck are you talking about?" Donnelly thundered.

Whitely blanched and took a step backward. She regretted it immediately. That firmed her determination to do this right.

"Sir, we've been through the exercises. You know the drill. We have to follow the process."

The president charged around the desk at her. Whitely nearly backed up another step. But she controlled herself and instead stood straighter. Adams, who stood slightly behind her and to her left, moved up half a pace to stand beside her.

"Do you know who I am, you stupid bitch? This isn't some drill. I'm the president of the United States, and you'll do what I tell you to do."

"Yes, sir, I will, as soon as we all identify ourselves properly and as soon as I'm certain you aren't under duress."

Hunter choked off a laugh.

The president whirled toward him, glared, then stalked back to the desk.

"Get someone in here who's going to follow orders, now," he shouted, then threw himself into his chair.

Hunter pursed his lips, and said, "Sir, I'll try to get one of the backups in here, but I suspect it won't be any different. Will it, Major? Captain?"

"No, sir."

Adams simply nodded.

Donnelly started to say something but clapped his mouth shut and slewed his chair around to look out the window. He pointed vaguely to the city beyond.

"You see that, Major? Do you? The smoke? That's my capital burning." He whirled around and bolted to his feet again.

"My buildings, mine. And you stand there and talk about *protocol*? I'm in a fight for my life here and you demand I *identify* myself? Are you an enemy agent? Are you? You are, all by yourself, keeping me from destroying my enemy. They should be your enemy, too."

Whitely was no longer nervous. But she controlled her voice and kept a barely respectful attitude. "No, sir, I'm not an enemy agent, and I am not trying to prevent any appropriate military action." She swallowed. "But every link in the chain from you to the men and women in the missile silos, bombers, and submarines requires identification and authentication. They will follow the proper process to release nuclear weapons. And I will damn sure follow it here, sir."

The stridence in her own voice shocked Whitely.

Donnelly and Hunter looked stunned, too. Silence reigned.

Hunter cleared his throat. "Perhaps, Mr. President, if we do as the major asks we can move forward?"

The president turned to glare at him for a long moment. Then, never taking his eyes off Hunter, he reached into his wallet and withdrew his White House ID card. He held it out in Whitely's direction.

"Are you satisfied?"

Whitely and Adams stepped forward and looked at the president's ID, then at Hunter's. She pulled out her own and held it facing the president, who never took his eyes off Hunter. Adams did the same.

"Sir, our ID?"

"Put it away. I know who you are."

"Yes, sir."

The men followed her lead through the proper procedures, though the president never once looked at Whitely. When they were done, the codes were relayed properly.

As they were leaving, the president spoke one last time.

"You're fired, both of you. Take off that uniform and leave the White House now. I don't ever want to see you again."

Never seeing you again would make me very happy, too, sir.

Aloud she said, "Yes, sir."

They both did a perfect about face and hurried out the door.

Hours later the Oval Office rang with more shouting.

"What do you mean the fucking codes were superseded?" shouted Donnelly.

"It's standard protocol when there's risk of compromise, sir," said Norton. He'd come in to explain why the order hadn't been obeyed.

"What compromise?"

"Sir, several nuclear capable platforms and bases were damaged—" Norton began.

"You're fired. Get out." Spinning to Hunter, he screamed, "Get me the next in line. Now."

Norton had no intention of being fired. But he did leave.

The firing of generals and admirals went on into the afternoon.

Eventually, a brigadier general who, up until now, had been the deputy Army G1 staff administrative officer, agreed to abandon protocols and direct STRATCOM to execute nuclear strike options on China.

Admiral Bing laughed at him when he called. "Surely, you don't think I'll follow orders from someone who's not been properly appointed chairman? All due regard, General, but you don't even have the codes. Sorry, no, I won't follow that order. Ya'll have a nice day, though. I've got a war to fight." The line clicked dead.

CHAPTER
TWENTY-THREE

1430 Zulu, 31 Oct
1530 Local Time
NATO Headquarters, Brussels

The television at the NATO ops center in Brussels wasn't normally the center of attention, but today was different.

On it, an attractive young blond woman spoke Russian. The sound was off in favor of English subtitles. At the lower right corner the logo of the "Russian News Network" featured prominently. Across the bottom scrolled mini-headlines in Cyrillic.

"—Kremlin spokesman told us, quote, 'attacks against Russian-speaking peoples in the Baltic regions have become intolerable,' unquote. The Foreign Ministry reports they have provided no less than thirty demarches in recent weeks, but to no avail. Instead, attacks have increased. More than ninety Russian-speaking citizens were reported killed, though we suspect the number is far greater." She glared into the camera. "An RNN reporter has this from Tallinn."

Another attractive reporter, this time a brunette, appeared on screen. "We asked for a statement from the Estonian Interior Ministry. But instead, they gave us twelve hours to leave the country. Officials have denied knowledge of any deaths, even when shown cellphone video of women and children beaten in the streets. One official claimed the video had been faked."

Here the feed cut away to images of a woman and two young children being clubbed by three men in masks. Offscreen the reporter continued.

The Polish ambassador, Długosz, turned to Doenitz. "The Estonians are right. That video and others were posted on social media today. They're actually from Chechnya years ago. The perpetrators were Russian soldiers in civilian clothes, the victims Muslim. They professionally deleted the woman's headscarf."

French Ambassador Lebeau grunted. "But this broadcast is primarily to justify to Russians why their military is once again on the move."

"They're drumming up support for their 'Make Russia Great Again' policy. The restoration of the Soviet Empire under the Federation name." Climber, the British ambassador, shook her head and grimaced. "Fools. Gregorivich has them completely bamboozled. He's leading them to disaster."

Lebeau shrugged.

Długosz opined, "Perhaps. But can we face them? Without the assistance of the Americans . . . ."

The four retreated into their own thoughts as they continued to watch.

"The Kremlin spokesman informs us that thousands of soldiers acted on their own in the face of this gravest provocation. These patriotic men crossed borders without orders. They moved to protect innocent women, children, and the elderly, people at the mercy of foreign monsters. The misguided actions of the last Soviet government allowed them to be subsumed into artificial constructs with no history of independence," the reporter continued.

"When these brave men arrived, they gave courage to the victims." She swept her arm behind her where the sounds of gunfire could be heard. "Faced with a population that will no longer allow themselves to be routinely beaten and murdered by a ruling minority, the supposed governments of these three regions have mobilized their soldiers to crush the innocents. We are told that the Kremlin has now moved to protect them."

The television cut away to the president of Russia speaking in front of Lenin's Tomb. The symbology was not lost on the men and women watching. Several Eastern Europeans bristled.

"Today, the Russian military is forced to intervene. Ethnic Russians are being murdered. For decades, these so-called governments have perpetrated genocide, driving Russians out of their homes. They repeat the Nazi depredations before the Great Patriotic War. But we will not stand idly by." The camera zoomed out to take in the Russian flag flying above the tomb.

"I have moved only those forces necessary to create zones of safety inside areas that border Russia. They will remain only so long as needed to ensure the lives of our people."

A reporter asked, "Mr. President, what about reports of attacks against NATO forces?"

The president frowned. "Those reports are lies by NATO leaders to justify intervention in our humanitarian operation. NATO has always hated Russia. But they also know their own people want peace. Their people understand Russia doesn't want war. Most importantly, their citizens recognize the legitimacy of protecting ethnic Russian peoples."

The camera zoomed back in on Gregorivich's face.

"The citizens of NATO applaud our actions, so their governments lie. But the people are smarter than that. It is in fact NATO's complete and abject failure to protect all their citizens that has led to this crisis, to our need to act."

Up to now, he'd faced the reporters. Now, he turned to look directly into the camera.

"I call upon NATO to respect the wishes of the citizens of the Baltic region. Stay out of our business. You chose to sit by and watch the slaughter of innocents. Now Russia will protect them. Interference will mean the deaths of millions." He paused. "To the citizens of NATO countries. Do not allow your governments to prop up the puppets in Eastern Europe. Respect the wishes of the peoples who live there to return to Mother Russia. Support their dreams of living freely under my protection."

The television cut back to the studio.

Doenitz spoke. "Well, he's presented his ultimatum and made his case for annexing the Baltic nations. It is Ukraine all over again."

A young Italian major waved his arm at the three ambassadors from the desk where he monitored chat rooms and radio circuits with NATO air defense sites. "My apologies. We have an urgent report from Poland." He took a breath. "American Patriot batteries have been hit by cruise missiles. So have Polish air defense radars and missile systems. Several network nodes have also been destroyed. There's a massive distributed denial of service cyberattack on all military networks in and around Poland."

Climber turned to the others. Her eyes blazed. "No, it's 1939 but with the sides scrambled." Her eyes swept to Długosz.

His face was set, eyes hard. He stared at the large screen in the center. On it, a map of Eastern Europe from the Finnish border south to the Dardanelles at the mouth of the Black Sea. As they watched, angry red circles appeared over sites that had been confirmed hit.

Climber continued, "I'm sorry, Jan. We all hoped this wouldn't come to pass. But we'll stand by you, as before. And we'll make a better job of it. I promise you that."

Długosz remained silent for a moment, his jaws working. "For millennia, my nation has been a battleground. East fought west in her fields and forests. We have been overrun by invaders seeking plunder, more land, or simply because they wanted to conquer someone." He turned to face the others. "But today we are more prepared than at any time in our history. We welcome your friendship and support, don't mistake me. But they shall pay a heavier price than they know. We will not be conquered again, not by anyone. Not ever."

He turned and left.

Doenitz shrugged and looked at his remaining companions. "I cannot help but feel he sees my nation's boots trampling through his countryside." He raised his hand as the others started to speak. "We will stand by our ally, perhaps more fiercely because of the history between us. But he is right. We *all* must make sure this can never happen again."

Climber and Lebeau exchanged glances.

CHAPTER
TWENTY-FOUR

1300 Zulu, 1 Nov
1600 Local Time
The Kremlin, Moscow

A fine dusting of early snow coated the Kremlin. Autumn had behaved very differently the past several years, veering wildly between record-setting cold and stunning heat.

"Tell him no, I am not available." The president of Russia slammed down the phone and turned to his visitor.

"That man must go. I am tired of his begging. It's too bad the Chinese didn't manage to kill him," he said as he pointed to the phone.

"Sir, while Donnelly may indeed be a maniac, you have to admit he's been useful. Who else could have so aggravated the Chinese that they felt forced into open war? Or so thoroughly alienate NATO?"

"Yes, yes. His sheer incompetence gave us opportunity." Gregorivich closed his eyes and took a deep breath. "But he must stop calling."

Remkin let the president fume. Things were going well militarily, and Remkin benefited when Gregorivich focused on managing relationships rather than meddling in military matters.

Gregorivich wasn't done yet. "He actually believes we have a personal relationship, one that transcends my own interests as the leader of the Russian people. He has convinced himself that I would forgo what is good for the *Rodina,* what is good for *me,* to help him out of this mess of his own making."

"You did encourage him, sir."

"Of course, I did. But he is so thick-headed, he didn't understand why." Gregorivich threw himself into the overstuffed chair that sat beside his desk.

"It is that thickness that makes him so easily manipulated, sir. Need I remind—"

Gregorivich waved his hand to cut him off. "Don't, Pavlov. I know." He sighed heavily.

Remkin smiled. "Mr. President, I bring more good news. Our intelligence has received a message from Donnelly's nephew, confirmed by a source within the American National Security Council." He had Gregorivich's full attention. "The commander of American forces in Europe has been ordered not to engage our forces."

"It confirms a complete break within NATO. Have you sent orders to avoid attacking Americans?"

Remkin nodded. "Of course, sir. Other than the necessary attacks on air defense sites, we were already avoiding American personnel."

The president sat, staring into the distance for a long moment before pounding his fist on the chair arm.

"So the United States is firmly out of the way. We finally have the chance to right the wrongs of the past thirty years. All the land stolen from us, the resources, the power. Once we've restored our position in Eastern Europe, we'll look to the south and regain the oil regions. Perhaps, if what's left of the American military degrades the Chinese sufficiently, we'll even retake Port

Arthur. My empire will be greater than that of Tsar Nicholas. Think of it, Pavlov."

Remkin *had* thought of it. While he lauded the president's goals, the old maxim about the enemy having a vote was also true. He wished he could remember who'd said it.

"Mr. President, remember that we must achieve one goal before we attempt another. Hitler's greatest mistake was never being satisfied with one war at a time. Besides, China is our ally."

The president missed the point. He shook his finger at Remkin.

"Hitler's greatest mistake was attacking Mother Russia. It would not have mattered *when*. That is what doomed him to failure. In any case, I shall have the foreign minister announce that we will avoid the American military, who have recently suffered such losses. Yes, we will be magnanimous in our victory. And China remains an ally only so long as they are useful. Excellent, Pavlov. Let us have a drink."

Remkin enjoyed it when the president offered him a drink. He always had the best Scotch.

0800 Eastern Time
Oval Office, The White House

Hunter closed his eyes and breathed deeply while the president raged.

"The sonuvabitch won't take my phone calls. What the fuck? I'm letting him off the hook for attacking those damned Patriot batteries. He should be grateful, the bastard. I could nuke his ass."

Hunter forbore mention that his previous attempt at "nuking" an enemy had come to nothing.

Hunter still searched for proof of a rebellion within the military, fruitlessly thus far. Nevertheless, he was certain once the "supersession" of codes was complete, they'd come up with some other excuse to ignore the president's orders.

Not that Donnelly would issue the order again. His notoriously short attention span had moved on to Eastern Europe.

The Russian move had caught them all by surprise.

In Hunter's opinion, everything boiled down to what was good or bad for business, especially in politics. He needed to determine how to best take advantage of the Russian attack, then guide the president in that direction.

But Donnelly had become more difficult.

The possibility that the president might be losing it came to Hunter's mind more often these days. He'd picked up whispers in the West Wing, as well.

"Sir, it makes sense they'd act now, given that our *allies* have abandoned us. It gives Gregorivich a free hand. He knows we won't intervene. In fact, it serves NATO right."

"But he's wasting his military power on Europe," the president whined. "He should be attacking China, not the Europeans. And he should have called and told me. God knows, I make sure he knows what I'm doing."

Hunter cringed. Donnelly had been holding private conversations with the Kremlin even before the election, but Hunter had deliberately avoided noticing. When he'd finally been forced to confront their existence, he'd strongly encouraged Donnelly not to talk about it. It wouldn't be prudent to acknowledge that America's president randomly passed some of the nation's most jealously guarded secrets to the president of Russia. He'd convinced himself that the president had the absolute authority to unilaterally determine what information could and couldn't be shared with foreign leaders. But when it came up, he still got nauseous.

"Sir, perhaps Gregorivich is just busy. He is, after all, trying to restore his nation's greatness."

"Damn it, he's going about it wrong, Jack. Yuri's my friend. My *friend* should attack my *enemy*, not my former allies."

"Sir, maybe he's punishing them."

Hunter grasped at straws, something he found himself increasingly doing. Donnelly hadn't even noticed that he'd completely contradicted himself in the space of a few minutes.

"We have an unspoken agreement, Jack, a gentleman's bond. You wouldn't understand. I'm trying to do here what he's already done for Russia." Donnelly's eyes roamed the Oval Office, finally stopping to rest on the presidential seal on the carpet.

"He's made them a great country again, a great country, like the Soviet Union. I'm doing the same here, Jack. We're on our way, and it's because I'm the only one with the balls to do what's needed. Those deadbeats in Congress are gone now, thank God. I can do what needs to be done without them whining about being consulted."

Hunter didn't interrupt. Better to let him rant.

"Too bad the Supreme Court didn't get bombed, too. But they won't dare meet. I'll make damned sure they rot in jail if they do."

"Sir, I just don't think you should jump to conclusions. Assume Gregorivich supports you. We, you, need all your friends now, sir. And I recommend fewer phone calls."

The president looked calmly at him and cocked his head. "Okay, Jack. Okay. I just wanted to talk to him, that's all." He sat at the desk and picked up the remote for the television. They'd gotten the local news back on to distract him.

Hunter breathed a sigh of relief. For the moment, the president would be reasonable. Donnelly smiled as he watched DC police shooting looters.

CHAPTER
TWENTY-FIVE

1300 Zulu, 1 Nov
1400 Local Time
USEUCOM Headquarters, Stuttgart, Germany

General Hornbeck, Commander USEUCOM, stood in her command center in Stuttgart, Germany, some three hundred miles from NATO headquarters in Brussels. She'd not moved far from it these past days. She'd slept in a small closet that passed for a bedroom, set aside for just that purpose in case of war.

She snorted as she asked herself. *Am I at war? It looks like it.*

Her nation was obviously at war with China. That was easy. But China wasn't in her AOR (area of responsibility). She'd sent a sizable chunk of her air assets to the western Pacific, but hadn't otherwise been affected. Now it looked like America faced conflict in her theater, albeit with a different enemy. A new, yet old one.

As she pondered, her hands clasped behind her back, her battle watch, Navy Captain Tanaka, stood and headed her way. He'd been hovering over the shoulder of the communications officer.

Her deputy, Vice Admiral Riley, moved up beside her. "Think this is the answer, ma'am?"

Without turning, she said, "I almost hope it's not. I'd like to believe the president is thinking about it for a change, instead of shooting off whatever comes into his head."

Riley shook his head at his boss's inappropriately political comment.

Tanaka handed over the sheets he'd retrieved. "It's from the acting chairman, ma'am."

She scanned the standard SMEAC format: Situation, Mission, Execution, Administration and Logistics, and Command and Signal. Skipping straight to the mission statement, she read: *Commander, US European Command, will aggressively defend American lives and property, using forces currently at her disposal, within the European Theater of Operations.*

Frustrated, she moved down to the paragraph on the Rules of Engagement.

Request for additional rules of engagement denied. However, Commander USEUCOM is reminded that aggressive and strict compliance with the peacetime ROE will be sufficient to permit mission success.

"That's not very helpful," sighed Riley, who'd read the message over Hornbeck's shoulder.

She turned to look at him, face red, nostrils flared. "That's the understatement of the friggin' year," she said.

She waved her hand. "Sorry, Adam. We've just had over a hundred American soldiers killed or wounded in unprovoked attacks by the damned Russians, and this tells us to pretend nothing happened."

"It doesn't tell us we can't fight back, ma'am," Riley advanced.

"Yes, it does. It emphasizes peacetime ROE. Sure, we can shoot at anyone we believe is getting ready to attack *us*, but specifically leaves defense of NATO off the table. Or am I missing something?"

Riley shook his head. "No, Ma'am, but I can't believe they'd do that."

She stared at him. "You saw the message from the NATO Council. I've been relieved as NATO Supreme Commander because our president threw another temper tantrum and told NATO to go screw itself. Hunter called Doenitz personally and told him we won't be helping them in *their* war."

Turning back to Tanaka, she stated flatly, "Send a message to the force, no change to the ROE. But tell them if they even think they're going to be shot at, they'd better damned well shoot first." She turned to leave but turned back when the comms major called out to her.

"Ma'am, wait. This P4 just came in for you from General Norton."

A P4, or Personal For, message was an informal way to provide additional information to senior leaders, beyond what might be put in formal orders. It was the equivalent of a hand-written personal note.

Tanaka and Riley moved away to give her privacy.

She raised her hand and stopped them. "You both might as well hear it now."

She began to read.

"1. Melissa, ROE change not approved by POTUS. I can't refuse a legal order. But this place is in chaos, nowhere more so than the White House. Therefore, I direct you to keep your reports to those absolutely, repeat, absolutely necessary for pursuing the war in Asia. Please understand my focus is there, and will remain there and only there. The National Command Authority and myself will have no time, repeat, no time to deal with European matters. I hope I've been clear.

2. Therefore, you are directed to use any and all forces you deem necessary, and to coordinate with foreign militaries as required, to protect and defend American lives and property. This is your primary duty.

3. You are also authorized to defend all, repeat, all assets, places,

and capabilities that are necessary for you to perform your primary
duty.

4. I trust your discretion.

Norton sends."

Riley snorted and crossed his arms over his chest. "Well, that's not much better. Says essentially the same thing. Waste of time telling us DC's in chaos. No shit, Sherlock. It's always chaotic there."

But Hornbeck wore a smile.

Riley saw it. "What's up, Boss? Something you want to share with us?"

She grinned and turned to Tanaka.

"Get the ROE message ready, Tank. But I want my own P4 to all commanders. We're going to give them a very liberal definition of what *assets, places, and capabilities* are required for me to accomplish my mission. I'd like to see it in, say, fifteen minutes. Meantime, I'm going for coffee."

She winked at Riley, turned, and walked out the door.

Riley and Tanaka looked at each other.

"I think the boss just swallowed a canary, sir. If she were Navy, I'd say she read between the lines. But she's Air Farce, so—"

They were interrupted as Hornbeck's head reappeared through the door. "We don't have any remaining diplomatic representation in NATO, is that correct?"

Riley blinked. "No, ma'am. Why?"

"Good. I need to talk with Doenitz."

She disappeared again.

Riley smiled and turned back to Tanaka.

"Don't assume she's like other general officers. She has a brain. Besides, even the Air Force expects their officers to go off the rails once in a while. It doesn't always work, but when it does, it can be handy."

"I'll take that under advisement, sir."

Hornbeck strode down the hallway, head high and shoulders back. She no longer had any doubt about if she was at war.

She knew the P4 wouldn't be enough to save their collective asses if something went sideways and the politicians came looking for a scapegoat in uniform. But she'd made a decision, one she could live with. The politicians could go hang.

Whatever politicians were left in the end.

CHAPTER
TWENTY-SIX

0515 Zulu, 4 Nov
1215 Local Time
USS *Nicholas*, South China Sea

Seated in his at-sea cabin on a couch that folded down into a bed at night, Bill read his novel, or tried to. Determined not to show how anxious he was, he'd been spending more time there. But it made his crew more nervous. They saw through his charade.

Nicholas had fought three battles now in under two weeks. Bill's crew were blooded veterans of naval combat.

With submarine USS *Annapolis* now on station, *Nicholas* had been relieved of ASW duties ahead of *Roosevelt*'s arrival. Seventh Fleet now directed them to a point twenty miles off the Mekong Delta to meet with Vietnamese warships.

The Vietnamese government publicly expressed their sorrow over the outbreak of war, adding that they expected both sides to respect its neutrality. But for over a decade the Chinese navy had used Vietnamese islands to play hide and seek. To add to the risk, the noise and shallow water near the coast worsened sonar conditions.

Bill had been given what the Navy called DIRLAUTH, Direct Liaison Authorized, to determine the level of support Vietnam might be willing to provide, and to accept it at his own discretion.

A knock on his door presaged the XO sticking her head in.

"Got a minute, Captain?"

Bill waved for her to come in and offered her the chair at the small desk.

She sat silently for a moment, blinking, her hands folding over each other repeatedly in her lap.

"Something on your mind, XO?"

"Well, sir—" She paused, then squared her shoulders and faced him. "Sir, my dad fought in Vietnam. I know that colored his perceptions. But he always said we couldn't trust 'em, even later when he was in the Foreign Service."

"Your father was in the Foreign Service? Where did he serve?" Bill asked.

"Pretty much all over the world, but mostly in the Middle East. He was fluent in Arabic, so we spent a lot of time there. Well, he did. The only places my mom and us kids lived with him were in Bahrain and the UAE. But he served in the Philippines, too."

"Well, that tour might have set his mind against the Vietnamese, too. The Filipinos don't have much love for them, especially lately, since both have competing island claims."

"Do you trust them?"

"I don't know. I haven't met them. I'd like to think anyone who's willing to meet with us right now can be trusted. Could they be luring us here to a Chinese trap? Sure. But that'd be pretty underhanded. Besides, the Vietnamese have no love for China." He ran his hand through his hair. "I guess I don't see them doing us dirty. They've been pretty happy to let us counterbalance the Chinese."

Irving looked doubtful. "I guess, sir. But dad always said a nation will only act in its own best interests. When those coincide with our own, great. But as soon as they don't, he said, expect them to cut you off at the knees."

Bill grinned. "Well, that's one way to think about it. I don't know your dad, so I can't argue with him. But it occurs to me that's a pretty pessimistic way to look at things. But he's right about how nations behave. They hardly ever act altruistically. Not even us, though we like to think we do." Bill stretched. "But we don't have a lot of friends right now. I'm willing to give them a chance."

Irving sighed and shook her head. "We sure could use a friend. And I don't mean to question your judgment, sir."

Bill shook his head and said, "I didn't take it that way. It's your job to tell me your concerns. I hope you're blessed with a good XO who does the same."

Irving blushed and stood. "Thanks for listening, sir." When she reached the door, she turned. "Oh, and Captain, if this pans out, will you ask them to take our prisoners ashore? We sure could use the security team back on the watchbill."

"Sure thing, XO. Thanks for reminding me."

The prisoners had been in the forefront of his mind since they'd taken them aboard. Not only did they take precious men and women off the watchbill, but they ate food Bill would rather save for his own crew. If the Vietnamese were willing to help, that would be one of his first requests.

The phone trilled and he picked it up.

"Captain."

"Yes, sir, this is the TAO. The helo's twenty miles from the rendezvous. Still no ESM on any Vietnamese ship radar. If they're there, they're in total EMCON, just like us. Commander Dix requests permission for one radar sweep."

"Negative, no radar. Tell them to keep to the plan, go in low and slow until they get a visual."

"Aye, sir, go with the plan, low and slow."

Bill leaned back and set his e-book down.

He was torn. That single helicopter was the totality of his

remaining air assets. It gave him both long-range surface surveillance and ASW attack. Losing it would be a disaster. But the helo's radar was distinctive. If there were enemy vessels around, using it increased the risk. But going blind was dangerous, too. He wiped his face with his hands, rose, and headed for the bridge.

Barrister was there, though not on watch. Whenever the ship was maneuvering close to land or in other restricted circumstances, the navigator's place was on the bridge.

She walked up to Bill as he entered.

"Afternoon, sir. We're twenty-six nautical miles from the rendezvous. It bears two nine five from our current position."

"Very well, Nav, thanks."

She was followed by the OOD, who gave him a complete status of the ship.

When that was done, Barrister still stood there, rubbing the back of her neck.

"Something on your mind, Nav?"

"Well, sir, sort of. If you don't mind." She paused and bit her lip.

"It's okay, Nav. Spit it out."

"Sir, I'm not telling you anything you don't already know, but, well, using celestial's great in open water. But close to shore, it's not fast enough." Seeing his eyebrows climb, she hastened to add. "I'm listening to the helo circuit. We used the islands they've been reporting visuals on, so we've got an estimated position. But this close in, we need fixes. Any chance we can use the Furuno, sir?"

"No. No way. We can't take the chance. The Chinese may tie the Furuno to us. Are you that worried?"

Barrister sighed and shook her head. "No, sir. We've got a good estimate for the currents here, too, so our ded reckoning should be pretty good. But 'pretty good' may not be good enough."

Bill pressed his lips together. "You think? That's not—" He closed his eyes and took a deep breath, rubbing the tip of his nose. Opening them back up, he added, "You're right to bring it up. You can log it if you disagree with me."

Her eyes widened. "No, sir, I'm not going to log it. I just wanted you to know." She shook her head. "Glad it's your call, sir, not mine."

He chuckled, the tension ebbing. "Well, Nav, stay in the Navy long enough and you'll find yourself making this kind of call. In ten years you'll have a ship of your own. You get picked up to be CO of a patrol craft, you could be in command in only, what, three years? Think now what you'd do in my place. Then you'll be ready when you are."

He turned to climb into his chair. Once seated, he said, "And ask questions, Nav. Always be willing to ask questions. Some senior officers will tell you it's a sign of weakness. But smart leaders would rather you ask intelligent questions than muddle through and screw something up because you couldn't admit you don't know everything. Pretending you know everything will destroy your credibility with the crew, too." He smiled. "I'm sure you've already figured that out."

She smiled back. "Yes, sir. That was another reason I boned up on celestial before I reported. I've always loved it, don't get me wrong. But it helps with my street cred."

Bill laughed. He'd figured it was something like that, though he was also glad to hear that she actually liked the old methods.

CHAPTER
TWENTY-SEVEN

0555 Zulu, 4 Nov
1255 Local Time
USS *Nicholas*, South China Sea

"Captain, TAO. Helo has visual on three small warships. I told them to close and use the flashing light recognition signal."

"TAO, captain acknowledges."

Bill leaned back in his chair. If he'd had his druthers, he'd have paced the bridge or gone down to CIC. But he had to project calm. He looked back down at his e-reader.

But five minutes later he still hadn't read a single word.

"Captain, TAO. Helo says they got the proper response. He's closing."

Bill sighed audibly and barely kept himself from wiping non-existent perspiration from his forehead. He dropped out of his chair and reached for the intercom.

"TAO, this is the captain. Tell the helo we're coming in." He redirected his attention to Barrister. "Okay, Nav, let's close the rendezvous."

"Aye, sir." Barrister nodded to the JOOD, who promptly gave the orders. But she remained standing near his chair.

"Sir, I will say it one last time, I don't think you should go. Remember the discussion we had right after I reported aboard? About leadership? You told me you thought Captain Kirk was an idiot 'cause he went on all the landing parties. You said it was Spock's job to command the away teams."

The XO spoke in a low voice so no one else on the bridge could hear her. She'd come up, face set and teeth clenched. The bridge team had seen it and edged away to give the two of them privacy.

Bill continued donning a bright orange kapok life preserver while they talked. He snorted and nodded. "You're right, it should be your job. But in this rare instance, it's mine." He fastened the last chest clip and reached through his legs for the straps. "Look, this could go south. All we know is they offered to meet us here. If they want to help, we don't know to what extent. Even if they're willing, I could say or do something they don't like and screw it up. If that happens, it needs to be me that does it."

He saw the frustration in Irving's eyes, so he said, "You know I trust you, Joanna. But the Navy's going to want someone's head if this doesn't pan out. Hell, the president will, too. I'd rather it be mine than have both of us go down." With the last strap run through the rings and tied off, he grabbed his ball cap and headed for the door.

"Besides, on the off chance it's a trap, I want you to get the ship out of here." He smiled.

Seeing her flush, he added, "No, I don't think there's even a remote chance of that."

The XO cocked her head, grimaced, and looked down her nose at Bill. "Really, sir? Here I thought you were just protecting me from being taken prisoner and thrown into their brig."

She took an expansive breath. "You know that's not what I'm concerned about, sir. I *am* worried if we find ourselves under attack while you're over there, and—" She held up her hand as Bill tried to speak. "No, sir, I'm certain we can fight the ship. But with you over there, will *you* survive? I'd like a command of my own someday, just not today."

Bill grinned. "Okay, XO, you've made your point. Now, let me get down to the fantail and go meet our friends."

They walked off the bridge.

On the fantail, aft of the flight deck, a Jacob's ladder disappeared over the port side. The ladder consisted of two ropes, each made off to a cleat on the deck. Rigid bright orange resin steps were fastened between the ropes.

Aft of the ladder and right up against the wire nets that marked the deck edge stood the ship's bosun, the first lieutenant, and the ops officer. Next to them stood the aft lookout, her ears covered by the sound-powered phone headset. Two seamen, one fore and one aft of the Jacob's ladder, tended lines that led over the side to the Rigid Hulled Inflatable Boat that lay alongside in the lee of the ship.

Campbell walked up to join them.

"RHIB's ready, sir."

"Alright, Ops, let's be about it."

The first lieutenant heard him and walked to the rail. He saluted the flag streaming from the mast, climbed over the rail, and descended. The lookout muttered into the microphone on her chest. Almost immediately, two double bells issued from the 1MC, followed by the BMOW's announcement.

"*Nicholas*, departing."

From below, the coxswain called out, "First lieutenant's aboard, sir."

Bill turned to the XO and saluted.

"You have the ship, XO."

Then he, too, climbed over the rail and down to the waiting boat.

As his left foot lifted off the steel deck to move down to the next rung of the ladder, he heard the single bell "stinger" that indicated he'd officially left the ship.

Bill normally eschewed tradition and stood near the coxswain driving the RHIB. Standing there, wind in his hair, knees bent to absorb the pounding as they fairly flew across the sea was exhilarating, and he loved every second of it. But today called for more formality, so he moved carefully to the seat in the stern where tradition bade him sit.

"Let's go, Boats," called the first lieutenant, and the coxswain eased the throttle forward to take tension off the bow line. At the same time, he called, "Take in the stern line." From above Bill, the seaman tossed the line into the boat and the first lieutenant expertly caught it.

When the forward line was slack, the coxswain called, "Take in the bow line."

The seaman in the bow caught that line as it, too, dropped, then coiled it. Turning the wheel to the left, the coxswain pushed the throttle farther forward. The RHIB moved out of the shelter of *Nicholas's* steel side, around the stern, and sped toward the waiting Vietnamese corvettes.

CHAPTER
TWENTY-EIGHT

Every sailor wanted to show off their professionalism and seamanship in front of foreign navies. The first lieutenant stood near the coxswain. Bill couldn't hear what he said over the sound of the engine, but the coxswain pressed his lips together and nodded curtly. Bill smiled as they smoothly made their approach.

Arriving alongside the flotilla's flagship, Bill examined the accommodation ladder they'd rigged. It descended from the deck to the water's edge more like a stairway. He also noted what appeared to be sideboys and a large welcoming party on deck. Two of the men wore dress uniforms, and judging by the amount of gold braid, one was clearly quite senior.

Bill hadn't been to Vietnam. Others had spoken of friendly people eager to host Americans, not at all reluctant to meet their former foe. The crews had enjoyed their liberty ashore.

According to tradition, Bill was the last to board the small boat and the first to debark. As he stepped onto the accom ladder, "Anchors Aweigh" sounded from the corvette's announcing system. Above, a sharp command brought the side-boys to attention. When his head reached the deck edge, the piercing sound of the bosun's call brought the sideboys' hands to their brows in salute. Finally, as he returned the salute, two double bell strikes sounded, then, "USS *Nicholas*, arriving."

The piping ended. He turned to face the more junior of the two men in dress uniform, hoping he'd chosen wisely.

"Request permission to come aboard, sir," he said.

The other man returned his salute and said in clear English, "Permission granted, Captain."

The senior officer stepped forward, offered his hand, and introduced himself.

"I am Commodore Tran Bihn. You are Commander Wilkins?"

"You are well informed, sir," Bill responded as he shook Tran's hand.

"Your embassy provided your name. They told me yours is the only surviving American Navy vessel in the East Sea."

Not the South China *Sea*, Bill noted. "We've had some, um, difficulty communicating," he said.

"To be expected. Your embassy communicates with your Seventh Fleet and tells me that the *Theodore Roosevelt* group is coming. They know you survive, though not your current status." He inclined his head. "Nor did they expect to, I believe. They said you'd been ordered to operate silently."

Bill was surprised at how much the embassy had shared.

"Let us go below where we can talk more," Tran said. He introduced Bill to the other man in dress uniform, the commanding officer of the corvette. Then he waved Bill to follow the captain as he led the way. Tran fell in behind.

Ten minutes later, he and the commodore were sipping brandy. They spoke more easily seated in the captain's cabin.

The cabin was tiny but well appointed. Light came from portholes that looked out to the starboard side. The first lieutenant had been taken to the officers' wardroom for coffee.

Tran spoke. "*Ly Duong* is a Russian-built *Gepard* class frigate. Despite our Russian ships and weapons, I have studied *your* naval tactics because I believe such studies make my navy more combat effective," Tran said. He leaned back in his chair and sipped his brandy, all the while looking at Bill. "You know, my father fought in the war. He was also in our navy."

Bill inclined his head and nodded. "My executive officer spoke to me just this morning about her father's involvement in the conflict. But those old animosities shouldn't stand in the way now."

Tran smiled briefly. "No, they will not. Perhaps I will meet her one day and exchange stories." He put down his glass. "However, that is neither here nor there. We are here to work together. Our government approached your embassy because we very much believe that without American assistance, we will eventually be Chinese puppets. Thus, we have common interests."

"Forgive my bluntness, but how much assistance are you prepared to provide? Can you provide fuel and food? Can we enter port, or must we keep our relationship secret?" He ventured further. "Will you fight?"

Tran smiled briefly again, eyes twinkling. "I have always found the American desire to *cut to the chase* admirable." He pursed his lips before he answered. "Yes, we will provide supplies, including fuel. But we cannot allow you in our ports. Technically, and I hope temporarily, we remain neutral. Our army is not yet ready, and our mobilization must be executed quietly." Shrugging, he continued. "But we will arrange for supply by ship. Moreover, we will provide you information about Chinese military activity. We have naturally increased the frequency of surveillance flights. We have the most recent information from an aircraft that flew only this morning. Your officer will have a copy of it by now." Tran looked at his watch. "Right now, he should also be on a tour of our bridge and combat information center."

Bill's eyes widened.

Tran laughed. "Do not be surprised. Since our short war in 1979, we have prepared to fight the Chinese again. In fact, I volunteered for this mission, knowing it will likely lead to war." His face grew serious again. "Commander, I am here, not only acceding to my government's instructions to conclude a working arrangement but actively supportive."

Bill remained silent for a long moment as Tran sipped at his brandy. *This could change everything.*

Aloud, he said, "I'm grateful for whatever you can provide, sir. I don't mean to immediately make demands, but I'm low on fuel."

Tran nodded but remained silent.

Bill continued, "For my part, what are your expectations with respect to my conducting combat operations? Obviously, I won't violate your neutrality. But if I were to engage an enemy outside, but close to, your territorial waters, are you concerned that the Chinese might, ah, suspect you were complicit? If so, these intelligence reports you want to give me might embarrass you."

"No, Captain. We anticipate you will operate aggressively. I personally wish that you do so. The Chinese threat must be eliminated." Tran rubbed his cheek. "Yes, you must respect our neutrality. I do desire, however, that you avoid combat too near to our coast. If the Chinese attack us before we are ready, it would be catastrophic." He downed the last of his brandy. "I will arrange for a fuel ship to meet you at sea. Would tomorrow be soon enough?"

"Yes, sir. And I'm grateful."

Tran leaned forward in his seat. "Now, as to the question I did not answer, and you were polite enough not to ask a second time." His eyes gleamed, hard and alert. "When the circumstances are right, we will fight. But you must not count on it, certainly not today."

He sat back again. "That said, I intend to take my flotilla on what we shall call extended maneuvers, beginning this afternoon. At some point, it is entirely plausible we might happen upon each other. If this were to occur and we are simultaneously attacked by Chinese forces, we may be forced to defend ourselves, unless it is clearly obvious that it is only you they are shooting at." He shrugged. "This, of course, can be very difficult to determine in modern naval warfare."

Tran shook his head again and laughed briefly. "Besides, Captain, I can't very well meet on the sea with an American warship, then return directly to port. My crews are loyal, but I believe you have a saying that *loose lips sink ships*? I do not want word of our *accidental* meeting today to reach unfriendly ears, especially when I drifted at this rendezvous point for three hours, apparently waiting for something, before then hosting an American officer onboard."

Bill thought about it for only a moment before he grinned back. He raised his glass to his host. "Well met, sir. I can work within those limitations." He drained it and set it down.

"Sadly, I'm not well informed about your ships' capabilities. I'll help you understand mine." He rubbed his hands together as the brandy's warmth spread. "Another question, sir, if you don't mind. Did the embassy have any other instructions for me?"

"I have a note from the ambassador, and another thicker envelope from the naval attaché. She wanted to come herself, but the Chinese and Russians watch the movements of the American staff quite closely. It would be imprudent for her to board an ostensibly neutral warship." He paused. "How well informed are you of events in other parts of the globe?" Tran asked.

"We listen to the BBC, sir. They seem the most informed. But even they don't know much about the situation at home," he said flatly. His stomach knotted.

Tran frowned, picking up the hint. "I do not know very much about the situation in the United States, other than what the news reports. The embassy had nothing specific, at least that I am aware of, for you or your crew." Tran leaned forward and put his hand on Bill's knee. "I'm sorry. I wish I possessed more." He sat back and looked up at the overhead before he began. "However, there is a great deal going on elsewhere."

.Tran laid out the European situation in short order. Bill's new optimism evaporated.

The information Tran shared contained more detail than the BBC broadcasts.

"So we really *aren't* fighting alongside NATO?" Bill clarified.

"It is difficult to know. According to your president, or at least communiques purported to be from him, American forces are neutral in the European war. However, there are reports of American units heavily engaged in Poland."

Bill could not believe that America would remain neutral. For his country to abandon her allies in the face of Russian aggression would be heinous. His heart raced and his temple throbbed. He couldn't sit still, so he stood and paced the tiny cabin.

Tran remained seated. "When I was a junior officer, I went to Vladivostok for training. My Russian instructors repeated one maxim over and over, that we could never trust you to do the logical thing or to follow your own doctrine. That Americans believe orders to be mere suggestions." Tran shrugged. "It is possible some of your officer corps have decided their orders are wrong."

He clapped his hands together. "Commander? While I applaud your concern, I suggest that our situation here is much more, ahem, close at hand?"

Bill sat quickly, nearly overturning his empty brandy glass. "You're right, of course. We've got a lot to talk about. I must read my orders from the embassy, but as of now, unless those orders prohibit me from doing so, I will use any intelligence you give me to hunt enemy vessels in the South, er, *East* Sea. I will pass anything I learn to you, as well."

Tran smiled briefly but said nothing.

Bill continued. "I'll do everything possible to keep my attacks from being linked to you. I'll make damned sure my targets can't tell anyone back home what happened."

Tran nodded. The two looked at each other, then Bill stood. "With your permission, sir, I'll go back to my ship and read the notes from the embassy. In the meantime, may I send my operations officer over to begin coordinating communications, and explore how we can most effectively assist each other?"

The XO bit her lips and a long breath escaped her when Bill stepped onto the fantail. The stinger still echoed along the deck.

"Well, XO, I'm back safe and sound," he said, a mocking lilt in his voice.

"I'm glad to see you, sir. What's the verdict?" She smiled.

"They're going to help us, XO. Ops, over here, please."

When the ops officer stood next to them, he continued, "Take a look at our new allies. Or, at least, the closest thing to allies we're going to find right at this moment."

The three turned to look at the small warships holding station near *Nicholas*, each lost in their own thoughts. Then Bill filled them in on what had transpired.

CHAPTER
TWENTY-NINE

1145 Zulu, 5 Nov
1845 Local Time
USS *Nicholas*, South China Sea

The next night, *Nicholas* steamed slowly toward a point ninety nautical miles due east of where the Mekong River met the sea. She had a full tank of gas, as well as fresh vegetables, eggs, and even milk from the supply ship Tran had arranged. Bill reflected on the US Navy's long history in these waters. Even *Constitution* had sailed them in 1847, visiting Hanoi and Cam Ranh Bay.

Ahead lay *Nicholas's* "appointment" with a Chinese naval auxiliary. A supply ship, it provided enemy warships with food and fuel, precious resources Bill intended to deprive the enemy of.

Nicholas's crew had gained confidence now that they were less blind. Twice a day the eyes of Vietnamese aircraft faithfully reported every surface contact out to 150 nautical miles from the coast. When ships belonging to the PRC were detected, they earned extra attention from the patrol aircraft. Bill sometimes even got hull numbers and names. Reports now came to Bill in near real time, only minutes old. When CIC correlated reports with the intelligence broadcast, miraculously still transmitting, it gave Bill a higher level of comfort that he knew what was around them.

Most important, the Vietnamese ensured he knew about any aircraft that flew without emitting any electronic signals, especially radar. Bill worried that, operating silently himself, a Chinese patrol plane might come upon him within visual range and report his position. He was able to detect and track those that used their radar. While *Nicholas's* slow speed, relative to a search aircraft, wouldn't allow him to run away, he'd been able to maneuver and use the ship's very small radar cross section to avoid attracting attention. To the enemy, he most likely resembled a small boat, mulling about a fishing ground. The ubiquitous rain squalls that scudded across the sea provided cover, and he often sailed in them for hours.

Thus far, of combatants there'd only been an occasional individual patrol craft, and all of those had been hundreds of miles to the northeast. Unless they moved nearer and congregated, Bill didn't consider them worth the risk to seek them out for destruction. He'd hoped to get reports of corvettes or destroyers.

The patrol planes remained clear of Chinese-held islands and reefs, of course. But Bill wasn't interested in tangling with them again, either. He wanted to make a dent in the Chinese surface combatant order of battle, and their new friends seemed willing to help him do that.

He stared out the bridge window in front of his chair. An hour ago, they'd briefed their plan for intercepting and sinking the enemy. The team had done a better job anticipating his "what if" questions this time. They only had to wait for darkness to execute it.

Around the ship the sea was already dark as the last bit of twilight faded to black. A gentle swell imparted a soothing lift and fall as *Nicholas* achieved the point and turned to make her way slowly northward. She showed no lights at all, not even required navigation lights. Those were for peacetime. The waxing crescent moon and nearly fifty percent cloud cover ensured little illumination, perfect for what they were about to attempt.

In the corner the BMOW phoned the master-at-arms and told him to walk the exterior of the ship and check for light leaks. The slightest illumination escaping outside could give away their position. Darken ship had been the routine for decades, long before the war. Now, however, it meant life and death. Even here on the bridge, they'd shut off the red fluorescent lights they sparingly used in order to eliminate every possible light source. All the instrument indicator lights were also turned down until they were barely visible, even to eyes adjusted to the dark.

The watertight door at the back of the bridge opened and two forms passed through, carefully moving to stand next to Bill's chair. Campbell's voice issued from the nearer of the two. "Evening, Captain."

"Hey, Ops, what's up?"

"Latest update on the target, sir. From its last reported position this morning, it kept a pretty steady eight knots, staying right at twenty-five miles off the coast. We got an update from the intel broadcast about ten minutes ago. It corresponded nicely with where the target should be. We ought to get her visually in about ninety minutes. I'm just headed down to Combat to take the watch."

The second form spoke in Dix's voice. "Recommend we get airborne, Skipper. It'll take a while to get enough separation for cross-fixing if they light off a radar."

"Have they used radar all day?"

Ops said, "No. But they might in the dark. It sure gives me the willies driving around blind."

Grinning, Bill said, "Okay. Go strap on your aircraft." His heart rate climbed. Exhilaration seeped into his body. "Let's be about it. Are we ready?"

Two voices replied, "Aye, sir."

Bill climbed down and Ops led the way. As they left the bridge, the BMOW passed the word to set flight quarters.

In CIC, Ops took a turnover brief from Lieutenant Commander Kam Bradran, the weapons officer. When finished, Campbell turned to Bill.

"Sir, request permission to relieve the watch as TAO. Course three five five, speed eight knots. Condition three watch set, warning yellow, weapons tight. Ready for surface engagement. Gun loaded to the transfer tray with HE-CVT. CIWS in Manual, key inserted. Sonar passive with tail at short stay. Nixie deployed, also at short stay, switched off."

"Permission granted. Relieve the watch."

Bradran announced, "Attention in Combat, Lieutenant Commander Campbell is the TAO."

Campbell immediately followed him. "This is Lieutenant Commander Campbell, I have the watch."

Sitting down at his console, Ops put on his headset. "SWC, TAO. All set, Chief?"

The Surface Weapons Coordinator, pronounced "swick", responded instantly. "Yes, sir. I got an SM-2 selected from the forward VLS. We'll fire it first to make sure the target can't get a message off. The gunfire control camera will give us target position and we'll light off the illuminators at launch. They'll get no warning, sir."

Bill looked over at the chief, her face set and focused. He thought he glimpsed a predatory gleam in her eye but decided it was his imagination. He looked around at the rest of the team. All hands were alert.

Gone were the nerves, evidenced before by pale faces, wide eyes, and perspiration despite the frigid temperature maintained in CIC. Still exhausted, these men and women were focused and calm. Bill's face wrinkled as pride welled up inside. Success had bonded them more than any pre-deployment training.

He was damned proud of them.

"This is the TAO, copy that." Campbell smiled and it snuck into his voice. "I presume the gun camera is trained in about the expected direction?"

Bill whipped around.

A grin blossomed on the chief's face.

"Why, yes, sir, it does appear to be. Amazing that those gun control FCs can get it right, isn't it?"

Bill found himself chuckling, too.

The fact that the gun control fire controlman on watch didn't provide a rejoinder told Bill that *someone* still recognized the modicum of discipline required. He nodded approvingly.

In due time, the bridge called. "Request green deck, sir. Flight quarters manned and ready, FOD walkdown complete. Helo reports ready."

"Very well. Green deck," Bill replied.

Once the helo got airborne and gave its state report, there was nothing left to do but wait.

The minutes passed glacially.

In Sea Hawk Six Zero One, Dix yawned. They'd been aloft for nearly an hour with nothing to show for it. Stretching, he said, "Zeke, take it."

"I got it," Craft replied. He was the ATO for this flight. Dix liked flying with him; he easily retained his calm demeanor under stress. Dix raised his night vision goggles and wiped his streaming face. "Hey, Carrie, you got anything yet?" he asked the sensor operator.

"No, sir. With traffic density what it is, I thought they'd have lit off a radar by now."

"Maybe they have but we don't recognize it."

The first class petty officer came back. "Well, sir, could be. You know me, I jess stare at the screen. I don' know nuthin'."

Dix chuckled. "I trust you more than I do that computer of yours."

"We got a full readout on this guy's radar from the Vietnamese. I know exactly what I'm looking for."

Dix laughed. "So that's how you do it. Here I thought you were magic. Guess that'll work."

He turned to Craft. "How you doing?"

Craft kept scanning the instruments in between watching out the windscreen. Even with night vision goggles, they flew at two hundred fifty feet to avoid unlit ships or flying into the water.

"Fine. Keepin' away from these fisherman's a bitch. The damned lights they use 'bout burn out the goggles. Sure feels good to be off the ship, though."

"I hear you."

They continued through the steaming dark, staying between thirty and thirty-five miles west of *Nicholas*.

Fifteen minutes later, the sensor operator's voice came over the internal circuit. "Skipper, I got a radar just came up on our ten o'clock. Looks to be a match. Give me thirty more seconds, I'll know for sure."

"Any chance they see us?"

She paused for a moment, then said, "No, I don't think so. Probably ought to turn away, though."

"Aye, report it. Let *Nicholas* figure it out," Dix said.

"Already sent it."

"Shouldn't we head over and take a look?" asked Craft.

"Nope. The CO doesn't want to risk it. They get a report off, there's less area for their patrol aircraft to search. Frankly, I'm surprised they haven't found us yet. The boat's doing a good job staying hidden."

"Shit. Based on cross-fix with *Nicholas*, he's only four, no, three miles north," reported the sensor operator.

"Dammit." To Craft he said, "Turn left, head one eight zero, kick it in the ass." The helicopter was already turning as he finished.

To the SENSO, he ordered, "Get ready on chaff and flare—"

"Missile flare, starboard side! No ESM. IR seeker," she called. "Popping flares now."

The cockpit lit with brilliant yellow as the helo spit flares, designed to decoy enemy missiles.

Dix keyed his mike. "Homeplate, Six Zero One. I got a missile inbound. Popping flares, evading. You got the position on the hostile?"

"Roger, Six Zero One. We got it."

"Hope they kill that fucker before he gets us."

Craft didn't respond as he twisted the bird around. Suddenly it jerked as a brighter light flared momentarily. Dix's eyes swept the instruments. Nothing out of the ordinary. *Near miss.*

"Second missile flare. Popping more flares."

"How many more we got?" Dix asked.

"Not enough if they shoot again."

To Craft, he said, "Get lower. We gotta get down."

"I can't see the water, boss."

"I know, but we stay up here, we're dead."

"Okay, but we hit water, we'll still end up that way."

The helicopter nosed down. Dix braced himself as he watched the altimeter roll down. At fifty feet, Craft pulled back and leveled out. Behind them, a fireball lit the water nearly a hundred yards back. The last of the flares hit the water, and it was dark again.

CHAPTER
THIRTY

1310 Zulu, 5 Nov
2010 Local Time
South China Sea

"TAO, helo reports missile launch."

Campbell looked up, mouth open. "Say again."

"Helo says there's a missile inbound."

"SWC, TAO, got anything?"

"No, sir—"

Bill interrupted. "Get the SPY up, now."

"TAO, SWC, gun control says they saw a flare on the horizon."

"Is the missile inbound to us or the helo?" Bill asked.

"I don't know, sir—" Campbell answered.

"TAO, helo says the missile's shot at them."

Bill swallowed hard. "Find the launch platform."

Campbell nodded.

"TAO, SWC. Gun camera's got a large contact bearing three two zero true on the horizon. They saw a flare near it. About right for the target. Matches ESM bearing, too."

Campbell asked about other surface contacts. There were

three of the ubiquitous fishing boats, but all were between *Nicholas* and the coast, the closest five miles or more away.

Campbell turned to him. "Request batteries release."

"TAO, SWC. Contact shows no, repeat, no, navigation lights. It's still hull down."

When they'd briefed the plan, Bill had emphasized how critical positive identification was, for two reasons. First, he didn't want to waste a missile on the wrong target. Second, and most important, they couldn't accidentally kill innocent seamen aboard a neutral.

The team waited for his answer.

Bill closed his eyes and nodded. "Tell the helo we're shooting. We'll vector them in once it's neutralized."

"Six Zero One, we're engaging the hostile. When we confirm hits, we'll vector you in for BDA."

"You mean we'll do it like we briefed?" Dix said. "Never mind." He took a breath. "We're still almost in visual range. I expect we'll know before you do." To Craft, he said, "Turn right, circle around. But stay low. Let 'em think they got us."

"Commander, we got more ESM off the target. Air search and fire control acquisition. They're looking for us."

"We below their radar horizon?"

"No, sir. Recommend we keep hauling ass outta here."

Dix nodded. "Yeah, let's do that. Zeke, keep goin' south."

Taking a deep breath to slow his racing pulse, Bill said, "Very well. Batteries released."

The SWC must have hit the *Engage* button as soon as the TAO acknowledged the order.

In the monitor, a glow reflected off the sea as *Nicholas's* missile streaked toward it at supersonic speed. In less than a second the intensely bright dot of the missile itself appeared, converging on the target. When they joined, a brilliant explosion blossomed and the target disappeared as the camera automatically adjusted light levels.

When it reappeared, flames engulfed the superstructure.

Bill put his hand on Campbell's shoulder as they listened to BDA from the gun camera operator. When he had Campbell's attention, he said, "Send the helo in. Tell the OOD to close the target and prepare to take on survivors. And be ready to engage with guns if they decide they aren't ready to abandon ship or surrender."

The cockpit again flared with light from an explosion.

"Is that a launch?" Dix asked.

"No, sir. I don't see nothing," the SENSO reported.

The radio spoke. "Six Zero One, close for BDA. We got hits. Looks like target's burning."

Dix heaved a sigh. "Six Zero One copies." He released the key. "Alright, Zeke, let's get some altitude and head back."

Craft grunted as he put the helo into a climb.

CHAPTER
THIRTY-ONE

1322 Zulu, 5 Nov
2022 Local Time
USS *Nicholas*, South China Sea

"Helo reports target burning furiously aft, sir."

Campbell pumped his fist.

Bill leaned back and heaved a sigh of relief. "Tell the helo to get back here. I want to see Dix as soon as he lands, too. We gotta figure out how to keep this shit from happening again. We can't risk losing our last bird."

"Aye, sir. I'll have the bridge set flight quarters."

Bill rose and put his hand on Campbell's shoulder. "Not yet. I'm going up there, so I'll tell them. I may wait til we see what's what on the target."

Campbell nodded as Bill turned toward the door.

The bridge was lit by the eerie orange glow of the blazing ship as *Nicholas* closed. The five-inch gun remained pointed at the enemy vessel.

"Let's get closer. I want to see what's happening on deck," Bill called.

As *Nicholas* continued to close, Bill moved to the port bridge wing.

Pettibone came up from Combat. "Sir, gun camera operator says he read the name off her stern: *Chong Lunj*. She's the one we were looking for." Pettibone looked over at their handiwork. "Those SM-2s are really effective."

On the enemy's main deck, the crew worked feverishly to save their ship. Some played streams of water at the base of the fire, while others moved stretchers. Aft on the superstructure, automatic sprinkler systems sprayed on the exterior.

Bill hoped there were sprinklers in the cargo fuel tanks, too, spreading foam on top to keep it from burning or exploding. The fire aft was out of control but hadn't yet spread forward.

He told Barrister to move within hailing distance.

"Sir?" she asked.

"Get us close enough I can use the megaphone." He turned to Pettibone. "Get CTI1 Kristophe up here."

Cryptologic Technician Interpretive First Class Kristophe was a Mandarin linguist. Bill hoped he could convince the enemy crew to abandon ship.

While they awaited his arrival, the XO joined him on the bridge wing. "Sir, why are we rescuing them?"

Bill turned to look at her. "Why not? We don't need to kill any more of them."

"Isn't that their CO's responsibility? Besides, the fishing boats can rescue them just as easily as us, maybe better. We should get away from here."

"If that was us, would you want to be left like this?"

Irving frowned and said, "Yes, sir, I would. I'd rather take my chances on a fishing boat than be a POW."

Pettibone looked at the XO then at Bill. He took a few steps back.

Bill stared at her, then turned back to the enemy ship. The XO stood silently, hands behind her back. Kristophe arrived out of breath. "Yes, sir?"

Pointing at the flaming hulk, he said, "Tell those people to abandon ship and make their way over to us."

"Aye, sir."

The small gathering on the bridge wing wilted before the heat of the flames. Even upwind, the stench of burning oil polluted their nostrils. Kristophe got the megaphone and called out in Chinese.

A few men looked over, seeing *Nicholas* for the first time. One ran aft to the man who directed the hose teams. He broke off and stared at *Nicholas*. Shaking his fist, he shouted something that didn't sound friendly. Then he returned to direct the fire-fighting.

"What'd he say, Kristophe?" Bill asked.

Kristophe frowned.

"Well, Captain, I'll leave out the insults. The short answer is he refused."

"Tell them I intend to sink their ship. I would prefer if they were not onboard when I do it."

Kristophe looked at him for a long moment, then passed on his message. He listened while Kristophe called across the water gap. The wavelets trapped between the two ships reflected the flames. Inside the pilothouse, Barrister gave engine and rudder orders to keep from drifting down on the burning vessel. Bradran joined the group on the bridge wing.

With no further responses, Kristophe turned to Bill. "Sir, he's ordered them to ignore us. He really seems to believe they can save the ship."

Bill agreed. They were making progress, beating the fire back slowly.

Bill had Kristophe tell them they had five minutes to abandon ship. Once the message was passed, Bill stepped into the pilothouse.

"OOD. Put us a thousand yards on her port quarter."

Striding to the intercom, he called CIC. "TAO, this is the captain. We're going to put her on our starboard beam at a thousand yards. Ten minutes from now, I want you to fire three five-inch rounds into her hull. Aim for her stern, as low as you can. Use HE rounds; I want her to go down fast so we don't get a big fuel spill that burns for days. I gave 'em five minutes. If they abandon ship, we'll hold fire and let them." He paused. He shivered, yet he was sweating. "If they don't leave after the first three rounds, we give them two minutes to think about it. Then fire another ten rounds. Is that understood?"

Campbell repeated his orders verbatim. Bill turned to go back to the bridge wind, then paused and flipped the switch again. "And call up before you start shooting. If they even look like they're going to do as they've been told, we'll wait."

Pettibone looked down at the wooden deck platform, while Bradran showed sudden interest in the stars above. The CIC phone talker, who'd come out to the bridge wing, stared first at Bill, then over at the enemy ship.

"Sir, I'll lay below to Combat," said Pettibone. He scurried away.

On the bridge wing again, Bill put his hands behind his back and stood up straight, back rigid, staring at the enemy ship.

As the heat receded, the night's cool humidity took its place.

Irving came up behind him. "Sir, there's no way this guy's going to be giving anybody gas or anything else. Hell, I don't think they can keep it afloat, do you? Sure, put a few more holes in the hull to make sure. After that, let the fishermen pick 'em up. It's the right thing to do."

He rounded on her. "No, the right thing would have been for them to do what I told them to do. They're being stubborn. And we're not letting the fishermen—" He flexed his hands and turned away.

"Sir . . ." She stopped.

As they waited, Bill silently prayed the captain over there would see reason.

The minutes dragged by like molasses on a frosty day. The pilothouse and bridge wing were silent save for occasional quiet helm and engine orders drifting from inside. The fishing boats, drawn to the flames, maneuvered around the two larger ships. But as soon as they saw the American flag on Nicholas's mast, they stopped, circling at a distance.

Bill finally allowed himself a glance at his watch.

It had to have been ten minutes, didn't it?

But it had only been eight.

An explosion aft rocked the burning ship. A mass of flames poured out of the stack and every opening in the superstructure as a fireball rose into the night. Its crew fell to the deck. The fire roared back, higher than before.

The heat hit Nicholas's bridge wing and everyone shrank before it.

He felt sick. "OOD, take us closer, a hundred yards."

Irving touched his shoulder and Bradran stepped closer.

The XO asked, "Sir, why? That was probably the ready service fuel tank in the engine room cooking off. That explosion could have breached the cargo fuel tanks."

Bradran added, "And if they're carrying ammunition . . . " His voice trailed off.

Bill turned to face them. But while Bradran was nervous, his fear was under control. Irving's face was hard, lips compressed into thin lines.

"You're right, Weaps, XO. But that's all the more reason to get those men off there, now." He rubbed his hands together. "Look, I don't have a death wish. But I want to give them every reasonable chance to prove they don't have one, either."

Bradran smiled briefly, though the smile didn't reach his eyes.

The XO turned. "Kam, why don't you head down to the main deck? Get the nets ready to go over the side, but don't put them over until the captain tells you to."

She moved closer. "Sir, we, you, are putting us at greater risk. The fishing boats can rescue the crew. The longer we stay here, the more chance the enemy has of finding *us*. Let it go. She's finished. There's no way they can save her."

Bill looked over at the enemy ship.

Aboard *Chong Lunj*, the situation had changed drastically.

The captain yelled at his crew, gesticulating. But the majority had decided to take their fate into their own hands. *Nicholas's* crew, gathered on deck, watched as they threw inflatable life boat canisters and anything else that might float into the sea. A few continued a desultory effort to pour water on the flames, but it lacked enthusiasm. More and more hoses were shut off and those men, too, ran to the side and climbed or jumped overboard. Their captain shouted at them, grabbed a few and tried to pull them back.

Bill turned and stared at Irving. Then he walked into the pilothouse. "OOD, let's get out of here. Set flight quarters. Let's get the helo on deck. As soon as you have manned and ready reports, give them a green deck." Turning to Petty Officer Kristophe, he said, "Talk to the fishing boats. Tell them — ask them to rescue the crew." Then he laid below.

In the wardroom, Bill found the XO filling her coffee cup. "Joanna, what makes you think we shouldn't save them?"

Irving finished stirring in some milk and turned to face him. "Sir, it's not that I want them dead. Or maybe I do, after what they did." She waved her hand. "I know it wasn't them who attacked us. But they're the enemy. We got a mission kill. Even

196 THOMAS M. WING

without sinking it, that ship was done for. And we don't need prisoners to guard and feed."

Bill sighed and rotated his shoulders. "You may be right. You probably are. But why couldn't their captain just do like I ordered?"

Irving tilted her head. "Because he's the captain of the ship you just blew up under him. He's just as angry as you'd be. Besides, he's got his duty, too. He's a Chinese naval officer. He's supposed to save his crew and his ship. That's what he was trying to do." She put her hand on his arm. "Look, sir, I'll support you. You know that, or I hope you do. But there are folks onboard who are getting mixed signals from their leadership. On the one hand, be aggressive and go after the enemy. On the other, be soft and try to save as many as we can."

"We can do both. If the Chinese would cooperate—"

She shook her head. "Sir, they won't. Just like we wouldn't." She took a breath and stepped back. "Sorry. You asked me what I thought. Now I'll give you a *cheery aye aye* and carry on." She sipped again and moved around him toward the door.

Bill closed his eyes and sighed. None of the Navy's predeployment training had prepared him for reality.

CHAPTER
THIRTY-TWO

0030 Zulu, 6 Nov
0730 Local Time
Presidential Office, Beijing

"I want that ship found, and I want it killed," a furious President Liu shouted.

Despite his own normally cautious nature, in his heart he'd believed the devastating blow they'd landed on the American military would end their resistance. They were made soft by decades of easy wins over third world countries. When faced with a true peer, they would back down. He would give them no choice.

They would *not* hit back effectively.

The defense minister's head bowed slightly as he said, "Mr. President, we were as surprised as anyone that this ship in the South Sea survived. We—"

"Stop. I do not want to hear what you *thought* would happen. I instead want to hear what you will *do* about it."

Blinking furiously, Huang paused. "Mr. President, I have sent a group of warships to hunt the enemy down and destroy it. Our aircraft scour the South Sea as we speak. We will find it. The missing submarine last reported in seventy-five miles southeast of Cam Rahn Bay. The attack on the supply ship took place twenty-eight miles east of Ho Chi Minh City. Therefore, the flotilla will search along the Vietnamese coast. He must be hiding along there, perhaps in the coastal islands."

Liu rubbed his chin. "You do not think the Vietnamese would dare interfere and help this enemy?"

"No, sir. There is much shipping along that coast, and we believe the enemy hides within it. The Americans tend to follow the rules. Their ship commanders are punished severely when they do not. The law of war forbids them to enter Vietnam's territorial seas. We will find it. I will ensure it is destroyed."

It was not lost on Liu that whenever Huang described a decisive act likely to garner approbation, he used "I". When he discussed intelligence reporting or anything that might earn later reproof, he said "we".

"You had better be right. If the Vietnamese are helping the Americans, it will cost them dearly. As for this enemy ship, our fleet grows smaller every time he strikes." He stared at Huang. "It is time for you to make good on your promises."

Huang swallowed hard, bowed, and left.

CHAPTER
THIRTY-THREE

1-5 Nov
Eastern Europe

Across Poland, NATO forces moved to reinforce those already in close battle with enemy columns. Russian generals, having been assured by Moscow that there would be no reinforcements, found themselves attacked on their left flanks.

But prudently, they'd planned for it. Years of bad intelligence and incorrect information from the Kremlin had taken its toll on the Russian army. And taught its leadership valuable lessons, written in blood.

The Russian plan had allocated more forces than they'd really needed to take the three Baltic states. The excess accommodated contingencies. These reserve formations pivoted and drove southwest. Thousands of soldiers who'd moved quietly into Kaliningrad over the previous two to three years now donned uniforms, manned equipment they'd hidden in warehouses, and moved.

Security forces along the route into Lithuania were already positioned to face the Polish border. They'd also had time to prepare fighting positions. Regiments that had ostensibly been moved to Chechnya magically reconstituted and moved quickly to fill in behind the security forces.

The fighting became brutal and bloody. It wasn't a stalemate, but movement slowed. Even so, the Russian front line continued inexorably forward past the Polish border. But as more NATO forces advanced into the fight, advances previously measured in miles per day became yards. To the north, the progress against the remnants of the national armies of the Baltic states nearly ground to a halt.

The slowdown worried the Russian military leadership.

***

0700 Zulu, 6 Nov
1000 Local Time
The Kremlin, Moscow

"Sir, we must exercise the Stalingrad Option." Remkin had come to the president's office through a driving rain. Reports of American units fighting alongside NATO, despite White House assurances, alarmed him.

Vilnius, the capital of Lithuania, had fallen quickly. Neither Riga, nor Tallinn, the capitals of Estonia and Latvia, had been taken. Yet. But those countries' forces were cut off. While for now they still held out, they wouldn't last much longer.

The naval war had been quick but bloody, and far less successful. The vaunted Russian navy had given a good account of itself, but in the end it had fallen prey to NATO ships and submarines.

Remkin had expected nothing less, given the Russian navy had long been a distant third to the ground and air forces. But the attrition they'd inflicted on NATO had been severe. More Russian submarines were enroute from the Pacific, transiting under the Arctic ice. They would break the back of NATO's maritime forces.

But he needed to stop the counterattack from Poland. That would give his generals a freer hand to smash the besieged enemy against the Baltic Sea. But until they blunted the attack from the south, they couldn't afford to move any troops out of that fight.

The Russian Air Force maintained superiority over the Baltic states, but the airspace over Poland was contested. Any attempt to conduct air attacks deeper into Central and Western Europe would be folly. Some aircraft would get through, of course, but not enough, and the cost would be too high. They needed something more.

"Something more" was the Stalingrad Option.

"Have we reached that point, Pavlov?" asked Gregorivich.

"Yes, sir, though not because of setbacks. We continue to move forward. But it will go faster if we do it. We thought NATO would take longer to decide to defend the Baltic states. We also believed they'd wait until all their reinforcements were present and integrated before they launched counterattacks. This is how they have always operated." He took a breath. "However, they hurt themselves by attacking piecemeal. Unable to drive at us with any particular strength, they only succeed in slowing us down. They cannot stop us."

"You believed they wouldn't fight at all." Gregorivich's mouth turned down at the corners.

Remkin began to respond, but the president waved for him to remain silent. "Never mind. What of the American units?"

Remkin sighed. "Reconnaissance tells us they are conforming to NATO movements."

Seeing the president's eyes raise to the ceiling and his head roll on his shoulders, Remkin hurried to add, "I know, sir. However, it appears either the general who heads their European Command has ignored her orders, or lower ranking officers are ignoring theirs. The Americans have a long history of disobeying orders, haven't they?"

"How many Americans have we killed, Pavlov?"

"I can't say with certainty. We found burned American tanks and dead Americans following a tank battle near Marijampole." He braced himself. "We've also captured wounded American soldiers."

Gregorivich's eyes went wide. He abruptly stood. "Why the hell do we have American prisoners?" He leaned across the desk, glaring now, the warm glow in his eyes replaced by fire. "We can't have American prisoners. Of all the things we cannot do, one of the most important is to not capture Americans."

Remkin blanched. "What would you have our soldiers do? We must not risk word getting out that we were killing prisoners, especially wounded ones."

The president closed his mouth and ground his teeth. Then he slowly stood up straight. Closing his eyes for a moment, he sat again. "Do not fear words. Words often kill those who utter them."

Remkin heaved a deep sigh. He'd been holding his breath.

Gregorivich spoke again, his voice steady. "All right. But can we not simply leave the wounded on the field? They will die, and we will not have a problem."

"I've already issued those orders, sir. That does not solve our problem with the ones we already hold. For now, they are at a site east of Moscow, isolated. We can hold them for quite some time without admitting it. But unless we are prepared to simply make them disappear permanently, we will eventually have to tell the Americans we have them."

"When I stand astride Europe, no one will question how I achieved it." An unblinking Gregorivich stared at Remkin. Then, he sighed. "We will deal with them later. Ensure they are guarded by the right men, men who will carry out my orders when I issue them."

"Yes, Mr. President."

It would not end well for the American soldiers. Remkin felt somewhat sorry for them, but not enough to act. This was war.

There were no rules in war, no matter what the West chose to believe.

"Yes, sir. Now, about the Stalingrad Option."

"Yes, yes, you have permission. I'd prefer to have held it until later, but you're right. If we wait, we might wait too long." His eyes bored into Remkin. "Do not make the same mistakes your predecessor made. You understand?"

Remkin gulped. "Of course, sir."

At midnight, fierce pulsing glows arose over bases across western Russia. The series of fires persisted for nearly an hour. Above the horizon the glows broke into hundreds of individual streaks climbing skyward. Each streak rose to a certain point, then cut off where the hum of a jet engine roared to life.

Dark shapes, conventionally armed SSC-8 cruise missiles, screamed back toward the ground, hugging it in their race toward self-destruction. They were banned under the Intermediate-Range Nuclear Forces Treaty, yet their numbers were far greater than any intelligence agency had uncovered. When America withdrew from the INF Treaty, any opportunity to limit their numbers vanished. Accompanying them were dozens of new hypersonic missiles. They would arrive much faster than their subsonic cousins.

At the ends of their flights were air defense systems, railheads, depots, assembly points, supply and ammunition depots, bridges, airfields and terminals, and even troop trains.

Dozens and dozens of shorter-range missiles streaked toward NATO positions in Lithuania and eastern Poland. Where they exploded, equipment was destroyed and men and women died. Many dropped small bomblets over residential areas in major cities near the front. Tens of thousands were buried in their bedrooms.

The Russian army now moved more swiftly into the heart of Poland.

Ahead of the advancing phalanx, hundreds of thousands of surviving civilians, generally unarmed men, women, and children, scurried away, carrying what possessions they could cram into their vehicles. They choked the highways, roads, and unpaved paths, hindering Polish and German efforts to slow the invasion.

Farther back from the front, they also slowed the work of surviving French, British, and American forces as they moved to establish a defensive perimeter around Warsaw on the flat plains of central Poland.

Transportation infrastructure had been ravaged and communications cut. Coordination was spotty at best. In some areas, short-range communications relied on old-fashioned written messages carried by messengers.

Elderly men and women experienced déjà vu, recalling the opening days of World War II.

CHAPTER
THIRTY-FOUR

2045 Zulu, 28 Oct
1545 Eastern Time
Niagara Falls Border Crossing

As the car approached the bridge that spanned the Niagara River from Canada into the US, Tim Neustein looked in the rearview mirror. Attorney General Karl Hauptmann sat in the back seat, a determined expression on his face.

Neustein served as Hauptmann's aide. He and his boss had been stuck in Toronto since the attack. No rental companies would allow their cars to cross the border, and no one would take a US Government credit card or voucher for payment. Neustein had convinced the Toronto city government to loan them a vehicle for their journey home.

Hauptmann had made his name by putting criminals behind bars. The crimes were unimportant; jail time was his·measure of success. Every sentencing recommendation sought the maximum. He particularly relished punishing street crime and blue-collar criminals. In his opinion, people were poor for two reasons: they were lazy, and God wanted them to stay poor. God favored those who worked hard, he believed, and wealth

206 THOMAS M. WING

resulted. Hauptmann's job as the AG was first to protect the presidency, and second to punish anyone who got in the way of the president and his friends. Neustein, a deputy prosecutor under Hauptmann, had been chosen to accompany him to Washington.

Tall and barrel-chested, Hauptmann intimidated witnesses and anyone else hapless enough to cross his path. By contract, Neustein was of medium height and carried several extra pounds in his belly. His full head of hair hung over his ears, with a lock forever falling over his eyes. He intimidated no one.

This day, no cars were in line ahead of or behind theirs. However, the opposite side of the road was bumper to bumper even on the Canadian side. Most had American plates.

"What the hell, Neustein? There's a lot of American cars over there. Why?"

Neustein had learned it was better to be silent than to have the wrong answer or speculate. Hauptmann hated speculation. He asked the Canadian border guard when they pulled up to the gate.

"Oh, we've had a constant flood of folks coming across," she said. "They want out. They're afraid the Chinese'll nuke the US. Line's about ten hours long on the other side."

Hauptmann leaned forward, face red and fists clenched. "You damned well better close the border, then."

The guard glanced at him. "Well, lest I get an order from my government, I can't really do that, now can I? Passports?"

Neustein quickly handed over their passports, trying to head off the outburst he knew was coming.

"You'll do what I tell you to do, young lady. I'm the attorney general of the United States. I'll have your badge."

The guard ignored him for a moment as she thumbed their passports.

She waited just long enough for Hauptmann to open his mouth before she interrupted. "Well, Mr. Attorney General of the United States, I don't work for you, thank God. If you really are who you say you are, of course, you can take it up with *my* government. But I don't think I'll be fired today nor any time soon." She smiled politely. "And if you *are* him, you might want to put your own house in order before you try fixing anyone else's. But you have a good day, now."

She stepped back from the car, smiling as she got in the last word, and waved them forward.

"You damned upstart. It's my border, and—"

Neustein drove quickly through.

Hauptmann shut his mouth and threw himself back in the seat. He turned his head away from the line of cars fleeing his country and stared across the open water.

"Neustein, I want the border closed when we get home. These cowards aren't allowed to run. Americans never run. And I want the Canadian government to deport all those bastards who've crossed the border. They're not going to get away with this." He stopped and sat silently for a few moments. "In fact, I want them arrested for deserting their country in its time of need. And I want *that* bitch's hide nailed to the nearest Canadian wall."

"Yes, sir."

Neustein made a mental note, though he didn't believe it would do much good. The border with Canada was too long and too porous.

And the border guard was too right.

Five days later they drove up to the Justice Department building in Washington. It hadn't been deemed important enough to receive treatment by the Chinese.

The trip had taken much longer because they'd had to navigate around National Guard roadblocks.

At the first one, the attorney general had laid into the master sergeant in charge. Had it not been for the tank actually blocking the road, Hauptmann would certainly have ordered Neustein to run it. As it was, the more Hauptmann harangued the sergeant, the more stubborn the soldier got. He'd finally ordered the car to turn around. At gunpoint.

After running into another roadblock on a different highway, Hauptmann hadn't even tried to control his temper. The result had been the same.

By the time they'd made a lengthy detour and reached a third one, the word was out, at least within New York, that a madman claiming to be the attorney general was trying to force his way through. The colonel controlling traffic through the area ordered him stopped and arrested.

The colonel didn't care if he really was the AG. He figured the president's poorly worded martial law declaration gave him all the authority he needed. Moreover, he intended to use it, especially if the person in question was a pain in the ass. Eventually, after demonstrating his authority, the colonel released them and provided an official pass for the rest of the trip.

When they arrived at Justice, Hauptmann's vile temper continued to overflow.

Not waiting for Neustein to open the door, Hauptmann threw it open and stormed up the steps as rapidly as his arthritic knees allowed. At his private elevator, he tore down the "closed" sign and shredded it, mashing his finger into the *Up* button again and again. Neustein caught up with him but stood back, letting his boss blow off steam.

The security guard in the lobby heard Hauptmann cursing and moved quickly to the private lobby entrance. When he recognized Hauptmann, he said, "Sir, the elevator isn't working. The generators get dragged offline when the motors start up. We can't use it."

Hauptmann spun on him.

"Get it working right now. I'll be damned if I'm going to walk up the friggin' stairs. We spent millions on generators for

these buildings. I don't believe for a second they don't work."
When the man hesitated, Hauptmann shouted, "Move!"

The guard pulled out his keys, opened the hidden door to the electrical panel and flipped the breakers.

Stepping back, he silently prayed as he gave Neustein a thumb's up. He had enough experience with the AG to know he shouldn't try to speak to the man directly. Once Hauptmann was angry, it could only be made worse.

The doors to the elevator opened and Hauptmann and Neustein stepped inside. Hauptmann continually jabbed at the *Close Doors* button and they eventually did. The instant the motor started, the lights went off, emergency illumination came on, and the elevator stopped.

Hautpman shouted, "Get these damned doors open, now."

Neustein tried to get his fingers between the doors to pry them open. Outside, the guard closed his eyes and silently cursed. Then he reopened the electrical closet and reset the breakers. The doors opened.

"You're fired, you stupid jackass," Hauptmann shouted as he and Neurstein walked to the stairwell in the corner of the marble-floored lobby.

CHAPTER
THIRTY-FIVE

2030 Zulu, 2 Nov
1530 Eastern Time
Justice Department, Washington, DC

In his office, Hauptmann sat in the luxurious chair behind the large oak desk he'd had installed. He took his perks seriously, including the well-stocked bar hidden in a bookcase in the corner nearest the desk. Behind him the damask curtains fluttered in the slight breeze. He'd opened the windows as soon as he'd entered. His nose wrinkled at the smell of burnt building materials that still hung over the city. After a few minutes, he rose and slammed the windows shut.

Just as he returned to his chair, Deputy Attorney General Doug Billingsley knocked, then walked into the office.

"Welcome back, Mr. Attorney General. How was Seattle?" Billingsley's smirk belied his almost jaunty tone.

"*How was Seattle*? You know damned well I never made it to Seattle."

"No, sir, I didn't expect you had. Just trying to lighten the mood. I do know you made it to, let's see, Orchard Park, along State Route 219. Also, East Aurora, on New York 400. Erie, or at least, the intersection of Interstates 90 and 79. And Salamanca, on I-86. After that, I lost track of you."

Hauptmann stared at him, opened his mouth to shout, then closed it again. Instead, he breathed heavily, staring at Billingsley's cold smile. Finally, he said, "If you knew I was trying to get back here, why didn't you help me?"

"Oh, sir, I thought you were doing fine by yourself." Billingsley stood with his arms crossed. He laughed briefly, then a hard stare replaced his smile. "Besides, the president made clear that *assistant* cabinet secretaries had no authority to challenge his ban on travel. I believe the threat to have someone shot for treason for interfering might have had something to do with that."

Billingsley sat without being asked. "A bit paranoid, that man. Apparently, he's concerned the Chinese sent a death squad to DC to assassinate him."

Hauptmann stared at him. Then, he asked, "Is he seeing any of the cabinet? Are any of the other members alive?"

Billingsley shrugged.

"Not many. Kingston's in Alaska. The Canadians told us he's alive. He'll fly out of Vancouver today. Right now, Phillips is acting, though no one's seen him since yesterday. SecDef Shackleton is dead. Wilson's acting for him. At least, he's pretending to." He looked up at the ceiling. Using his fingers, he enumerated. "Let's see, Northman at Homeland Security's dead, as is the Deputy. The Chief of Staff refused to act, so Admiral Threadman is it for now." He looked back down. "Although she was thrown out of the Sit Room a few days ago, so we're not entirely sure who's acting. Treasury's also dead with Tillghman acting. That's the big ones."

Hauptmann sighed and looked out the window. "Not a competent one in the bunch, of course. Our government is being run by a bunch of deep state bullshit artists whose sole claim to success is having climbed to the top of the shit pile."

Billingsley thought he could have dropped "deep state" then

stopped after the word "artists." That would certainly have applied to the situation before the attack. He stopped himself. Not that he cared if Hauptmann knew how he felt, but because it would gain nothing. Now with Hauptmann back in town, he had to at least pretend the man was in charge.

After a moment, Hauptmann continued. "Who's leading the investigation into how the hell this happened? It had to be treason."

Billingsley grimaced. "No, we're not investigating yet. I talked with the director of the FBI. We agreed to wait until the situation stabilized. We obviously want leaders, especially military leaders, focused on fighting back."

"You agreed to what?" Hauptmann shouted and half rose from his chair. Then he threw himself backward and nearly tipped it over as he landed. "What you mean is you gave the guilty parties time to come up with some lame excuse and coordinate their stories. I was right, not a competent one among the actings." He glared at Billingsley.

Billingsley shook his head. "You'd be surprised what happens when people involved in a conspiracy try to coordinate their stories. That's usually when they become so implausible, it's easy to rip them apart," he replied, voice steady and measured. "You can, of course, overrule me now that you're here. See for yourself if an investigation helps or hinders. I'll be happy to go back to keeping the routine stuff going. Not that there's much of *that* right now, since the country is pretty much shut down."

He stood. "I'll be in my office if you need me. Glad to have you back, sir."

He turned and walked toward the door.

Hauptmann fumed. As Billingsley reached for the door handle, he called out, "Wait. Wait just a damned minute."

Billingsley turned and cocked his head.

"Get back over here and sit down. I need to know exactly

what you said to the FBI, and what else is going on," Haupt-mann said.

Billingsley shrugged and returned to the chair. "All right, sir."

He'd already decided not to tell him about Hunter's order to arrest Admiral Threadman. He'd never passed the order on and had no intention of ever doing so. The federal government needed *one* person in leadership who wasn't crazy.

Hauptmann sat alone, nursing a scotch and staring out the window at the altered skyline.

Billingsley had talked for an hour. Nothing the FBI could point to indicated malfeasance on the part of anyone related to the attack. The intelligence agencies agreed.

Of course, they do. They were probably complicit.

He sipped, rolling the liquid around, enjoying the fire on his tongue.

There's no way the ChiComs could have done this without help.

But that was the rub: who and how?

He'd watched the other cabinet members for nearly two years, and competed with them for Travis Donnelly's attention. Watched as they tried to undercut each other to curry favor. He'd fought them at every turn and held them at bay. But the situation had changed. Some of those he considered the greatest threats were dead.

That's good, isn't it? They were in the way and the commies took them out for me. Accidentally, of course. But the results are what matters.

Hauptmann thought about who remained.

Hunter, of course. He'd always been the biggest threat. He had Donnelly's ear in the West Wing.

Next was Threadman. *That bitch.* He'd have to watch her. *No one that ugly could be dumb. God either gives them looks or brains, so she must have at least half a brain. Gotta get rid of her. Martial law allows the death penalty* . . . .

If no one with investigative power was willing to find those who'd sold out their country, he would. He was the only one left with the courage and the knowledge to act for the good of the nation. He would wield the power his God intended for him.

First, though, his president, his Leader, had obviously fouled up. Therefore, he must be judged and replaced.

The attorney general's job included monitoring the workings of the executive branch to uncover misconduct and deal with it swiftly. God had shown him Donnelly's failure and wanted him judged.

He would do just that.

CHAPTER
THIRTY-SIX

0705 Zulu, 4 Nov
0205 Eastern Time
State Department Building, Washington, DC

Secretary of State Herman Kingston rubbed his temples against the two-day headache that still plagued him. In a moment, he'd be back in his office, where it could only get worse.

Kingston had come to Donnelly's cabinet from business. The CEO of a textiles company, he'd diversified it into electronics, appliances, and furniture, all manufactured in third world countries. His task from the new president had been to shrink the State Department, get rid of career officials, and stay out of the limelight. Part of staying out of the limelight involved not "wasting time" traveling overseas or meeting with high-level foreign officials.

So Kingston met with the same business leaders as when he'd been a titan of industry, and went on hunting trips.

He'd been in Denali National Forest in Alaska during the attack. With his security detail unable to contact Foggy Bottom, he'd eaten supper and gone to sleep, planning to rise early and hunt moose.

However, his aide, keeping abreast of the news, had convinced him to return home.

But getting back to DC had proven difficult.

After hiking out, they'd managed to puddle jump through small airfields to Vancouver. Once there, Canadian officials had arranged a private jet back to DC.

Now, a week later, his vehicle approached the State Department building.

Kingston climbed wearily out of the Suburban and stretched broadly before he headed for his office.

"All right, someone bring me up to speed on this clusterfuck," he said to Todd McClusky, deputy assistant secretary of state for Asian affairs, the senior assistant secretary in the building.

McClusky had twenty-three years at State, and he'd learned to be skeptical of rumors. He chose to deal in facts and opinions based on facts. That hadn't made him popular with this administration, but he figured he'd outlast it and continue to make a difference in the inevitable next administration.

Now, he wasn't sure of anything.

For months he'd worried about how the Chinese viewed the president's behavior, so he'd kept his fingers on Beijing's pulse as closely as possible. But none of his contacts, even the highly placed ones in the State Council, had warned him of anything this drastic being contemplated. He now questioned everything he thought he understood about Chinese culture, the current government, and the men who controlled it, because nothing had led to this point.

"Well, Mr. Secretary . . . "

McClusky told him about the attack, the aftermath, and what the Chinese diplomats had been saying since. He also went into the Russian attack on NATO at great length, ending with the president's order to stay out of the war.

He'd contemplated mentioning the reports of US troops "defending" NATO forces but decided to leave that out until he determined where the secretary stood.

He also mentioned Phillips' sudden absence. He refrained from conjecture on why he'd disappeared, though the building roiled with speculation.

When he finished, Kingston leaned back in his chair and stared up at the ceiling for a long time.

"Well, that's just dandy," he said when he looked back down. "I told that stupid son of a bitch you can't push countries around like that, but did he listen? No. He figured they were just like the kiss-asses who've always worked for him: he could say or do whatever came to mind, and they'd take it because he was the American president. He literally told me to stay out of his business. Told me not to worry about foreign affairs, he'd handle it all. Well, here we are."

He looked at McClusky. "Is there any indication at all he knows how royally he fucked up?"

McClusky looked at Kingston's aide. "I, uh, that's not . . . ." He couldn't go on.

Kingston looked at him and snorted. "Don't worry about it. I won't hold it against you, and I won't repeat what you tell me. We both know Donnely's an arrogant bastard and an idiot. You all probably think I am, too, but at least in my corporate career, I didn't bully my foreign partners. *He* made his fortune bullying *everyone*. So tell me, please, please, that he realizes, finally, that he's clueless."

McClusky sighed. "No, sir, nothing's changed. There's a rumor, and I'm passing it on only because I have good reason to believe it's factual, that he tried to order a nuclear strike on China a few days ago."

Kingston sat bolt upright. "Obviously, it didn't happen. Did someone talk him out of it? SecDef?"

"No, Shackleton's dead. Wilson's acting."

Kingston grunted and ran his hands through his hair. "That weasel? I bet he's running scared. He wouldn't have the balls to talk his mother off a ledge."

McClusky bit his tongue. He still wasn't sure how much he should share, so he simply said, "Well, sir, I'm sure he's finding the situation a strain. We all are."

Kingston barked a laugh. "Yeah, well there are those who adapt quickly and the rest are left in the dust. What about the chairman of the Joint Chiefs, then?"

McClusky realized he should have walked the secretary through who was alive and who wasn't.

"Sir, the chairman is in the ICU at Bethesda. I don't know how he is. Last I heard he was critical. In any case, General Norton's acting."

Kingston's eyes narrowed and his face took on a grim frown. "Well, *he's* no patsy. I wonder if he did it. Hmmm . . . ."

He sat staring off into space for a few moments, long enough for McClusky to get uncomfortable. Suddenly, his eyes regained focus and he looked back. "Do you know what's going on militarily?"

"The Vietnamese told us about a destroyer in the South China Sea that's been kicking up dirt. They've told our embassy they're supporting it with food and fuel."

Kingston whistled. "Who'd have thought the Vietnamese would get in a stand-up slugging match? There must be some powerful motivation."

"Maybe they want back some of the land they lost in '79."

The secretary thoughtfully eyed him. "Did they lose much? Back then, I mean."

"Not a lot, but what they lost was good farmland, primarily occupied by ethnic Chinese. When the borders were formalized in the '90's, what few ethnic Vietnamese were left relocated farther south, away from the border. They've always feared being a vassal state."

Kingston nodded. "Well, we need to take advantage of it."

He rose and strode around the office.

McClusky thought he looked like a caged lion and involuntarily shivered. He'd never reacted to this secretary that way before and it unnerved him. In fact, he'd had little to do with this secretary at all since the man's confirmation. He hadn't seemed interested in hearing specifics about anything, or his job in general.

Maybe I've misjudged him. What he said about the president's guidance explains a lot. But how far can I trust him?

Silence reigned for minutes more. McClusky wondered if he should just leave. He was about to get up when Kingston returned to his desk and opened his laptop.

"It's Todd, right?"

McClusky nodded.

Kingston continued. "Todd, I need to talk with the acting chairman first thing in the morning. Stop trying to contact Phillips. He's out, and you're my new deputy, at least until the Senate gets around to confirming whatever new jackass the president foists on me." He looked at McClusky. "What?"

"Congress is, uh, out of session. Rather permanently, I'm afraid. At least, until we get a new election. You hadn't heard?"

"I heard a bit from the Canadians, but I had them focus on the international situation, not our government."

"Congress was in session during the strike. Seventeen representatives and three senators survived because they were out of town or not in the Capitol building. The president's martial law declaration didn't grant an exception for them to travel back. I'm surprised you made it."

"I had to, shall we say, overrule a couple of overzealous National Guardsmen at airfields along the way, but fortunately, they accepted the idea that perhaps the president's staff had made an error in drafting the declaration."

Kingston smiled, remembering the look on the face of one young captain. He'd known he'd convinced the captain to let them through when he'd suggested to the young man that the president's staff might be incompetent boobs. The captain had been taken aback, then a twinkle had appeared in his eye. He'd not only let them refuel and take off again but given them a written pass for the rest of the trip.

Kingston had enjoyed the interplay. He had always been pretty good at reading people and had found it no less useful during his short stint in government. "Well, Congress never did anything useful. Not for the past few years, anyway. In any case, you're it. Get hold of my assistant and get him back to work ASAP." Then, he blinked, asking, "What time is it?"

Checking his watch, McClusky answered, "It's just after two in the morning. Can it wait until six? I'm guessing you could use some sleep, too, sir."

McClusky had been driving those few people he could get into the building hard. Many had left less than an hour before the secretary's arrival.

"Okay, but I want a staff meeting first thing, say, seven o'clock. I want suggestions on our own diplomatic messaging, that sort of thing. What can we do to repair our relations with NATO? What can we leverage to get more Southeast Asian nations to come in with us?"

"Well, sir, that's exactly what we've been working on. With Phillips out, however, no one in the White House will take my calls. He's an excuse for ignoring us."

Kingston replied, "Good. I'm done being window dressing. It's time I earned my pay."

McClusky felt slightly energized. Perhaps this secretary would be all right, once he had a chance to act like one.

CHAPTER
THIRTY-SEVEN

2100 Zulu, 5 Nov
1600 Eastern Time
The Pentagon, Washington, DC

General Norton received the secretary's meeting request, hand-carried by a State Department courier. He'd let her know he had no intention of kowtowing to a political toady or to go running when called.

However, the note itself was polite to a fault. It suggested that the secretary come to Norton's office. It made him wary.

Norton had had little use for the secretary. The man constantly traveled at the taxpayer's expense, normal under other circumstances. But this SecState's trips always seemed built around events that smacked of vacation and leisure. And they rarely included meetings with foreign political leaders.

By statute, Kingston was fourth in succession. Given the deaths of the vice president, speaker of the House, and president pro tem of the Senate, now he was next. If he'd been energetic enough to get back from wherever he'd been, maybe he'd be active in the post-attack American government. But Norton didn't know what that role might be or how useful. So, he agreed to meet and see if he could gauge him.

He greeted Kingston at the door. "Welcome, Mr. Secretary. I would have come to you, sir. But I appreciate the chance to talk and still be close to my temporary command center."

They shook hands and Norton waved him toward the sofa he'd had moved in just for this meeting.

"Thank you, General, I'm happy you're willing to meet with me."

Kingston sat first and Norton followed. When they were settled, Kingston surprised him by diving right down to business.

"General, I'm not going to pussyfoot around here. It's pretty obvious the president's nuclear attack hasn't happened. I need to know if it's *going* to happen. Obviously, if it does, that will have, shall we say, enormous consequences internationally. I need to be able to react."

Norton pulled his head back and examined Kingston's face. "Well, sir, you don't mince words. From State, that's refreshing." He smiled, but his eyes remained cold. "No, sir, there's been no strike. We can't carry one out right now even if I wanted to. We have to replace the codes."

Kingston sat back, a look of relief sweeping his face. Silence lingered. Kingston broke it. "Thank you for your honesty. You said *even if I wanted to.*" Seeing Norton bristle, he raised his hand. "Don't worry, General, I'm not suggesting anything nefarious. Nor am I putting words in your mouth. But if that was your way of throwing bait out to see what I really think, I'll take it."

He took a breath. "We cannot use nuclear weapons because I know what the fallout would be, no pun intended." He paused briefly. "Look, in my previous life, I did a great deal of business with foreign partners. So I've always paid attention to international relations. I'm not the neophyte that idiot in the White House made me seem. He told me to stay out of foreign affairs, he'd handle it all." Kingston snorted. "Clearly, he handled it superbly, the moron."

Norton sat quietly and listened. He found Kingston's candor refreshing. At the same time, it raised red flags. How open would he be with others, people with whom he ought to be more guarded? He'd have to be careful. "Well, Mr. Secretary, I take my orders from the president. It would be treasonous for me to disobey."

Kingston sparked a laugh and shook his head. "I'm not suggesting you're involved in treason. But it may surprise you to know I'm familiar with the concept of an illegal order. I also know that though he demanded one, you have *not* taken an oath of loyalty to him." He twirled his college ring on his finger before looking back up. "Cabinet secretaries also take an oath to the Constitution, General. Some of us took it seriously. Unfortunately, too many took that oath to *him* seriously. Many of those are dead, of course . . . "

Norton stayed silent, hoping Kingston would continue.

"But I don't intend to let him destroy our nation," Kingston finished. He took a deep breath and smoothed his trousers. "You should know that I had an agreement with the secretary of defense." Kingston frowned for a moment. "I'm certain the acting secretary doesn't know about it. The chairman was also part of our agreement. However, I understand he's in the Bethesda ICU, in a coma?"

Norton pursed his lips. He needed more. "What kind of agreement would that be, Mr. Secretary?"

Kingston didn't hesitate. As he said it, he stared directly into Norton's eyes. "That if this president ever ordered a nuclear attack, the order would not be carried out until all three of us had conferred and agreed. It didn't cover existential threats that called for retaliation. As I understand the current situation, the Chinese have specifically *denied* being an existential threat and have worked hard to prove it."

Norton sat back. "Well, Mr. Secretary, that jibes with what

Hopalong Cassidy told me the other day. He's not in a coma. He needs to stay in intensive care, but he's conscious and coherent. I've also brought Admiral Bing in since he controls the strategic nuclear force. We have control of all those forces. And we've made sure the president can't go around us."

Kingston smiled. "I'm glad we understand each other. I also get why you forced me to come out with it instead of admitting you already knew. You don't trust me. Given all the water under the bridge, well, I'd be surprised if it'd been any other way." He slapped his hands on his knees and said, "Tell me then, how goes the war?"

Norton hesitated. He'd been a young lieutenant colonel during the invasion of Iraq in 2003. From his seat in the Time Sensitive Targeting Cell in the Combined Air Operations Center, he'd seen firsthand the disruption created by a micromanaging secretary of defense. That meddling had directly led to the post-conflict security disaster that had pocked the Iraqi landscape and extended the war.

Kingston saw the concern in his face. "Don't worry, General, I won't get into your knickers. You have your area of expertise, I have mine. Let's help each other, first by not interfering with each other."

Norton nodded. "Well, Mr. Secretary, we're doing the best we can. We have two carrier strike groups moving into the western Pacific, and one coming from the Indian Ocean. The JTF commander is Commander Seventh Fleet aboard *Blue Ridge*. I'm letting her fight the best way she knows how."

"Her? The Seventh Fleet commander is a woman? Is she, well, is she aggressive enough? I've rarely seen a woman aggressive enough in business. Pretty sure that's worse in a military context."

Norton sighed deeply. After a few seconds, he said, "She wouldn't be in command of a forward deployed fleet if she weren't. She's already engaged an enemy submarine force and killed most of them. She's as aggressive as anyone could ask for." He smiled coldly. "We've found that women in command are just as good as the men, sir."

Kingston seemed taken aback by Norton's fervor but recovered quickly. "I meant no disrespect, General. Merely that my observations are that women don't have the killer instinct. Perhaps you're able to train it into them."

"Actually, sir, I suspect it's that we give them the freedom to fully exercise their talents."

Kingston looked ready to rebut, so Norton quickly waved him off. "Sir, that's neither here nor there. You want to chat about that over a beer someday, we can. Meantime, the Vietnamese are a godsend. I think we're doing well, given our losses."

Kingston dismissively waved his hand. "I wasn't suggesting you weren't." His demeanor suggested he wasn't certain, however. "But it would be easier, would it not, if you had more resources?"

Norton shrugged. "We're moving ships and aircraft as quickly as possible to the theater. We *were* moving a four-ship surface action group through the Red Sea, but someone laid mines. Sixth Fleet identified a Chinese merchant that they were pretty sure was the culprit. I hope it was, anyway."

He paused, and Kingston obliged him. "Why is that, General?"

"Because we sank the son of a bitch, Mr. Secretary. The CO of one of our recommissioned frigates put two Harpoon missiles into it, all on her own authority. Sufficiently aggressive, don't you think?"

Kingston grimaced. "I guess you're right."

Norton bowed his head slightly. He finished his not-quite-detailed report.

"Finally, the *TR* sank the Chinese counter-piracy ships in the Indian Ocean."

Kingston looked alarmed. "Is that legal? Can you sink ships not in the war area, if they haven't done anything?"

Norton smiled.

"Mr. Secretary, *every* Chinese warship is an enemy, no matter where they are. Those were warships. Our rules of engagement allow us to destroy any ship or aircraft that is positively identified as belonging to the PRC."

Kingston queried further. "Does that include merchantmen, I mean ones that haven't been identified as making attacks, like the one your frigate sank?"

"Yes. Every Chinese merchant contributes to the war effort through trade. Thus, every ship is a valid target." Norton's eyes held a predatory gleam. "Welcome to war, Mr. Secretary. During World War II, we brought our enemies to their knees in part by destroying their merchant marine and making sure they couldn't move cargo by sea. In my opinion, if we as a nation had girded our loins and fought an all-out war against the Taliban and Al Qaeda, we'd be far better off than we are now, they'd be far worse off than they are, and it wouldn't have taken so long." He paused. "But we fight the way civilians tell us to. So, even when it makes sense to do something different, we follow *legal* orders."

He paused and looked directly into Kingston's eyes. "But, if civilian leadership is wise, it will at least listen to and seriously consider our advice. After all, we've studied the conduct of war for all our careers. That includes the utility and impact of politics and diplomacy." He leaned back on the sofa. "On the other hand, I've rarely known a diplomat who'd studied the conduct of war." He tilted his head as he finished.

Kingston opened and then closed his mouth.

CHAPTER
THIRTY-EIGHT

0900 Zulu, 7 Nov
1600 Local Time
USS *Nicholas*, South China Sea

Bill wished he'd gone over to the Vietnamese flagship. He wouldn't have minded a small glass of brandy right about now. He and Tran sat in Bill's in-port cabin.

Rather more quickly than anyone had anticipated or desired, relations between China and Vietnam had come to a head. Tran had sought out *Nicholas* to work out a plan for the coming fight.

"Their dispatch of three ships to hunt you surprised us. They must have more information than we gave them credit for," Tran was saying. "In their exercises, they do not react without having complete intelligence."

It had only been thirty hours since *Nicholas* had destroyed the supply ship. Both Vietnamese intelligence and Bill's own cryptologic systems said it hadn't been able to report the attack. So they'd only expected increased Chinese reconnaissance flights while the enemy figured out what had happened.

Tran seemed less concerned than Bill.

"The flotilla appears to be combing the waters along the

coast. During the day, they use helicopters to increase the area they can search without using radar."

"Yes, sir, but that's not normal. Even accounting for the old adage that 'the Book goes over the side when the first bullet flies', if I were them, I'd keep my more powerful surface ships in the north to defend against our subs and wait for the carriers. I definitely wouldn't risk them down here. Especially with one of our attack boats running loose."

"Commander, they know how capable you and your ship are. They have told the world they achieved their objectives. One of those is control of the East Sea. *Your* presence here contradicts them. *Your* presence, combined with the battle group that is coming, are what encouraged my government to take action. You are the proverbial thorn in their side, and they must act. It is unlikely they know yet about your submarine."

Bill shook his head. "But we haven't done all that much—"

Tran laughed. "Not done much? Come, come. You sank a frigate on the first day of the war. You seriously damaged their land base. I am certain they suspect you had something to do with their missing submarine. And you destroyed their supply ship. And may I remind you, we still do not know *why* that ship was here nor where he was headed." He shook his head. "No, Commander, they honor you. They fear you."

Up until yesterday, only a few maritime reconnaissance aircraft patrolled the area. Now there were multiple flights daily.

"I could do with a bit less honor, then." He stood and looked out his porthole. Whitecaps flecked the sea. The wind had picked up and visibility had shrunk to less than five miles in haze. "Hiding from aircraft is now virtually impossible during the day."

He turned back to Tran. "They'll be here tomorrow afternoon or evening. We'll have to take them on, but in a stand-up fight against three *Luyangs*, I'll get beat. My only hope is to catch them by surprise. If they know where I am, I can't do that."

Tran said, "It would not do for the enemy to have destroyers hidden in the shipping outside the Singapore Strait when your strike group arrives."

Bill agreed. International law allowed the group to operate aircraft in the strait. But the carrier had to be able to maneuver or go very fast to launch fixed-wing aircraft. They could do neither in the cramped and crowded waters. Sending helicopters alone to tangle with three destroyers would be a suicide mission. If they sent the escorts through by themselves, the Chinese could engage them one at a time as they exited the strait.

Tran seemed to read his mind. "Captain, I am confident we will be able to help you, even fight, by the time we intercept the enemy."

Bill shook his head.

"Sir, I know you mean well. But I can't count on it, especially when your headquarters keeps telling you to wait. Besides, if we base the plan on you not being able to help, it'll be that much easier if you can." He smiled though his heart wasn't in it.

He hadn't slept much last night. The *Luyang*s were the newest guided-missile destroyers in the Chinese fleet, armed with their newest missiles. He'd have to hit them quickly and hard to knock them out. If he didn't, it would be a bad day for *Nicholas* - a very bad day, indeed.

He wondered why he even considered engaging them alone. But he saw no way around it.

"I think the plan we have now is the best we're going to put together. But it has to be executed violently and fast, and that means you must have physical separation from *Nicholas*. It won't be helpful if I accidentally hit one of your ships."

Tran laughed lightly. "No, Captain, nor would it help me or the men under my command." He leaned forward. "But all jesting aside, we will not be in your way. And with luck, we will provide more assistance than we currently have planned."

The two men talked for another hour. By the end, they were exchanging stories of their families and careers. When Tran left, Bill missed having him aboard.

As midnight crawled by, *Nicholas* cruised due west at a leisurely thirteen knots through a wine dark sea.

The moon had set, so she stayed close to the normal shipping lane that ran from Singapore to Cebu in the Philippines. They'd rigged extra lights topside to make them look somewhat like a cargo carrier. A totally dark ship moving along a shipping lane would be suspicious. Unfortunately, there was only so much they could do to not look like a destroyer.

The ship would go to General Quarters in fifteen minutes. Bill stood on the bridge. Pettibone was TAO in CIC.

Thirty miles ahead and to the south-southwest, the Vietnamese flotilla executed their part of the plan, radiating all their radars and steaming northward toward the enemy. Commodore Tran would steam a dozen miles west of the Chinese ships and pass targeting data to *Nicholas*. If they were fortunate, the enemy would be too distracted by the Vietnamese to notice as *Nicholas* approached.

Just as she had done with *Chong Lunj*, *Nicholas* would then close to within visual range and launch SM-2 missiles to kill the enemy's radars and radios. The surprise might keep the *Luyang*s from launching missiles in return, or at least slow their reactions. *Nicholas* would wait until the Vietnamese were well past to give them plausible deniability.

Bill had no illusions about whether Tran would be able to engage the Chinese themselves. He thought it very unlikely.

"Request permission to relieve the officer of the deck, sir." The voice came from the dark, Barrister's voice.

"Permission granted, Nav. Up early for GQ?"

"Yes, sir. Thought I'd get a good turnover, let the watch settle down. Besides, sir, Bob can get down to DC Central and get set up, too."

Bill listened as she took the watch from Lieutenant Johnson. Tradition had it that the OOD should be the last position on the bridge to turn over. Bill applauded her initiative to violate the inviolate. Within the next few minutes, all the watch standers were turned over.

He smiled to himself.

"Well, sir, will they help us out tonight?" queried Barrister's disembodied voice.

"I don't know, Nav. I'd like to think so. If it were up to Commodore Tran, he'd shoot missiles right along with us. But it's hard for their government to commit. They've got a lot to lose, and we don't have the resources we once had. If we pull this off tonight, though, it'll certainly help."

"I'm sure we'll pull it off, sir. If nothing else, tradition says we have to, right? *He who will not risk, cannot win,* and all that. Besides, how can we let those guys from World War II down?"

The voice sounded like a smile.

"Oh, we won't, Nav. In fact, if you believe in ghosts, I'd expect some of those guys are aboard now, helping us out."

"Okay, sir, that's not gonna help anybody relax. We're sailors, after all. We're superstitious as hell." Now, she laughed.

"Nav, surely you've heard of Casper the Friendly Ghost?"

They continued their patter and the tension on the bridge eased.

After a few more minutes, he went below. Time for him to get ready, too.

CHAPTER
THIRTY-NINE

1805 Zulu, 7 Nov
0105 Local Time, 8 Nov
USS *Nicholas*, South China Sea

"Sir, gun control reports several fishing boats twenty-five degrees off the starboard bow."

Bill's blood pressure shot up at the first four words. He took a deep breath, then laughed at himself. They'd seen dozens of fishing boats and small coastal merchants all day.

"Very well. What's the range to the enemy?"

"Just a second, sir, Vietnamese are reporting now. Should be about fifteen, maybe eighteen miles."

Bill turned up the volume on his right-side headphone and listened in, though he couldn't understand a thing. A few minutes later, Operations Specialist First Class Vuong, the son of a Vietnamese refugee, came across his left headphone.

"Sir, Alpha Six reports lead ship of the enemy SAG bears one five three degrees true, seven decimal nine nautical miles from them. That makes the bearing and range from us two four nine, eighteen nautical miles."

"Based on that, sir, we ought to see them pretty soon. Recommend we change course, just a bit southerly, sir."

"Go ahead." *We're committed now,* Bill thought.

"TAO, Gun Control. I have a possible target, bearing two four six decimal five, range estimated at thirty-four thousand yards."

Seventeen nautical miles. Bill closed his eyes and clamped his teeth together.

"Gun Control, TAO, confirm this is one of our targets?" Pettibone asked.

An agonizing minute passed.

"Sir, I can't be for sure, but I'd bet a week's pay on it. They're showing no lights. There's some fishing boats the other side of 'em . . . makes their silhouette easier to see."

Bill smiled weakly. His blood pressure hadn't returned entirely to normal and now it soared again. Sweat broke out on the back of his neck. He looked at the set faces around him. It might be his imagination, but they looked pale. CIC fell quieter than ever before. Even the phone talkers, who usually carried on whispered conversations through their phones, quietly watched the displays.

This battle would be different. Up to now, they'd had the advantage in firepower. Not this time.

Pettibone turned to Bill. "Sir, request permission to target the contact."

Bill nodded, not trusting his voice.

They waited. They had to make sure all three enemy ships were in sight before they attacked.

It didn't take long before the second and third ships heaved into view. While they waited, silence reigned in CIC. The closer the lead ship got to *Nicholas,* the more likely the enemy would figure out she wasn't a merchant.

"TAO, EW. I've got a radar just came up on the same bearing as the lead ship, two four one. It's a commercial surface search, but it's the same kind we've seen on Chinese warships, sir."

"SWC, TAO, engage all three targets."

Bill leaned forward, willing the missiles out of their launcher cells.

There could only be one reason the Chinese had turned on their surface search radars: they were suspicious.

"TAO, what's the del—?" Bill started to ask, but the first two missiles roaring out of their cells interrupted him. Two more quickly followed, then the final two.

But were they in time?

"TAO, Bridge. Missile launch, broad off the port bow. Multiple missiles."

A pause, then, "More launches from a second target."

Dammit!

Pettibone brought the rest of the Aegis system online. The CIWS had been in Standby and came to Auto quickly. The rest of the combat system would take a minute or so.

Reports flew across internal voice nets. It would be close, very close.

The five-inch gun forward spoke, banging out a round every three seconds. Bill pounded his fist on his thigh.

The *Luyang* destroyers carried YJ-83 advanced subsonic anti-ship missiles. From launch, they would quickly reach maximum speed, leaving very little time for *Nicholas* to respond. The EW operator had launched chaff and begun jamming as soon as he'd heard the bridge call missile launch.

Once the Aegis system came online, its automatic defense doctrine would take over. But it was taking too long. The supersonic SM-2s would quickly kill the archers. But the return fire was already in flight.

Nicholas accelerated rapidly and turned, heeling sharply to starboard as the OOD changed course to two three five, directly at the enemy.

These were pre-planned actions, plotted well in advance to counter as many possibilities as they'd come up with. So far, they'd been executed smoothly. But it would've been much better if they hadn't had to exercise them at all.

More missiles finally left their cells. This time they were Evolved Sea Sparrow Missiles. They were shorter range, but allowed *Nicholas* to save her SM-2s.

He heaved a short sigh. Nothing more to be done. The gun still pounded out rounds. More decoys were launched. The EW called for reloading the chaff launchers.

Then came the sound he'd dreaded and feared.

The *brrrrrp* as the CIWS fired.

Seconds later he heard and felt a powerful wallop as the CIWS target exploded close aboard. The clatter and bangs as debris hit the ship.

The CIWS barely paused before it engaged another inbound.

All the while, more missiles left their VLS cells. More shrapnel hit his ship.

"Sir, we lost comms with the bridge."

Bill pulled off his headphones and whirled around.

"What do you mean?" he demanded.

The CIC watch supervisor's face blanched and he stammered. "The phone talker w-w-went off su-suddenly, mid-sentence. We tried phone and intercom. Nothing, sir." His voice faltered.

In the background, the gun paused for a moment, then began again. Two more missiles roared away. Pettibone interrupted.

"Sir, we killed eight inbounds, decoyed two. Gun and CIWS got three. Gun camera reports all three enemy burning, but I want to make sure they can't hit us anymore." He paused to listen to something. His eyes went wide.

"Sir, they split their missile launches between us and the Vietnamese."

He paused again, listening to something else. "Signal bridge says our bridge got hit, sir—"

Pettibone abruptly turned back to his screen. "SWC, TAO, take with birds." Turning back to Bill, he said, "Gun Control says the leftmost target opened fire with its gun."

Bill's heart tried to beat its way out of his chest. "You know what to do, Andy. Kill them."

He turned to the CICWO. "Get comms with after-steering and drive from here. You have the conn. I'm going to the bridge."

He unbuckled, swiveled out of his seat, and hurried out of CIC. His journey through the passages and up the ladders was made more difficult as the ship slewed back and forth to confuse the enemy gunfire solution. At one point, his uniform shirt snagged on a fire station, tearing a wide hole.

Over the 1MC, Bonnet's shaky voice announced, "Executive Officer, your presence is requested in after-steering. Request you contact CIC first."

Why isn't Joanna on the bridge? he thought as he ran.

CHAPTER
FORTY

1812 Zulu, 7 Nov
0112 Local Time, 8 Nov
USS *Nicholas*, South China Sea

Bill ran into the damage control party one deck below the bridge. Seeing him, the team leader called out, "Make a hole."

Despite their bulky gear, the team backed up and pressed themselves to the bulkheads to let him through.

At least there's no fire up there, Bill thought as he hurried up the ladder.

The scene that greeted him resembled a page from a World War II picture book.

Wires and cables hung from the overhead. Broken glass littered the deck, and shredded metal was strewn everywhere. The eerie red light from the emergency battle lanterns splayed over the wreckage. But it was the smell that hit hardest. The stench of burned insulation and electronics mingled with that of hot steel and scorched paint.

Wind blew through several holes in the port side bulkhead, one large enough for a man to climb through.

Doc Wells and the corpsmen, as well as the stretcher bearers from Repair 8, huddled over figures lying prone on the deck.

Bill moved toward them. BM1 Lenz appeared, holding a bloody rag over the left side of his face.

"What happened, Boats?" Bill asked.

Lenz looked at him for a moment, then blinked and shook his head. "I dunno, sir, not really. CIWS started firing then I heard this big bang. Next thing, I'm on deck on the other side of the bridge, feeling like half my face is missing."

"Captain, I need you over here, sir."

Doc crouched near another of the wounded. Bill rushed over, nearly tripping over a piece of the helm console, torn and bent outward.

"What is it, Doc—"

Barrister lay in a pool of blood, propped against the bulkhead. His stomach heaved at the long narrow chunk of metal that protruded from her right side. Her face twisted in pain.

Unable to speak, he tried and failed to absorb the scene. Then, his eyes welled up. "How are you, Nav?" He cursed his stupidity.

"Been better, sir," she said, then coughed. "I think I screwed up." Foamy blood dribbled down the side of her face.

"Doc, you need to get her out of here," he said, standing up.

Doc shook his head. "I can't move her, sir. The other end of that metal bar's embedded in the bulkhead."

Bill stared at him. It didn't make sense. Then, it suddenly did. Ice spread through his body.

"Can the repair team pull it out?"

"They'll try, sir, but it'll make it worse. Though I'm not sure how. Her lung's punctured, and I can't get at it."

He looked Bill carefully in the eye, made sure he had full eye contact, then slowly, hesitantly, shook his head.

Bill's head reeled. Closing his eyes, he knelt back down. "It's okay, Nav, you did fine. We're still here."

He became aware of the absence of sounds: the gun had

stopped firing and missiles no longer flew. "Sounds like we got 'em."

She coughed again, trying to breathe, to speak. "Good thing, sir. Can't afford to take any more hits."

Her voice faded, trailing off into nothing.

"We're tough, Nav. Nav?"

She was gone.

Bill stood up, willing the tears in his eyes to vanish. There were others, dead, dying, badly wounded. *No time to grieve.*

"Doc, how many others?"

"Two more dead, sir. LTJG Houseman was on the port bridge wing when we got hit. Seaman Jastrow, too. A piece of what hit us cut him in half. Isn't pretty, sir."

Bill swallowed bile flooding his throat. "Will the wounded make it?"

Doc shrugged. "I don't know, sir. I'll do what I can, but we need to get them off ASAP. I don't have enough blood plasma. Most are gonna need surgery to remove shrapnel. I'll get most of it, but there might be some I can't. I wish I could promise, sir, but I can't." He shook his head. "My first job's to make sure XO doesn't lose her hand."

Doc's face was set, but his eyes threatened to spill over.

Bill automatically reached out and squeezed his shoulder. "I know you'll do your best. They have the best care there is, Doc. I'll get out of your way."

Bill turned, unsteady on his feet. He willed himself to walk to the door and head back down to Combat. Just before he closed the watertight door, he added, "And let me know as soon as you can about the XO."

From there he had the word passed for the chief engineer.

"CHENG, we need to find a way to get the bridge back up, at least enough to steer from."

Only silence came from the other end of the phone. Lieutenant Orlando Martinez, the chief engineer, always paused to think before answering.

"Landy, can you do it?" Bill asked.

Finally, "Well, sir, I don't know. The report from the repair locker leader's pretty bad. I'll get my guys up there and take a close look. But we can't make new parts, and if it's as bad tore up as it sounds, well, I just don't know."

"Give it your best shot. If we can't steer from there, we might just be out of the war. And right now, we're the only ones *in* the war, at least, hereabouts."

He hung up.

Pettibone demanded his attention. "Sir, two of the targets are dead in the water, burning. I don't think they're a threat. But the western target's still underway. She's withdrawing at nine knots. I don't know how badly she's hurt, and I don't know if she'll be able to call for help. They're out of gun range. Request permission to close and sink her. We can put a fish into the other two, to finish them off."

The blaze in Pettibone's eyes worried Bill. He took a deep breath.

"All right, CSO, close the moving target. Sink him. Leave the others alone. We may need the torps for other targets." Another breath.

"After that—" Bill shook himself, then finished. "We accomplished our mission. They're finished as a fighting force, and we're hurt. We need to lick our wounds. Get hold of the XO—" Then he remembered.

Bill put his head down in his hands, raised it up again. He couldn't show weakness here in Combat, not with his crew watching. He counted on Joanna. He had no bench to fill holes. The XO would be a big hole.

"All right, CSO. You're acting XO, effective immediately. Tell Ops I'll want him on the bridge as GQ OOD. I want you down here. Got it?"

"Aye aye, sir. What's up with Nav?"

He looked at him, unable to say it. "I'm headed for the wardroom."

The bright surgical light that hung over the table lit the wardroom stark white. Beneath it, Doc sutured a wound. Bill covered his mouth and nose with the t-shirt from under his uniform blouse.

Doc looked up. "Whatcha need, sir?"

"XO?"

Doc waved a forceps toward the door. "She's in the navigator's stateroom."

Bill retreated to the passageway. He took three steps to the next door. He gently fingered the name plate.

Barrister and Houseman, both dead. His dead.

Steeling himself, he knocked then entered.

The XO lay asleep in the lower bunk. One of the mess attendants put another blanket over her as he walked in. A junior seaman, she was assigned as a stretcher bearer and had helped move Irving from the operating table to the stateroom.

"How is she, Seaman Myers?"

Myers looked down at the XO, then back up at Bill. "She's, uh, she'll be okay, 'cording to Doc. She almost lost a hand, though, sir. He sewed it —" Her voice broke.

"It's alright, Myers. She'll be alright. That's good, isn't it?"

Myers nodded.

"I've got to get back to CIC. Take a minute, then get back and help Doc."

He left quickly.

CHAPTER
FORTY-ONE

1824 Zulu, 7 Nov
0124 Local Time, 8 Nov
USS *Nicholas*, South China Sea

Nicholas closed the wounded enemy as it tried to slink away.

They kept their speed down since they had to steer by remote. The rudder commands went via sound-powered phone from CIC. No one there could see where they were going.

Sitting in his chair in CIC was no good. Barrister's face haunted him.

"Shit." Pettibone's curse stabbed through his mental haze.

"What's going on?"

"EW reports missile seekers. Looks like the Vietnamese fired on the Chinese again, sir."

"Did they hit?"

It took a long while for Pettibone to answer. "Waiting for gun control to report, sir."

Bill looked at him. His face was ashen, his eyes downcast.

"What's up, CSO? You look like you've seen a ghost."

"Nothing, sir. Just, uh, tired. Relieved the Vietnamese are with us, though."

He smiled weakly but it quickly vanished.

ENS Bonnet stood behind Bill and tapped him on the shoulder before she whispered in his ear. "Sir, we got word down here about the casualties just before you came in. Mr. Pettibone took it pretty hard, sir."

Bill suddenly understood.

"I'll be fine, sir," Pettibone said in a low voice.

"I know you will, Andy. I also know it hurts."

Pettibone lowered his head and closed his eyes. After a moment, he whispered, "I lost them, sir. It was my job to protect them. I lost them." He leaned back and raised his head, but kept his eyes glued to the displays.

Bill reached over and touched his arm. "You didn't lose them, Andy. The enemy took them, right out of our hands. If anyone lost them, I did."

"TAO, Gun Control. Explosions on the moving target, sir. More on the two that's DIW. Wait one—" An interminable pause.

"Son of a bitch. Closest target just disappeared, sir. Massive secondary."

Bill reached to respond when he heard a *whump* and felt the ship jiggle.

The shockwave.

The two remaining enemy ships sank, one just before 0300 and the other at sunrise. *Nicholas* moved off while two small merchants and three fishing boats rescued survivors. When they rendezvoused with the Vietnamese, Commodore Tran's ship still fought a large fire amidships.

0645 Local Time, 8 Nov

Bill took the RHIB over to Tran's ship. With assistance from the surviving Vietnamese ship and *Nicholas*, the fire was out and flooding under control.

Once aboard they escorted him to sickbay. The foul odors of

burnt electrical insulation, paint, and metal assaulted him, plunging him into renewed sorrow. In the sick bay, Commodore Tran lay in a cot, his left arm and head swathed in large bandages.

"Congratulations, Captain. You single handedly defeated three of China's best destroyers."

Bill blinked and his head jerked backward. "No, sir, we did it together. I got a few hits, but you finished them off. Thank you."

"Do not thank me. The enemy made it easy. They attacked me." He winced. "I must say, my crews executed their responsibilities well. I am proud of them. However, this ship and I are out of the war."

Bill licked his lips. He didn't want to ask but couldn't avoid it. "How bad is it, sir?"

"Bad enough. My doctor tells me I will lose my arm. And we have lost what you call your CIC. I have issued orders to the captain of *Da Nang*. He will be at your command."

Bill stared. Both the severity of Tran's wound and the easy way in which he described it shocked him.

He shook his head. "My ship's also out of action, sir. Our bridge took a hit and we need to at least be able to steer from there before I fight again."

Tran looked at him calmly. "Then I wish you the best, Captain. I will see if our shipyard at Cam Ranh Bay can help."

He groaned and shifted in the cot. Bill reached out to his good hand. Tran continued. "Do not be concerned. Between our two nations, we will defeat the enemy. Now, I will ask that you take your leave. Your ship needs you, and I must begin my journey home."

Bill took his leave. He would be eternally grateful for the sacrifice Tran had personally made and for their alliance.

CHAPTER
FORTY-TWO

1553 Zulu, 8 Nov
0053 Local Time, 9 Nov
USS *Blue Ridge*, **Western Pacific, south of Japan**

Aboard *Blue Ridge* everyone not on the mid-watch was supposed to be resting. Admiral Simpson had been adamant: she didn't want her staff wearing themselves out trying to be superhuman. She'd seen before the unspoken competition to see who could get the least amount of sleep and still be semi-functional. The problem was just that: they were only semi-functional. And she would not tolerate it.

So when LCDR Jason Hillerman, the current battle watch captain, called her stateroom, he expected a sleepy response. Instead, she sounded fully awake.

"Admiral, it's zero zero fifty-three. We just got a report from the embassy in Hanoi. *Nicholas* engaged in a surface action off the southern coast of Vietnam about twenty-four hours ago. I made sure it's in your inbox if you want to see it, ma'am."

"I'll look at it later. Why don't you give me the highlights now?"

"*Nicholas* and three Vietnamese combatants took on three Chinese DDGs. *Nicholas* took a hit, but she's still able to fight. The Vietnamese lost one corvette sunk and a frigate damaged. The frigate returned to port. That's how we got the CO's report. The surviving corvette remained in company with *Nicholas*. It also says the Vietnamese will let *Nicholas* pull into Cam Rahn Bay for repairs."

"How badly damaged is she? What kind of casualties?"

"Three dead, seven wounded, ma'am. The bodies and four of the wounded went ashore with the frigate, to the military hospital in Ho Chi Minh City. The CO said they'd jury rigged the bridge so they could handle the ship from there. He says they're fully mission capable, though he'll need to re-arm as soon as they join up with *Roosevelt*."

"So the Vietnamese are in this. That's great news. Is that all?"

He scanned his computer screen. "That's the important parts, ma'am. It's a standard SITREP, so there's more on equipment status, etc., but nothing that can't wait til morning."

She thanked him and hung up.

Hope she gets some sleep tonight. I'd hate to have to report her for violating her own orders. He smiled to himself, then re-focused on the watch. She hadn't said it, but their new ally probably made her just as happy as did *Nicholas's* survival.

A hundred miles west, USS *Goldsborough* (DDG-160) steamed slowly southwest ahead of the core of Seventh Fleet's strike force.

The group was spread out to make it harder for the Chinese. Carrier *Ronald Reagan* and command ship *Blue Ridge* were separated by nearly fifty miles. Communications were relayed by an LCS stationed halfway between them using very low power UHF radio. There were two screens around the high value units. The closest in formed a ring of anti-air warfare ships, including three Aegis cruisers and two Aegis destroyers. The farther out consisted of a cordon of Aegis destroyers, two Japanese frigates, and another LCS, all to defend against submarines. At this range from the Chinese mainland, submarines constituted the greatest threat.

Aboard *Goldborough*, the Anti-Submarine Warfare Evaluator reported to the TAO, "Ma'am, we've got something on the tail, broad on the port bow. Range is between fifty and sixty thousand yards. Not sure what it is. Nothing solid enough to call a contact, but this is the third time Sonar's reported something there."

The TAO drummed her fingers on her console. She'd never entirely trusted sonar. School had taught her the basics of sound propagation through the water column, but even now as a department head, she still believed it to be PFM – Pure Fucking Magic. It sometimes worked, though.

"Can they give me anything solid? Something I can tell the CO without sounding like a voodoo practitioner?"

She looked over at the ASWE as he sat at his console. Shoulders hunched and bent forward, he stared intently at his screen. "No, ma'am, I can't, I mean, they say they can't. The conditions are right for a deep sound channel, so in theory we could get something at that range. I mean, if it's putting enough sound in the water."

His voice faded out. He'd been onboard for two years but had just moved from Engineering to Combat Systems. He'd only recently qualified ASWE. Moreover, his self-confidence was mediocre at best.

She sighed heavily. "Very well. Continue to monitor it. I'll call the captain."

She saw him wince, but she'd prefer to call the captain for nothing. They couldn't risk it being Something.

Thirty minutes later, a helicopter lifted off their deck and moved out ahead of the ship to investigate.

As the helo reached the closest range Sonar had estimated, it dropped sonobuoys, the objective to confirm or deny the possible contact's existence.

The captain was in Combat now, seated next to the TAO, with the ASW picture dialed up. They waited as the helo repositioned out to the furthest estimated range and dropped another sonobuoy pattern.

In only a few minutes, they got a response.

"Buoys nine and twelve hot."

Both the TAO and CO listened in on the helo control channel. Strobes appeared nearly simultaneously on the large screen displays, indicating the bearings to whatever the sonobuoys had detected. The strobes crossed at a point only twenty-eight miles ahead. The CO nodded at the TAO's questioning look. She spoke into her throat mike.

"Tell the helo to prosecute. Designate the contact Skunk Zulu 1."

Aboard *Blue Ridge*, Hillerman again called his admiral.

"Yeah?" answered a sleep-soaked voice. She cleared her throat. "Admiral Simpson."

"Good morning, ma'am. This is the Battle Watch. It's zero one forty three. I just got a report from the ASW screen commander. Seven minutes ago *Goldsborough*'s helo detected a possible submarine, confidence high, bearing two five nine, range one hundred thirty-five miles from the force, twenty-five miles from *Goldsborough*. They're prosecuting it passively. I've given them weapons release authority. I checked. There are no friendlies in the area." He paused. "Just a moment, ma'am."

Hillerman bent his head and read an urgent chat that had just come from the Supplemental Plot, where the ship's special intelligence systems were monitored. He raised his head in alarm.

"Ma'am, SUPPLOT just reported someone's sending a coded radio message from the same vicinity as *Goldy*'s POSSUB."

"On my way."

Gone was the misty sound of sleep, replaced by her cool command voice. Hillerman gulped and hung up.

He wished she'd gotten more sleep. He shuddered, glad he wasn't an admiral.

CHAPTER
FORTY-THREE

1646 Zulu, 8 Nov
0146 Local Time, 9 Nov
USS *Blue Ridge*, Western Pacific, south of Japan

"What do you have?" asked Simpson as she arrived in TFCC. She was still pulling on her jacket against the chill that pervaded the command center. Her eyes adjusted quickly to the dimness.

"*Goldsborough*'s helo got a solid track on the sub. They're making a second attack run now. First one missed. They don't know if the fish malfunctioned or if the sub used some kind of decoy. We should be hearing—"

"Seawolf Five Four Six reports weapon in the water, ma'am," called the assistant battle watch.

Both Hillerman and Simpson moved toward her. Sensing their approach, she pulled down the comms menu and clicked to put the ASW circuit in the speaker overhead so they could listen directly.

"Ranger, Seawolf Five Four Six. Fish is running. Estimated time to target is one one nine seconds."

Silence swept through the space as whispered conversations died.

Time passed glacially before the radio beeped as the crypto synched.

"Oh, crap. Ranger, this is Five Four Six. I got tubes opening." A pause, then, "Something just launched. Multiple somethings. Ranger, you better duck."

The command center became a cacophony as warnings went out on all radio circuits.

Simpson continued to listen.

"Permission to bring up the link, sir?"

Hillerman blinked at his assistant. "Hell, yes. Radio silence is pretty much OBE at this point."

"Mark intercept. Noth—" A pause, then, "Yeah, baby. We got an explosion on all buoys, bearing — wait one — bearing three four two, three hundred yards from estimated target position. Waiting for BDA."

The battle watch waited, studying their screens for inbound missile tracks. The ships in the anti-air warfare screen brought their radars up.

In another moment it was no longer a *probable* weapons launch. Five, then six, then eight missile tracks appeared from where *Goldsborough*'s helicopter had attacked and hopefully destroyed an enemy sub.

Simultaneously, two radio speakers burst out. First came a frenzied transmission from the helicopter, then over the top of that came the more measured words of the anti-air warfare commander.

Simpson whirled around, but Hillerman beat her to it and turned the second speaker down.

"—breaking up noises. I think we got 'em."

The assistant battle watch demanded their attention.

"Ma'am, Delta Mike reports at least forty-four inbounds from four locations. Two positions are close together to the northwest, one is *Goldy*'s target, and one's to the southwest. Everybody's engaging."

Simpson and Hillerman looked at each other. Simpson shrugged and took off her jacket.

There was nothing to do but wait. Somehow, however, she didn't feel cold any longer. Her heart pounded and her throat constricted.

The Chinese either detected us or anticipated where we'd be, dammit. How do we get closer? If we survive.

She listened to the reports as they flowed around her. She'd never felt so useless in her life.

Over a two-hundred-mile plus radius, invisible radar beams stabbed the night, searching. Death, barely visible as it streaked toward the fleet, hugged the wave tops at just under the speed of sound.

As quickly as each enemy missile was detected, dazzling sun-like fireballs leapt from vertical launcher cells on half a dozen ships, reverse meteorites rising from the surface and rocketing skyward, then dropping back down to engage the unmanned adversary in mortal combat. Often a brief flare marked where an interceptor warhead killed its target.

Too many times just a hidden splash signaled that a friendly missile had impacted the water and flown apart, allowing the enemy to continue its deadly approach.

"Track six five nine one, splash nine, continuing."

The call indicated that nine of the twelve enemy missiles in one group had been killed. The defenders continued to fire on the surviving inbounds.

She said a silent prayer. But as often happens, as soon as she thought it, Murphy came to visit.

"Delta Mike, this is November. We're hit aft. We've lost steering and the aft VLS cells. Continuing to eng—"

The transmission cut off.

Simpson closed her eyes and prayed again, this time for the lives of the men and women in *Cochrane*, the destroyer who'd just reported being hit. *The transmission might have been cut off because they lost power,* she kept telling herself.

Regardless, she had to wait. *No, there are things I can do.* "Jason, make sure all the enemy launch points get appropriate attention from ASW platforms. I want them dead. I also want you to launch the alert five aircraft from *Reagan*. I want F-18s standing by overhead the carrier and us."

"Aye aye, ma'am. CAP over both."

CAP would be armed with air-to-air missiles to protect against air attack. They could be used against missiles but were much less effective than ship based interceptors. They'd also get in the way of ships' weapons fire.

"No, Jason, not CAP. I want Hornets with bombs. And I want them prepared to drop their weapons close aboard us and the carrier. Close enough to sound like the enemy hit us."

Hillerman's brow furrowed, his eyes narrowed and then suddenly went wide with understanding. "Aye aye, ma'am. All three ready aircraft have a mixed load."

He turned and typed the order into the chat room for the carrier and the air wing.

The battle raged for what seemed like hours, but it lasted only twenty-nine minutes.

The enemy submarines tried to reposition to launch a second salvo, but to do that they had to move fast. When they moved fast, they made noise. When that happened, they found themselves attacked by helicopters, and in one case by a Japanese frigate.

That ship was particularly motivated to sink the enemy who'd struck first. The other Japanese frigate lay dead in the water and on fire, its crew fighting to keep it afloat.

The attacking frigate succeeded. A Chinese *Song*-class submarine became a piece of twisted, crushed steel on the sea bottom.

Around the battlespace, some enemy missiles found unintended targets.

A sailboat with an Australian couple aboard sailed alone, homeward bound after a summer cruising the Bering Sea and Alaskan coast. A radar reflector hung from atop their mast, meant to ensure no large ships ran them over in the night. Unfortunately, it drew the attention of a different radar. The missile sheared off the top of the mast and nearly capsized their boat. But they were lucky and survived. The warhead didn't explode until the torn missile body hit the water a hundred yards further on. A week later they would be rescued by the Japanese Coast Guard as they drifted northeastward in the Kuroshio current.

The second accidental target was not so fortunate. A Japanese fishing trawler working the waters between Guam and Iwo Jima had headed home when news of the war broke. A missile hit her amidships and exploded. A spreading jumble of flotsam marked their grave.

As the air battle finished, the last of the enemy cruise missiles either died or were decoyed off to explode uselessly in the back of a wave.

But too many had found a valid target.

Simpson sighed heavily and twisted the Naval Academy ring on her left hand.

Captain Brickman, the Ops boss, had stayed in the background during the battle so as not to distract the team. Now she came forward and stood with her boss. "We got hit pretty hard, ma'am."

Simpson looked over at her, then closed her eyes and shook her head. "It could have been worse. There were four subs out there, Letty. There may be more. I wish to God we had land-based air cover. It's impossible to sanitize our route without long-range aircraft and their big sonobuoy loadouts."

That had been an ongoing discussion. They'd taken what they'd hoped was a minimal risk route. Most of the limited anti-submarine aircraft available in the western Pacific had been destroyed on the ground. The remainder searched for Chinese submarines near important naval bases around Japan.

Thus, Seventh Fleet relied solely on their helicopters and an old-fashioned anti-submarine destroyer screen.

"I know, ma'am, but we do the best we can." Brickman's shoulders were slumped but she offered a partial smile. "There's nothing else we *could* have done."

Simpson turned to Hillerman. "Give the order, Jason."

He looked sheepishly at her. "Ah, I already did, 'bout five minutes ago. I figured the bombs should go off pretty much the same time some of those missiles ought to get here."

His eyes reflected concern that she'd be angry. She reinforced his initiative. "Nope, Jason, you did exactly the right thing. Thank you."

She turned back to Brickman, who said, "Once we know what the damage is, ma'am, we need to send home those ships who can make it." Her eyes passed unspoken words.

Simpson nodded. "And we'll sink those who can't."

Brickman winced and nodded.

Two hours later, they had the tally.

Seventh Fleet had sunk three enemy submarines. The fourth had escaped after firing three torpedoes at its pursuer, and an anti-aircraft missile at the helicopter that dogged it. All four weapons had missed, but the submarine escaped by diving deep and running.

The fleet's casualties were bad. One Japanese frigate was sinking. The crew had been taken off by their countrymen.

Cochrane had sunk already after taking two more missile hits. Only half the crew had survived. Two LCS were dead in the water, their crews trying desperately to fight fires and flooding.

Talbot remained behind to provide assistance, tying up another destroyer critical to keeping the carrier alive.

Worst were the lost Tomahawk Land Attack Missiles — TLAM — and the helicopters aboard *Cochrane*. None had gotten airborne before the ships were hit. But as bad as it was, it would have been worse if they'd been flying around during a missile engagement. *Goldsborough's* helo had been an unwitting victim of friendly fire.

By evening, both LCS crews had been rescued and their ships sunk by gunfire. *Talbot* raced to rejoin the force.

The fleet moved inexorably toward the second island chain.

Individual officers and crews had learned hard lessons and suffered loss. But they were more determined than ever to hit back, hard.

CHAPTER
FORTY-FOUR

1545 Zulu, 8 Nov
2145 Local Time
Entrance to the Strait of Malacca

Theodore Roosevelt sliced through seas that were calm — not quite flat but nearly so — under a quarter moon. Behind her in the darkness flowed a river of phosphorescence. Ahead of the big carrier, two destroyers listened intently for submarines, a nearly impossible task at twenty-five knots.

But speed was their friend, especially here. Once they passed into the strait itself, they would slow and be more methodical.

Slowing would also keep them from sticking out like a sore thumb. Merchant ships just didn't fly through crowded shipping lanes; it put them and others at risk. Warships did. Rear Admiral Gupta wanted to pass through the most crowded areas at night to minimize risk of detection by Chinese intelligence.

They planned to launch attacks once they got into the relative openness of the South China Sea. Every man and woman in the group looked forward to the fight. Sinking the Chinese SAG in the Indian Ocean had been satisfying but not enough to sate the bloodlust. For that they needed to take the fight to the enemy in his own backyard.

Gupta sat in TFCC, face wan, dark circles under his eyes. He sipped his fourth cup of coffee.

"All right, so the Vietnamese have come out in the open. They've got very little to fight with, but we need all the help we can get." His fingers drummed on the arm of his chair. His Ops and intel assistant chiefs of staff stood near him.

Heaving a sigh, he said, "That leaves us exactly where we were two days ago. We're about to steam into the South China Sea. *Nicholas* is there but she's hurt. We've got an attack boat there, too, but she's most likely hunting enemy subs. We don't have a good operational picture of the battlespace, and we can't fly or use our organic sensors yet to build one. There are probably enemy submarines in the strait and we'll be hard pressed to find them. Malaysia and Indonesia are *not* willing to step up and support us in any way. Let's see, have I forgotten anything?"

Just as Delawr was about to speak, Gupta interrupted.

"Oh, that's right, the oiler is now two *days* behind us and the escorts are going to need fuel before she catches up. Not to mention *Nicholas* is asking to be re-armed."

The two captains looked at each other. Gupta was normally pretty reasonable. But as he'd grown more tired and as more problems had asserted themselves, he'd become more and more difficult.

"Well, sir, Hanoi offered to have their tanker meet us just the other side of the Singapore Strait. They've given us the latest intel *they* have on Chinese movements. And our intel broadcast is still up, though degraded." replied Darling, the ACoS for Intel, N2.

"Yes, but the Vietnamese info's twenty hours old. And they notably did *not* include intel on subs."

"Sir, they don't have much ASW capability." Seeing Gupta's face darken, Delawr quickly added, "And yes, sir, we know, that's the gravest threat. But the only way to deal with that threat is to go active and pound hell out of the water as we transit."

"You said yourself there's enough shipwrecks to confuse the shit out of sonar. Plus, it'll tell anyone listening that a group of American warships is in the area. Right after they hear us, *we'll* hear *them* as they come to periscope depth and report in. Even if we kill them then, it'll be too damned late," Gupta said. He closed his eyes and leaned back. "I know, I know."

Breathing deeply for a moment, he continued. "Yes, alright. Tell *Briscoe* to go active. She can be a lily pad for *Oldendorf*'s helo det, too. The helos can drop sonobuoys in front of the group to help make more noise. But arm them with Hellfires as well as torpedoes. That way they can handle a surface or subsurface target. Then have *Coeur d'Alene* take station ahead of the force. Let's take advantage of her high-end ASW suite."

Both Delawr and Darling heaved sighs of relief.

"Aye aye, sir. I'll also have the airwing put a couple sections of CAP on alert, two with full air to air packages, and two with mixed air to air and anti-surface," said Delawr.

Gupta rolled his head to both sides. His neck cracked audibly, even over the air blowing through the vent diffuser above the admiral's chair. "Okay, Ham. Get a P4 ready for me. I want all ships at Condition II for ASW, starting as soon as we're within thirty miles of One Fathom Bank."

"Aye, sir."

The word went out and the strike group girded its loins for war.

The TAO in USS *Coeur d'Alene* (LCS-91) looked at his console. They were deep in the Strait of Malacca, approaching One Fathom Bank. Their Raytheon commercial navigation radar was piped into the ship's combat system, giving him a plot of the ships around him. He also saw what *Oldendorf*'s helicopter, Sea

Hunter Two Five Two, saw ahead. Or rather, he saw what the sonobuoys reported.

Coeur d'Alene had been configured with an ASW module. This made her the best choice for leading the group through the strait. But that had also left her with only limited capability to defend herself against surface or air attack.

Unfortunately, when they'd first brought the sonobuoy processor up, it had pretty much blanked the screen with the bearing lines of detected machinery noise. The helo had worked feverishly to correlate sound with ships, but it had taken nearly an hour to get tracks on all of them and filter out the merchant traffic.

But over two dozen unknown sound sources remained. The TAO figured most were small fishing boats, wooden and unlighted. What the helo couldn't see, it couldn't filter out.

Add to that the contacts his own sonar operators had picked up and were busily trying to classify, and data filled his display, none of which made for useful information or contributed one iota to his understanding of the battlespace. It would make little difference if they operated their sonar passively. In the shallow, crowded, and confined waters of the Strait, trying to find a submarine could be described as near to impossible. At least by pinging away, they might intimidate an enemy. Passively, it was just too noisy.

It was aggravating. Worse, it was dangerous.

The CO knew it, too. Which is why he sat behind the TAO, fidgeting. Preferring to micromanage everything, there was little he could do to micromanage the helo, though he'd tried. They'd ignored him, diplomatically at first, then more pointedly until even the CO got the message.

The TAO sighed. Nothing was ever easy aboard *Coeur d'Alene.*

"Hydrophone effects, bearing one two six. Recommend all ahead flank, hard left rudder."

The call from Sonar shocked all hands. The TAO stood

motionless for a moment. Then he reached for the intercom. "Bridge, TAO. Hydrophone effects, bearing one two six. All ahead flank, hard left rudder."

His entire body went cold as he released the switch.

We can't do that.

"Belay my last. *Right* hard rudder. Get on bridge to bridge. Tell everyone around us what's going on. And don't hit anything."

The CO grabbed his arm. "What the hell are you doing? Sonar said hard left."

"Yes, sir. But there's three large merchants to port, one on the beam and two on the bow. We can't turn into 'em, and we can't go between 'em."

The CO opened his mouth, then closed it again. He looked at the display, his jaw working, then looked again at the TAO. He wanted to say something, but instead spun and returned to his chair. "This better work." He settled into his seat and stared at the display.

The TAO hoped it would, too.

The ship heeled to starboard as the rudder bit. All hands grabbed for something to hold onto as she accelerated.

The ASWE activated the Nixie torpedo decoy streamed astern.

The TAO ordered, "Get a torp over the side. Shoot back." In less than a minute, *Coeur d'Alene* had a torpedo racing down the bearing from which the deadly fish came.

"Pike, Sea Wolf Two Five Two, dropping now, now, now. Fish is away." The helo had dropped a torpedo at the point where the enemy had launched its own.

The ship lurched as the rudder was thrown back hard to port. The TAO nearly fell as the ship came upright then heeled to the opposite side.

"Pike, Sea Wolf Two Five Two, we've got an explosion. Waiting for the noise to clear. We'll go look for debris."

The radio seemed far away.

He found he was sweating. His hands didn't shake, but his heart pounded.

He looked at the CO, who sat head up, face calm. He returned the TAO's look and shrugged. "You did right."

The TAO smiled briefly.

The torpedo wasn't fooled by the decoy or by the turn. It hit *Coeur d'Alene* dead amidships, penetrating the forward fuel tank. The explosion ruptured the bulkhead between the tank and the engine room, the fuel bursting into the hot engineering space. There were only a few seconds, during which just the right concentration of fuel mist existed for it to combust explosively, but it was long enough. The engine containment module had broken open, and the gas turbines were plenty hot enough.

The resulting explosion broke through more bulkheads. Burning fuel spread throughout spaces above and aft. One of those was the torpedo magazine. The warheads quickly cooked off, tearing the ship in half. The released torpedo fuel formed a cloud of corrosive toxicity that shot outward from the explosion with the shock wave, shredding metal and people. Those who miraculously survived the explosions were slain by the poisonous cloud.

The helo nearly went into the water as the blast wave hit. When they recovered and looked at the scene, the ship was gone. Damaged themselves, they had no time to look for survivors.

Several small craft who'd been near *Coeur d'Alene* when she blew up were also damaged. Helicopters and boats spent the next several hours rescuing injured sailors and civilian mariners.

CHAPTER
FORTY-FIVE

0045 Zulu, 9 Nov
0645 Local Time
USS *Theodore Roosevelt*, Strait of Malacca

The watch in TFCC listened to the radio calls between Sea Wolf Two Five Nine and *Coeur d'Alene*. When the report came that *Coeur d'Alene* had simply disappeared, shocked silence reigned.

Lieutenant Commander Howard, the battle watch, picked up the phone to the carrier's Pri-Fly, where aircraft launch and recovery operations were controlled. "Launch the alert helos. Get a couple of SAR birds up ASAP. *Coeur d'Alene* just sank."

Next, he picked up the handset that connected him directly to the admiral's cabin.

"Admiral Gupta."

"Sir, I just copied a transmission from *Oldendorf*'s helo. The submarine put a torpedo into *Coeur d'Alene*. She's gone."

He still heard the admiral breathing. "Say that again, Willy."

Howard repeated it, adding, "I've ordered the alert helos launched to prosecute the sub, and told the carrier to put up search and rescue helicopters ASAP to look for survivors."

Howard heard Gupta replaying the info before he said,

"Okay, thanks. We're going to take a break and come down. I know you don't need help, but you're about to get a whole lot of it."

"Aye, sir." He hung up.

When he'd been a junior officer onboard a frigate in drydock, there'd been an electrical fire on the mess decks. Nearly every officer onboard had come running to see what was going on. As he himself walked calmly by, a first class petty officer had said, "Every damned bad thing that happens is a friggin' khaki magnet." The phrase had stuck with him.

The "help" took longer to arrive than expected. By the time Gupta and the rest walked into TFCC, the second and third helos had reported on station. Sea Wolf Five Three One had peppered the area with active sonobuoys and were pinging the water mercilessly. Just as they considered moving the sonobuoy pattern farther east, they got a solid contact.

"Contact, bearing one eight zero, range one five five zero yards from buoy six. No Doppler."

The second helo, callsign Sea Hunter Five Four Nine, answered. "Roger. I just placed a pattern west of yours. If it comes this way, wait one."

A minute passed.

Five Four Nine continued, "Contact bearing zero nine nine, range five nine zero zero yards from my buoy one. Make that two zero one, one six zero zero yards from your buoy six. Strong up Doppler. He's moving west. Estimate speed five knots."

Now Sea Hunter Five Five Three joined in.

"Copy. I'm eight thousand yards out. I'll make the firing run."

A deathly silence prevailed in TFCC, save for the hum of electronics and the gentle whisper of the air conditioning.

Howard had highlighted Sea Hunter Five Five Three's icon on the large screen display on the bulkhead.

"Dropping, now, now, NOW," came the report. After a short

pause, the voice said, "Fish is running true. Time to impact, two six seconds."

An eternity passed as the digital clock marked off the time. But at twenty-two seconds, "We've got a bubble. The fish hit something."

More life drained from those in TFCC as the helos used their sonobuoys to determine if the enemy had been hit.

"Contact. Maneuvering contact, bearing zero seven six, range five eight two zero yards from my buoy one. She's still there," called Sea Hunter Five Four Nine.

Sea Hunter Five Five Three replied, "Shit. Fish took a quick right turn just before it blew. There must be an obstruction."

Delawr said, "Probably one of those wrecks or other crap. The torpedo might home on it if the angle's right."

Gupta nodded and continued to listen.

The helicopters expended their five remaining torpedoes. Howard had already ordered two more birds launched. Those helos expended two more torpedoes before they finally got a hit on the submarine.

Sea Hunter Five Six Six saw it first.

"Broach. Target's broached off my right side, range . . . range about three thousand. Gonna drop another fish."

Gupta leaned forward and grabbed the handset.

"Negative, Sea Hunter. This is Hammer actual. Get BDA first. We don't have an unlimited supply of fish."

But he needn't have negated the attack, for just as he finished transmitting, the helo called, "Negat fish. Target just rolled on its side. It's got no stern."

The blow by blow account of the enemy submarine's death throes commenced.

"There's a couple of guys climbing out of the conning tower hatch."

"Forward hatch just opened. They're climbing on top of each other to get out."

"Crap. She just rolled, forward hatch went under. One guy got sucked back in."

"She's belly up."

"She's gone."

"Homeplate, there's about a dozen guys in the water. Request SAR helos pick them up."

Howard looked at Gupta, who shook his head. "You said there's Malaysian Coast Guard headed for the scene, right?"

Howard nodded.

"Let them pick them up. I'm not bringing prisoners aboard. Let the SAR birds focus on *Coeur d'Alene* survivors."

Then he turned and walked out of TFCC. Delawr followed.

Howard relayed the order to the helicopters. Then he moved *Oldendorf* to take the spot in the formation left vacant by *Coeur d'Alene*'s demise. The strike group continued toward the Singapore Strait.

Howard fervently hoped they wouldn't run into any more enemy submarines. They couldn't afford to fight a war of attrition, not with a one-to-one loss ratio.

"Enter," Gupta called.

The door to his cabin opened, and Captain Max Jarvis stepped through. Gupta expected him, having been tipped off by his deputy commander that the commodore wanted to see him. Jarvis commanded Destroyer Squadron Thirty Nine, permanently assigned to Gupta's strike group. Three of DESRON Thirty Nine's ships formed part of the strike group.

This morning there had been four.

"What can I do for you, Max?" asked Gupta.

"You can tell me what the hell you were doing putting *Coeur d'Alene* in harm's way this morning. Sir."

Gupta sighed.

"And what did you think I intended when I told your staff to put their most capable ASW platform in the lead?" Gupta asked.

"Don't you dare try to blame my staff for this clusterfuck. They were carrying out your orders. *You* killed those people."

Gupta sat back and stared at Jarvis. He'd only known the man eleven months. In that short time it had become obvious: Jarvis was a schmoozer, competent enough to achieve and survive command at sea, but not a risk taker. In fact, he'd shown himself to not only be a risk avoider, but also quick to shift blame to his subordinates when things didn't go exactly as planned. He had excellent men and women on his staff, but nothing in military operations ever went perfectly. When it didn't, Jarvis looked for a scapegoat.

"The enemy killed those men and women, Commodore. Not me, not you. Certainly not your staff. We knew there could be an enemy sub hiding in the strait. But what option did we have other than try to find it or scare it off before it could take a shot at us?"

"We could have avoided the strait entirely. Why go through right where they expected? Why not go around south, through the Sunda Strait?"

Gupta shook his head. "No, that's where *they* expected us to go. You saw the intel. There were reports of three enemy subs down there. That's why I sent our own attack boat and the SSGN through there. *Idaho* had the best chance against those enemy boats. She took on two of them and won. We can't and you know it. And *Georgia* can hold her own, too. Hell, they won't even hear her."

Jarvis raised his hands to the overhead. "You're damned right, surface ships have no business fighting subs. That's why we shouldn't have transited until the strait was cleared. We could have stayed in the IO until we could sanitize the route with aircraft. It's unbelievable you'd put lives at risk that way."

Gupta closed his eyes and sighed. "How long would it take to sanitize four or five hundred nautical miles of strait? Days?

Weeks? Even if we had the aircraft to do it. We can't wait that long." He shook his head again. "The enemy is raising hell across the Pacific. We're at war, Commodore. We have to accept risk, even loss. Why are we having this conversation?"

Jarvis glared at him, hands clenched. "Because as soon as I can do it without giving up our position, I'm sending a message off to Seventh Fleet to let her know that the *aviator* in command of this strike group has a cavalier disregard for human life, and no grasp of naval warfare."

Gupta snorted and leaned forward. "You may do that. In fact, if you write that letter tonight, I'll see that it goes ashore if and when we send anything to the embassy in Hanoi. But you are still going to follow orders and do your job as I direct. Is that clear?" He stared hard at Jarvis until he nodded.

"I will, for now. But I will damn sure protest if you ever unnecessarily endanger my ships again. You can count on it," Jarvis added.

"Oh, I expect you will. But you can expect me to give your arguments all the consideration they deserve. Dismissed." Gupta returned his attention to his computer screen.

Jarvis stared at him for a moment, then turned and left, not quite slamming the door behind him.

Gupta rubbed his eyes and took a deep breath.

The Navy had plenty of risk-averse officers in command, men and women who'd grown up under the threat that if everything didn't go perfectly, they'd be fired. They polluted the younger generation with the same fears and unwillingness to face the reality that naval operations were never risk-free.

Jarvis would continue to be a problem, but Gupta couldn't just get rid of him. That would create havoc within the group's command structure and be bad for morale. He'd just have to keep him on the margins. But it would wear on both his and Jarvis' staffs.

CHAPTER
FORTY-SIX

0400 Zulu, 9 Nov
1200 Local Time
Presidential Office, Beijing

President Liu whirled and stomped around his office. Surrounding him in overstuffed chairs or on the sumptuous sofa were the members of the Military Committee.

Reports from the field were mixed. If he were completely honest, they were not good.

Admiral Yu Hua, head of the PLAN, tried to calm him. "Mr. Secretary General, these are minor setbacks. We agreed any elements of the American Navy that survived would individually be formidable, that it would be costly to hunt them down. But we will prevail."

Liu barked, "So you say. But every time we fight, we lose more ships than they do. You *believe* you may have sunk as many as three American and two Vietnamese ships. But at the cost of at least four submarines, four destroyers, and a supply ship. That is *not* a good ratio, Admiral."

He turned to Zhang Yongyi, the foreign minister. "And you said no Asian nation would dare stand against us. That ASEAN had no stomach for fighting, especially with the American navy neutralized. And yet, the Vietnamese have taken a side and it was *not* ours."

He strode to his chair and threw himself into it. "Tell me again how you intend to destroy the two, no *three*, aircraft carrier groups that are coming. Aircraft carriers you told me would not survive our first strike. And do not even *think* about putting our own aircraft carriers at risk. The Americans have a century of experience fighting with aircraft carriers. Ask the Japanese how well they fared in battle. We will need ours to control our expanded waters after we send the Americans home." His fingers drummed on the desk.

Yu studied his hands, which were folded in his lap. "Mr. Secretary General, we will destroy them with the weapons we specifically developed for this purpose."

"You're supposed to have studied their naval tactics when they fought Iran in the 1980s," said Liu. "You said you knew what wouldn't work. Yet you sent our ships, my ships, to die. What makes you certain *this* will work?"

"We have practiced this with superb results. This is the one weapon the Americans fear above all others because they cannot defeat it. This has always been our plan for destroying their carriers." He straightened his shoulders. "As the enemy approaches, we will attrite them with our ballistic missiles. We have already ordered preparation—"

"But you don't know where they are."

Yu set his jaw and blinked. "Precisely? No. But we know within five hundred kilometers. That is sufficient to focus our search. Once located, our very large numbers will overwhelm their defenses. They cannot counter these missiles at all, let alone in large numbers. We will use all our missiles and sweep them from the sea."

Liu took two deep breaths before he spoke through gritted teeth. "Does that not leave us with no arrows in our quiver, when it fails?"

General Sao Yide, commander of the Rocket Force, took the lead. "Mr. Secretary General, their navy is extremely vulnerable to what they call our carrier killer. We have far more of them than they know. Each one can destroy, sink, an aircraft carrier."

"What of their vaunted missile defense systems?" asked the president.

"The American systems were designed for missiles that follow an entirely ballistic profile. We maneuver the warhead after it reenters the atmosphere. It impacts the target at supersonic speed, perhaps penetrating all the way through the ship and out the bottom. Even if it does not, the impact of such a mass of steel at such velocity will pulverize ships' systems and wreak destruction. Even if they do not sink, they will be useless."

Liu snorted. It was the most optimistic model, the result of some engineer's fantasy. He'd just be happy if the damned thing hit its target. An idea flitted into his head.

"How will it know which target it should hit? How will you identify the carrier from its consorts?"

Yu took the question. "The warhead, using its own radar, will automatically attack the largest target."

"When?"

"In four days. The enemy is still out of range. But when they reach that point, they will get no closer."

Liu wished he had their confidence. Too many things hadn't gone as planned, despite months of carefully accounting for every foreseeable complication. The Americans had proven surprisingly resilient. After years of studying their tactics, their doctrine, and their actual operations, they'd still managed to astonish the People's Army.

What other surprises did the Americans still hide?

0400 Zulu, 9 Nov
0700 Local Time
The Kremlin, Moscow

The Russian president also paced, also furious.

Remkin had delivered more reports of American soldiers fighting alongside NATO. The Russian offensive had ground to a halt in central Poland, though Remkin called it an "operational pause." Despite massive damage from the Russian cruise missiles, NATO had managed to scrape together sufficient force to stop the revamped Russian army. Worse, they'd reacted quickly when his generals moved to outflank them.

As Gregorivich paced, his eyes burned into Remkin. "This is unacceptable. Nine days of glorious success. Now you've been motionless for nearly twenty hours."

"Mr. President, this is how military operations work, is it not? We have discussed this. We cannot allow ourselves to get overextended. We must move carefully."

"You told me our missile strikes had neutralized *all* enemy reinforcements. Where did these new ones come from? And how are they replacing all the munitions and weapons we supposedly destroyed?"

"Sir, I admit, they had better hidden and more widely distributed stocks of munitions and weapons than we knew. And we did not strike the Americans because they were not supposed to fight. But we can still succeed."

"How? For yours and everyone else's health, you better come up with the answer quickly and make it work." He stared at Remkin. "Remember your predecessor committed suicide after he failed me in Ukraine. I suggest you not make the same mistake."

Remkin closed his eyes and pinched his nose. His hands shook so he took a deep breath.

"Sir, if you will give us another twelve hours, we will consolidate our gains and move our own reinforcements up. We

AGAINST ALL ENEMIES   273

continue to hammer at the enemy with artillery and air attacks. We attrite their air forces as we fight to establish air superiority. We still have a large quantity of old Soviet airframes. We simply take old planes from storage, make them airworthy, and send them up. We will over-mass them. We can lose three for every one we kill."

"What of pilots?"

"We have great depth of reserves. We conscripted civilian pilots and provided them sufficient training so they don't kill each other. Now we send them into battle. We can do that for quite some time. The enemy cannot replace their own pilots for the same reason they cannot replace their aircraft."

Remkin shifted in his chair. Now, to his main point. "Sir, there is one more recommendation."

CHAPTER
FORTY-SEVEN

1400 Zulu, 9 Nov
1700 Local Time
The Kremlin, Moscow

That afternoon, Gregorivich and Remkin made a call to Washington, DC.

They did not use the hotline established after the Cuban missile crisis. Instead, they used an encrypted Voice Over IP phone secretly installed shortly after Donnelly's inauguration. The encryption came not from the NSA but from a Russian security firm.

Gregorivich spoke first. "Mr. President, it is good to talk to you again. I have been very busy, as you know. You, too, have a great deal to contend with. I appreciate you taking the time to speak with me."

The conversation was on speaker, the only translator on the Russian end.

"You're damned right I've been busy, Yuri. You're ducking my calls, my *friend*. What suddenly has you interested enough to call *me*?"

Truculence clouded his voice. When the translator finished, Remkin cringed and Gregorivich rolled his eyes.

Remkin signaled him to remain calm. The American president was a master of provocation.

"Please, Mr. President. I have not been avoiding your calls. We are both engaged in a war for our lives. Our commitments to our people must always take priority."

"You rotten sonuvabitch. We had an understanding. War for *our* lives, my ass. *I'm* the one who's fighting for my life. You *started* your war. Mine started when I was attacked. You're supposed to be helping me. You owe me that."

Gregorivich closed his eyes and took a deep breath. "Mr. President, let us not descend into name calling. I admit, you have been hurt much worse than I. In fact, my country is, for the moment, holding its own." He looked at Remkin while he spoke. "My intelligence services tell me, however, that your navy has won some important victories. The Chinese will regret going to war with America."

"You damned betcha, Yuri. My carriers have really pounded those bastards. We're gonna destroy their miserable country. My generals begged me to nuke 'em, but I told them they just have to come up with something else. You know, I've got the greatest military this planet has ever seen. If they knew as much as I do, they'd see how easy it is."

"Yes, Mr. President, that's excellent," Gregorivich said as he closed his eyes and shook his head, nostrils flaring. "I'm certain you can defeat them easily." He took another deep breath. "I have another request, Mr. President. My intelligence people say that some of your soldiers are fighting alongside NATO forces. I have tried very diligently not to harm them. But it is difficult. The longer the fighting goes on, the more difficult it will become. It would be helpful if you would reiterate your orders to remain neutral."

Silence from the other end of the line. Finally, "Yuri, none of my people would ever disobey orders, so your intelligence prob- ably sucks as much as mine. I'm sure none of my guys are fight- ing. But I'll send the order again just to make you happy. Now I need to ask you something. I've been trying for days to get hold of you. This is important, Yuri. Are you listening?"

Gregorivich rolled his eyes.

"When the fuck are you going to attack China? We had a deal, Yuri. We're supposed to help each other out. I promised to kill NATO. I stopped helping Ukraine. I got rid of those stupid sanctions my predecessor hit you with. All so you could win there. Now, it's your turn."

Now Gregorivich was silent. Finally, he replied, "Mr. President, I will work to make the attack happen as soon as it is prac- tical. Goodbye, Mr. President."

As the translator hit the speaker button on the phone, Donnelly began to expostulate. "Yuri, don't you dare—"

Gregorivich excused the translator and sat down facing Remkin. "I am ever surprised and pleased that he doesn't see the need for a translator on his side," he said. "I may tell the world whatever I wish with regard to what was discussed, with no record or witness on his side to contradict me."

"He contradicts himself constantly," Remkin replied.

The president snorted. "Pavlov, the man is completely oblivi- ous. I have heard him argue both sides of a question in the same sentence and be blissfully unaware. No, I am convinced he is supremely ignorant. He has no filter between brain and mouth. He is also unable to remember his own words, the rambling thoughts projected as they manifest themselves, dissipating as quickly as they come."

Remkin's eyebrows raised. But it wasn't relevant to what they needed to discuss. He asked, "What of your request? Do you believe him?"

"Yes, and this removes any consequences for American deaths. You were right to ask me to call him."

In Washington, the president hung up the phone.

The conversation appalled Hunter. The president, *his* president, had openly admitted to making under-the-table deals with Gregorivich. Worse, he'd apparently made an *alliance* that no one else knew about.

He needed to get out of there.

"Well, I sure as hell told him off, right, Jack? He'll think twice about going off on his own again."

Donnelly sat behind his desk, rubbing his forefinger along the edge admiringly, apparently enjoying the silky touch of the varnished oak. "Now we'll get the help we need against China."

Hunter cleared his throat. "Uh, yes, sir, I think you conveyed what you expect. Do you really think he'll do it, though?"

The president smiled. "Of course, he will. He knows who the most powerful man in the world is. And he knows not to piss me off. He'll attack China, then he can have whatever he wants once we take those cocksuckers down. It's going to be great, just great. An American-Russian alliance, telling the rest of the world where to get off. A new world order."

He sat back, still enjoying the moment. The sun reflected off his bald spot.

"Sir, don't you think it might send the wrong signal if we appear to be allied with the Russians right after they've attacked NATO?"

"I don't want to hear any bullshit about NATO. Those bastards are traitors. They abandoned me. They deserve to rot in hell. I hope Yuri kicks their asses up around their necks. I made an agreement with him, and I'll stick by it."

"Sir, the Constitution doesn't allow—"

"The Constitution says what I say it says. I have total authority to do whatever the hell I want. What's wrong with you today?" Donnelly stared at him, breathing heavily. Then he turned and looked out the window.

Feeling nauseated, Hunter said, "Nothing, sir. Well, I'll excuse myself. I know—"

The president wasn't listening, so Hunter did something he'd never done before: he simply walked out and closed the door behind him.

There was much to do.

CHAPTER
FORTY-EIGHT

2350 Zulu, 9 Nov
0850 Local Time, 10 Nov
USS *Blue Ridge*, Western Pacific

Letisha Brickman knocked on the bulkhead next to the Flag Cabin door and entered. As she did so, she said, "Admiral, the gravity sump's coming online again."

Admiral Simpson scowled. "Who's asking and for what?"

Brickman replied, "PACFLT, ma'am. They're asking us for a full SITREP. I guess someone there has forgotten the concept of radio silence and that that's what's keeping us alive."

Simpson sighed. Thus far, "higher headquarters" at levels above Seventh Fleet had not interfered, nor asked her to provide the myriad reports that accompanied all military missions these days. On a normal pre-hostilities day, those headquarters consisted of PACFLT and the Navy's Operational Staff, called OPNAV. Depending on where her ships were operating, she sometimes had reporting responsibilities to US Forces Japan or US Forces Korea. Then there were the thousands of administrative offices across the Navy, who had a stake in something or someone aboard one of her ships, aircraft, or submarines.

"Alright, Letty. Let's gin up something but don't send it. For now, like Arleigh Burke, we're going to ignore the request. If the cries get too raucous, we'll find a way to fend them off. But I don't intend to sacrifice anyone to the Gods of Admin, at least not yet."

Brickman smiled broadly. "Aye aye, ma'am. No sacrifices today. Great minds must think alike, because I told Lieutenant Chrisman to go ahead and assemble one but not send it. I also told him that anything he can't get by flashing light probably isn't important enough to put in a report."

Simpson smiled. "Thanks, Letty. Anything else?"

Brickman's smile died. "Unfortunately, yes. Fuel status is in from all ships. High speed during the battle, then station changes to cover for losses, left a few of the destroyers mighty low. Still no word from Japan on fuel."

Simpson took off her glasses, rubbed her bloodshot eyes, and pinched her nose. She wished all her ships were nuclear-powered just so they didn't have to ever worry about fuel. Or at least only about aviation fuel. But they weren't and she did.

"Okay, Letty. What's the bottom line? How long do they have?"

"About another day and a half. *Goldy's* the worst; she's at twenty-two percent as of 1300 today and estimates she'll be at fifteen percent tomorrow around 1800. And if the weather worsens and the sea state goes up, so does the risk. And if the weather really goes to shit, we'll have a helluva time UNREP-ing."

Both women had seen their share of Underway Replenishment operations. Two or three ships would steam along at fifteen to eighteen knots. Between them were strung automatically tensioned wire ropes with either fuel hoses hung below to transfer fuel, or slings to pass pallets of food and ammunition. Sometimes foul weather made an already dangerous evolution much more so. It was like driving two cars down the freeway at normal speed, pumping gas through a garden hose, and passing beer and pretzels through open windows, all using clotheslines.

"There's more, ma'am. Everyone's worried about JP-5 fuel for the aircraft. We used a lot chasing down those subs, and we're burning it fast with three helos up twenty-four/seven."

"Send the messenger planes. I hate that we have to burn so much fuel to set up a refueling." She rubbed her eyes with her palms, then looked up. "And make damned sure those pilots know the return to force procedures. We can't afford any blue on blue engagements." Glancing out the porthole, she asked, "What's the weather guesser say?"

"She says the barometer is holding relatively steady, so no changes. But, as always, she caveats the hell out of it."

Brickman began to mimic the meteorologic officer. *"Even with the weather satellite photos, any of the systems currently west of us could change course, and the weather patterns could bring a storm or clear weather. Without access to the models the Naval Oceanographic Centers have, I'm taking a shot in the dark."*

Simpson chuckled. "She hates the possibility she might be wrong. The fact she rarely is makes her paranoia worse. But I'd bet on her over the models any day."

Brickman smirked. "Yes, ma'am, it's a real break having a *bone-i-fied* weather goddess onboard."

"Get out."

"Aye aye, ma'am."

Brickman's face continued to be split by a grin all the way out the door.

Half an hour later, five F/A-18 Superhornets shot off the *Reagan*'s flight deck and headed northeast at low altitude. All five carried extra fuel tanks and only minimal air-to-air armament for self-defense. Four also carried a refueling kit so they could refuel each other and the fifth aircraft.

An hour into the flight, one of the aircraft refueled the remaining four and turned around to fly alone and unafraid back to the carrier. A second aircraft went into an orbit to await the return flight.

At the second hour, another aircraft refueled the remaining two and headed for home. At the third hour, the last tanker aircraft refueled the messenger plane and went into an orbit.

The messenger plane continued for another ninety minutes, went into an orbit, and began broadcasting a recorded burst message on HF radio. It circled for ten minutes, rebroadcasting the message for five seconds every minute, then began the trek back to the carrier.

At Headquarters, US Naval Forces Korea, the chief of staff called his counterpart on the staff of the Republic of Korea Navy headquarters.

"Dong, we got an update from Seventh Fleet. Can your tanker refuel them?"

The ROK Navy chief of staff replied, "Yes, he is ready. Please pass to us the rendezvous position, and we will order him to meet there. If he cannot, I will tell you. We are glad to help, Glen."

Captain Lavender closed his eyes. "Dong, the US Navy is incredibly grateful. I am personally grateful. The fact that you and your navy stand by us demonstrates the depth of commitment we have to each other. Thank you."

CHAPTER
FORTY-NINE

0240 Zulu, 10 Nov
1140 Local Time
USS *Blue Ridge*, Western Pacific

Aboard *Blue Ridge*, Admiral Simpson picked up the phone. Brickman and Proudfoot were lunching in her cabin.

"Ma'am, this is Lieutenant Commander Hillerman. NAVFOR Korea says the ROK oiler will meet us at the rendezvous tomorrow morning, 0400 local. I passed UNREP instructions to the force. With your permission, we'll move into the UNREP formation at 0330."

"Sounds fine, Jason. Make it so."

Hanging up the phone, she turned to Brickman. "All right, Letty, how do we integrate the *TR* group into our plan?"

Brickman quickly chewed her bite of pork chop and swallowed. "Well, ma'am, they have the pre-hostilities target lists. They're supposed to be able to operate in our AOR, too. The hard part's getting them intel updates. Hell, it's hard enough to get them ourselves."

Proudfoot interjected. "We're still getting some data. It's not a lot, but it's telling us where at least some of their fleet's operating. It even suggests that a couple of ships have returned to port, apparently for resupply. Though I'm not sure why they need to resupply. Their surface fleet hasn't been engaged at all, except for that group *Nicholas* sank. The stuff from the Vietnamese helps, too."

Simpson asked, "Why haven't they? They've been bragging for years about their new combatants."

"I suspect they know they really can't compete with our experience. Sure, they have great new toys. But what *Nicholas* has done to them may have scared them. Looks like their surface fleet's staying close to home.

"Any chance they're spoofing us? Making it look like they're rotating through homeports when they're really out looking for us? Or making it look like we know where their surface fleet is when they're actually elsewhere?"

"There's no indication that's happening, ma'am. Don't get me wrong, they're good at counterintelligence and deception. But I'm fairly comfortable with what we think we know. We're looking closely at all of it and filtering out what's suspect. So I'm good with the target sets I gave Ops."

He nodded at Brickman.

She smiled at him then turned to Simpson. "We're building the strike plan, allocating targets to either TLAM or aircraft. To be honest, we're getting some pushback from CAG. He wants more targets but Air Ops doesn't want to commit that many airplanes to high risk targets. We can't replace aircraft, so I want to keep them for targets that really need a pilot." The CAG, or Commander Air Group, was the captain in command of the aircraft aboard the carrier.

"We can't replace TLAM, either, Letty," Simpson reminded her.

"I understand, ma'am, but pilots are way more expensive. I want to use TLAM on well-defended fixed targets and use air against mobile ones."

Simpson nodded. It made the most sense from both risk and preservation of assets perspectives.

She shuddered at having reduced pilots and multi-tens of millions of dollar airplanes to "assets," but that was her job. If she worried too much about them as people, it might be impossible to send them into harm's way.

On the other hand, she could never completely divorce herself from the fact that they were flesh and blood men and women. It was a tense balance. She mourned the losses of the other night. "All right, it sounds like *we've* got a good plan. Now, back to my original question. How do we integrate *TR*?"

Brickman nodded. "Yes, ma'am. Sorry." She took a quick sip of water. "We've got a strawman Operation Order we'll pass them. It assigns roles and responsibilities, allocates targets, and provides fighting instructions. Most important, it gives them your JTF mission and objectives, and measures of performance and effectiveness. It's gonna be difficult to coordinate without direct radio comms." She scratched her nose. "At minimum, we can assign times for strikes and hope they make them. We know their weapons loadout, so we haven't overtasked them. We'll keep about fifteen percent of our TLAM in reserve for pop-up targets."

"Sounds good. What about the Vietnamese? Can we give them targets?"

Brickman shook her head. "No, ma'am. They really don't have any capability. The best use we can make of them is intel gathering, message passing, and anti-surface warfare. They've got six Kilo class subs, but we think only four are operational. The other two are in overhaul. Kilos pack a helluva punch against surface ships and should be fairly decent against Chinese subs. The problem is, we don't know how proficient they are, especially against other subs. So I think if we incorporate them into our plan, we use them for tracking and killing enemy surface combatants. Their ships can continue to operate with our surface platforms. That all assumes they're willing to give us tactical control of their ships and subs."

"Okay, let's not put too much on them. Assign their subs a geographic operating area and let them do what they can in that area, using their own assets as they know how. Make damned sure there's a good buffer zone between their subs and ours, and that our surface folks know where their subs are operating. We don't want an errant bubblehead sinking any of our allies, or vice versa," said Simpson.

Brickman looked down at her now empty plate, then back up at her admiral. "Aye, ma'am."

"Alright, lady and gentleman. When can I see the draft?"

Brickman smiled again. "Well, ma'am, this evening work for you?"

Simpson grinned back. "Why yes, that'll be just fine."

She turned to Proudfoot. "Have you seen it, Pete?"

Proudfoot also smiled. "Seen it? Ma'am, my people *contributed* to it. You don't think we'd let the Ops folks get all the credit, do you?" Turning more serious, he added, "Yes, our teams are working well together. I think it's a good plan."

Simpson looked back and forth between the two, both of whom were looking quite pleased with themselves.

"I don't know if I can stand you two. This could be a record: Ops and Intel working together without chaos and flames? What next, solving world hunger?"

Brickman and Proudfoot laughed.

0400 Zulu, 10 Nov
1100 Local Time
USS *Theodore Roosevelt*, South China Sea

In the staff spaces aboard *Theodore Roosevelt*, Captains Delawr and Darling discussed the OPORD they'd received.

Darling had just walked into the staff operations office, located on the 03 level forward above the massive hangar deck. He grabbed a metal chair from the desk next to Delawr's, turned it around, and sat in it backward.

The strike group steamed now in the South China Sea proper, having passed Singapore abeam just before dawn. The city had been well illuminated, as usual. It reminded all hands that, while they were at war, much of the rest of the world was not.

Or, if they'd asked Admiral Gupta, it wasn't at war *yet*.

"Hey, George, I was just about to call. Do we have good data on the target lists?" asked Delawr.

"We do. We had several CD's worth of Seventh Fleet data, so we uploaded it to the servers. I heard we got orders."

Delawr and Darling had a rocky relationship. Darling had joined the staff right before deployment. Delawr said, "Well, the strike team should work together with your folks to build the target packages."

"Already ordered. We're using the templates to build a strawma—"

"George, I get it, your guys are on top of it." Delawr took a deep breath and rubbed his eyes. He'd had enough. "You know, you don't have to try to prove how good your folks are at what they do. I know they are. So are you. Let's just get this done. Agreed?"

Darling looked quizzically at Delawr, cocking his head. "I don't know what you're talking about."

Delawr stared at him for a moment. "Alright, George, forget it."

He turned back to his computer screen and pulled up the OPORD, looking for the Operations Annex that included the target list and instructions for servicing them.

"So, how does it look? In terms of weaponeering, I mean?" Darling asked. He'd remained seated.

Without looking at him, Delawr responded, "Well, the strike team has to do the pairing. We'll bring the carrier's planners into it. They'll build the aircraft loadouts. But your team's input is gonna be key. We'll need to know how defended each target is, and how hardened. For example, the sub bases look to be hardened pretty thoroughly, but anything your team knows about them will help my guys figure out how to attack them."

Darling waved his hand. "Got it. I'm sure my guys *are* on it. But my question is, do we have *enough* weapons?"

Delawr shrugged. "No way to know. I doubt it, especially since we're talking the entirety of the country. We'll need to prioritize the targets even within the priorities Seventh Fleet gave us."

"What do we do when we run out?" Darling avoided his eyes when Delawr turned to look at him.

"We hold back a reserve," Delawr said. "OPORD says hold back fifteen percent. I'm gonna recommend we make that twenty. We'll service some targets with bare minimum for a mission kill instead of destroying it. That's the boss's call, but I think it's reasonable."

Darling nodded. "Makes sense. So you're going to need to know what we think a mission kill looks like. I'll tell my folks."

He started to stand, then paused. "You didn't answer my question, though. What happens when we run out of ammo?" While he stood, he cracked his knuckles.

Delawr shook his head. "That part of the script isn't written yet. Hopefully, we inflict so much punishment they negotiate," he said. "But all the planning we've done for war with China over the past fifty years doesn't mean squat right now. Those planners tried to envision every possible scenario. But not one of them envisioned *this* scenario."

Darling smiled briefly. "Yeah, I know. I was on one of those planning teams when I was stationed at INDOPACOM. I helped prepare the Most Likely Enemy Course of Action. My wife worked the Most Dangerous Enemy Course of Action. That's how we met. But in all our brainstorming and nug work, we never figured on something like this."

Delawr suddenly remembered something that made his gut tighten. He didn't want to but he asked, "George, your wife still active duty?"

Darling looked down at his fingernails as he spread his hand in front of him. "Yeah. She'd just reported back to INDOPACOM after a tour at Third Fleet. We were going to geo-bach for a year or so, 'til I could wrangle early orders back to Pearl." He continued to look down at hands that now shook.

Delawr reached out and squeezed Darling's forearm. "Hey, I'm sure she wasn't in the building when it got hit."

Darling looked up, eyes misty. "She's still a junior commander. She was on duty rotation, would've had the morning watch. She'd have just been getting off when INDOPACOM got it."

He turned and strode to the door, closing it quietly behind him.

Delawr stared after him.

The Tomahawk officer spoke up quietly from across the space where he'd been watching.

"Holy shit, sir. I know most of us know someone who might have bit the big one. But I can't imagine if it was my wife."

Delawr turned back to his computer. "Nope, neither can I. But all of us have to just keep going."

He turned to glance at the closed door again. "He has so far. I hope he can keep it up."

CHAPTER
FIFTY

1210 Zulu, 10 Nov
0710 Eastern Time
National Security Advisor's Office, The White House

Jack Hunter sat head in his hands.

General Norton had just reported not one but five tactical nuclear detonations in Poland. Worse, USEUCOM believed thousands of American soldiers had been killed or injured.

Hunter hadn't asked why. The answer would be that US soldiers had been stationed there before hostilities and been caught in the crossfire.

But it didn't matter. They'd been killed and this time it couldn't plausibly be called an "accident," as had been the case with the Patriot batteries. And Hunter needed to decide what to do about it.

Norton had come to him instead of going to Donnelly. Norton had shrugged and said he knew Hunter wanted everything to go through him. Since the president didn't attend meetings in the Sit Room, Hunter must be the lead.

Hunter couldn't argue the point, having deliberately cultivated that belief. Now he found himself with knowledge that might send the president over the edge.

Not that he has far to go.

The president had shown himself a thin-skinned bully from the moment they'd met. But Hunter had worked for men with all sorts of foibles and figured he could deal with anything. But after the attack, in the innermost part of his mind, Hunter began to wonder if the man was unhinged. Moments of rationality were interspersed with moments of unthinking rage. These were followed by moments of serene calm, surreal to observers.

But removing a sitting president wasn't easy.

Hunter pulled a rarely opened copy of the US Constitution from his bookshelf and reread the pertinent section of the 25th Amendment.

The problems were manifold.

First, there was no vice president. The secretary of state, next in line, was newly returned to Washington, but Hunter had never been a fan. He was too self-confident, too hard to intimidate. He had to be gotten rid of.

Half the remainder of the Cabinet was dead or missing, so an outsider might question whether an acting secretary could be part of a "majority of the principal officers of the executive departments."

Finally, the big question revolved around the fact that there was no Congress to whom to transmit such a written declaration.

Hunter himself had no issue with any of the clauses. From his perspective, he'd just as soon make the written declaration himself, stick it in a filing cabinet against the time someone questioned it, depose Donnelly, and move on.

But the legalistic types, especially here in the West Wing, would need more. Hunter considered simply removing them with the Capitol Police or Secret Service, but that would be a bit more dramatic than would be helpful.

And then there was the Secret Service.

He didn't know for certain where their loyalties lay, but he was sure he didn't want to test them and find out.

But there had to be a way.

CHAPTER
FIFTY-ONE

1230 Zulu, 10 Nov
1330 Local Time
Brussels

In Doentiz's Brussels home, the NATO council's executive committee met. General Hornbeck, unofficially serving as deputy NATO supreme commander, looked out from a video teleconference screen.

Doenitz spoke. "This was a message. Yes, yes, it killed our soldiers, disrupted supply, and forced us to avoid the blast zones. But it also tells us how far Gregorivich will go." He sipped from a water bottle. "I no longer believe he intends to keep Poland, else he would not have deployed atomic weapons," he continued. "He will use Poland as a bargaining chip, offering to return it in exchange for the Baltic republics."

"Surely you do not suggest giving in?" asked the Latvian ambassador, Aivars Vanags. He was both angry and frightened. Angry that his country was almost completely occupied by invading Russians and terrified Gregorivich might use tactical nukes in Latvia.

"No, of course not," Doenitz replied.

Lebeau spoke up. "To me, it does not matter why they have done this. What is important is how we respond."

"I agree, Mr. Ambassador," said Hornbeck. "How we respond *is* critical. But we must understand how *Gregorivich* believes we will react. Otherwise, we may have to deal with unintended consequences."

"What the bloody hell difference does that make?" stuttered Climber, her arm now resting in a sling strapped securely to her abdomen. "There are always unintended consequences, and they're nearly always bad."

"But if we understand Gregorivich, we may avoid the worst." Her image momentarily glitched as the crypto resynched.

"NATO has always eschewed use of nuclear weapons," Doenitz said. "America is the only nation who ever really considered using them tactically, and even that differed from president to president."

He stood and paced, warming to his topic. "NATO has spent billions on defenses against radiological and chemical weaponry. During the 2003 invasion of Iraq, did not the Americans and your own soldiers, Madame Ambassador, carry or wear chemical suits?"

Climber nodded.

Doenitz continued. "Where we suspect use of a chemical or biological agent, it is doctrine to avoid those areas. The message to the world, then, is we will go to great lengths to avoid fighting on a battlefield where weapons of mass destruction have been used."

He stopped to face the group. "Politically, what has happened when terrorists attack our cities?" He didn't wait. "Populations grew angry and turned to the political right. Nations that endured such attacks became more insular, more unwilling to extend themselves for fear of attracting even more attention from the attackers."

Both the British and French ambassadors spluttered and

interrupted. Climber spoke over Lebeau. "But we rooted them out. We continue to fight."

Lebeau chimed in, "And our capabilities are improved. We keep them from crossing our borders. If they do enter, we find them."

Doenitz smiled. "Yes, but we haven't gone to the source. We have not been willing to do what the Americans do, destroy their home bases."

"That would mean forever war. We do not make the same mistake as the Americans," said Lebeau.

Hornbeck interjected. "I won't waste time defending our approach. But, from the Russian perspective?" She paused and cleared her throat. "The Russians perceive NATO's unwilling-ness to conduct offensive operations outside our own borders as weakness. Gregorivich sees nukes as exerting leverage, to make us withdraw. He doesn't believe we're truly committed to Poland or the Baltic nations. Just as we finally gave up in Ukraine, he wants us to abandon them out of self-protection. He believes he'll win an armistice that enshrines his territorial ambi-tions." She shook her head. "He's not afraid of us."

Długosz spoke, his voice a raspy whisper. "I for one say we must respond with atomic weapons. But not in Poland. We must hit the Russian fatherland."

A pin drop would have had the impact of a blockbuster bomb.

The meeting went into the early morning. When it ended, NATO would not abandon any of its members.

They would raise the stakes.

The next day, two nuclear-tipped missiles rose from the stormy waters of the North Atlantic between Iceland and the Scottish coast.

They climbed rapidly and turned eastward. Twenty-three

minutes later, five warheads separated from each of the missile bodies and screamed down toward western Russia. Anti-aircraft missile systems, modified to try to emulate the United States' ballistic missile defense, fired more than two dozen missiles against the man-made meteorites.

Two were stopped. The remainder obliterated five major Russian Army and Air Force centers, destroying munitions, airplanes, tanks, other vehicles, radars, all the equipment and supplies necessary for waging war. Thousands of Russian military personnel were also incinerated.

The bases had been chosen carefully for their size and contribution to the Russian war effort, and for their distance from civilian population centers.

At the same time the missiles clawed their way skyward, surviving NATO formations moved forward to resume an offensive that hadn't ended in Russian nuclear fire after all.

CHAPTER
FIFTY-TWO

0335 Zulu, 11 Nov
0635 Local Time
The Kremlin, Moscow

"Remkin, you said they would not retaliate."

A livid Gregorivich towered over his desk. Spit flew as he spoke. With every word, he slammed the palm of his hand against the desk.

Remkin had not been invited to sit. So he stood, trying to emulate some form of attention. "Mr. Pres—"

"Do not speak. No excuses."

He spun round and looked out the window. Winter quickly approached and frost etched the glass pane.

The bombs had fallen at just after 7:00 p.m. local time, ensuring most civilian workers had left. The message was clear: "We are not fighting the Russian people; we are fighting the Russian government."

Unfortunately, the message appeared to have gotten through to more Russians than Gregorivich would like, aided by a barrage of propaganda broadcasts. The security services and Ministry of Information had made every effort to block them, but they came from a cloud of nano-satellites seeded into existence almost overnight, broadcasting on entertainment bands, as well as all the frequencies used by the Russian government.

"Mr. President, please." He waited. He fought hard to keep his voice from quivering.

Remkin found himself way out of his depth. He did not fear dying in a nuclear-fueled fire. He dreaded what special agony the president might direct.

Finally, Gregorivich nodded curtly, though he kept his back turned.

"The Europeans are behaving in most unprecedented ways. They—"

The president whirled on him. "Don't tell me what they *are* doing. I want to know how to dissuade them from continuing to do it."

He stalked around the desk and glared down at Remkin.

Gregorivich stood a few inches taller than Remkin did under normal circumstances, but this morning he towered over Remkin, his bearing accentuated by rage.

"I can *guess* they're not behaving as you expect. There are over fifteen thousand dead Russians to vouch for your complete failure. I must completely crush NATO. I want to know what is the best way, the fastest way, to do it."

"Sir, my advisors believe it will take a full-scale nuclear strike on the United Kingdom. Intelligence believes, er, *I* believe the reason the French did not use their own weapons is they fear retaliation. The British have always been less easily intimidated. If you destroy Britain, you will destroy NATO's only backbone."

The president stared, then turned and stomped back to the window.

Remkin waited.

After a few minutes, the president turned back, his face more composed. He seemed nearly calm.

"Very well, Remkin. I agree," he said. "In fact, I came to the same conclusion myself. I ordered the attack prepared nearly an hour ago. We should be ready to launch in —" He consulted his watch. "—in just under thirty minutes."

He turned to face the window. Remkin sighed quietly, relieved.

Then he noticed Gregorivich studying his reflection. His mouth went dry, and he couldn't speak.

The president had bypassed him. Gregorivich had given the order to *someone else*. He wondered who. Most of all, he wondered what that meant for himself.

The president faced him again and leaned across the desk. He put both hands on top and said, voice low and controlled, "You are finished, Remkin. I have informed your deputy you have left your post and that he had better not fail me." He straightened and let his arms hang at his sides. He smiled coldly. "And you better ask whatever deity you believe in for mercy. You will need it. Get out."

As Remkin hurried from the room, he did something he had not done since he was a small child: he prayed.

He didn't even make it to the street.

When the elevator opened on the ground floor, three security men met him and took his arms. His head swam as his legs gave out, partly from the stark icy terror in the pit of his stomach, and partly from a sharp blow behind his knees.

His entire life had come to this moment. A sob escaped him.

"Here, Minister, let us help you. The president told us you didn't feel well."

The mechanical voice wasn't meant to persuade any witnesses that Remkin was sick, just to dissuade them from paying attention.

They ungently ushered Remkin into a side room. The man behind him thrust a hypodermic forcefully into his thigh.

He was dead in moments, his foaming mouth covered by a hood.

Colonel General Yeltsin, deputy commander of Russian Rocket Forces, stepped carefully into the president's office.

"Excuse me, Mr. President. We are ready to launch on your order. I have also arranged for you to watch the progress of the attack in real time from here. With your permission, we will install the necessary software." He waved at the classified computer that sat on a stand near the bookcase.

The president sat behind his desk, signing papers. He looked ordinary, calm.

Gregorivich smiled slightly and nodded.

Yeltsin briefly bowed his head. He opened the door again and gave a curt nod toward the hallway.

Two technicians hurried in. One quickly logged into the computer using a master password while the other watched. Then, they swapped places. A second password logged the system directly into the feed. Once they finished and the map display became active, they rose and hurried out the door. One nodded slightly as he left. Yeltsin heaved a sigh of relief.

"It's ready, Mr. President. You may issue the order yourself by clicking on this icon, here, and typing in this code."

He handed the president a small yellow sticky note with five handwritten letters, a number, and an asterisk. The president sat and did as instructed.

The two men watched as fifty icons, each indicating a nuclear-tipped intercontinental ballistic missile, rose from fields in Siberia and streaked westward.

CHAPTER
FIFTY-THREE

0602 Zulu, 11 Nov
0602 Local Time
North Sea, 35 nautical miles east of Scapa Flow

Aboard USS *Robert G. Bradley* (DDG-149), the TAO chatted with the CIC watch officer.

The upside to operating in the North Sea was that they were in what was called short haul communications range, that is, using low-power UHF to exchange messages with headquarters. It also let them receive regular supply and mail runs, which kept the ice cream machine full.

The downside was they could get messages *from* their head-quarters, which entailed the usual administrivia. *Bradley's* commanding officer sat reading a message draft.

Robert G. Bradley currently operated under the TACON of the Royal Navy as part of a flotilla of Ballistic Missile Defense — BMD — capable ships. Their mission was to defend the United Kingdom. They also launched occasional Tomahawk missiles as Russian military targets beckoned.

The CO had worked with NATO for over half his career. They were people he'd grown to like and respect for their professionalism and dedication. Now, he fought alongside them in a war for NATO's existence.

"Missile in flight. Missile in flight."

The monotone computer voice interrupted him.

"We've got launch indicators. Enemy missile launches, composition many. Conducting radar search," called the ADC.

Immediately, the TAO turned back to her console, her diatribe in support of black and white thrillers forgotten. The CICWO had likewise moved to ensure the alertness of his watch team. He needn't have worried. The announcement galvanized them. This would be the first time they'd ever used their BMD capability in combat — and they were ready.

The CO put the message down, almost grateful for the interruption. He flexed his hands as he looked at the angry red icons on the display.

Bradley defended northeastern England, from the Scottish border to Peterborough in the south. He smiled slightly. He defended Boston, a town far older than the Boston he'd grown up in.

"Radar horizon in . . . twelve minutes," said the TAO.

The CO nodded. Over his own headset came the clipped accent of the flotilla commander aboard HMS *Green Sea*.

"Hotel Bravo Eight, this is Hotel Bravo Eight actual. The game's afoot. Report only missed intercepts. We'll see you all on the other side. Out."

The CO smiled. The calm, cultivated British voice was so colorful.

The time slowly dragged by. With no radar contact, they had only an imprecise idea of the targets' locations. The reports came from satellites designed to detect the heat of rocket motors. Once the rockets burned out, the satellites were blind.

Finally, "Radar contact. One, no . . . three . . . now five, repeat, five contacts. Bearing zero six eight through zero seven two, max range."

Hundreds of miles away and over a hundred miles above the

earth, the powerful beams of the SPY-6 radar had found the inbound missiles coasting along a ballistic path.

She expanded the range on her console and looked up at the status display. "All headed for the UK, sir. Nothing at any other NATO country. 'Least, not yet."

The CO nodded. He wiped sweat beads that had formed on his dark shaved head, then rubbed his hand on his trousers.

"We should be seeing more as they come in range. Looks like they went for simultaneous impact, sir. Not very well executed, if you ask me," the TAO offered.

The CO smiled briefly. "That's in our favor, Tanya. Don't look a gift horse in the mouth."

A launch designed for simultaneous impact meant that since each missile had a different target, the launches were spread out in time. This allowed defending forces to engage them singly or in small groups based on their time of flight and target.

A simultaneous launch put all the weapons into flight at once. Even though they originated from three different locations, creating three different "clouds" of missiles in flight, they could overwhelm defenders since each cloud traveled together, dozens of missiles all needing to be engaged simultaneously.

The next few minutes flew by with the rapidly decreasing range.

"You may fire when ready," said the CO. He'd done it so the CIC watchstanders could hear his paraphrase of Admiral Dewey's command at Manila Bay.

The TAO smiled. "Aye, sir. Eighteen seconds."

The first missile roared out of its cell, shaking the ship. A second, a third, a fourth, then a fifth leapt into the sky.

"Sir, we've got skin on nine more but I told radar not to track them. They're engaged by other units, and they'll just clutter our screens."

Jacobson grunted. "Understood. But don't ignore them completely. If someone misses and we have a shot, I want to take it."

Bradley's missiles bolted out of the atmosphere toward a point in space where they'd intercept the attackers, destroying them with a skin-to-skin impact at a closure rate of over ten thousand miles per hour. All five seeker systems detected and acquired their targets.

However, in an incalculably bad coincidence, a nanosat passed through the same space as *Bradley*'s missile. The two collided. The only indicator the ship got that something had gone wrong was a blinking alert on the missile control console. In the heat of battle, the operator missed it.

"Radar contact on second wave, composition six. Firing."

Six more interceptors streaked from their cells.

"Sir, *Sea Green* and *Halyburton* both report missed intercepts. We're to engage," Callaghan said, leaning toward him.

He nodded.

Two more interceptors raced skyward.

At this rate, we'll be out of Schlitz pretty quickly.

In the near regions of space, warhead met warhead and explosions silently bloomed. The bridge watch saw pinpricks of light that expanded into glowing clouds of debris and slowly dissipated. But the OOD didn't need to report. CIC had their own ways of "seeing" whether they'd killed enemy missiles, and he knew better than to interrupt the flow of the battle being fought below. Instead, he perversely enjoyed the light show.

Finally, the pace slackened, the final enemy destroyed.

"TAO. Missed intercept on track six nine three four! Looks like the interceptor self-destructed before impact."

Blood drained from faces in CIC.

The TAO's head swiveled around to look at the missile operator, who stared at his console.

"TAO, aye. Fire again."

"It's inside minimum range."

The CO bristled. "Fire again. The p-sub-k of a missile sitting in our magazine is zero. Dammit, take the shot!" The probability of kill was the percent likelihood a weapon would kill its target.

Another interceptor streaked from its cell toward space.

The CO's heart had leapt into his throat at the missed intercept call. Now he prayed silently. His hands shook, so he put them on his knees and held on tightly.

"Fuck!"

He heart froze and he looked at the TAO. Pale, her mouth worked noiselessly.

"Shoot again, Tanya. Keep shooting as long as you can," he said, his voice gravelly and cracking.

"Aye, sir. ADC, TAO, shoot again."

Silence for a long moment.

Then, "Ma'am, I can't. The system won't let me engage a target that's past us. There's nobody in position to get that one."

The ADC's deadpan voice broke. There was nothing more to do.

"Where's that one headed?" the CO whispered hoarsely.

The TAO blinked. "York."

In a quiet street near downtown York, a dustman used the automatic arms on his lorry to pick up a dustbin that sat alongside the curb. He looked up to the east at a bright shooting star. He watched it with excitement. He'd loved meteor showers since he'd been a child. He knew this was none of the major showers, so he figured it to be some bit of random debris burning up. As he did, he noticed many glowing clouds to the east and grew uneasy.

It was his last thought as the meteor burst into a nuclear sun.

Aboard *Robert G. Bradley*, the CO stayed in Combat long enough to assure himself there were no more enemy missiles to engage. Only the hum of the electronics disturbed the funereal silence.

"Have the DCA work up the fallout pattern. If we need to, issue radiological protective gear to the crew. Tell me if we need to shift our station. Let the commodore know, too." Then he left, climbing the ladders wearily to his cabin. Locking the door, he lay face down on his rack and wept.

CHAPTER
FIFTY-FOUR

0715 Zulu, 11 Nov
0715 Local Time
The Bunker, United Kingdom

The British prime minister sat rigidly, hands folded on the desk. His home secretary stood swaying before him, visibly shaking. Next to her stood the defence secretary. He appeared to have more control over his autonomic functions. By contrast, his face was beet red.

"How bad is it?" asked the prime minister, staring straight ahead.

He still wore his bathrobe. Within minutes of missile launch detection, Royalty and Specialist Protection officers had rushed him to his armored Jaguar and driven him to a bunker well outside London.

The home secretary took the lead.

"As bad as it could be, Prime Minister. Actually, there's no way to know."

She motioned toward the ceiling. "The RAF will send reconnaissance flights as soon as they can. They'll take photos, of course, and measure radiation levels, but we still won't *know* until we get people into the devastated area." She scrubbed at her cheeks. "We've got fire and police coming from all over the kingdom. We don't know what to do with them, yet, of course. Civil defence, too. Hospitals across Yorkshire are calling everyone in to handle the injured."

The prime minister looked at them for the first time. "How many casualties?"

The two secretaries traded glances. Defence answered. "We don't know, sir. York's population is nearly two hundred thousand." The prime minister winced, so he hurriedly added, "It won't be that many. But it could be half that. It was an air burst, eight hundred kilotons, forty times the size of the bombs dropped on Japan. Given how densely packed the older part of the city is . . . ." He paused and swallowed hard. "It could be as low as fifty thousand, or as many as a hundred."

He lapsed into silence. Only the ticking of the grandfather clock to the side of the windowless room disturbed the quiet.

"It could be days, weeks, perhaps months, before we have any idea, Prime Minister," continued the home secretary. "I don't know that the Japanese have ever determined how many people disappeared."

The prime minister lowered his gaze and reached out to twiddle with a paperweight. When he looked up again, fire blazed in his eyes.

He looked first at his home secretary. "Do whatever you must to help the people of York. Expend any moneys you need. If anyone stands in your way, I want to know immediately."

Then he looked at Defence. "Select *two* Russian cities the size of York. I want them destroyed, is that clear? I want that right bastard in the Kremlin to see we will not be cowed, by God. We will burn his country for him, city by city, if he chooses."

Defence breathed heavily. "Yes, Prime Minister. It shall be done."

"I don't care a whit what it takes. Use every missile you need. I want him to know what this feels like."

Seeing their looks, he waved his hand. "Oh, yes, I know he doesn't give a damn about his people. But, by God, he cares about power. If we can shock his people into realizing what he's got them into, maybe they'll throw him out."

He thought for a moment. "When you look for targets, choose places where there is something Gregorivich cares about, like his dacha, a girlfriend, a bank, something."

Defence said, "I'll bring the nuclear release codes in a few moments."

"What of Parliament, sir? The king?" asked Home.

"Once I'm dressed, I'll notify the king and the shadow prime minister. I presume they are also in their bunkers?"

"The king is at Birkhall, sir. Parliament is scattered, but yes, the opposition leader is in the bunker."

"Well, there's little doubt of their support." He rose and tucked his bathrobe more tightly around himself, then pushed past them. As he did, he said, "Get a move on, Alistair. I want two Russian cities in flames by midday. Sooner, if possible."

Defence called after him, "Do we want to limit casualties?"

He turned and regarded them for a moment, then shook his head firmly. "No. We are past that. Don't misunderstand, I've no taste for killing civilians. But it is time we took the gloves off. They were looking to obliterate us, our people, our country. By the grace of God and the Royal and American Navies, they failed. Now it is our turn."

The prime minister closed his eyes then looked at Defence again. He said quietly, "We're burning his cities, Alistair. Is there any meaningful way to reduce casualties?"

Defence shook his head. "Not really, sir."

The prime minister turned and continued out the door.

Two hours later a second Royal Navy submarine opened its missile tube doors. Two missiles emerged. When they popped to the surface, their rocket motors ignited and they sprinted skyward.

At apogee, the shroud that protected the warheads from the rush of air fell away as they climbed into space. Five warheads separated from each of the missiles.

More alert, the result of the previous attack, Russian defenses shot down six of the ten.

However, four were enough.

The city of Smolensk disappeared in a single burst of atomic fire.

The city of Kaluga, on the outskirts of Moscow, suffered not one but three manmade fireballs.

CHAPTER
FIFTY-FIVE

1630 Zulu, 11 Nov
1930 Local Time
The Kremlin, Moscow

Had he been looking out his Kremlin window, Gregorivich would have seen the fireballs. Instead, he'd been hustled to a bunker deep below Moscow as soon as the British launch was detected.

But he'd felt the tremors in the floor and shaken with rage.

He returned to his office well after dark. A glow arose on the horizon to the south from fires that still raged in Kaluga.

His secretary knocked gently and tiptoed in. The foreign minister begged for a moment of his time.

"Does he not realize that when he arrives without an appointment and asks for a minute, that he is saying his time is more valuable than mine?"

She stood mute, staring at the carpet.

"Oh, very well. He'd better have good news, or he'll end up like Remkin."

She scurried out. In a moment, Ivan Kolchavin walked in.

"Mr. President." He bowed his head slightly as he spoke.

"What do you want?"

Noting the acerbic tone and Gregorivich's immediate turn to business, Kolchavin went straight to the point.

A tall, spare man, bald with a fringe of white hair that wrapped around the back of his head from ear to ear, Kolchavin's face was heavily wrinkled, his voice raspy from years of smoking.

"Mr. President, I wish to express my sorrow on Remkin's death. His suicide, I mean."

The president snorted and looked up, locking Kochavin's eyes with his own. "*Spacibo*. My hands are full fighting a war he appeared intent on losing. The deaths of so many thousands of our people weighed heavily on him. Perhaps it is better."

Kolchavin looked down, breaking eye contact. The president relaxed and sat back.

"Very good, Mr. President. But I wonder if it is time to end the escalation? Perhaps a covert message to NATO that we have ended the, ah, nuclear phase of the conflict?"

The president regarded him. Then he rose and walked around the desk to the corner table. He poured himself a drink, which he sipped as he turned back. He did not offer one to his visitor. "What makes you say that?"

His voice was cold, tone flat. Kolchavin took a deep breath. "Mr. President, I simply offer options, which you may accept or reject." He adjusted his cuffs. "My UK experts assess the British will not back down. They will instead continue to escalate until they believe it is no longer necessary. After all, these same people survived the Blitz." He tapped his hand on the back of the chair in front of him. "I agree with my analysts."

"You only remember part of your history. The Russian people also survived the Nazis. The toll was far higher, the destruction much greater." Gregorivich took another sip. "We have a far greater capacity to absorb loss than they do. If they insist on bringing complete destruction on themselves, so be it."

Kolchavin stopped himself from twisting his watch. "Mr.

President, you are, of course, correct." He leaned forward. "But to what end, sir? There is no need. I believe we can defeat NATO despite American assistance. It will take longer, but victory is inevitable." He paused. "However, if we fight an all-out nuclear war, even with just England, we will lose more cities, more industrial centers, more resources. Those losses will make it more difficult to maintain your position as the most powerful man on earth."

The president set his empty glass on the tray and grunted. "They will find it hard to strike back once we destroy their blasted submarines. Once that is done, we will annihilate England." He moved behind his desk and sat.

Kolchavin nodded slightly. "Yes, Mr. President, I expect you will succeed," he said. "But I have spent years working with NATO diplomats and their military advisors. Should we destroy the UK, France will fear they are next. They will act."

He raised his hand as the president began to respond. It was now or never. "I do not doubt we could then destroy France. But before we do, they will inflict significant losses on the *Rodina*. To avoid that necessitates we launch a preemptive attack on France at the same time as the UK."

He lowered his voice and pushed his shoulders back. "I do not question your decisions, sir, nor your authority. Far be it. However, I give you my best assessment to inform your decision-making."

"Do you think I am ill-informed?" Gregorivich's eyes were steely. His shoulders were hunched and taut.

"Of course, not, sir. However, Minister Remkin's, ah, suicide, suggests he did not present you with good estimates of NATO's probable reactions. I suspect he gave you only military assessments, not understanding of their leadership."

The president visibly relaxed, his shoulders sank back into the chair. After a moment, he said, "You are correct about his failures."

Gregorivich rose and strode about the space between the

desk and window, pacing between the bookcases and the wall. "But the very fact you have spent so much time with them casts doubt on your advice. It influences your perceptions. You are no longer objective."

He waved his hand dismissively and returned to behind the desk, his back against the wall. "The French are not stupid, but they are not brave. They have sold us weapons and ships because I am strong. They respect and fear me. They only fight now because battlefields in Poland are far from their borders. But they will hesitate when they have seen what happens to their precious allies. When radioactive debris is strewn across England, they will bow to the inevitable." He smiled coldly. "Once France withdraws, NATO will collapse, and we will move swiftly through Poland into Germany. Once there, the Germans will be repaid for what they did to us. Russia will be the dominant nation on this planet."

Kolchavin thought, *But he is wrong. The French will not back down.*

He had little hope Russia could find and kill the British submarines. Nor could they attrite the ships defending England. And if even one of those submarines launched all their remaining missiles—.

He could not let that happen.

Kolchavin rose and said, "Very well, Mr. President. I will, of course, obey your orders. Good evening, sir."

As he moved quickly through the door, he hoped he'd last longer than Remkin.

CHAPTER
FIFTY-SIX

1445 Zulu, 11 Nov
2345 Local Time
USS *Blue Ridge*, **Western Pacific**

Vice Admiral Simpson read over the intel operator's shoulder. South Korea would deploy an ASW task force to support sub-hunting operations in the East China Sea. That would relieve some of her worries as her own force moved to where it could strike.

"Missile launch. Multiple missile launches." Every head turned toward the large screen display. Angry red symbols indicating ballistic missiles proliferated over central China.

"How many?" she asked.

The operator was silent. Simpson stifled her impatience.

After a moment, he answered, "At least thirty. Two locations, one we knew about and one we didn't."

"What types?" She hadn't been able to bite off the question. Her fingers drummed on the back of his chair.

"Unknown, ma'am. We gotta wait for first stage burnout. But the trajectory looks medium range. Definitely not ICBMs."

She relaxed but only a little.

316 THOMAS M. WING

It could still be against Guam, or Japan, or . . . .

"Initial impact prediction is . . . well, not us, ma'am."

The operator looked up at her as he finished. She released the breath she'd been holding. Someone else's night was going to be interesting.

"Aye. Where're they headed?"

"Well, if the *Kearsarge* is still on the track COMNAVFOR-JAPAN passed us, they're the target."

Simpson sighed. "Make sure our BMD ships have the launch points in case they throw a second set at us. Then pray for our friends up north."

She strode to her command chair, forcing herself to walk slowly. There she sat, chin in hand, elbow cocked nonchalantly on the chair arm. She even forced a yawn, though her fingers kept drumming.

Those had to be the carrier killers. She'd wondered when they'd come.

Well, tomorrow we'll get a piece of our own back.

Simpson closed her eyes and sighed.

"You read it, I take it, Letty?" Simpson handed the short message back to Brickman.

"Yes, ma'am. Pretty bad. Not counting the dead and injured, losing those twelve JSF aboard *Kearsarge* is a punch in the belly."

Simpson agreed. She had only one squadron of F-35 Joint Strike Fighters aboard *Reagan*. They were the most advanced aircraft available, theoretically able to penetrate Chinese missile defenses to hit well-defended targets F-18 Hornets couldn't go against. She'd been amazed the *Kearsarge* squadron had survived in the first place.

"Okay, Letty, adjust your plans. When you're done, tell me how bad it is."

"We'll nug it out, but it'll be a helluva lot harder. I'll know more in a couple of hours." She moved to leave, then turned back. "At least most of her escorts survived. We'll need those TLAM. And the Japanese destroyers should help our own survivability. Especially since they validated the anti-ballistic missile tactics."

Simpson smiled. "Thanks. Keep focused on any kind of silver lining."

Twelve hours later, Seventh Fleet executed their first attacks.

As the first Tomahawks roared from their launchers, crews cheered. Simpson watched from the *Blue Ridge*'s flag bridge. They'd fought so hard to take the offensive, to seize the initiative.

Thirty minutes later, dozens of aircraft lifted off *Reagan's* deck and headed west. She could replace neither the men and women flying those planes nor the planes themselves, but she had no choice but to send them into harm's way.

She'd flown over and spoken with them in their ready rooms. They'd made it clear they were ready and wanted to go — and would have roasted her head on a spit had she not sent them. She smiled ruefully.

The silent wait in TFCC was excruciating. Around her, the staff quietly performed their duties. The time of impact for the Tomahawk strike came and went.

"Initial BDA looks fairly good, though we can't be sure that some of the sites didn't go down to hide from follow-on strikes," reported Proudfoot. He'd been watching the intel broadcast, the only source they had. "Their IADS were as tough as we expected, but I don't think they knew about our anti-radiation homing capability, or how good it is. So I think we degraded about forty percent of it with the T-birds. That should help the Hornets. Plus, the stealth of the F-35s was as good as advertised, maybe better. We didn't lose a single one." The Integrated Air

Defense Systems was China's system of systems to defend its airspace.

"What about collateral damage?" Brickman asked.

"Impossible to estimate without imagery. We have reports from pilots, of course, but that's usually low accuracy. It looks pretty minimal, though, since most targets were pretty far from civilian centers."

Simpson nodded. Her guidance had been clear: avoid civilian casualties, if possible. She doubted the Chinese had been quite as careful. Her lip curled into a snarl.

The Hornet sorties suffered losses, at least some due to her directive. In all, they'd lost eleven of sixty F-18s. Given the distance there'd been no radio comms, so they had no idea if any pilots had survived. She prayed but the odds were against them.

"Ops, what's our next move?" she asked, swallowing her worries.

"Well, ma'am, we need to know how successful *TR*'s strikes are. For now, I think we can continue with Phase 2 ops against targets ashore. If they have the same level of success, we might be able to initiate Phase 3 ops at sea, establishing maritime superiority. I'm certain we can do that in the South China Sea, thanks to *Nicholas*. Chinese bombers are still a threat. And we don't know if they have any more of those ballistic missiles they used to take out *Kearsarge*."

Proudfoot scowled. "The Japanese were pretty damned effective in countering them, but a saturation raid against us would be bad. The chaff worked some, but not as well as we'd need. Same with the jamming."

Kearsarge now formed a reef in the cold waters of the western Pacific. The crew had fought valiantly, but firemain breaks had kept one of the ammunition magazines from flooding. The resulting explosion had killed and wounded hundreds of sailors and blown out watertight bulkheads. The flooding heeled the mighty warship dangerously to starboard, and the XO had reluctantly ordered her abandoned. She'd still taken over two hours to go down, as if fighting for every breath as she died.

Simpson gathered those of her staff not on watch in the conference room.

"All right, people, what are we missing here?" she asked.

As she swiveled her chair around, her eyes swept her staff. Most met her eyes directly, calmly. Only a few, mostly younger members, looked elsewhere. She smiled. They'd gelled into a fine team.

"Ma'am, where are our strategic bombers?" asked one young lieutenant.

Simpson grimaced slightly.

"The answer isn't one we like. The bombers survived, though fuel and weapons are a major challenge. But," she paused for a moment, "we're not going to use them."

A few murmurs broke out, and there were more than a few surprised looks.

"Look, it's a difficult decision," she said. "But the acting chairman's logic is solid." She sipped her coffee. "The enemy has a pretty good idea of the damage they inflicted. Unfortunately, their imagery satellites are still working. Even if they weren't, there's enough commercial satellite imagery available to let them know what survived. Leadership did their best to force companies to make the photos inaccessible, and the Chinese did a fairly good job of that themselves with cyber and physical attacks against the internet. But not enough." She shrugged and shook her head.

"If we use the big boys, it'll look like we're upping the ante. The fact that both Russia and NATO have traded nukes makes it even more likely. That means they'd respond with both tactical and strategic nukes. We have a lot more strategic nukes than they do, so they'd assume they were in a use-'em-or-lose-'em scenario. They'd launch everything they have. And we'd be on the receiving end of the tactical stuff."

She chuckled mirthlessly. "I'd very much like *not* to face tactical nukes. We've got enough problems."

The men and women in the seats were deathly quiet. A few shifted uneasily. Most looked down at notebooks they held. They didn't like it.

She continued. "So, as much as we could use the help, there'll be no long-range bombers. We're not hitting their nuclear capability, either, and that sends a strong message. Hopefully, that reduces the risk of things going high order." She looked around again. "Anything else?"

After answering a few more questions, the meeting adjourned.

"Should we have been that upfront, telling 'em we're out here alone and unafraid?" Brickman asked.

Simpson nodded. "No point hiding it. They need to know what we're up against. You know me, I believe in telling it like it is."

Brickman and Proudfoot looked doubtful but said nothing more.

Three hours later the next wave of Hornets, JSF, and Tomahawks were outbound toward the Chinese coast.

CHAPTER
FIFTY-SEVEN

0005 Zulu, 12 Nov
0905 Local Time
USS *Blue Ridge*, Western Pacific

Simpson took the opportunity to shower, following the night spent in TFCC. As she finished soaping her face, the speaker outside the head in her cabin erupted.

"General Quarters, General Quarters. All hands man your battle stations. Enemy missiles inbound. General Quarters. Make manned and ready reports to the bridge and DC Central."

The *bong-bong-bong* of the GQ alarm followed.

But before the repeat even started, she turned the water back on, hurriedly rinsed off, and jumped out to towel off. In less than two minutes she walked into TFCC.

"What's going on?" she asked as she took her command chair.

"Multiple ballistic missile launches from one of the sites that hit *Kearsarge*, and a new one."

"Is it our turn?" she asked, then didn't need to hear the answer. The beads of sweat on Hillerman's face said it all. She leaned back in her chair and looked up into the overhead.

Around her drawn faces stared intently at consoles and computer screens. She needed to say something.

"Well, we've once again proved that emergencies only happen when someone tries to take a shower, and only after they've fully soaped their face."

A few chuckles and small smiles rewarded her. She sighed. The tension wasn't gone, but it was more pliable.

"How'd they find us, ma'am?" Hillerman asked.

"Probably tracked returning strikes. No matter how careful, we're in their backyard. The closer we are, the harder it is to hide." She shrugged. "It was bound to happen. I just wish it had been later."

The icons inexorably closed her force.

Her stomach tightened. She looked down at her hands, tightly gripping the arms of her chair. She forced them to relax. She wanted to put them in her lap and rub them. But that would make her look nervous. So, she simply put her chin in one and tried to look bored.

"*Shiloh*'s ordered the force to light off radars," reported Hillerman.

Simpson closed her eyes and breathed heavily. They had no choice, but it was like turning on a beacon.

As radars detected targets, she blinked. Dozens of aircraft flew in five straight lines, all within a few hundred miles east. All were quickly identified as commercial aircraft.

She'd so completely shifted to war-fighting mode that she hardly remembered what a non-military airplane was. Above the dark sea, passengers and cargo flew, peacefully pursuing their own business, while beneath them her fleet would soon be fighting for their lives.

The radio speaker above her chirped as *Shiloh* passed another directive. "Zulu, this is Charlie Zulu Six. We put out a warning on International Air Distress telling those COMAIR to get the hell out of the area. Make sure you don't accidentally engage them."

Brickman came to stand by her. She shrugged. "Can't afford to waste missiles."

Simpson smiled.

Then, the fight began in earnest.

"*Shiloh*'s engaging, ma'am. Chaffing and jamming, per the plan," reported the battle watch.

For the next twenty-two minutes streaks of outbound missile fire sought inbound enemy warheads. The superheated bodies of the carrier killers glowed brightly, illuminating the black night. Soon the twinkling lights of small explosions intensified the show as missile met missile.

"Alpha Alpha, Charlie Zulu Six. Lima Kilo Echo's been hit."

Simpson winced. They couldn't afford to lose ships, especially not *Lake Erie* with her large load of cruise and anti-air missiles.

The wave of red icons was slowly culled. But those that remained relentlessly closed her fleet. The display operator kept zooming in so the tracks didn't become a red and blue mass at the center of the screen.

"Missiles inbound. All hands brace for shock." The call over the ship's announcing system caught her by surprise.

She looked up. Seat belt already fastened, her hands still automatically reached under the arms and locked tight to the chair frame. Her left eyelid spasmed. She took a slow deep breath to counter her short shallow ones. Brickman grabbed a handhold in the overhead and the arm of Simpson's chair.

From topside came the roar of Sea Sparrow missiles leaving launchers. But they had no chance. Time slowed until she was thrown from her chair and the lights went out.

———

The warhead penetrated deep into *Blue Ridge*'s guts before exploding. It passed through the flag intelligence space where Proudfoot and Percy were updating target lists.

The blast created an empty space filled with fire. It buckled watertight bulkheads and smashed systems, cables, and pipes.

But *Blue Ridge* was fortunate: though gravely wounded, the hull didn't rupture.

The ship that had saved her was not so lucky.

Destroyer *Hoel* had been on station astern of *Blue Ridge* to provide anti-missile defense. When her CO saw three of the warheads on a direct path to strike the ship he was supposed to protect, he'd ordered full speed and brought his ship close alongside to starboard. His helo laid a chaff cloud ahead and just to starboard of the two ships so they'd pass through its edge.

He succeeded in fooling the warhead seekers into thinking the chaff cloud was a carrier. Unfortunately, the solid steel of *Hoel*'s deck convinced the electronic brains she was the center of their target.

One impacted just aft of the bridge, breaking the ship's back. The second hit the water just feet to starboard, abeam the ship's smokestack. When it exploded, it blew a hole in the starboard side below the waterline. As the ship died, she folded up, bow and stern rising as she sank by the middle, crushing the superstructure. Then she rolled slowly to starboard and disappeared.

Rear Admiral Sam Hiakawa, commander of the *Ronald Reagan* strike group, stared at the display in his own TFCC. The icons that represented *Blue Ridge* and *Hoel* blinked silently. Solid only a moment ago, now they showed the last known position of ships that no longer transmitted their location in the data link.

He silently prayed for a malfunction, but he knew at least two of the three missiles must have hit.

He cleared his throat. "Ops, try to raise *Blue Ridge* or Admiral Simpson, please."

The Ops boss shook himself and reached for the radio handset. As he touched it, the bitch box above his head blared. *Reagan*'s Combat Direction Center, the carrier's equivalent of a combatant's CIC, reported, "TFCC, CDC. Helos report *Blue Ridge* is burning. She's dropping out of formation. But *Hoel* . . . . She's just — gone."

Hiakawa broke the stillness. "Ops, pass the word on the command circuit. I'm assuming command of the force."

The operations officer regarded him for a moment, then said, "Aye, sir."

He stared for a second at the handset, then put it to his mouth and keyed it.

CHAPTER
FIFTY-EIGHT

1300 Zulu, 11 Nov
0800 Eastern Time
National Security Advisor's Office, The White House

Hunter's head hurt.

When Donnelly had attempted a nuclear strike, it had all been academic. Casualty counts were mere numbers, potential American losses purely notional.

But the fighting in Europe had seared reality into his brain. He'd tried to ignore news video. But in the end, human fascination with horror had forced him to look.

The president hadn't exploded over the loss of American lives. But his moments of lucidity were fewer and farther between.

Hunter was grateful they'd avoided such devastation on American soil. For now. He paced his office. It couldn't be allowed to happen.

For one thing, I live in a primary target.

Both the attorney general and secretary of state had refused to come to the White House, despite his best efforts. Hauptman put it bluntly when he said, "If the president wants me there, he'll ask me himself. I don't take direction from you."

Kingston used ongoing diplomatic efforts as his excuse.

But Hunter needed them. Of the thirteen surviving cabinet officials, two were in hospitals and three more were out of DC. Apparently unwilling to return, they remained wherever they'd been stranded. The remaining six would resist. Their positions had been rewards for campaign donations. They'd support Donnelly to the end.

Then he had a thought. "Ann, get your ass in here!"

Selstrom scuttled through the door, tablet in hand. He sneered when her dress caught momentarily on the doorknob.

"Get the attorney general on the phone."

"The national security advisor, Mr. Hunter, for the attorney general. It's about treason," said Selstrom.

When Hauptman himself got on the phone and told her to get her boss on the line, she buzzed the intercom. Hunter picked up.

"Hi, Karl. Thought you'd talk to me this time."

Selstrom wanted to hang up, but the word treason frightened and excited her. Instead, she clicked her mechanical pencil near the receiver and listened.

"You better not be fucking with me. What's this about?" asked Hauptman.

"It's a bit complicated—"

"Cut to the chase. I don't have all day."

She heard Hunter chuckle

"All right. The president is a traitor."

The line went silent.

"What the hell are you talking about?"

"I mean I was on the line when he talked with Gregorivich day before yesterday. He mentioned a deal they'd made. When

China attacked us, the Russians would attack *them*. It was a plan, Karl. He *goaded* them into it. He just didn't know they'd do such a bang-up job."

Selstrom's eyes went wide. She nearly dropped the phone.

"Are you sure?" Hauptman asked. "You didn't dream this?"

"Come on, Karl. He thinks Gregorivich is going to attack China. You and I both know the man's not that stupid. And he's got enough to deal with in Europe. We can't let that nut in the Oval get *us* into a nuclear war. We need to act. You're the AG. Do something. Arrest him."

"Ha! And let that idiot Kingston take over? Not on your life. We need someone strong in there. Kingston's a snowflake. He'd probably surrender."

"I'll let you and he figure out who gets to sit on the throne. I sure as hell don't want the job."

"Of course not, you're a coward." Hauptmann's voice paused. "Hmmm . . . . Maybe there's a way. We need to talk to Kingston."

Selstrom bobbled the receiver when Hunter yelled from his office. "Ann! Get the secretary of state on a conference call."

"Y-yes, sir. Right away."

She quickly flashed the phone and dialed. "Conference call with the AG and Mr. Hunter, for the secretary."

Kingston picked up. Selstrom clicked her pencil again.

"Kingston. To what do I owe this, um, pleasure? I have a job, you know."

Hunter laughed. "Herman, you can't hide forever."

The two men quickly brought Kingston up to speed.

When they'd finished, Kingston whistled. "Well, I told the stupid sonuvabitch that someone who knew what they were doing ought to run foreign policy. This is where it got him, by the balls. You gonna arrest him, Karl?"

"I don't see a choice. Why don't Hunter and I go over there this afternoon and confront him. We'll see what he has to say. Assuming he doesn't have a good explanation, I'll go back to

Justice and bring in the FBI. Then we'll get the chief justice to swear you in."

"You don't think I should go with you?" Kingston asked.

"No, no. You there makes it look like a coup. You need to keep out of it," Hauptman replied.

"Let me know what happens." Kingston hung up.

Hauptman said, "I need time to set up the FBI. Give me three hours."

The phone clicked off. Selstrom hurriedly hung up.

CHAPTER
FIFTY-NINE

1600 Zulu, 11 Nov
1100 Eastern Time
The Oval Office, The White House

Three hours later, Hunter was in the Oval Office. Donnelly appeared rational. For the moment.

"Jack, how are you? What have you got for me? How goes the war?"

Hunter hesitated. "Well, Mr. President, the Navy's conducting missile strikes on China." Hunter found himself talking to the president like he would a toddler.

A knock sounded. The attorney general walked in, the door held by the Secret Service agent outside. The president had forbidden them to be inside during meetings.

"Karl. How are you? Welcome back," the president gushed, all smiles.

"I'm fine, Mr. President. A bit tired from the long car trip back."

"Damned airlines. They ought to be flying."

Hauptman and Hunter exchanged a glance. Hauptman walked up to the edge of the desk.

"How are you, sir? I imagine it's been rough. Thank God the White House has power. So much of the country is still dark."

The president stared at him as if he'd spoken a foreign language. "What do you mean? Why aren't there lights?"

"The attack, sir. A lot of the power companies are still making repairs. But the fall leaves were beautiful."

"Ah, the fall leaves. I wish I were back in Boston. The colors are so beautiful. But Hunter here's keeping me too damned busy."

Hauptman looked at Hunter again and raised his eyebrows. Hunter just shrugged slightly and shook his head.

"Well, sir, perhaps we can do something about that."

Hauptman pulled out an odd-looking object. He shot Donnelly in the chest.

Hunter froze.

They were supposed to steer the discussion toward the telephone call with Gregorivich. Hauptman would record it, then go back to Justice and get a warrant for the president's arrest.

Hunter's head swam.

The president's eyes went wide, then closed as his body crumpled behind the desk.

Hunter's eyes swung to the door. It was just opening, the agent coming to investigate. Hauptman spun and shot the agent. The man's body splayed back and to the side, falling as he brought his own weapon out of its shoulder holster. But he never got off a shot. In seconds he lay on the floor, his stare glassy.

Hunter turned back to Hauptman. He noted the tiny thread of smoke rising from the gun barrel.

Hauptman moved to the dead agent and picked up his weapon. Hunter belatedly moved as the barrel swung to point at him. He barely had time to register Hauptman's finger tensing on the trigger before the barrel filled with smoke and jerked backward. Hunter felt the bullet enter his chest. He lost control of his legs. The office spun as he fell to the carpet.

His last sight was the blue and white threads of the carpet as darkness closed in.

————————

Hauptman hurried to Hunter's body and placed his own gun in the right hand. Holding the dead hand around it, he aimed at the wall to the right of the president's desk, fired twice, then dropped the weapon and hand to the floor.

Rising again, he hastened back to where he'd stood when he shot the president and peeled a thick layer of dried glue off his hand. He crumpled it and stuffed it into the water bottle that sat on the president's desk. Closing the top, he shook it vigorously for a few seconds. Time rapidly running out, he dumped the contents into the floor planter next to the desk, recapped the bottle and put it back. He returned the agent's gun and collapsed on the sofa.

The Secret Service quick response team rushed through the door moments later. Hauptman dropped to the floor on command. They quickly searched him and cuffed his hands behind his back. The agents roughly grabbed his elbows and lifted him, throwing him back onto the sofa. An agent covered him with his weapon.

With the scene secure, the agent in charge questioned Hauptman.

After nearly two hours of interrogation and detailed examination of Hunter's body with a mobile test kit, the AIC ordered Hauptman uncuffed. He apologized for the rough handling.

"That's all right, Agent Elliott. I expect you to do your job, and that includes making sure you have the facts before you jump to conclusions. Thank you. I just wish I'd been able to save the president. Who knew Hunter had become so power hungry and deranged?" he said, rubbing his wrists.

He left the White House. There were no records of the

conversation with Hunter before they'd brought Kingston in. It would be his word against Kington's. He'd testify that he'd urged Hunter and Kingston not to try to remove the president. His phone call to the FBI would confirm he'd been worried about a coup.

Hauptman would step up to save a government that hovered on the brink due to the treasonous behavior of some of the president's senior advisors. He would act to preserve the Republic. Kingston would be imprisoned.

He smiled coldly. Yes, it would all work out.

Kingston nearly leapt out of this seat.

"He WHAT?" he shouted.

McClusky replied, "I said, Hunter shot the president. The AG was there. Hunter seems to have thought the AG was on his side, so the Secret Service had time to get in and take out Hunter."

"How the hell did Hunter get a gun into the Oval, for God's sake?"

McClusky shrugged and raised his hands to his waist. "Three-D printed plastic. Secret Service speculates Hunter had been smuggling pieces in over time and reassembled it inside the secure area."

Kingston sank back down. Madness.

Ann Selstrom sobbed at her desk. Despite her mistreatment at Hunter's hands, she hadn't wanted him dead. Nor did she believe him capable of murder. During the phone call, no one had said anything about killing the president.

There was nothing she could do. However, she knew

someone who might. She'd briefly dated an FBI agent. It hadn't worked, but they'd parted as friends.

She lifted the phone.

CHAPTER
SIXTY

00315 Zulu, 11 Nov
1015 Local Time
USS *Nicholas*, South China Sea

Bill stood on the starboard bridge wing and stared at the paper.

Simpson had been chief of staff when he'd been a flag aide years before. Bill had worked closely with her.

"Fuck!"

The information technology specialist blanched and shrank back against the bulkhead. Bill took a quick breath and let it out slowly. "Sorry about that, Petty Officer Cooper. Do you know what's in here?"

Cooper quickly shook his head. He *had* read it, of course. Radiomen had been reading messages since radio first arrived aboard ships. But he certainly wasn't going to admit it.

Bill closed his eyes for a few seconds and pretended to go along.

"That's all right. I'm sure someone will fill you in. It's not good news. Not catastrophic but certainly not good. But it's going to be okay. Thanks for bringing it up."

He turned and raised his binoculars to stare out at nothing.

Cooper left quickly.

Hearing the watertight door close, Bill lowered the binoculars again but kept staring out to sea.

The wind had kicked up. Whitecaps, big ones with staying power, stretched to the horizon. The sky to the west was dark with rain. It competed strangely with the bright sun and painfully blue sky overhead. The ship herself rolled ponderously. They were low on fuel again, but unless something bad happened, they'd refuel in the next several hours.

Nicholas steamed slowly south.

The task of cleaning up the bridge and making it functional had consumed most of two days. Once the grisly aftermath had been removed, the damage controlmen had welded a patch over the hole where Barrister had died, a few feet from his chair. Unfortunately, the scene remained vivid in his mind's eye. So he avoided it. The starboard bridge wing was his new habitat.

They'd also patched the port bulkhead as best they could. But they'd had to tac weld shut the door to the bridge wing where Houseman and Nelson had died. Too badly holed, they'd cut most of it away and thrown it over the side to keep the bent and twisted steel from increasing their radar cross section. They'd been extremely lucky the port side radar array had escaped serious damage.

As if they'd known about the Vietnamese offer, the Cam Ranh Bay shipyard had been bombed the morning following the battle. *Nicholas* was on her own again.

What's next? Or, perhaps more to the point, who *is next?*

For the first time his hands twitched, so much he stopped taking tea on the bridge, drinking only in his cabin or the darkened CIC.

It wasn't fear for himself. He feared more of his people would be hurt or die. He saw the torn bodies in his sleep, life seeping from them. Sometimes they spoke, their eyes accusing.

Barrister was the worst. He would meet her supply officer fiancé someday, assuming they both survived. Would he accuse

Bill of complicity in his love's death? An irrational fear, but no less real for it.

"Sir, lookout reports a pair of aircraft, low and fast, dead ahead, position angle one."

The OOD's voice sounded urgent but calm. Even fatalistic. In the back of his mind, he rebuked himself for not growing hard himself.

Bill raised his binoculars.

Two dots quickly resolved themselves. The OOD stuck his head out the door. "TAO says they've got 'em on gun camera. Confirms Hornets, sir."

Bill relaxed.

The aircraft sighted *Nicholas* and broke left and right, increasing speed and circling at a distance. They'd confirm whose warships they faced before they got too close.

Apparently satisfied, they continued their approach. A couple of miles out, the fighter coming in from starboard broke south while the one approaching from port flew directly over-head, waggling its wings as it marked on top. The ship shud-dered with the jet noise. Cheers came from the main deck, several of his sailors having come out to catch a glimpse of the first American aircraft they'd seen since well before the war.

The planes repeated their performance over *Da Nang*. He'd stationed her on *Nicholas's* starboard quarter at only two thou-sand yards to make clear she was a friend. She also flew a huge Vietnamese naval ensign.

When they flew off north, his tension eased. It would be nice to operate with air cover.

CHAPTER
SIXTY-ONE

0430 Zulu, 11 Nov
1130 Local Time
USS *Theodore Roosevelt*, **South China Sea**

When *Nicholas* reported for duty as tradition demanded, the admiral summoned Bill. Thirty minutes later he landed on *Theodore Roosevelt*'s flight deck, courtesy of his one remaining helicopter.

He stepped out amidst the controlled chaos and heard the two double bell strokes followed by the announcement, "*Nicholas*, arriving."

Quickly escorted to the island, a petty officer stood just inside the watertight door. She took his helmet and life jacket, and another petty officer whisked him down a ladder and through the long, blue-tiled passageway to the flag cabin. Arriving at the royal blue door with the big brass plaque that told him Commander, Carrier Strike Group Seven, resided there, Bill knocked then entered.

"Reporting as ordered, sir."

Rear Admiral Gupta rose from his desk chair and strode to

the door, smiling with hand outstretched. The other three officers also rose.

"Captain Wilkins, it's great to have you with us again."

Bill shook the proffered hand and replied, "Believe me, sir, the feeling is mutual."

The relief in his voice must have been evident as Gupta cocked his head slightly. He said nothing and motioned Bill to the sofa that sat to one side of the cabin. Bill greeted each of the others and moved to stand next to Captain Delawr. As soon as the admiral sat down, they did, too.

"I'd offer you something stronger but the best I can do is coffee, Bill. Or you prefer tea, don't you?"

Without waiting, the admiral poured a cup of tea from a pot placed strategically on the coffee table and offered it to Bill.

The joke was one of the oldest in a Navy that hadn't allowed alcoholic beverages aboard ship for over a hundred and fifty years. That, combined with the fact that the admiral had a pot of tea ready for him, told Bill he wasn't here to be reprimanded. The others already had coffee.

"The embassy forwarded your report." Gupta smiled. "I must say, you've had a bit of excitement."

Bill carefully considered his words. He'd been prepared for almost any kind of reception, from standing at attention getting his ass chewed to something akin to what seemed to be happening.

"Yes, sir, a bit. I acted as I thought best. We didn't get much in the way of rudder orders. I did what I could to bring a little pain to the enemy."

"You did well, damn well. You were here by yourself, outnumbered, with little in the way of intel, and you kicked ass and took names. I'd say you did more than bring a *little pain* to the enemy." This time, he grinned. "And I didn't send you orders because I trusted you."

"We had a lot of help from the Vietnamese, sir," Bill said. "I admit, I had some qualms about them, but they came through in spades and more. They took some hits for it, too."

Captain Wendy Paxton, chief of staff, replied, "Yes, we know. The embassy shared their after-action report. They got hit pretty hard. Do you know what else is going on between them?"

At Bill's head shake, she continued. "The Chinese moved several divisions into northern Vietnam and started driving toward Hanoi. The Vietnamese were as ready as they could be, but they're a bit outclassed and certainly outnumbered. They're still falling back, but they're slowing them down as much as they can."

"Commodore Tran told me they'd do what they could. His government was willing to take the risk. Are we going to help them out?" Bill asked.

"We already are. Most of the aircraft from CENTCOM are being moved from Australia to bases in Vietnam. From there, they can give the Chinese ground forces a pasting. They'll be pretty useful to us, too. CENTCOM's rounding up the elements of two brigades that were in theater and sending them, with gear from the Maritime Prepositioning Squadron, to Vietnam, too."

Bill sat back, realized what he'd done, and leaned forward again. "Aye, ma'am, that's good to hear." He turned back to Gupta.

"Sir, I really haven't had much news other than listening to BBC and Al Jazeera. I heard about the Brits and Russians trading nukes. Any risk of that here? I had my DCA prep and issue CBRN gear just in case." Chemical, biological, radiological, and nuclear defense gear was designed to protect the crew in a weapons of mass destruction environment.

Delawr piped in. "God, I hope not. No, unlikely we'll see nukes here. Something the acting chairman is working to make sure of."

Gupta leaned forward, elbows on his knees and hands clasped in front of him. "There's been some chaos in DC, as you might imagine. We don't honestly know what's going on ourselves. I suspect our military leadership feels we have plenty to do out here without giving us more to worry about. But we're obviously listening in on comms from the Pentagon to Seventh Fleet. And everything we're hearing, and I mean all of it, is coming from the acting chairman. SecDef is dead. But we don't know why nothing's coming from the deputy secretary, who's alive. The White House's also been silent the last forty-eight hours."

He leaned back and rubbed his hands together. "Not that anything we'd heard from the White House has been all that useful lately."

Bill looked quickly at the other three and saw their grim expressions.

Silence reigned for a moment. Finally, Gupta broke it and changed the topic. "How are you managing around your personnel losses, Bill?"

He gulped. "We're working around them, sir. We have strong chiefs in the divisions that lost their officers. We're making due across the gaps where we lost enlisted. The XO's a tough one. She almost lost her left hand, and she did lose a lot of blood. But she's conscious again and helping out. My combat systems officer's filling in for now."

"I can let you have people from the DESRON or my staff, if you need. And we've got a volunteer to come be your XO. I know Commander Pettibone's a good man, but I'm sure you don't want to crush him with extra responsibilities, either."

Bill shook his head. He'd thought about it as they'd steamed to the rendezvous. He'd even talked to Pettibone and Irving. "No, sir. I'm grateful for the offer, but honestly, Pettibone needs the distraction. He was TAO when we took the hit. He's feeling a bit responsible for the dead."

The look on Gupta's face made Bill hasten to add, "Don't get me wrong, sir, he's going to be fine. He is fine. But if I bring another officer aboard to take the XO job, it could look like I don't trust him. That would do more harm than good." He grimaced. "Besides, sir, I think the XO would pin my ears back if I let her get dragged off the ship."

Gupta didn't look convinced but said, "Okay, I trust you on this one. But say the word and I'll get you help."

"How are *you* doing, Bill?" asked Paxton softly.

Bill found himself blinking furiously as his eyes threatened to overflow. He cleared his throat. "I'm alright, ma'am. It's been a bit of, uh, a challenge." He paused to swallow. "I don't like losing anyone, ma'am, truth be told. But I'm fine."

He didn't dare continue.

She looked closely at him, nodded and leaned back in her chair. When she spoke, it was gently. "Not many of us have lost people under our command. Even fewer in combat. We're dealing with it ourselves. You hear about *Coeur d'Alene*?"

He shook his head, so she filled him in.

Then Gupta took over again. "There's nothing I can say to make it easier. We have to focus on making the bastards pay. That's what gets me through the night. He who will not risk, cannot win."

Bill nearly lost it. He choked back a sob as he remembered the last person who'd spoken those words to him.

Yes, I will make the bastards pay, for her and for all the others. He took several deep breaths.

Gupta rose. "I'm told it's fish and chips for lunch in the wardroom. The ship's XO, Captain Lopez, has kindly invited us to join the mess today. Or, if you'd prefer, we can have some brought up to the flag mess. You're likely to find yourself the center of attention since you've been responsible for pretty much all our victories at sea so far."

Bill swallowed again. It would be miserable and he knew it. So did Gupta. But he had no choice. "That's fine, sir. I know Cal Lopez. He was one of my instructors at Department Head School. It'll be good to see him again."

The admiral led them from the cabin.

CHAPTER
SIXTY-TWO

0001 Zulu, 12 Nov
0900 Local Time
USS *Theodore Roosevelt*, South China Sea

The next day, Bill sat in Gupta's conference room. *Nicholas* had rearmed and additional repairs had been made. Now the strike group leadership listened to the next few days' ops plan.

"That's about it, sir. Subject to questions, that concludes my brief."

The current operations deputy had just finished presenting a set of PowerPoint slides, detailing how the strike group would establish air and maritime superiority over and on the South China Sea as it steamed north to launch air strikes against Chinese bases on Hainan Island and the southern coast. They would bypass the islands and reefs of the Spratly Group in favor of targets that would impose greater cost on the enemy. The Air Force, operating out of Vietnam, would deal with the island bases.

Bill shifted in his chair, but he remained silent.

"Bill?"

The admiral must have seen. There was no dignified way out.

"Sir, I appreciate the work *TR*'s folks have done to get us fixed, and I almost have a full magazine. But I'm not sure *Nicholas* is the full-up round you need to lead the SAG. Not to mention other COs who're senior to me." He nodded at two who were seated at the table.

The admiral regarded him quietly for a moment, which made him shift again.

Then Gupta shifted in his seat. "I hear you. Especially with these modern systems, once you shake them up it's hard to know if something's going to fail at a critical moment. But I need you out front for a lot of reasons." He smiled.

"First, you've seen more sea combat in the past weeks than any naval officer currently on active duty, and you've won every fight. That's a statement about you and your crew. And, hell, you know as well as I do it's a powerful talisman.

"Second, the Vietnamese know and trust you. They'd wonder why you weren't part of the SAG, and it might make them hesitant.

"Third, you're more familiar than anyone else with Chinese wartime operational patterns. I choose experience over seniority, and Phil and Elliott both know that."

When Bill opened his mouth, Gupta held up his hand. "I know, you were operating in EMCON. You didn't have a great operational picture. Certainly not a geographically wide one. But you got the Vietnamese picture and the intel feeds. That's a helluva lot more than we've had. What's more, we've only been here for three days. There's no one in this strike group who can lead it as well as you."

He leaned back slightly and looked around the table at the other ship COs and his own staff. "Any more questions or concerns?"

There were none, although Commodore Jarvis glared at him.

"Very well, we execute as soon as the UNREP's complete tomorrow evening," Gupta said.

While the admiral remained seated, everyone else rose and moved toward the door.

"Bill, stay for a moment, won't you?"

Bill closed his eyes and sat. The admiral remained silent. Soon, the only ones left were Paxton and Delawr, standing expectantly by the door. At the admiral's nod, they exited and closed it behind them.

"There's one more thing. The Vietnamese came into this fight because of you. *Only* because of you."

Bill cocked his head.

Gupta continued. "Tran told their CNO he trusted you. He said you wouldn't let them down, that you'd defend them as if they were Americans. That sealed the deal. So for that reason, too, I need you leading."

"Why not have Commodore Jarvis lead?"

Gupta sighed and spread his fingers out on the table in front of him. Looking at them, he said, "I need him commanding the screen. Let's say it's a better use of his talents."

Bill sat silently.

"What's troubling you?" Gupta asked.

Bill thought for a moment. "Sir, you know my worries about the systems. I'm also concerned about my folks. They've been out here fighting or preparing to fight every day. It's wearing."

"Are you concerned about anyone in particular? We can replace them, you know."

Bill's eyes widened. It was harsh, but in the back of his mind he knew it was true.

"No, sir, it's not that. But they're tired. Tired men and women make mistakes. I'd hate for us to make a critical mistake in something this important."

The admiral sat back and regarded him closely. "We're all tired. We've been operating under tough conditions since this thing started. We'd all been at sea for at least a couple of weeks before the attack." He shrugged. "Everyone's worried about family and friends back home. All we have is speculation based on news feeds." Pursing his lips, he asked, "Is that a concern?"

Bill shook his head. This wasn't going well.

"Then what is it? Are you worried about yourself?"

There it was. The admiral had said it. A roaring erupted in his ears. "No, sir, of course not," he lied. As he did, he saw Barrister's dead face in front of him, accusing eyes vacant and staring.

Silence lay between them like a thick fog. Gupta let out a deep breath. "Bill, you're human. You've lost people under your command who looked to you for leadership. You think you let them down, that it's somehow your fault. But it's not."

Gupta paused briefly. "Let me tell you a story. I was a young lieutenant flying off *Nimitz* during the invasion of Iraq. On the third night I was flight lead for a four-ship sortie. We were supposed to hit Republican Guard positions south of Baghdad. It was overcast, so we were supposed to come in high to the release point, then get the hell out." He closed his eyes in remembrance.

"The cloud cover broke ten miles out, so I ordered five hundred feet for the run in. One of my wingmen, in fact, my roommate, took small arms fire. The bullets went right up through the fuselage. Killed him. They're not supposed to be able to do that. There's armor along the bottom of the cockpit. But the patrol's fire was at just the right angle." He waved his hands toward the bulkhead.

"I blamed myself. I almost resigned my commission. A couple of years later I ran into a British Tornado pilot who'd done a similar mission that same night. I told him my story over beer at the Sigonella O-Club. He laughed at me. *His* flight leader decided to go in high as ordered. They got hammered by triple-A fire. He said every one of their aircraft took shrapnel. They lost one plane and the pilot, and two other pilots were wounded. They never even dropped their bombs. So my decision let us get in, drop, and get out. We got the mission done." He shook his head.

"It sucks, don't get me wrong. But that's the job. Isn't the mission more important than our lives?" He paused. "Isn't that what we signed up for?"

Bill didn't answer; he couldn't. He simply stared first at the admiral then across the table at the wall clock. After a moment, he said, "Yes, sir, I suppose it is." He stood. "With your permission, sir, I'll get back and make sure we're ready."

The admiral nodded, then added, "Remember, he who will not risk, cannot win."

Bill's body trembled. He flashed back to a dark night five days and a thousand years ago.

In the end, they were both right. He brought himself back to the present, swallowed, and said, "Aye, aye, sir."

CHAPTER
SIXTY-THREE

1900 Zulu, 11 Nov
1400 Eastern Time
Secretary of State's Office, Washington, DC

"Hello, Herman. Have a good vacation? Sorry you didn't get a chance to tell me all about it the other day." Hauptmann's voice dripped with sarcasm.

Kingston could hear the smirk. Controlling his own voice, he said, "Well, it wasn't much of a vacation, now was it? Especially coming back as we both did to a disaster."

A sharp chuckle came over the phone. "Well, you can certainly say that again. But then, you've pretty much been on vacation since you joined me and the president, haven't you?"

Kingston refused to rise to the bait. Instead, he said, "We all serve at the pleasure of the president and in the way he wants us to, don't we? One serves by his silence, another as a personal minion, yet another as an attack dog."

The silence told him he'd scored. Another part of his brain regretted it. He needed to mend fences, not build walls. "I'm sorry, Karl, that didn't come out right. We all do — did — our parts, the way the president needed us to. Now we need to work together to rebuild and carry on as he would have wanted."

"Yes, and I intend to do that. The first step, of course, is swearing in a new president. I presume that's what this call is about?"

"Yes, it is. I hear it'll take place in the Oval Office in two hours, is that about right?"

"You obviously know that. You also know I'm taking the helm. I hope you're calling to congratulate me."

Kingston took a breath. "Not exactly, and I think *you* know *that*. Let's talk about the order of succession, as codified in the Constitution, in law, and in precedent over the past hundred and sixty years or so."

Another harsh laugh. "Precedent? Don't talk to me about precedent. There's no *precedent* for what's happened, or do you know even your most basic American history? We've been attacked, our government destroyed, our institutions savaged. We need a leader, not a fisherman. We need someone strong, who's not afraid to make hard choices, who will rule with the force of law."

"Don't you mean *lead within the bounds* of the rule of law?" Kingston carefully asked.

"No. I mean exactly what I said. The opposition's insistence on the *rule of law* is what got us into this mess. They made us weak. They nibbled away at our strength with their mealy-mouthed hand-wringing about respecting the rights of others. They let external threats breed that challenged us for world leadership, and internal enemies who only want to suck the blood from those of us who are successful. They wanted to drag our whole society down." Hauptman snorted. "Well, we're done with that. My first act will be to ban the opposition party and arrest their leaders. *They're* the ones who are *really* responsible for this mess."

Kingston's eyes widened. *He's lost it, completely lost it.*

Hauptman wasn't done yet. "And you call to tell me *you*

ought to be the president? You're a power monger. But you don't know what to do with it. I do. I'll fix this country and make sure that no one can ever hurt her again. I'm the only one who can."

His voice calmed. "Besides, the president declared martial law, Herman. That suspends a wide variety of laws. Who knows, maybe all the laws. That means *Donnelly* could determine who his successor would be. And his last words as he lay dying in my arms were that he wanted me to finish what he'd started."

It was worse than Kingston had thought. The man was not only power hungry. He'd also gone over the edge into mega-lomania.

"Karl, you can't do that. The Constitution—" he started.

"I don't give a fuck what the Constitution says. The Founding Fathers never foresaw this. Well, I know how to handle it. I've suspended the Constitution until the crisis passes. And the FBI ought to be over in a few minutes to visit you. I might have you executed for treason."

The receiver clicked.

Kingston held the phone for a moment more. Only when the recorded voice told him that if he wanted to make a call to hang up and try again did he put the phone down.

He didn't seek the power and prestige of the presidency. He sought to prevent more harm.

Kingston had never been a deeply patriotic man. He'd been successful, enormously so, thanks to America's laws and institutions. He'd never worried much about his fellow citizens, either, and he'd always voted to make sure the government represented *his* interests over those of anyone else. Didn't everyone?

But a Hauptman presidency had the potential to destroy everything. He didn't for a minute believe the man wouldn't arrest anyone who might pose even an imaginary threat. He was fairly sure that institutions like the FBI wouldn't submit easily, but there were plenty of militia groups who would follow him to hell, if need be. They'd welcome suspending the Constitution, especially if there were vague assurances it would be restored "after the crisis was past." He'd been at the rallies. He'd seen them.

With the military fully occupied fighting the Chinese and perhaps the Russians, or trying to keep people alive while the national infrastructure was brought back online, there would be little to stop the man from consolidating his power. Once ensconced in the White House under a dictatorship, he might not be assailable.

Kingston knew he needed to act. Now.

CHAPTER
SIXTY-FOUR

1330 Zulu, 12 Nov
0830 Eastern Time
The White House, Washington, DC

Kingston walked into the White House feeling like he'd entered a prison. What he was there for only cemented that feeling. If he weren't able to prevent it, he saw all of America becoming one.

He moved toward the metal detector and removed his keys and smart phone and placed them in a container on the conveyor.

"Sir, your security detail will take longer to clear than before. We're a bit on edge, as I'm sure you'll understand," said the young woman in the uniform of the Capitol Police.

Kingston grunted but acquiesced.

"We'll be up as soon as we're cleared, sir," said the senior of the three men who had followed him in.

Kingston nodded. "All right. Wait for me outside the Oval."

Kingston retrieved his keys and phone and headed for the elevator.

Three Secret Service agents stood beside the door outside the

Oval Office. He allowed one of them to frisk him. The man then opened the door and stood aside for Kingston to enter.

Inside, Tim Neustein stood beside the large desk. Behind the desk sat Hautpman himself.

"Getting comfortable before the ceremony, Karl?" he asked.

Hauptman laughed. "You better get used to saying Mr. President, Herman. The ceremony was half an hour ago. We can't have the nation without a leader for that long, now can we?"

Kingston ground his teeth. "Well, *Mr. President*, I suppose congratulations would normally be in order. But, as you said earlier, these are unprecedented times."

Hauptman's eyes narrowed, and he frowned slightly. "Neustein, get out of here. Now."

Neustein looked at Kingston, then turned back to Hauptman. "Alright, Mr. President." He picked up a paper, placed it in a folder, and left.

Hauptman returned his attention to Kingston. "What do you want? Here to beg for your job? Not happening. My foreign policy lead must be someone who believes in the strength and greatness of America. You're not him."

"No, Karl, I'm not."

Hauptman bristled at the deliberate use of his first name but said nothing.

"I'm here to suggest you bow out gracefully."

Hauptman laughed harshly and leaned back in the chair, which squeaked. "You really are a piece of work. You've got balls, I'll give you that. But there's no way I'm stepping down. I'm the president. And you, Mr. *former* Secretary, are out." He reached toward a buzzer on the desk.

"I don't think I'd do that until you hear me out."

Something in his tone made Hauptman pause.

"Did you swap out the chair and curtains out after you murdered our former boss?" Kingston asked.

Hauptman's eyes narrowed. "What are you talking about? Hunter killed my predecessor."

"Did he, now? Well, that's not how I hear it."

Kingston started to enjoy this. The startled look in Hauptman's eyes, though quickly dispelled, told him all he needed to know. He was on the right track.

Hauptman rose and turned to look out the windows at the Rose Garden.

The gold curtains that normally hung there had been pulled down, Kingston presumed because of blood spatters. He noted that only the ones on the left side were gone. It merely confirmed what he already believed. Kingston waited.

"Hunter was an overly ambitious man, Herman. He told me what he planned to do." Hauptman turned to look at Kingston, hands clasped behind his back. "He told me, you understand. He told me on the phone that he intended to remove the president. You were on that call, as I remember."

He turned his face away again. "Naturally, I didn't think he'd kill the man. I found it difficult to believe, but something in the tone of his voice . . . well, I was concerned. That's why I came over, to be here when they met."

"That's not how I remember the conversation, Karl."

"Regardless, that's what I told the FBI." Hauptman changed topics. "There's a lot of work to do, Herman. First, I crush the Chinese, wipe them off the face of the earth. They can't survive to try again. After that, I eliminate the opposition. Execute their leaders. We can't let them peddle their bullshit theories and ideals." He waved his hand to the city beyond the window. "Then, I rebuild. We can never be *weak* again. Those who weakened this country will never be allowed the opportunity to do so again."

He whirled around and moved behind the desk. Leaning across, he braced both hands on it. "Do you understand what it's going to take? Do you?" He stood back up and laughed. "It's going to take the strength of an ogre. You rebuilt a company after a decade of weak-minded CEOs ran it into the ground. This is like that, only a thousand times bigger. People like you, the consensus builders, have no idea how to *really* fix problems this big. There's no room for people like you at the table. And if you try to stand in my way, I'll crush you as mercilessly as I'll crush the yellow menace. Do you understand me?"

It was meant to frighten Kingston. It did, but not in the desired way. "You forget that's not how our system works, Karl."

"You will call me *Mr. President.*" Spittle flew from Hauptman's lips.

Kingston inclined his head. "Very well."

Hauptman visibly relaxed and sat.

Kingston leaned forward slightly. "But before we go too far down the authoritarian path, let's examine a few facts, shall we?" He smoothed his trouser legs. "First, the American people threw off an authoritarian king around two hundred and fifty years ago. Second, they've stood against authoritarianism wherever it's reared its ugly head for nearly a century. Third, your predecessor's base has argued for years that they sent him to Washington precisely *because* they feared a dictatorship. Of course, what they really feared was the other party and the fact there are more of them than of us."

Hauptman swept a hand across between them. "Bah. The American people, *real* Americans, have always respected strong leaders," he replied. "I say again, you don't know your history. Even Hitler was widely respected in America, right up until he foolishly declared war on us. If not for that, he'd have ruled Europe for decades."

Kingston shook his head. "Yes, there were fools who liked him. But even those who'll initially support you will one day wake up and realize you duped them. And when they do, look out. Their retribution will be quick and mighty. Because you'll have empowered them. They won't hesitate to step in and throw you out in favor of the next guy."

Hauptman leaned back and laughed. "You truly are blind," he said.

He rose and reached again for the buzzer. Kingston had to

make his point now. "Karl, I *know* who killed the former president. I know it was you. And I'm not the only one who knows."

Hauptman's hand hovered over the button. Then he smiled and sat. "Fine. Regale me with a bedtime story. How could I possibly have done it when Hunter was found with the gun in his hand?"

Kingston began. "Your first and biggest mistake was trying to dissolve your glue gloves in the potted plant. The agents who cleaned up the scene couldn't figure out where such a large quantity of glue came from. So, being curious types, they took samples and investigated it. Imagine their surprise when they found human DNA."

Hauptman scoffed. "Of course there would be human DNA. A *human* had to have poured it there, probably one of the cleaning people. Once they have time to analyze it, they'll find out whose it is. But it'll be a waste of taxpayer money and time to do that."

Hauptman looked pale.

"I'm sure they will once they have time. But, funny thing, they don't need to analyze it other than to verify what they've already found." He paused. "The Secret Service agent had no powder burns on his hand, but his gun killed Hunter. That confused them. So they began looking harder at everything." He crossed his legs to keep from jiggling. "The glue didn't dissolve completely, Karl. They found a partial fingerprint." He let it hang for a moment. "And one complete thumbprint."

Hauptman stared at him, then visibly shook himself. "All this speculation is well and good, but I've got a country to run. Goodbye, Herman." He reached for and pushed the buzzer.

Hauptman's eyes went wide when the Secret Service agents followed three other men into the room. He rose to his feet unsteadily. The man in the lead introduced himself.

"Good afternoon, Mr. President. I'm Special Agent Harold, FBI." He already had his badge out. The other two had their right hands inside their jackets.

"What are you doing in my office?" Hauptman demanded, his face ashen and his hands shaking.

Kingston spoke. "They're here to arrest you, Karl, for the murder of your predecessor."

Harold nodded. "Secretary Kingston is correct, though it is *my* job to inform you of that." He put his badge away. "We've been listening to your witty repartee, Mr. President. Your intentions are, to say the least, alarming. However, they will not be the star witness in your trial." As he spoke, his compatriots moved around the desk and took Hauptman by the arms.

"How dare you listen in on conversations in this office? There are no listening devices here. They were removed by my predecessor."

Kingston held up his smartphone. "Not this one," he said. "Oh, and it turns out Hunter's assistant listened in when we were on the phone. She called the FBI, too."

Hauptman's legs gave out. The two agents nearly dropped him before they guided him back into the chair.

"Karl Hauptman, you have the right to remain silent . . . ."

Kingston didn't listen to the rest. He walked out to the presidential secretary's desk.

"Get the judge back here. We're going to have another swearing in ceremony, now."

The first orders President Kingston issued were to the acting chairman of the Joint Chiefs of Staff. American forces in Europe were to support NATO forces wherever they were engaged.

He and Norton worked out a communique to the Chinese government. The goal was to provide the PRC a face-saving way to end hostilities, known as an off-ramp in military parlance.

At the same time, they sent a carefully worded message to the Russian Federation to the effect that there was a new sheriff in town, and that the adventurism that had previously been tolerated was at an end. It also warned the Russian government that any further use of nuclear weapons would result in a massive, full-scale retaliation.

Finally, he released a statement to the American people. It was the first to actually come from the American president since the initial attack weeks earlier. In it, Kingston promised a return to the rule of law and the transparency they should expect of their elected leaders.

The responses to these four pronouncements were swift.

American forces were already engaged with the Russians but were buoyed by their new commander in chief's endorsement. So were NATO forces. Both fought with renewed vigor.

The American people were divided, as they'd been for more than thirty years. Militia groups in several western and southern states acted on their threats and rose in armed insurrection.

However, the US Army, kept in its garrisons thus far during this war, vented their frustration and quickly crushed the rebels, showing little mercy. It took direct orders from the president to force them to give quarter.

The rebellion was short-lived but costly.

By the end, over seventy thousand Americans were dead.

CHAPTER
SIXTY-FIVE

1500 Zulu, 12 Nov
2200 Local Time
USS *Nicholas*, South China Sea

Nicholas sprinted through heavy seas, her happy disposition lifting the spirits of her crew despite the tang of fear that pervaded. The upcoming battle could be decisive. Grey skies and low overcast failed to dampen tense anticipation.

Intelligence said the Chinese Navy knew *TR* and her strike group were loose in what they considered their bathtub. It also showed additional enemy warships and aircraft searched for it. With time running out, Admiral Gupta adopted Halsey's World War II guidance: hit hard, hit fast, hit often.

Behind and to both sides of *Nicholas*, five other destroyers of Surface Action Group Bravo charged along, spume flying aft as their bows drove through seas. With six miles separation, the ships ranged to both sides as far as the eye could see. Over the horizon to the west raced a Vietnamese flotilla of eight corvettes and frigates, allies come to play. Scouting ahead of the ships flew four helicopters at low altitude, visually sweeping the air and water.

Their path was populated by fishing boats and small trading ships. The larger merchant traffic seemed to have disappeared since the carrier and her escorts had passed the Singapore Strait.

Despite the great firepower at his command, Bill remained nervous.

The Chinese had already gleaned some lessons from previous fights with *Nicholas*. Their ships and aircraft relied exclusively on visual search. It took longer but held far less peril. Simultaneously, it increased risk to the Americans. Just as in World War II, before radar became ubiquitous, ships might stumble upon each other without warning. When they did, victory would go to those most ready and who reacted fastest.

Bill had done everything possible to ensure his force's readiness but dreaded what he didn't know. He'd grown up in a navy that feared no one and operated with impunity. One that saturated the ether with electrons to make sure it knew everything that moved nearby. But as the sun set on the port beam, the detection range of their mark one mod zero eyeballs shrank.

"Sir, message from Vietnamese naval HQ. They're missing a maritime patrol aircraft. It should have checked in fifteen minutes ago. It was searching an area a hundred twenty nautical miles northeast of our current position. They're worried."

Acknowledging Campbell's report, Bill sipped his tea. He'd ordered Pettibone to his rack to get some sleep before the coming battle. The man was exhausted due to performing the XO's duties as well as most of his own. Irving still wasn't on her feet yet, but as Bill had predicted, she'd fought being left behind and made herself available to Pettibone for help.

Bill had also forced Pettibone to delegate his routine responsibilities to his division officers. He suspected *Nicholas's* dead still weighed heavily on Pettibone's mind, and he couldn't help but sympathize. The admiral's story had been all well and good, but losing one man didn't compare to losing seven.

"Assuming an enemy combatant were doing twenty knots

and positioned itself at the closest edge of that search box, when would they be in surface search radar range?" he asked.

Campbell used the cursor on his console to enter a test track and lay out a trial intercept. "Just a bit under two hours, sir."

"All right, Ops, in one hour slow the formation to twenty knots. That'll be a good time to start looking like a group of merchants trying to sneak through a war zone."

The radio speaker over his head sprang to life. "SAG Bravo, this is Strike Group Seven. We are under attack by at least forty short-range fixed-wing aircraft. Maintain radio silence. I repeat, maintain radio silence. Execute assigned mission. Be alert for fixed-wing enemy air. Strike Group Seven out."

"Sir, EW just picked up two SPYs and the carrier's radars coming online. At least five Hornet radars went active, too — wait, one."

Campbell listened, his hand pressing the headset to his ear.

Bill reached for his.

" . . . crapload of Hornet radars up, sir. Looks like they got as many airborne as they could, fifteen or so," the EW supervisor reported.

Bill touched Campbell's arm and pointed to his headset.

"TAO, aye. *Captain's online*," Campbell intoned.

The EW's abashed voice came back, "Aye, sir, uh, yes, sorry, sir."

Bill smiled slightly, then frowned. Where did forty fixed-wing short-range attack aircraft come from? He wished for the millionth time he could use his own radar.

Lieutenant j.g. Hawke provided the most likely answer. She moved over from her Cryptologic Technicians at the consoles.

"Sir, what if their carrier's out here?" Without waiting, she added. "We picked up four merchant radars in a group to the southeast an hour or so after we left the strike group. We haven't seen their carrier underway since this thing started. She was supposedly in port the day before the attack. What if they got her underway without us noticing?"

"That makes more sense than anything else. Do the Chinese have that many fighters on the islands?" he asked.

"No, sir, not even if they've tripled what they had there the day before the war. Besides, the Vietnamese would have seen them moving."

Bill thought hard. If there were an enemy carrier out there and they'd caught *TR* by surprise, it could be bad, very bad.

Bill had by far the majority of Tomahawk land attack missiles in the ships under his command. But the planes aboard the carrier packed an equally big punch. Moreover, they could deliver that punch several times compared to the one-and-done a cruise missile brought to the fight. If they lost the carrier—

"Ops, send a signal to turn the formation around. And double the lookouts. We need to find and sink that carrier."

Campbell stared at him for a second, then responded, "Aye, aye, sir." He turned to call the signal bridge.

The signal went out by flashing light, requiring acknowledgement by all ships before it could be executed. It took nearly seven minutes before the formation reversed course and increased speed to thirty knots. As it turned, it girded itself for a three-dimensional battle against ships and aircraft.

The waiting let him dwell too much and too long on what might happen when they met the enemy.

As they steamed back the way they'd come, Bill still hoped against hope to hear more from the strike group. If the carrier was lost, that would leave only one operational carrier in the theater and no reinforcements available anywhere on earth.

How could they possibly give the Chinese the bloody nose they deserved? Not to mention, how would the rest of the strike group survive bereft of air cover? He didn't even know how to contact the US aircraft moving into Vietnam.

It had been bad enough when *Nicholas* alone faced a force of surface ships searching for her. Facing an enemy carrier and land-based bombers might prove impossible.

Finally, the speaker came alive again. His heart soared. "SAG

Bravo, Group Seven. Attack beaten off. Carrier sustained light damage, flight deck operational. War at sea strike launched against enemy carrier. Do not acknowledge. Maintain silence. In view of carrier being localized, strike timetable advanced to seventeen hundred Zulu. Imperative your force arrives launch baskets on time. Repeat, launch window opens 1700 Zulu. Group Seven out."

Bill's heart plummeted. The turn back toward the carrier had cost them the ability to transit looking like merchant traffic. Now to get into position they'd need to race at maximum speed, with no certainty they'd make it.

If they didn't, they'd have to launch from outside the designated launch areas, throwing off the carefully timed missile impacts.

His blunder had sowed the seeds of disaster. He closed his eyes and clenched his fists under the table, letting the anger wash over him.

When he opened them again, he took a deep breath and acted. "Ops, get the formation turned around again. Then stay at max speed. I know the Vietnamese can't keep up, but that's okay. They aren't part of the overland strike, anyway."

"Aye, sir. The helos are due to HIFR in about thirty minutes. I'll stagger them so we keep at least two out front."

HIFR, or Helicopter In Flight Refueling, took less time than landing to refuel. The helo hovered over the flight deck until a fuel hose could be connected to its belly. The helo then gently pulled it taut while fuel flowed into its tanks.

"That's fine," said Bill.

Campbell looked at him for only a split second then turned away to make it happen. Bill closed his eyes again and kept them shut.

CHAPTER
SIXTY-SIX

1620 Zulu, 12 Nov
2320 Local Time
USS *Nicholas*, South China Sea

An hour later Bill awakened with a start.

He'd been asleep. Self-loathing, a feeling he'd come to know well, crept through his mind like black tar, blanketing his thoughts.

"Ops, what's our status? And don't let me sleep like that again."

Campbell jumped, not having noticed his captain was awake. "Aye, sir, sorry. I thought you could use some rest."

Regaining his composure, Campbell continued, "We're about thirty minutes from the launch areas. We've been making thirty-one knots speed over ground, so we'll just make it by the time the launch window opens. The last two helos are about to get back up. The other two are off the port and starboard edges of the formation at five miles. Visibility's closed in and that's as far out as we can maintain reliable comms."

"Great. Let's set GQ in fifteen—"

"TAO, Bridge, lookout reports multiple flares on the horizon, bearing three two zero to zero four zero relative."

"Shit." Campbell looked guilty for a moment as the expletive escaped him, then his reflexes took over and the ship's combat system quickly woke.

"EW, anything?"

"No, sir. Uh, yes. Yes, sir. I got seekers on those bearings. Five, six, seven—there's a shitload, sir."

"Sir, the rest of the ships are bringing their systems online," Campbell said.

Bill nodded. "Cancel GQ, Jason,"

Campbell barely nodded. Once again, Bill was an observer.

He flipped the switch on the intercom. "OOD, captain. Pass the word. The ship is under attack. We'll fight in Condition III. Man Damage Control stations but combat systems watches remain on station. No reliefs. Pass to brace for shock, too."

"Aye, sir," came the response.

He swiveled his chair to face the CICWO. "Call the CSO. Tell him what's going on."

She nodded and hurried to a phone.

As he finished, the first missiles raced from their cells to intercept the incoming fire. Very quickly the five-inch gun joined in.

"Sir, I'm using the gun to kill the launch platforms," said Campbell.

Bill nodded. Survival in a missile exchange depended on "shooting the archers" so they couldn't fire again.

Then came the sound he'd dreaded as CIWS engaged an inbound. He closed his eyes and forced his hands to relax their grip on the chair arms. He winced as he thought once more of his dead.

In the blink of an eye, a force heaved him up and halfway onto the TAO table. As the ship flexed, he fell between his and the TAO's chairs. The lights blinked then went out. The screens on all the consoles, the status boards, and the large screen displays all went out. The eerie stark red glow of the battle lanterns came on.

Bill picked himself up and took inventory. Blood dribbled from a gash on his forehead. There was soreness in his knees where he'd hit the table, and where he'd landed on his right arm. He applied his handkerchief to his forehead and looked around.

Others in CIC, who hadn't buckled their seat belts, picked themselves up but no one appeared down for the count. Two petty officers helped OS1 Willard up. His face was covered in blood, but he was able to stand once they had him up.

Bill walked over and looked closely. Willard's nose was smashed to one side.

"Get him down to the Wardroom. Doc and his guys should be set up."

"I'm alright, sir. I can stay."

Bill shook his head. "No, get below. Doc makes the call. If he says you can return, okay."

He turned back to find Campbell trying to get someone on the sound-powered phone circuits. "How bad is it, Jason?" he asked.

"I got DC Central. Investigators are out. They have comms with Repair Two and Five, but they were only partially manned up. Nothing from Repair Three or Eight, yet."

He paused to listen, then relayed what he heard. "They've got a pressure drop on firemain aft by the hangar."

The intercom demanded his attention. "TAO, bridge. We lost comms with aft lookout. Forward lookout says there's a big-ass fire in the hangar."

"This is the captain. Do we still have propulsion? How's the rudder?"

"Yes, sir, we've got engines and steering. We lost comms with After Steering, though."

"Send someone down there to check." *Dammit*! He'd known this would happen. He'd tried to tell the admiral, but he wouldn't listen. "What's going on with the rest of the force?"

"I already told DC Central to check After Steering." A pause. "We got some hits on a couple of them before we took the missile, sir. There's two off the port bow, both burning, and another one to starboard. Looks like there's more fighting to both sides — holy crap." There was a moment of silence, then, "Sorry, sir. One of the enemy ships to port just exploded."

"What about the rest of *our* force?" he demanded, irritated.

"Uh, sorry, sir. *Halsey* and *Horne* are shooting. I see missile fire beyond them. It looks like us, sir." Another pause. "Uh, sir there's a big fire off to starboard, about where *Hepburn* is."

Bill closed his eyes and stretched his neck. "Very well. Send flashing light to *Berkeley*. Tell her to take TACON and proceed to the launch areas. Say we're trying to get our systems back up. Then turn *Nicholas* away and slow down, say, five knots. Better yet, ask DC Central what course will help firefighting. And see if *Hepburn*'s okay."

Not waiting, he picked up a sound-powered handset and selected the 1JV circuit to listen in.

"—DC Central. I'm trying to get power restored to the combat systems. EOOW says generators are still online, but a bunch of relays and breakers tripped. They have to isolate faults. It must be worse aft, 'cause I show the emergency diesel kicked on back there."

Campbell looked up and shouted across CIC. "Shut everything down that's not on a UPS. They're restoring power. Shut down the consoles and displays."

Most of the computers and monitors were on Uninterruptible Power Supplies to prevent them from being damaged or losing data if power was lost. But the rest of the combat system was not. It required far too much power. If power were restored with switches in the on position, they risked blowing out electronic components.

All around CIC people began scrambling to make sure their equipment was set to off or standby before electricity came back.

As they worked, the air took on the foul odor of burning fuel oil and something else, something sweet. A swirl of smoke eddied in front of the battle lanterns. An image of barbecue blasted through his mind. He quickly dismissed it.

He blinked as the blue lights flickered on and steadied. The hum of ventilation returned. Around him, switches clicked as consoles were turned back on and his crew began resetting electronics. Flickers began to fill the space as the big displays powered up.

Bill tried to be patient but couldn't keep from asking. "How's the radar?"

"Too soon to know, sir."

Turning to Pettibone, who'd come through the door into CIC shortly after the hit, he said, "Andy, I need you to get the systems up, anything. We're sitting ducks out here."

Pettibone spun and hurried out the way he'd come.

"How many enemy, Jason? Were you able to get a count before we got hit?" Bill asked.

"Maybe, sir. There were two groups of fishing boats along our track and a few contacts that looked like stragglers strung out between them. The helos looked at both groups but the fishing lights blinded them. After they launched, radar showed five targets shooting at us. Three of them were what we thought were stragglers. My guess is they used bright lights like the ones the fishermen use to fool the helos."

Bill closed his eyes and clenched his fists. *No, the enemy isn't stupid. I wish they were.*

"Combat, Bridge. Sir, it looks like the rest of the force got more hits on the bad guys. There's seven burning, plus the one that exploded."

"That means collateral damage, sir," Campbell said, his voice low.

"Damn it, I kn—" Bill snapped his mouth shut and looked up at the overhead. After a steadying breath, he continued. "I'm sorry, Jason. Yes, I know. I hate it. But there's not much else we could have done."

Campbell and Bill both sat and studied their displays. Systems and people struggled to re-identify the contacts around them. As they did, Bill saw *Hepburn* was dead in the water.

Campbell hadn't asked but he'd brought the powerful Aegis radar online along with the surface search radars.

Not much point in trying to hide now, Bill thought.

"Captain, DC Central. Repair Three's manned up, but I don't have comms with them. Handheld system's fried. We're jumpering around a break in the 3JV sound powered circuit to get them up." The DCA's voice quivered but didn't hesitate. "We took at least one missile hit in the hangar, sir. I don't know how many casualties. We're trying to get in there but it must've ruptured fuel lines. The fire's really hot. It's already spread down to the main deck. Some of that's probably burning fuel leaking through holes. I set fire boundaries on the main deck below, and on the oh-one level forward of the hangar." After a moment, he continued, "Smoke's the real problem, sir. We were pretty much at Zebra already, but the blasts tore through bulkheads. Smoke's everywhere. I'm setting smoke boundaries—"

The DCA paused, obviously consulting his damage control charts. "Smoke boundaries at frames 400 aft and 220 forward. Fire boundaries on the main deck are the flight deck aft, and frame 230 forward. We're trying to get in 'n set up smoke curtains, but we need to get at the fire, too."

Bill whistled. Nearly a third of his ship was inside the smoke and fire boundaries.

"Sir, there's more. It looks like we took something below the waterline, too. We've got high bilge alarms in the port shaft alley."

Bill shook his head. *How much worse can it get?*

CHAPTER
SIXTY-SEVEN

1635 Zulu, 12 Nov
2335 Local Time
USS *Nicholas*, South China Sea

But it did. The DCA continued, "Forward, there's a fire in Ops berthing. Repair Two's fighting it. Said it looks like at least three holes."

Bill slammed his fist on the table, making those around him jump. He took a deep breath. "All right, I got it. Keep me informed. But don't let it interfere with what you've got to do. CHENG available?"

Almost instantly, Martinez was on the line.

"Landy, how's the port engine and how stable is power? We need to keep fighting."

There was a moment of silence on the other end. "Well, number two port line shaft bearing is running hot. We don't need to shut it down yet, but there's something going on. That also tells me the high bilge alarms aren't false.

"As for power, well, it's as good as it's going to get. We got all non-essential breakers open and we're tracing grounds and shorts as fast as we can, but there's probably a few hundred.

We'll keep it as stable as we can but I can't promise anything. We'll try to give CSOOW as much head's up as we can if there's an issue."

The Combat Systems Officer of the Watch was the senior enlisted tasked with managing the Combat System during his or her watch, just as the EOOW managed the engineering plant. If they knew there was a power issue, they could at least try to protect the electronics.

"All right. Let me know how it's going."

Bill reflected on the hundreds of damage control exercises he'd been in. None of them had prepared him for this complete feeling of helplessness. His ship was damaged, he didn't know how badly, and in this too, he was an observer. He needed to trust his people to do their jobs. It was agonizing.

"Sir, OOD here. We have bridge to bridge comms with *Hepburn*. She took at least one missile hit in number two engine room. She had to go all stop to keep from going in circles 'cause they lost steering, too. They're rigging casualty power to after steering. But their Aegis system is up, sir, and they said they can defend themselves."

Bill sighed and shook his head. This was a clusterfuck! Two of six ships out of action.

He reached for the intercom to answer. "Bridge, this is the captain. Copy all. Take TACON of *Hepburn*. Tell her to maneuver independently for damage control. Make sure *Berkeley* copies."

A hand touched his shoulder, and he spun around. The air boss, Dix, stood before him, face ashen and eyes wide. His shoulders and arms shook. Bill's heart climbed into his throat.

"Sir, I, um—" Dix's face sank until he stared at his shoes. He cleared his throat but remained silent.

"Tell me, Nelson. How bad is it?" Bill prodded gently.

Dix shook himself and looked up. The water in his eyes swam under the dim blue light. But he refused to let it run down.

"It's bad. We, I, had folks working on Six Zero Eight,

installing the parts we got from *TR*." His voice broke. "They're all gone, sir."

"You can't be sure," Bill said.

Dix hiccuped. "The OOD ordered an all hands muster. Most of my det were in their bunks, least 'til they heard the missiles. They were headed up to the hangar when we took the hit. Petty Officer Swanson was standing near the door, about to open it. The blast blew him ten feet down the p-way. If he hadn't hit a couple other guys, he'd've been pretty badly hurt. No way anyone in the hangar survived."

Bill just stared at him. Then he reached out and squeezed Dix's shoulder. He couldn't speak. His heart reached out to the broken young man before him. Then he dropped his arm and turned to Campbell.

Just as he opened his mouth, the intercom blared. "Captain, OOD. Sir, we have the muster, sort of." The OOD paused. "Sir, we've got twenty-eight missing. Eleven from the Air Det, five from Engineering, six from Ops, three from Combat Systems, and four from Supply."

As he reached to acknowledge, Engineering broke in. "Sir, this is the CHENG. Repair Three says there's at least four bodies in the sonobuoy locker. Repair Five says they found five more in the p-way below the hangar. I suspect we're going to find a lot of the missing that way."

Bill paused, his arm raised, almost touching the switch.

In his mind he saw the black spaces filled with smoke, lights from the helmets of the damage control team barely penetrating, swinging wildly back and forth as they moved. He saw them stumble and look down to find the upturned face of someone they'd known, now a lifeless doll, broken and burnt.

Something in him snapped. He reached the rest of the way and flipped down the switch. "Captain, aye."

He turned to Campbell. "Jason, get to the launch area ASAP. I know we need to worry about wind fanning the hangar fire, but we've got to fight. Tell the OOD and DCA to figure it out. You and I are going to determine how to send the fucking Chinese a message they'll never forget. Let's get Andy back up here."

CHAPTER
SIXTY-EIGHT

1715 Zulu, 12 Nov
0015 Local Time, 13 Nov
USS *Nicholas*, South China Sea

For the next forty minutes, Pettibone worked furiously with his team to build new target packages.

Bill sat in his command chair, willing the ship forward. She struggled through the building seas with only one healthy shaft; the other was limited to a standard bell to keep from overheating the line shaft bearings.

His eyes kept going back to the large-screen displays. They showed both distance to their launch area and time remaining to 1900 Greenwich Mean Time.

He'd given up on their original launch area. He counted on the new solutions to let *Nicholas* serve out more punishment, repayment for what she, they, *he*, had suffered.

"Sir, surface contact closing fast, thirty-one thousand yards, bearing two two six. No emissions. I'm locking her up with fire control."

Bill nodded. "Kill it."

He'd ordered *Hepburn* to shut down her sensors, reducing the enemy's opportunity to target her. Their own SPY was also back down. But *Nicholas*'s commercial navigation radar was up. The rest of the SAG had sprinted ahead, radiating everything, since the Chinese already knew where they were. That also allowed him to see the air picture via old style HF data link. But he needed his own sensor for nearby surface tracks.

"Combat, Bridge. Flashing light. I think that corresponds to skunk alpha x-ray. Wait one, the QM's trying to copy it."

Campbell said, "Sir, he's right, that's the one we just locked up. I'll hold fire but we're ready with the gun if she shows even a hint of hostile intent."

The seconds passed like hours. The ship rolled twice, three times.

"Captain, Bridge. Sir, it's one of the Vietnamese ships, the *Tran Hung Dao*. Recognition signal checks, sir. Want me to talk to 'em on bridge to bridge?"

"Yes. Find out—"

"Captain, DCA. Fire in the hangar's out of control. Fire watch on the mess decks boundary says the bulkhead insulation just burst into flames. They tried to put it out, but it spread too quickly. They had to leave. I'm moving the rest of the boundary, too. Losing that space puts two more spaces at risk from two sides. I have to move the boundaries down on the second deck, too, since now they have fire above."

Shit, I'm losing my ship!

Campbell added to his woes. "Sir, CSOOW reports the aft SPY face is down. He's investigating."

Bill wanted to pound out his frustration on the table. But if he couldn't control these impulses, the real impact would be on his crew's nerves. "Very well, Jason. We'll have to make sure the enemy doesn't know that and sneak up on us from that direction."

"Sir, can I have a moment?"

Bill turned to find the XO at his side. She swayed slightly. He didn't know if it was the wound or the ship's motion. Together, they stepped back to the middle of CIC. The CICWO moved quietly aside, taking the watch supervisor with her.

"What's on your mind, XO? Should you be up and about?"

"Sir, I heard the DCA's report. You may want to order preps to abandon ship."

Bill stared at her, eyes hard. She shrank under the glare but didn't back away.

After a moment, she added, "Captain, I know you don't want to, but if we have to bail, we'll need at least a half an hour to destroy all the classified material and crypto. We can't wait. The water depth isn't enough to keep the bad guys from getting it."

Bill tried to be reasonable, to think it through, to see it from Irving's eyes.

He'd often heard the term "seeing red." He'd never truly experienced it. He did now. The blood pounded in his ears and the lighting in CIC took on a red tinge. His vision narrowed, as if he were in a tunnel. He felt disoriented.

"No. No! It isn't that bad. And if I say it, the crew will think we're lost. They can't fight if they think we're already licked. I won't give in as long as I have a gun that fires. *I'm* not afraid to keep fighting."

The XO straightened. Her eyes took on a deadly glint.

"Sir, I'm not afraid. But I wouldn't be doing *my job* if I didn't bring the possibility to your attention. Sir."

She turned and began to move gingerly back toward the door. Bill reached out, hesitated, then took her elbow.

"I'm sorry. Again. You're right." He swallowed hard. "But I'm right, too. If we pass the word, it'll be a morale blow we won't recover from." He thought for a moment. "So here's what I want. Go down to Radio. Tell them to start emergency destruct procedures. Also tell them if I hear a single peep about what they're doing, they'll regret it. Then tell CSOOW the same thing. I'll talk to Emily and have the watch supe start up here. Alright?"

Irving breathed a sigh. "Yes, sir, I'm on it."

She turned and left.

Bill explained to Hawke what he wanted, left her to do it, and returned to his chair.

"That bad, sir?" Campbell asked.

Bill looked at him.

Campbell shrugged his shoulders. "I saw the watch supe head for the filing cabinets and start pulling stuff out. Hard to miss. I told everybody on the circuit it's just precautionary, that we're gaining on the fire. I don't want them thinking about it."

Bill nodded and sat down. "You're right, it's just a precaution. We're not done yet."

The bridge called again.

"Sir, Vietnamese ship wants to know how they can help. They said another ship's helping *Hepburn*."

Bill's surprise turned to gratitude. "Tell them whatever the DCA says."

He released the switch, then thought better of it and pressed it again. "And tell them thank you. Thank you very much."

Fifteen minutes later, *Nicholas* had slowed to bare steerageway. The Vietnamese frigate steamed alongside, pouring water into the hangar from several fire hoses. Bill prayed it would be enough.

The attack team re-wickered the Tomahawk solutions again.

As he continued to ask himself at what point he might be forced to take more concrete steps and order his crew to leave their home, *Nicholas* plowed ponderously toward her new launch point. She rolled more slowly and didn't rise to the waves as quickly. As fast as the pumps took water out of the bilges, firefighting hoses poured water in even faster, and not all that water made its way to the bilges.

That alone wouldn't sink her. It would take a couple of days for that to happen. But as the weight of water increased in spaces above the waterline, her center of gravity moved higher. Hundreds of ships over the centuries had rolled over when their center of gravity rose too high, or when such heavy weight flowed from side to side.

"Thirty minutes, sir." Campbell spoke quietly, looking intently at his console. Then his eyes went wide and he keyed his mike. "Unidentified air contacts, composition many, bearing zero five three, range three hundred miles. Assumed hostile. EW, whatcha got?"

Bill reached for his own headset and put it back on.

"—yet, sir," came the response from the EW Supe.

He touched Campbell's arm. When Campbell looked over, Bill cocked his head.

Campbell shook his own. "No ESM, yet. I'm bringing up SPY, sir?"

Bill shook his head. "We've got the link picture from the SAG, let's stay quiet for now. Make sure *Tran* knows there's enemy aircraft inbound. And let's shut down our surface search radar, too. Those aircraft are a bigger threat than surface ships, at least for the moment."

A few minutes later, *Tran* had shut down her fire hoses and moved to a point four thousand yards on *Nicholas's* port side. A radio talker passed her range and bearing to the inbound aircraft so she could be as prepared as possible, since her radar was also silent.

"The rest of the SAG's under attack," Campbell reported.

Bill sat tightly, gripping the arms of his chair. He prayed his task group would survive the night.

"Six of the aircraft broke off to the east, sir." reported Campbell. "We're watching them."

As the minutes passed, Campbell kept up a litany of reports. Twelve aircraft, Chinese-built versions of the Russian Badger long-range bomber, launched two missiles each at the rest of the SAG, but the group defeated all of them either through hard or soft kill. Then the enemy turned away, missiles on their tails. Four of them died. The other eight got away.

Bill heaved a sigh of relief, but it was short lived.

"The group of six just turned inbound to us, sir."

"Shit."

Campbell didn't turn from his console, but his eyes widened.

Bill thought recklessly, *Well, they're just going to have to get used to hearing me curse.*

The countdown began.

"Range, one hundred ninety-seven miles."

"One seventy-five."

They continued to close the force. Bill wasn't sure how long he could stand it.

"Bring SPY online."

Bill had just been about to order it himself when Campbell spoke.

As the radar came up, it detected and began tracking the aircraft. Almost instantaneously, the EW Supe and Tactical Information Coordinator both called out.

"Missile launch. Multiple missiles inbound. Engaging."

Bill watched the deadly dance.

"Mark intercept. Splash two, continuing."

"Splash three more."

"Missed intercept. Firing again."

The choreographed moves continued. The enemy missiles, supported by jamming from the strike aircraft, continued inbound. *Nicholas* loosed return fire, slowly killing them.

Campbell was trying hard to kill the launching aircraft, too, but the inbounds were so close they needed to take priority. The gun joined the fray, rhythmically banging out an invisible curtain of steel designed to shred missile bodies approaching at supersonic speed. Then it came again, the horrible tearing sound of the CIWS firing. A massive *thud* shook the ship and Bill winced as if he'd been impaled.

"Damage report," he called into the intercom.

"Combat, Bridge. CIWS got that one, sir. It was awful fucking close, though."

Bill smiled briefly, mirthlessly.

"Captain, DCA. Repair Two reports pieces of that one came through the hull forward. There's a small fire in Combat Systems Berthing. They're on it."

Bill's breath exploded. *More holes. Who knows how many more injuries?*

Another thud, not as strong. He waited. A few seconds later another followed, this one enormous, though not nearly as strong as the missile hit in the hangar.

"Combat, Bridge. The frigate got it, sir. The whole ship disappeared. It's just — gone."

Bill's heart broke. Would there be no end to death?

"Strike's outbound, sir. That was the last of the inbounds."

Bill looked around at Campbell.

Campbell stared back, sweat beaded on his forehead.

"Kill the bastards, Jason. Don't let them go home to rearm."

Campbell stared at him, hunger in his eyes, and something else. Profound sorrow.

"I can't, sir. We've only got two birds left. We may need them later. I wish to God I could, sir, but I recommend against it."

Bill stared at him then let his shoulders sag.

He nodded, unable to speak.

After he ordered the RHIBs launched to search for survivors, he sat and waited. *Nicholas* continued toward the place where she would launch her retribution.

The phone on the desk trilled.

"Captain."

"Sir, XO here. We can't launch the RHIBS, it's too rough. We could lose the boat and its crew. There's probably no survivors anyway."

"Dammit, XO, I want boats in the water. They trusted us, they trusted *me*. I won't leave them to drown or let the sharks get at 'em."

"Sir, there're fishing boats headed this way. We can let them pick up anyone who did make it." She paused. "Sir, it's an empty gesture. And the Vietnamese are warriors. They know the priority must be the fight."

Bill closed his eyes and took a deep breath. "Put one RHIB in the water. Empty gesture or not, do it." He hung up.

An hour later the fire in the hangar was finally out, victim of a combination of the Halon deluge system the repair locker personnel had finally managed to activate, and aggressive fire-fighting.

"Captain, CHENG here. The chief in Repair Three got burned personally leading a hose team. Ensign Sandstrom took charge. He did a bang-up job, sir."

"Very well. Tell him Bravo Zulu. Tell him, tell him I'm proud of him." He reflected a moment on how much the young officer had matured since the first attack.

Bill got launch reports from *Berkeley*, then fifteen minutes later *Nicholas* launched her own TLAMs.

He heaved a sigh of relief as he ordered both groups of ships to turn back toward the rendezvous.

As they passed, *Nicholas* recovered her RHIB. The boat officer reported they'd found five survivors in the heavy seas, all badly burned. Two had died so they'd slipped them gently over the side. The remaining three were moved to sickbay. Doc had very little hope for one of them but thought the others might make it if they could be gotten to the carrier. The boat officer didn't know how many the fishing boats had picked up.

The dismal dawn brought a drenching rain. Amidst the downpour, a mist rose from the sea. Bill and his crew drooped with fatigue.

But he couldn't rest. He had to take reports from the other ships.

A near miss from a missile had crumpled *Berkeley*'s hull forward, smashed a SPY radar face, destroyed the captain's cabin, and caved in the forward superstructure on the starboard side. The rest of the SAG had come through unscathed. But they were down to half their missile load outs. There were just enough TLAM for a few follow-on strikes once they knew how effective these had been.

But were there enough anti-air missiles to protect themselves and the carrier?

The worst were the casualty reports.

Berkeley had only suffered one killed and three injured. *Hepburn*, on the other hand, had lost thirty-seven killed and fourteen wounded. Two of those were so badly burned, they weren't expected to live. *Nicholas* had twenty-nine dead and eleven wounded.

But the Vietnamese had suffered the most. They'd been attacked by a second flotilla of Chinese corvettes. While they'd destroyed the enemy, they'd lost two ships sunk and two badly damaged, one so severely that she'd been scuttled after removing her surviving crew. Added to the toll was the total loss of the *Tran*.

Bill didn't have numbers, but he knew they had to be in the hundreds of dead and injured.

He dreaded reporting to Admiral Gupta.

He dreaded writing letters to next of kin even more.

CHAPTER
SIXTY-NINE

1000 Zulu, 13 Nov
1300 Local Time
The Kremlin, Moscow

Kolchavin eyed the stains on the rug with distaste. He hadn't sought bloodshed. But knowing Gregorivich, he wasn't surprised.

He and six others had come to this office the day before to reason with the now former president of Russia. But prepared for him to refuse to listen, they'd had a backup plan.

Soldiers loyal to the head of the Russian military awaited a pre-arranged signal. If it came, they would move quickly through the presidential suite, eliminating any resistance from bodyguards, break down the door, and arrest the president. The goal was to move so quickly, he couldn't call for help.

But nothing came off as planned. The large number with Kolchavin had tipped off Gregorivich. He'd warned his body-guards, slowing the soldiers and allowing the president to make a stand in his office. He'd seized a pistol none of them knew he kept in his desk and killed two of the delegation before he'd been overcome.

384 THOMAS M. WING

His own deputy foreign minister and the minister for the interior had given their lives to save the *Rodina*.

Now it was up to him to clean up the figurative mess, just as cleaners would remove the bloodstains. The men and women seated around the table in the next room would assist him.

He turned the doorknob and entered.

They rose to greet him, standing in variations of rigidity or feigned relaxation, depending on their level of fear.

The majority remembered the Soviet days, the coup against Mikhail Gorbachev right before the end. Though some had been children, they remembered the fear and uncertainty. It was reflected in their faces now.

"Please, sit. Now is not the time to place exaggerated emphasis on protocol. We have too much work to do."

Several faces relaxed a little. The others feared they, too, would be deposed.

One, however, was not fearful.

"Where is Yuri?" demanded Peotr Ornikov, head of state security.

Taking his seat at the head of the table, Kolchavin noted Ornikov still stood. He leaned forward, face flushed, hands on the table.

"Relax, Peotr," Kolchavin said. "I intend to tell you all what has happened."

He stopped and regarded Ornikov, his expression mild as he waited.

Ornikov looked rebellious, but eventually sat. The hand of the deputy interior minister on his elbow helped convince him.

Kolchavin looked around the table, trying to hold the eyes of each in turn. Some refused.

Ornikov spoke, though he controlled his tone. "Again, I want to know where Yuri is, or the prime minister? They should be here. Why do you chair this meeting?"

Kolchavin sighed. "The president is indisposed. Actually, he's in hospital. I have chosen to move forward. As for Mikhail, he told me himself he did not want to attend. I believe he felt strongly his attention was best directed elsewhere."

This was strictly true, after a fashion. Medinsky had decided he wanted no part of the coup. He had a knack for finding ways to protect himself regardless of the impact on the rest of the government or the nation.

"Ladies and gentlemen, I think no one in this room would disagree that this war has not been the resounding success predicted at the outset," Kolchavin continued.

Grumbling rose from expected quarters. Ornikov leaned forward. "The bungling of the Foreign Ministry is to blame, and the failure of the military to properly prosecute the enemy. In any case—"

Kolchavin pounded his fist on the table and said, "Enough."

Ornikov looked like he would start again, so Kolchavin held up his hand. "Enough. If anyone in this room raises his or her voice again, I will have the guards step in and remove them. Is that clear?"

Ornikov calmed himself.

Kolchavin continued. "I also do not want to hear blame apportioned. There is blame enough around this table. That is not what we are here to discuss." He looked around again. They were at least listening. "We are here to determine how best to save our country."

Someone muttered "and ourselves," but he ignored it.

But Ornikov still couldn't resist. "Save it from what, exactly? We are not under imminent threat. Our army holds half of Poland and nearly all the Baltic states." He sneered. "What exactly are we to save ourselves from?"

Irina Blogovich, the Information Minister, spoke angrily. "Perhaps we should ask the people who lived in Kaluga or Smolensk that question. If you can find any who are alive."

Kolchavin once again raised his hand.

"The threat is the loss of our legitimacy. The loss of our

ability to recover from this disaster. The loss of our position in the world." A pained expression crossed his face.

He looked at Ornikov. "What makes you think that NATO and the Americans will stop at the western border of Ukraine or Belarus? Do you believe they will allow us to maintain our land corridor to Kaliningrad, or keep the Baltic states?"

Ornikov snorted derisively. "Of course they will. They have no stomach for the dead we would inflict on them should they *not* stop. They are weak-minded fools and will be happy with the status quo. Ukraine and Belarus are ours, have always been ours. So is the Baltic region. They will recognize our right to annex them. Even they have to realize we cannot tolerate oppression of Russian-speaking peoples." He slammed his fist on the table. "But we must act now and counterattack."

Kolchavin regarded him quietly, frowning. "Peotr, you are wrong. They will demand that we return—" He avoided the word *retreat*. "—to our pre-war borders. It is even likely they will demand that we give back Ukraine and the Crimea."

Ornikov leaned forward and glared. "Never. And if they demand it, they will continue to feel our wrath. We will push them back and back until we enter Germany. If they still do not understand, we will continue to push, even through France to the Atlantic. Let us see at what point they acknowledge our right to a buffer between ourselves and enemies bent on our destruction." Spit had begun to fly as he ended his rant.

The minister for internal affairs spoke up. "At what cost? We are nearly bankrupt now, and this war is eating what reserves we had. We cannot continue to provide munitions or food to sustain a war of that length. And if the enemy continues to destroy our infrastructure, and especially if they again use nuclear weapons, we will have nothing left to protect within your buffer."

"The enemy will never again use atomic weapons. We will ensure they cannot by destroying their weapons in their silos and at sea," Ornikov replied.

Astounded, Kolchavin started to reply, but was interrupted by the deputy minister of defense. "Minister, how did that work for us the first two times? Our attack against the United Kingdom was easily defeated by the enemy's ballistic missile defense ships. Our submarines have had little success in defeating those ships. In the North Sea, the enemy's submarine fleet reigns supreme. Our own anti-ballistic missile systems proved much less reliable than we'd expected." She firmly shook her head. "We cannot prevent a massive retaliation. We will lose many cities, perhaps even Moscow. And with the Americans now openly against us, we face thousands of their atomic warheads. Even if we destroyed all the enemy's land-based weapons, their sea-based missiles would destroy our country." She locked eyes with him until he looked away. "Do you understand? Our nation would cease to exist," she finished.

Ornikov fumed, breathing heavily. But he wasn't ready to give in yet. "This is the result of the obstruction you all have used to keep Russia weak. You fought the president in every way, and now you sit here talking of defeat. I will not have it. I still have authority, and I *will* ensure that any government sitting in the Kremlin will defend Mother Russia to the last extreme."

He rose and stormed from the room. Consternation broke out. Many of those present rose, fear on their faces.

Kolchavin waved them to sit. "My friends, I know he controls the state security apparatus. But the army will ensure they do not interfere with the properly constituted authority of the office of the president. I have given the army the authority to arrest the leadership and engage their forces, if necessary."

His words did not erase the fear, but they sat.

"Now, ladies and gentlemen, we must discuss our offer to NATO to attempt a negotiated peace."

CHAPTER
SEVENTY

0200 Zulu, 15 Nov
1000 Local Time
Office of the President, Beijing

"Comrade President, Ministers Zhang, Dong, and Peng, and General Jiang ask to see you."

Liu frowned, wondering why they hadn't made an appointment. The current crisis didn't justify abandonment of proper protocol. He also wondered why Jiang wasn't attending to his duties.

The American attacks had hurt far more and destroyed much, much more of their defense infrastructure than they'd thought possible. He thought Jiang ought to be finding a way to defeat the American navy, which slowly punched its way through every barrier the PLAN and PLAAF had erected.

He sighed. "Send them in."

They all looked both angry and determined. They skipped the preliminaries and went straight to business, another protocol violation.

"Comrade President, we have come to end your disastrous war," said Dong. The people's deputy from Hainan Island, Liu wondered why he was here. *Such discussions should not involve deputies from such small regions.* The theory that all people's deputies were equal in stature was just that, a theory.

"And who has decided it is a disaster?"

Zhang responded. "Comrade President, even you must admit that events are not proceeding exactly as we would desire?"

"Gentlemen, war is never a certain thing," Liu said. "We knew there would be reverses when we embarked on this course of action, perhaps even significant ones. But we are not losing."

The four men looked at one another. Dong opened his mouth, but Zhang shook his head and turned back to Liu. "No, we are not winning, certainly not anymore."

General Jiang added, "Comrade President, perhaps you are not aware of the latest damage assessments? They are rather dire."

Liu had seen them, at least in summary. He had no need for details. "I have. But they are nothing compared to the losses the Americans have sustained. Have we not sunk three of their aircraft carriers? That is on top of the ones we destroyed in their ports. They have, what, perhaps three left that are operational?"

Jiang flushed and jabbed his finger at Liu. "No. We face *four* enemy carriers. Initial reports have been in error. Two groups are nearing the first island chain and wreak destruction out of proportion to their size. A third group operates in the South China Sea. That group sank one of *our* carriers." Nostrils flaring, he angrily gestured with his hands.

"We have lost nearly half our Air Force, Comrade President. Over half of our naval strength. Our non-nuclear ballistic and cruise missiles are reduced to one-fifth of pre-war levels. Had we not fired so many in our attempts to defeat the enemy naval forces, most of them would have been destroyed in their bunkers." He stopped. His face said it was much worse than just the numbers.

"Can we not replace all those weapons, Comrade General?"

Liu asked quietly. "Do we not outproduce the Americans in weapons and platforms by four or five to one?"

Jiang blinked. "Yes, given time. But at the rate the Americans are destroying them, we will still be without weapons in a week, perhaps ten days. And the Americans have targeted our missile factories. They surprised us with how thoroughly they succeeded in identifying even our most secret manufactories." He snorted. "They have also managed to degrade our ability to locate them. Their ballistic missile defense ships have destroyed three of our intelligence satellites. Their submarine force has been singularly successful in eliminating our submarines. We counted on them to track and destroy their naval forces, or at least to decrement them so our surface force could close for the kill. It has not worked out that way."

It was Peng's turn. "Worse, Comrade President, our renegade province has refused continued meetings with our reunification delegation." He heaved a sigh. "We have achieved our objectives. Some, anyway. To continue to fight risks losing what we have gained."

Liu was angry now. "Where is Huang? Why is the deputy defense minister in my office, speaking to me of losing?"

Peng shrugged, and said, "Minister Huang is, shall we say, ill. He was unable to attend. However," he paused, his eyes taking on an intensity Liu hadn't seen before, "he has briefed me on the original plan. He has heard my arguments, and I could say he agrees with me."

Liu sat back in his chair. "I doubt that very much. What I do not doubt is that you have moved Huang out of your way."

Peng didn't respond. Instead, he walked to the sofa placed beneath the large bookcase that lined the wall to the side of the office and sat. The others also moved to chairs or the sofa and took seats.

Zhang spoke next. "We four have been asked by the State Council to speak on their behalf. In the past three hours, Comrade President, we have received communiques from several NATO nations and the NATO council itself. They have reversed their previous positions and have aligned themselves with the United States. The Thais have also found their courage and announced they will support the Americans." He paused to let that sink in. "Finally, the Australian navy has ordered a five-ship task force to join the American carrier in the South China Sea. And there has been a marked increase in communications between Australian naval headquarters and their three submarines." He shook his head. "You should note, Australian submarines are armed with Tomahawk cruise missiles, as are three of their surface ships."

Liu's eyes had widened and his pulse quickened. "Why would NATO and Australia join the Americans?"

Zhang looked at him with contempt. "Perhaps you have not been told the biggest news of all. The Americans have a new president. It is their secretary of state, Herman Kingston."

Liu squinted as he tried to remember what he knew of Kingston. If he recalled, the man had been a do-nothing Cabinet member, sidelined by a president who preferred to run his own foreign policy, such as it was. The man had no military training or background. In fact, his entire experience was in business.

Liu responded, "He is no threat. He is completely ignorant of military affairs. He knows nothing of how to fight a war."

Zhang responded, "Perhaps not, but he knows how to build teams. He has already reversed the damage done to NATO by his predecessor's bluster."

"They cannot fight us. They are fully committed to fighting Russia."

"Ah, that is another one of the many ways in which you are wrong. Kingston has openly committed American forces in Europe to fight. And I would remind you that the war with Russia is a land war. Ours is in the air and on the sea. The NATO navies have decimated the Russian navy. Not sufficiently to allow them to send ships to fight us, which in any case would not arrive for weeks. But the shift in the balance *is* sufficient to let them redirect naval and air forces that were moving toward Europe back to the war here." His neck cracked as he moved his head from side to side. "Finally, there is also a new president in Russia. His Foreign Ministry approached NATO three hours ago to obtain a ceasefire."

Liu reeled with shock. "Where is Gregorivich?"

"It appears Gregorivich was arrested. For all we know, he is dead. A very Soviet-style coup has taken place. The new president is Foreign Minister Kolchavin."

"We believe it is now time for us to have a new leader," Peng said, smiling grimly.

Liu looked at the four. They were in a greater position of power than he'd expected. "What if I do not go quietly into that good night?"

"Comrade President, we do not propose to replace you at this time, only to, shall we say, curb your more dangerous proclivities and limit your decision-making. You will remain president, but henceforth foreign relations will be conducted by us."

Dong added, "And should you not agree, *Comrade*, it is entirely possible you might suffer an illness very similar to that which afflicts Defense Minister Huang. It might perhaps even be fatal."

"We do not want the world to know there has been a coup," Jiang said. "We cannot afford to appear weak. However, we also cannot continue the war." He shook his head. "The objectives you laid out to us and to the world have been achieved. We have limited the power of the United States to act with impunity in the western Pacific. We have likewise limited their ability to interfere with our sovereignty in the South China Sea. They will no longer be able to arm Taiwan, and so we will avoid, for now, a war over reunification." He ticked the points off on his fingers as he spoke. "They also no longer threaten North Korea, nor will they be strong enough to prevent us and others from modernizing that country's economy. They will simply have to accept the Kim regime. And with you remaining in the office of president, we will avoid the appearance of error." Jiang locked eyes with him.

Liu looked away.

Jiang continued. "In the circumstance you resist, however, you will become ill. Perhaps a stroke or heart attack. One way or another, you will not again have the authority you misused to lead us into war."

Liu's mind raced, looking for a way out. But every path wound up at the same point. In the end, he had little choice.

"You seem to have thought of everything." He breathed a heavy sigh. "I accept your proposal."

CHAPTER
SEVENTY-ONE

0700 Zulu, 14 Nov
0800 Local Time
Interim NATO Headquarters, Brussels

"I believe only a few of you have seen the Russian offer," said Doenitz. "For those who have not, I will summarize." He read from the single page in his hand.

"One. The Russian Federation will withdraw from Polish territory to the pre-hostilities borders. Two, they will move forces into garrisons in Estonia, Latvia, and Lithuania, with the exception of those security forces required to maintain stability. Three, they will conduct elections for local government in the Baltic *regions* and Ukraine, within six months."

Murmuring broke out, and he waited. When it was quiet, he continued to read. "Four, a ceasefire will go into effect at midnight Central European Time tomorrow while negotiations proceed, with all military forces remaining in place."

He looked up and placed his glasses on the table in front of him.

"Our tasks are simple. We must decide if we should accept these terms. If not, we must counter them. However, before we

AGAINST ALL ENEMIES   395

begin, I wish to welcome our new temporary American representative."

Murmured greetings swept around the table. The ambassador smiled warmly.

Up until yesterday, he'd led a trade delegation trying to mitigate the negative effects of the now-former president's massive tariffs against the European Union. When the war erupted, he and his people had gone to their hotel rooms. Thus far, they'd sat it out. He had no military background. He was an economist. His post had been a reward for an economic paper written years ago.

Now, as the new Atlantic Council representative, the only way to close the gap with the NATO allies was to be friendly, accommodating, and endorse whatever the allies wanted. These were also his instructions from President Kingston.

"I'm happy to be here, Mr. Secretary. The United States looks forward to renewing our relationships with our allies, and to working closely with you to end this devastating conflict and establish a just peace that protects NATO and the interests of its members. *All* of its members."

Several ambassadors relaxed and a few returned his smile.

"Thank you, Mr. Ambassador." Doenitz turned back to the rest of the room. "Now, with respect to their offer, is there anyone who suggests we accept it as written?"

The answer was a resounding "no", so he didn't bother with a voice vote. "Then, ladies and gentlemen, what should our response be?"

It took only two hours to hammer out the terms NATO would demand. They were not at all close to what had been offered.

Along with the new terms, a note informed the Russian Federation that fighting would continue while negotiations were ongoing.

2048 Zulu, 14 Nov
2348 Local Time
The Kremlin, Moscow

Kolchavin sighed and kneaded his brow.

It was nearly midnight as he and his much smaller war cabinet met to finalize their response to NATO's demand. He'd not included the holdouts from the former president's cabinet.

"Are we about done?" he asked.

He looked around. He hadn't yet taken the title, but he was effectively the president now, and these men and women acknowledged it. The Russian populace seemed content with his explanation that the president was ill and had stepped aside. For now.

Given what they'd endured, he wasn't surprised.

"Yes, I think we are," said the finance minister.

"I will have my spokesmen prepare to release it publicly at the same time as we transmit it to NATO, Mr. President," said Blogovich.

"Wait until we are sure *they* will accept it," he said. "We don't want to be seen as presenting them a *fait accompli*. We want them to see us as cooperative, not antagonistic." He rubbed bloodshot eyes and leaned back. "And do not call me 'Mr. President'."

She smiled briefly, then nodded.

He turned to Admiral Gorshkov, newly promoted, and to General Bovarin. "Are the orders to withdraw ready?"

"Yes, sir. I've also issued orders to certain army units whose loyalty I can be sure of to make sure those *unconventional* forces in eastern Ukraine withdraw, as well. I anticipate some resistance with all the fighting these past several years. They will not want to give up what they believed they had finally won."

"I know that, but NATO has made it clear eastern Ukraine must be able to decide its own fate. Legitimately, that is." He closed his eyes and pinched his nose. "We must accept it. And while they rejected the land bridge to Kaliningrad, their offer of a neutral zone along the main highway is generous, given that we both started this war and initiated the use of nuclear weapons. No, ladies and gentlemen, we are fortunate to be given this much. If we are to salvage any dignity, we must acquiesce."

"Too bad Ornikov couldn't see that."

Peotr Ornikov had been killed earlier in the day, while leading a state security paramilitary attack on the Kremlin. Many of his most rabid followers had also died, unwilling to surrender even after their leader's demise.

Kolchavin kept it to himself, but he suspected the elimination of those fanatics would be a good thing for the nation in the long run.

He was tired, but perhaps in a few days' time he might sleep.

No, he reflected. *There will still be no time for sleep. We must rebuild.*

CHAPTER
SEVENTY-TWO

0500 Zulu, 14 Nov
1200 Local Time
USS *Theodore Roosevelt*, South China Sea

Ding-ding. Ding-ding.

"*Nicholas*, arriving."

Bill stepped out of the helo as the announcement boomed. He nearly fell as the strong wind across the flight deck grabbed him.

An anonymous petty officer wearing a cranial helmet and dark flight deck goggles saluted him and indicated he should follow. He ducked his head beneath the still spinning rotors as she led him to the island and held the watertight door, closing it once he ducked inside. Bill removed his goggles, helmet, and float-coat and handed them to another petty officer. A young officer stepped forward.

"I'm Ensign Williams, sir. May I escort you to the flag cabin?"

The woman had severely cut, short dark hair. Ice stabbed Bill's heart as he remembered Barrister. He followed mutely. He barely noticed the eyes of the sailors who moved against the bulkheads as they made their way down to the flag deck.

Inside, the admiral's cabin was the same as the last time he'd been there.

Was it really just forty-eight hours? His head spun slightly.

This time only Gupta and his chief of staff greeted him.

The admiral rose immediately and strode to shake Bill's hand. "Welcome back, Bill. Welcome back."

Paxton's handshake was equally warm as Gupta waved them to sit.

Gupta leaned forward and clasped his hands together. "How bad was it? I read your report, but I want to hear it from you."

Bill leaned back. He'd gotten a couple of hours of sleep before they'd rejoined the strike group, but his hands still shook and he fought to keep his voice clear.

"Bad, sir, but I hear we got the job done."

"You did, and I'll tell you about that, too. But how are you and your crew?"

Bill stumbled through it. Additional details were drawn out by questions from both. Only once did he slur his answer so badly he had to repeat it.

When he finished, Gupta leaned back and gave Paxton a significant look before addressing Bill. "You did a helluva job. I know it cost you, but you did well, extremely well. Bravo Zulu!"

Bill smiled slightly but couldn't hold it. The faces of the dead kept running through his mind. "As I said before, sir, I've got a damned good crew. So do the other COs. In particular, Phil Ridgely in *Berkeley* should be commended. He took command after *Nicholas* had to fall back and did a nice job of fighting off the air raid."

Gupta smiled. "He and I go back a ways. He was a JG when I was a squadron department head aboard *Nimitz*. He and I met one night when a couple of my guys got brought back aboard ship a bit, shall we say, under the weather? We had a few words. I suggested he and the Navy might be better served if he decided to go be a farmer somewhere. But he stood his ground. I've always liked shoes who can give as good as they can take."

Gupta slapped Bill's knee. "And you are one of those, truly."

Bill didn't know what to say so he said nothing.

Paxton said, "Bill, we're sending *Nicholas* for repairs. The Vietnamese offered to take you into a shipyard in Ho Chi Minh City for voyage repairs, enough to let you go home via the Suez. It's too risky to send you via the Pacific. There're still too many Chinese subs missing and the Indonesians didn't take too kindly to warships transiting their waters. They're neutral, so we have to honor that."

"What about Australia or Singapore?" Bill asked.

Paxton shook her head. "The Aussies are joining the fight, but they don't have the capacity to fix your weapons and sensor systems. Singapore is still on the fence."

Bill sighed. He'd feared being sent out of theater. He'd also welcomed it and yet was unhappy, all at the same time.

He and his crew had suffered great losses. They were tired and beat up. But they were strong, stronger than he'd believed possible. And they were proud of what they'd done. But their ship was hurt and couldn't fight anymore without a lot of work.

At the same time, he couldn't help wishing they could stay and see it through. The Chinese were far from down for the count. *Nicholas* and the rest of Seventh Fleet had done a lot of damage, but China could absorb a lot of damage. Who knew how long they could keep up the fight?

In the end, that was the best argument for going home and getting fixed. They'd come back as a full-up round, ready to take on whatever China had left to throw at them.

He squared his shoulders. "Aye, sir. I wish we could stay. But we'll be back, better."

Gupta smiled. "I know you will. And we'll need you. *Hepburn* will go with you, but you're senior, so you'll have TACON. We'll keep your helos here, unfortunately, to augment our air wing. The planes we're putting in Vietnam will provide air cover for the straits transit. I believe you know Lieutenant

Commander Dix volunteered to stay. What do you think about that?"

Bill had spent twenty minutes talking to Dix about just that. The young man still grieved, but he'd recovered his equilibrium. He wanted to make sure his people hadn't died in vain. Bill worried he might be too shaken to be effective, but Dix had shown a certitude Bill couldn't argue with. "Sir, I think that's a good idea. He'll do a good job."

"Good. Now, we've got a draft of folks we'll transfer over to you to supplement your crew—"

"No, sir."

"Excuse me?"

"I said, no, sir."

Gupta sat back and put his arms behind his head. Bill stared back at him calmly. Finally, Gupta ran one hand through his hair then put both on his knees. "Why not?"

"Sir, I believe my crew has earned the right to take *Nicholas* home on our own. Besides, you need every man and woman you have here where the fight is." He took a deep breath. "So, no, sir, we don't need help. Thank you all the same."

Gupta regarded him silently.

Paxton broke the silence, clearing her throat. "*Franklin*?" she asked Bill.

Bill turned to her for a moment, then nodded. "Yes, ma'am, if you want to put it that way."

Paxton nodded and looked at Gupta. "USS *Franklin*, the World War II carrier. Remember, sir? She was horribly damaged, lost over eight hundred of her crew. But her CO insisted on the surviving crew taking her home by themselves. They did it, too."

"I remember my naval history, but thanks, Wendy," Gupta said, smiling.

Then he turned back to Bill. "Alright, if that's what you want. You're sure?"

Bill nodded.

Gupta stood and shook his hand. "Good luck, Captain Wilkins."

CHAPTER
SEVENTY-THREE

14 Nov to 1 Dec
Western Pacific Area of Operations

The Chinese were as prepared as possible when the waves of TLAM roared in from several different directions. But no system they'd fielded could do much to stop them. A few missiles were lost to lucky shots. But thanks to the guided-missile submarines, who'd clandestinely arrived within striking range, over seven hundred total missiles hammered at air defenses and fighter bases, leaving burning rubble in their wake.

Behind the missiles came manned aircraft from the four carriers, nearly two hundred in total, each carrying a loadout optimized for their particular targets. Moreover, almost every aircraft had three targets loaded in its computer.

Without air defense missiles and fighter aircraft to oppose them, most prosecuted at least their primary and secondary targets. Thousands of Chinese military personnel perished, and critical capabilities were destroyed.

With each capability they lost, the rest of their military machine became that much more vulnerable to follow-on strikes, and the American military took advantage of it.

The Air Force and Marine Corps scraped together a few planes in Okinawa, raised like a phoenix from the ashes. From Guam came more. American bombers based in Australia added to the mix. US planes in Vietnam plastered Chinese forces moving toward Hanoi, stopping them.

Slowly, the US military machine rolled back the Chinese military. As good as the enemy was and as numerous, the Americans adapted and overcame the deficit.

CHAPTER
SEVENTY-FOUR

0630 Zulu, 4 Dec
1530 Local Time
USS *Ronald Reagan*, 300 nautical miles northeast of the
Philippines

"Carrier Strike Group Seven's reporting for duty. They're taking station as assigned."

Rear Admiral Hiakawa made his report to Commander Seventh Fleet.

Simpson had shifted her flag to *Reagan* when it became obvious *Blue Ridge* was too badly damaged and needed to go back to Japan.

The crew had fought hard and saved their ship. But they hadn't been able to restore sufficient power to keep the flag spaces online. Coupled with personnel losses, the need to move had been obvious.

Now the *TR* strike group had joined up with what remained of Task Group Seven Zero Point One, as had the ARG Third Fleet cobbled together around *Peleliu*. Along the way, an Australian SAG had joined the *TR* force. Task Group Seven Zero Point Two,

406   THOMAS M. WING

consisting of *Nimitz*, *Stennis*, and escorts, had taken position five hundred miles to the north.

A ceasefire had been in effect since the day before yesterday, but no one was taking any chances. Negotiations had only just begun.

Simpson grunted as she shifted in her seat. The cast on her right arm went nearly to her shoulder, making it difficult to get comfortable.

"Thanks, Sam. Did we give the Vietnamese a good screen position?"

"Yes, ma'am. Their flagship is in the lead carrier position, right in the middle. She's off *TR*'s port bow and *Reagan*'s starboard bow. They should be very pleased with themselves."

The Vietnamese Navy had suffered severe losses and Simpson wanted them to know the US Navy honored their sacrifice. Yes, it had been an act of self-interest, but few other nations had been willing to make that commitment.

"What about the subs?"

Hiakawa smiled, the smile of a raptor.

"They're on station, too. The Chinese won't even know what hit 'em if they violate the ceasefire. Two more SSGNs, each with a full load of TLAM? Oh, yeah, they'll regret it, and quick."

Simpson smiled. The weeks since *Nicholas* had departed the theater of war had been bloody and painful, but they'd met the enemy and defeated him soundly. The end of the war in Europe had allowed US reinforcements to flow to the Western Pacific, especially munitions.

Chinese losses were heavy, more than America's, even accounting for the wide-ranging losses from the sneak attack. Simpson was certain the damage done to Chinese infrastructure was what had really led their government to sue for peace. Their claim to have "met all their objectives" didn't wash.

But if it made them feel better and still ended the bloodshed, she was fine with that. They'd been punished for their perfidy.

And the United States had the Seventh Fleet's four carriers ready to make sure they negotiated in good faith.

She said a silent prayer for those who'd been lost along the way.

It had always surprised her that civilians with no ties to the military believed so strongly that military people, especially senior officers, *wanted* war. She'd never found that to be true. Those who served knew who bore the brunt of the cost. The men and women in uniform did not shrink from it: they understood when they took the oath that death or dismemberment was a possibility. But she'd rarely met anyone who actively *sought* war.

She shook her head, then groaned. They'd just removed the stitches from her forehead a few days ago, revealing a jagged red scar where the torn table edge had split it.

"What's that, ma'am?" asked Hiakawa.

"Oh, nothing. Just thinking about what it cost to get here."

Both turned and looked out the windows of the flag bridge at the proud formation of battered warships. Most showed rust, the result of the never-ending battle against the elements. A few showed battle scars, testament to what they'd been through.

Yet they were magnificent vessels, who'd fought through and won against an adversary that outnumbered them and had also fought hard.

Simpson was proud of them.

EPILOGUE

1800 Zulu, 12 Jan
1000 Pacific Time
Naval Information Warfare Center Pacific, San Diego

Captain (Select) Bill Wilkins stood before the tall pile of rubble, all that remained of the building where his brother had perished. Beside him was his old friend and the new lab CO, Captain Geraldine Maxwell.

She'd taken command the week after the attack. Both the CO and XO, as well as the rest of the civilian and military senior leadership, had been killed.

The two stood in the middle of the road that ran in front of the ruin, near the short set of stairs that had gone up to the lobby and now went nowhere.

A short, athletic woman, normally energetic and full of verve, today Maxwell's face was drawn, with bags under her eyes and a somber expression.

"We found the bodies pretty quickly once we started recovery. Search and rescue didn't take long. There weren't many survivors. Your brother was in the wreckage of the cafeteria, so he was identified about three days after. The stench was awful."

Realizing what she'd just said and who she was talking to, she cringed and her face colored.

He smiled. "Don't worry about it. War is messy. It's been three months, and I'm not squeamish. At least, not anymore," he added barely above a whisper.

She looked gratefully at him and turned back to consider the pile.

To their left, two enormous dump trucks took on concrete, rebar, and debris from two loaders that worked their way through the pile. To their right, another set of dump trucks and loaders worked the building from that end. They'd cleared nearly half the rubble.

"I appreciate you bringing me up here. I just wanted to say goodbye, I guess. I missed his funeral, and I know there's a part of him still in there."

He pointed with his shoulder at the pile.

She reached out and squeezed his forearm gently.

"No problem, Bill. I've known you and your brother a long time. I'm so sorry."

He smiled sadly and put his hand on hers, returned the pressure, then let his hand drop.

He breathed deeply. "Well, I'm supposed to have dinner with Jenny and the kids. They miss their dad a lot. I told them I was coming up here. None of them wanted to join me."

"How are they doing?"

He shrugged. "As well as can be expected. She's moving them back to Jacksonville to be near her parents. She says it's too hard living in the house with the memories. They've been there nearly fourteen years. The school's great, but the kids are ready to leave it behind. It's just too much," he said, choking as the last words came out.

He stood quietly, breathing deeply and rapidly.

There was nothing more to say so they stood there for a few more minutes.

He turned to go but stopped and faced Maxwell again.

"There's been so much death, Dina. I lost a bunch of great kids. One of them was as fine a navigator as anyone could ask for. She'd have been a great XO and CO." He sighed. "What was it for? No one won or lost. No borders shifted, no treasures or resources were taken. The Chinese still have their damned islands, for God's sake. Nothing was resolved. Does that mean we'll do it again someday, maybe in twenty or thirty years?"

She didn't speak as her eyes welled up. Finally, she said, "I can't say, Bill. I wish to God I could. But I can't. But you brought your people home, Bill. As torn up and hurt as *Nicholas* was, you brought them home."

"Not all of them."

She reached out and squeezed his arm again. "But you brought everyone you could, and they're with their families again, because of you."

Bill smiled sadly and walked back to his car. And every step of the way, he tried to decide what he should say to his brother's widow and children.

ACKNOWLEDGMENTS

No author ever wrote in a vacuum. Each had someone who believed in them and their story, in order to get it published. I've been blessed to have several someones. I thought I didn't need anyone else, but I quickly learned I needed at least support from my family. As I've matured, I've realized I need support from a host of family, friends, and acquaintances. As John Donne so famously said, "No man is an island." And so it is with me.

First and foremost, I must thank my wife, Elisa, and my daughter, Emily. They have suffered and supported me longest, giving up hours and days I could have spent with them to let me put words on paper. Elisa first learned of my writing in the second or third year of our marriage, when I finally had the courage to share that last secret and let her read something I'd written. She has always supported my writing since, despite my serious lack of confidence, encouraging me to pursue it. Here we are thirty-some-odd years later, and I'm finally publishing a book length story. Emily has consistently encouraged Dad to keep making up stories and writing them down. I can never sufficiently express my gratitude to them!

Next, to my extended family and friends, who have put up with my tentative admission that I write fiction, then with requests for readers, and finally, for reading not just one draft, but in some cases, several drafts. In no particular order: friends from thirty-eight years of military and civil service: David Wallace (who also suffered through being my roommate on our first ship), and Don Ditko; my other beta readers and reviewers,

George Galdorisi, Tammy Taylor, Seamus Beirne, Kathy Taylor; Jara Tripiano, and my cousin Marc Wing. All of them endured to make what you, gentle reader, hold in your hand into something worth reading, if indeed that is your judgment.

Few authors, if any, are successful without an editor. My first editor, the late Jean Jenkins, was the voice of encouragement I needed to keep working on this project. She was terrific, identifying plot holes and bravely tackling my overuse of, well, lots of errors. She said she thought I could compete with "the big boys." We will see, but I cannot adequately express my gratitude for her confidence, and for the kicks in the pants she gave me to keep me moving. I hope she knows how much she helped me. My second editor, Jennifer Silva Redmond, built on what Jean had taught me and encouraged me to "kill my darlings" — cut scenes that weren't necessary but that I liked. She was right, and this is a much better story for it.

My friend, Laura Taylor, deserves all the accolades I can give her. She has encouraged my writing for the last six years as facilitator of a Rogue Read and Critique at my favorite writers' conference, and as the editor who pulled me across the finish line. I've grown tremendously as a writer under her tutelage. Thank you!!

I also must thank the writers and friends I've made through the Southern California Writers' Conference, run by Michael Steven Gregory and Wes Albers. There I joined a community of like-minded people who are mutually supportive and encouraging. In no particular order are friends and other authors who have encouraged me: Ara Grigorian, Janis Thomas, Jennifer Silva Redmond, Rick and Linda Ochoki, Mike Murphey, Laura Rader, Seamus Beirne, and George Galdorisi. My apologies if I have missed someone, as is likely the case. It takes a village!

I must also give enormous thanks to the whole Acorn Publishing Team, especially Holly Kammier, Jessica Therrien, and Jessica Hammett. They decided to take a chance by working with me to get this book in print. They were easy to work with, answered all my questions, dealt with my anxiety and doubt, and all in all made it a good experience. My deepest thanks to you all!

Last but not least, I am deeply grateful to my late cousin Jackie Ward and her late husband, Richard Keith Taylor. Richard was a writer of the first magnitude, and it took quite a while for me to risk him reading my writing. His response was way, way, way over the top, but I think he knew I needed something to keep going. From that moment, he and Jackie encouraged, cajoled, and wheedled me to keep me going. (Not to mention the brandy with which they plied me when I'd visit!)

I must also note that while each of those whose names appear here have striven to make this novel of a certain quality, my own efforts, and very likely my pride, have pulled in the opposite direction. Any merit you find in these pages is the result of the input of these gentle people; the corollary is that all errors or failures are mine and mine alone.

Lastly, I must thank you, the person who holds this book in your hand or on your screen. You've taken the risk of opening it, perhaps reading it, and thus I am indebted to you, as well.

ABOUT THE AUTHOR

A Naval Academy and Naval War College graduate, Thomas M. Wing retired after thirty-two years as a Navy Surface Warfare officer. He served in guided missile destroyers and frigates, as well as with destroyer squadron, cruiser destroyer group, numbered fleet, and Joint Task Force staffs, where he planned  and executed real-world joint operations at the operational and strategic levels of war. He also participated in naval combat during Operation Praying Mantis in the Middle East in April 1988.

He has taught Coast Guard licensing courses and has held a variety of sailing licenses, including Master and Master of Sailing Vessels, Upon Oceans. As well, he founded and served as executive director for the Continental Navy Foundation, which conducted experiential education at sea for young people 13-17 years of age. He also commanded the foundation's tall ship, the brigantine *Megan D.*

His novel, *Against All Enemies*, resulted from a random thought during a period of political tension between China and the U.S. What if that political tension included cruise missiles flying in from the sea to strike the San Diego waterfront?

Thomas M. Wing resides in San Diego with his wife and daughter, two cats, and a dog. He still spends whatever free time he has on the water.

GLOSSARY

1MC - Ship's announcing system
ACoS - Assistant Chief of Staff
ADC - Air Defense Coordinator
AFCENT - Air Forces Central Command
AIC - Agent In Charge
AM - Amplitude Modulation
AOR - Area of Responsibility
ARCENT - Army Forces Central Command
ARG - Amphibious Ready Group
ASAP - As Soon As Possible
ASEAN - The Association of Southeast Asian Nations
ASROC - Anti-Submarine Rockets
ASTAC - Anti-Surface Warfare/Anti-Surface Warfare Tactical Air Controller
ASUW - Anti-Surface Warfare
ASW - Anti-Submarine Warfare
ASWE - Anti-Submarine Warfare Evaluator
ASWO - Anti-Submarine Warfare Officer
ATACO - Air Tactical Control Officer
AW or AAW - Air or Anti-Air Warfare

AWACS - US Air Force Airborne Early Warning Aircraft

Bitch Box - Intercom between ship control stations; in older ships, called the 21MC

BDA - Battle Damage Assessment

BIT - Built-In Test

BM1 - Boatswain's Mate First Class

BMD - Ballistic Missile Defense

BMOW - Boatswain's Mate of the Watch

Bolt from the blue - A completely unanticipated attack

Bravo Zulu or BZ - Navy term telling someone they've done a good job

Bridge/Pilothouse - Bridge is the space where the ship is controlled while underway and includes the bridge wings on both sides of the ship; the pilothouse is the interior space from which the helmsman steers the ship. The two terms are essentially interchangeable on modern warships.

C2 - Command and Control

CAG - Commander Air Group

CAP - Combat Air Patrol

CBRN - Chemical, Biological, Radiological, Nuclear

CCS - Central Control Station, where the engineering plant is monitored and controlled

CENTCOM - US Central Command

CEO - Chief Executive Officer

CHENG - Chief Engineer

CHT - Collection, Holding, and Transfer

CIC - Combat Information Center, where all sensor information is monitored, correlated, and weapon systems are controlled

CICWO - CIC Watch Officer (pronounced sick-wo)

CIWS - Close In Weapon System

CNO - Chief of Naval Operations

CO - Commanding Officer

Commo - Communications Officer

COMNAVFORJAPAN - Commander Naval Forces Japan

Condition II - Wartime steaming with approximately half the weapons systems fully manned; can be modified to focus on one warfare area, e.g. Anti-Submarine Warfare

Condition III - Wartime steaming, but allows for rest; usually three section, e.g. four hours on, eight hours off

CONPLAN - Contingency Plan

CSG - Carrier Strike Group

CSO - Combat Systems Officer

CSOOW - Combat Systems Officer of the Watch

CTF - Commander Task Force or Combined Task Force

CTG - Commander Task Group or Combined Task Group

CTI - Cryptologic Technician Interpretive

CUB - Commander's Update Brief

CZ - Convergence Zone

DC - Damage Control

DCA - Damage Control Assistant

DCC, DC Central - Damage Control Central, where damage control efforts are coordinated

DDG - Guided Missile Destroyer

Ded or Deduced Reckoning – An estimated ship's navigation position based on accounting for winds and currents

DESRON - Destroyer Squadron

DIRLAUTH - Direct Liaison Authorized

DIW - Dead In the Water, unmoving

EMCON - Emission Control

EOOW - Engineering Officer of the Watch

ESG - Expeditionary Strike Group

ESM - Electronic Support Measures, or radar emissions from a ship, aircraft, or submarine

EUCOM - US European Command; also USEUCOM

EW - Electronic Warfare

EW Supe - EW Supervisor

EXORD - Execute Order

FBI - Federal Bureau of Investigation

FM - Frequency Modulation

FOD - Foreign Object Damage, anything that might get sucked into a jet engine, causing damage

FONOP - Freedom of Navigation Operation

Foxtrot Corpen - Course for launching and landing helicopters and fixed-wing aircraft

GIUK Gap - The two oceanic passages between Greenland, Iceland, and the United Kingdom

GPS - Global Positioning System, a constellation of satellites that permits very precise navigation on land and sea

GQ - General Quarters

Green Deck - The ship is ready for the helicopter to launch or land, and the helicopter has permission to launch or land.

Homeplate - Unclassified callsign for the ship a helicopter is based on

HE - High Explosive

HF - High Frequency

HIFR - Helicopter In Flight Refueling

HMMWV - High Mobility Multipurpose Wheeled Vehicle

HQ - Headquarters

HVU - High Value Unit, usually the aircraft carrier or amphibious assault ship, or a supply ship

IADS - Integrated Air Defense System

ICBM - Inter-Continental Ballistic Missile

ID - Identification

INDOPACOM - US Indian Ocean Pacific Command

ISR - Intelligence Surveillance Reconnaissance

JFMCC - Joint Force Maritime Component Commander

JMSDF - Japanese Maritime Self Defense Force

JP-5 - Aviation fuel

JSF - Joint Strike Fighter

JTF - Joint Task Force

JOOD - Junior Officer of the Deck

LCS - Littoral Combat Ship

Material Conditions:

X-Ray - Set in port. All watertight doors marked with X are closed, but not dogged tightly, and can be used as needed

Yoke: Set at sea and at other specified times. Watertight doors marked with X or Y are closed, but not dogged tightly, and may be used when needed.

Zebra - Set during General Quarters and at other specified times, usually involving physical threat to the ship. All watertight fittings marked with X, Y, or Z are dogged tightly throughout the ship. Permission to transit such doors must be obtained from Damage Control Central.

MIDPAC - Naval Forces Middle Pacific

N2 - Staff code of Intelligence

N3 - Staff code for Operations

N6 - Staff code for Communications, Networks, and Computers

Nanosat - A very small satellite, often called a cubesat. Less than eighteen inches in all three dimensions

NATO - North Atlantic Treaty Organization

NAVCENT - Naval Forces Central Command

NAVFOR Korea or Japan - US Naval Forces Korea or Japan

NCA - National Command Authority

NORTHCOM - US Northern Command

NSC - National Security Council

OBE - Overcome By Events

OOD - Officer of the Deck, the officer in charge of the ship during his watch

OPCON - Operational Control, authority to provide general tasking to ships/units, but not direct their individual movements (see TACON)

OPLAN - Operational Plan

OPORD - Operational Order to execute an OPLAN

OPNAV - Operational Navy staff at the Pentagon, headed by the Chief of Naval Operations (CNO)

OPREP THREE - Heavily formatted message sent by units under attack to the chain of command up to and including the president and secretary of defense

Ops - Short for Operations Officer

P-Sub-K - Pk, Probability of Kill, a statistical probability of a single missile killing a single target based on conditions

P4 - Personal For message

PACFLT - US Pacific Fleet

PFM - Pure Fucking Magic

PLA - People's Liberation Army, the People's Republic of China's army

PLAAF - People's Liberation Army Air Force, the People's Republic of China's air force

PLAN - People's Liberation Army Navy, the People's Republic of China's naval service

POSSUB - Possible Submarine contact

PRC - People's Republic of China

PTDO - Prepare To Deploy Order

PTSD - Post-Traumatic Stress Disorder

QM - Quartermaster

Red Deck - The ship is not ready for the helicopter to launch or land

Repair Two - Repair Locker with equipment and personnel tasked with controlling damage in the forward half of the ship

Repair Three - Repair Locker responsible for controlling damage in the after half of the ship

Repair Five - Responsible for damage control in the main engineering spaces

Repair Eight - Responsible for damage control within Combat Systems spaces

RHIB - Rigid Hulled Inflatable Boat

Rodina - Russian for *Motherland*

ROE - Rules of Engagement

ROK - Republic of Korea

ROTC - Reserve Officer Training Corps

RTB - Return(ing) To Base

SAG - Surface Action Group

SAR - Search and Rescue

SATCOM - Satellite Communications
Schwacked - Military slang term for killed or destroyed
SecDef - Secretary of Defense
SecState - Secretary of State
SITREP - Situation Report
SLQ-32 - Radar Warning receiver, detects radars from other ships, aircraft, and missiles
SOCOM - Special Operations Command
SM-2 - Standard Missile Type 2, an anti-aircraft/missile interceptor missile fired from ships
SM-3 - Standard Missile Type 3, anti-ballistic missile interceptors fired from ships
SM-6 - Standard Missile Type 6, anti-air and anti-ballistic missile interceptors fired from ships
SNAFU - Situation Normal, All Fouled/Fucked Up
SPY-1 or 6 - High-powered phased-array radars used aboard Aegis-equipped combatant ships
SSGN - Nuclear-powered Guided Missile Submarine
STRATCOM - US Strategic Command, responsible for Intelligence, Surveillance, and Reconnaissance, global communications, and nuclear weapons
SUPPLOT - Supplemental Plot, where cryptologic systems are monitored
SWC - Surface Weapons Coordinator
TACON - Tactical Control, authority to direct movements of individuals ships/units
TAO - Tactical Action Officer
TFCC - Tactical Flag Command Center
TLAM - Tomahawk Land Attack Missile
UHF - Ultra High Frequency
UNREP - Underway Replenishment
UPS - Uninterruptible Power Supply
VCNO - Vice Chief of Naval Operations
VHF - Very High Frequency
VID - Visual Identification

VLS - Vertical Launch System

WARNORD - Warning Order

WAS - War At Sea strike; attack on a maritime target by carrier based aircraft

XO - Executive Officer, second in command

RANK STRUCTURE

Enlisted:

SEAMAN / FIREMAN RECRUIT (E-1) - Lowest rank in the Navy
SEAMAN / FIREMAN APPRENTICE (E-2)
SEAMAN / FIREMAN (E-3)

Author's Note: All Seaman/Fireman ranks are either "designated" or "undesignated". Undesignated means the person has not yet been chosen for a specialty, such as Engineman, Fire Controlman, or Quartermaster. Designated means they have selected a specialty, and they take on the initials for that specialty when referred to. When a specific person is indicated, the rank is combined with the rate, that is, their specialty. For example, a Seaman designated as a Quartermaster specialist will be referred to as QMSN. Fireman is the title used for personnel in the Engineering fields. Seaman is the title used for personnel in the Weapons/Combat Systems, Operations, Supply, Administrative, and Aviation fields.

PETTY OFFICER THIRD CLASS (3/C) (E-4)
PETTY OFFICER SECOND CLASS (E-5)
PETTY OFFICER FIRST CLASS (E-6)

CHIEF PETTY OFFICER (CPO) (E-7)
SENIOR CHIEF PETTY OFFICER (SCPO) (E-8)
MASTER CHIEF PETTY OFFICER (MCPO) (E-9)

Petty Officers' rank is always combined with their rate, therefore a Quartermaster Third Class will be referred to as a QM3. Petty Officers are non-commissioned officers. A chief's rank will also be combined with their rate, e.g. Boatswain's Mate Chief will be BMC. Chief Petty Officers, including Senior and Master Chief, are often given responsibilities nearly equal that of officers because they are technical experts in their field, having a minimum eight years' service.

Officer:

ENSIGN - Lowest officer rank
LIEUTENANT JUNIOR GRADE (JG)
LIEUTENANT
LIEUTENANT COMMANDER (Army, Air Force, Marines, and Space Force equivalent is Major)
COMMANDER - Commanders normally command smaller ships, such as destroyers, frigates, smaller amphibious ships, and Littoral Combat Ships (LCS). (Other service equivalent is Lieutenant Colonel)
CAPTAIN - Captains normally command larger ships such as cruisers, aircraft carriers, and larger amphibious ships. (Other service equivalent is Colonel) A captain commanding a squadron, such as a destroyer squadron, will also be called a Commodore.
REAR ADMIRAL (LOWER HALF) - This one-star rank used to be titled Commodore but was retitled to avoid confusion with the honorary title Commodore given squadron commanders. (Other service equivalent is Brigadier General)
REAR ADMIRAL (UPPER HALF) (Other service equivalent is Major General)
VICE ADMIRAL (Other service equivalent is Lieutenant General)

ADMIRAL (Other service equivalent is General)

Author's Note: Rear Admirals of both halves command Strike Groups. Vice Admirals command Numbered Fleets. Admirals and Generals command Geographic Combatant Commands, such as CENTCOM, INDOPACOM, etc.

Made in the USA
Columbia, SC
16 September 2024

41950621R00262